Mythangelus

Mythangelus

A Collection of Stories

Storm Constantine

IMMANION PRESS
Stafford England

http://www.stormconstantine.com

Cover and Interior Illustrations by Danielle Lainton
Design by Storm Constantine

Set in Souvenir

IP0024

An Immanion Press Edition
8 Rowley Grove
Stafford ST17 9BJ

http://www.immanion-press.com
info@immanion-press.com

ISBN 978-1-904853-59-6

Books by Storm Constantine

The Wraeththu Chronicles
*The Enchantments of Flesh and Spirit
*The Bewitchments of Love and Hate
*The Fulfilments of Fate and Desire

*The Wraeththu Chronicles (omnibus of trilogy)

The Artemis Cycle
The Monstrous Regiment
Aleph

*Hermetech
Burying the Shadow
Sign for the Sacred
Calenture
Thin Air
The Thorn Boy

The Grigori Books
*Stalking Tender Prey
*Scenting Hallowed Blood
*Stealing Sacred Fire

Silverheart (with Michael Moorcock)

The Magravandias Chronicles:
Sea Dragon Heir
Crown of Silence
The Way of Light

The Wraeththu Histories:
*The Wraiths of Will and Pleasure
*The Shades of Time and Memory
*The Ghosts of Blood and Innocence

Wraeththu Mythos
*The Hienama

Short Story Collections:
Three Heralds of the Storm
The Oracle Lips
The Thorn Boy and Other Dreams of Dark Desire
*Mythophidia

*available as Immanion Press editions

Contents

Paragenesis

I have scars upon my left hand, but not upon my right. If I hold my hands up to the eternal sun, light shines through the flesh. But there is no flesh. I am idea, essence. I am the flash of sunlight off chrome; I am the seasons; I am the shadow beneath the eaves; I am a scrap of litter scratching across cracked asphalt. No, I am bones and blood. I am crude and heavy. I am what I am.

When I was sixteen, I ran away from my leaf-shrouded home in the enclave for the rich, about twelve miles from the city centre. Perhaps it began as a suicide bid. All I did was move my limbs, without conscious volition, toward the wilderness of stone and glass that circled the city itself like a plague. It was the hinterland of decay, spreading both outward and inward, threatening city core and enclave alike. People could lose themselves there, and I wanted to be lost.

I remember that day. She was standing at the kitchen sink with her back to me. She could always sense when I walked into the room. I'd see her spine tense beneath its dress of cotton, its caul of skin. How cruel had Mother Nature been to make her spawn a child she could only fear? Blessed was the day when she no longer had to touch me; when I could feed and bathe myself, tie my own laces, rub my own hurts. I could not despise her, for I shared her bewilderment, her bitterness. When I'd been born, no doubt she'd decided to make the best of it. I was a beautiful child, but for those hidden abnormalities. Later, she probably realised that even monsters could be beautiful. My father was a non-entity, consumed by work. We rarely saw him. Our home always seemed empty when she and I were in it together. The spaces between us were too great, and as I grew older, they became gulfs.

On that final day, I could not bear to see that stiffening spine any longer. She had birthed me and raised me; now her responsibility was over. I turned around and walked away; out of the shady house into the sunlight; past the bike lying on the tarmac, where a few red leaves had drifted down; past the rope that hung from the old willow, still swinging and where I never played. The street was devoid of children; empty. Empty. This had never been my home.

On the horizon, a grey green cloud hung above the city. It was a walk of about four hours to reach it along the main highway. Sometimes, a bus might come, rattling and armoured, but not very often. People with eyes like pebbles rode the bus; not coming from anywhere, going nowhere, just riding. Perhaps they thought time would stop for them in that way. I would not ride the buses, for I was afraid that if I did, I would be absorbed into that shadow community and never leave it. Another freak on the back seat.

It was mid-morning when I left the enclave, and already the sun was fierce in the late summer sky. At the high metal gates, the eyes of the guards were hidden behind black glass. They stood motionless, like automatons. I passed between them, showed my ID card, and the gates slid open. A minute later, someone else might come by, and the guards would come alive. They'd touch their helmets, grin to show their white teeth and utter a pleasantry. But not for me. After I'd gone, one would say, 'That's the weird kid from Acacia', and the others would sneer.

I walked along the slip road that led to the highway. It seemed hotter beyond the enclave, and the air shimmered about me. Vigilantes had strung someone from a pole. I could see the body dangling on the other side of the road, surrounded by trees. A cloud of flies danced around it. Beneath it, someone had left some artificial flowers. Perhaps the enclave guards, high up on the gates and watchtowers, had seen it happen.

I cannot remember feeling anything then. I just walked, kicking up dust that smelled of metal and age, buffeted by the searing wind of passing vehicles. After an hour, a truck stopped to offer me a lift. The back was filled with people, crammed together like pigs on the way to a slaughterhouse. They were probably just crop-pickers, returning to the city. My feet were aching, so I hopped up into the back. Certain people always picked up on my strangeness, and this occasion was no different. My fellow travellers were like frightened animals: I saw furtive shuffling, and nervous eye movements. I didn't say anything. Eventually, one of the men offered me a cigarette and I smoked it, looking out through the truck canopy at the passing road. My mother will have missed me by now. Her relief will fill the silent house, washed by waves of shame. She will grip the edge of the sink and blink at the garden, where the sprinkler slowly turns on the lawn.

I did not resent being born different. The resentment came from other people's reactions. I was so ordinary in most respects. Dogs had never liked me; we could never keep one. Sometimes, things happened around me over which I had no control. It wasn't my fault. It was the look in her eyes. I made the saucepans fly once, but not toward her. She just screamed, her hands pressed to her face, staring at the mess on the floor. Other kids didn't like me very much, despite my parents' efforts to find me friends. I didn't mind being alone. I'd tell my mother things she thought were her private thoughts, and then her mouth would compress into two white lines. Later, I'd hear her telling my father about it: 'He must *listen* to us, for God's sake! Do something!' I didn't listen. I just knew. It was like she told me things herself without words.

It was the doctors I hated the most. There was nothing wrong with me; I wasn't ill. But my mother kept taking me back to that neat office that smelled of nothing, and let the white coats prod at me. I said, 'just let me be', and they would smile tolerantly, spreading my legs on the table for another look. They must have taken a hundred photographs.

'It isn't Froehlichs syndrome,' I heard a doctor say to my mother, 'because apart from the genital abnormalities, there are no other physical deformities.'

Her reply: 'Then what is it? Can you operate?'

'That is a decision your son will have to make for himself later on. We have counsellors...'

She thought I should have been twins: a boy and a girl. But it wasn't that.

I got out of the truck on the outskirts of the city, in an area called the Longhills. Once, it would have been a thriving neighbourhood; now a ruin and an ideal place to hide, to think, to do whatever would come next. Tall buildings with broken crowns reached towards the veil of evil cloud that always hangs above the city. I think it is the city's aura, an expression of its soul, soiled and poisonous. The people who live in that place are barely human, but then I had been taught to think that neither was I. Perhaps this was the place where I belonged. I wanted to cast off the trappings of affluence and live close the edge of survival. Discomfort did not bother me.

I walked as best I could along the sidewalks, avoiding debris, bundles of cloth that may have been corpses and the smouldering remains of fires. What did people burn here? Sometimes, it seemed they burned their own possessions. I saw fragments of books, jewellery and crockery blackened among the embers. The smoke was toxic. Someone had burned a wasps' nest. A substance like syrup leaked from its collapsed mass. I saw few people. They kept out of the sun during the day. They slept then. Welfare trucks occasionally slid across an intersection ahead of me. They might contain bodies or miscreants or supplies. Perhaps all three at once.

At three o'clock in the afternoon, when the sun was at its most vehement, I stood in the centre of a street and looked up at the sky. Buildings loomed over me, derelict and rotting. I wondered what the point of it all was. Why do we continue to live? What drives us to survive in an environment so hostile to life, an environment we have made for ourselves? Civilisation was a Leviathan whose limbs were too weak to support it. Now it sank to its knees, bones cracking beneath its weight. And all who rode the Leviathan were tumbling down, their screams thin like that of insects. My difference was just one more symptom of this fall. Our purity was mangled and dysfunctional. In those moments, I saw myself as the avatar of the world's destruction, a cruel joke in the distorted form of the primal human. I could do as I pleased, for it did not matter what would happen to me.

Soon, I began to feel hungry, but willed the pangs away. I could see no way to feed myself. It was cleansing to be able to step aside from human needs. I felt excoriated, but also renewed. For a while, I sat inside a broken building, where the walls were black. I listened for sounds: the faraway throb of rotor blades, the occasional human cry, cut off short, and once the distant bark of a dog. I watched the sun slide down behind the splintered towers, and thought how in the enclave, the day would be drawing to a close. Men would be emerging from the units in the nearby industrial park. They would climb into their sleek transporters, hail a manly good-night to the guards on the wall, and drive the short distance up the tower-studded avenue to the gates of the enclave. Here, wives who sought to enact the rituals of a past Golden Age would be waiting in kitchens that were devoid of stain. The women wore aprons and smiled at their children, keeping back the pain, the fear, the utter chaos that massed on the horizon of their fantasy world. None of it was real, but then I had never really conspired in my parents' dream. My very existence cracked its fragile shell.

At dusk, a gang of girls stole in through the windows of my sanctuary. They saw me crouching in the rubble, which I quickly realised was *their* rubble, and began to snarl at me and utter strange ululating cries, their bodies dipping and rising like snakes. Their leader rushed at me a couple of times, brandishing a knife near my body, but I sat as still as I could, looking at her face. Presently, she came to a decision and gestured for her minions to get on with their business. They unfolded loot from tattered sacks, and set about dividing it amongst themselves. The leader flicked glances at me occasionally. I recognised something within her that later I identified as the indomitable human spirit. Society no longer existed for her, yet she continued to thrive, albeit in a debased fashion.

The girls ate and laughed together, handing round a plastic bottle of murky liquid. After an hour or so, their leader offered it to me. It was a vile, base alcohol that left a trail of fire in my throat and tasted only of chemicals. The girls asked me nothing about myself, even though they must have made judgements about my cleanliness, my neat clothes. They were separatist females who hated men. They could have killed me, perhaps, but it seemed they recognised something within me with which they felt comfortable and could accept.

I ran with them for a week or so, raking over the ruins, pillaging the debris. They seemed to repel rival male gangs by the strength of their voices alone, using a repertoire of chilling screams and cries. Boys would lope away from them like chastened dogs. Often, the leader would climb to the highest, most precarious point around and stand there with arms outflung, uttering a world-filling shriek of anger. They did not know about despair. I envied them.

In the asphalt wilderness of Longhills, there were few adults. Perhaps they had wisely moved away, or else been killed. Sometimes, choppers would drone over the streets and emit a stinging spray, which the girls told me was supposed to kill disease. Why would the city authorities bother? I didn't believe it. The spray probably just killed fertility.

I felt more at one with the desperadoes of the wilderness than any of the people who hid within the enclave. It was because these outsiders expected nothing and gave little in return. They did not make demands upon one another. Co-existence, and therefore a certain amount of co-operation, was the only remaining aspect of community. Pleasure was without contrivance: a good find among the rubbish; a chance meeting with a group who had something to barter; a basement found untouched, like an unopened tomb full of treasure; an abandoned welfare truck still laden with vitamin-enriched gruel. We were grave-robbers, really, for most of humanity had already died in that place. But I liked the simplicity and honesty of their lives, the fact they did not judge me.

One day, one of the gang was shot by a sniper and the leader told us we would have to move area. A sixth sense told her this was the beginning of something bad. So we gathered up what little we had and left Longhills behind, burrowing off through the darkness, and into another decayed sector called Coldwater Valley. It must have been an industrial complex at one time, and here the survivors were older and hostile to strangers. We prowled carefully between the arching metal structures that were now smothered with tendrils of quick-growing vines. Echoes were strangely muffled by the vegetation. Any human group we came across yelled and threw things to repel us; we were not welcome. Finally, one group, crazier than the rest, directed a fire cannon on us and killed all but five of us. Our leader was among the fallen; a blackened crisp in the road. How quickly life can be expunged. It seemed inconceivable that what was left of our companions had ever housed souls. We, the survivors, went back the way we had come, but it was the end of our group. We split up, and I went alone deeper into the madness of the ruined land that surrounded the desperate core of the shrinking metropolis. Its towers seemed to have huddled together, as if in fear.

There was much activity in the air nearer to the city core. Choppers roared through the skies, and once I saw one crash. People emerged from the jumbled ruins like cockroaches and swarmed all over the wreckage, picking it clean. I did not look like an enclave boy any longer. My head was thatched with lice-infested hair; my clothes were tatters, to which I was forever adding more layers, whatever I could find. I had learned to snarl in the way that meant, 'stay away if you value your health.' I also learned much about myself. Because the convenient utensils of life were no longer available, I was forced to live on my wits, and in this way discovered that the boundaries of my difference were much further than I had imagined. It began this way.

I'd been going through the belongings of a dead man on the street, who had died of a sickness rather than murder. He had many treasures, which I was greedily transferring to my own pockets. Then a group of tearaways came slinking along the spiky walls around me, uttering low, hooting cries. Their message was for me to leave, to abandon my find. I do not think they would have attacked me if I'd simply obeyed this request. But there was too much for me to leave. I growled back. They must have thought I was mad; there were at least seven of them. Their leader dropped down from the wall and sauntered toward me, looking to either side all the time. I remained hunkered down beside the corpse, my hands dangling between my knees. I did not feel afraid at all. It was as if there was someone else inside me, far wiser than I knew; someone fierce and confident. An arrow of indignation flew out of me, and somehow touched the crumbling substance of the wall behind the gang leader. There was an explosion, a gust of dust and rocky debris, and then my would-be attacker was on his hands and knees before me, his head hanging down. He shook his hair and drops of bright blood flew out. At once, I jumped to my feet and snarled. My eyes felt full of sparks that I could shoot like bullets from a gun. The gang just melted away, dragging their fallen leader with them. After this incident, I felt so much stronger, safer.

Perhaps I underestimated my strength.

Some days later, I found a hole for myself deep beneath an old department store. It had been cleaned out thoroughly years before, but some people must have lived there for a while, because I found a few mattresses, some of which had not been burned. Rags had been hung from metal beams in what remained of the ceiling. It was a musty labyrinth full of silent ghosts. I imagined it had once been home to a whole community, who

15

had either been smoked out or died from some contagious infection. There were no bones about as evidence, but the wilderness scavengers are very thorough, so that meant little. In this place, I made myself a nest. I did not think about the future, but took simple pleasure in surviving from moment to moment.

The wilderness was the garbage heap of the world, yet I learned to see beauty in it: the different colours of the sky at various times of day and how they conjured sculptures from the rubble; shining through blown out windows; making a cathedral of light of the starkest structure. The passing of civilisation in itself was a wondrous thing. I would walk the cracked streets marvelling at the way stringy vegetation was slowly reclaiming the land. Mother Earth had learned the saying that revenge is a meal best eaten cold. She was implacable, eternal, and the green tidal wave of her reclamation was evidence of humanity's frailty and insignificance. The people had regressed, but in their barbarity possessed a startling innocence. The complex rituals of life had been pared away, and if the people were dying, at least they would do so with swift dignity, rather than being hooked up to machines in a long coma of slow decay. Those who lived in the cities, the enclaves, were deluding themselves. They should give themselves up to the inevitable. I thought I too would soon die, and these were my last days. Each one dawned fresh and vital. I wanted to experience life through my senses to the full, and because of this, learned how my touch was death.

He was older than me, yet seemed younger. We met when he strayed into my lair, and after a few warning shots of snarls and aggressive gestures, realised we were not enemies at all. He was like me: a runaway from the theatre of luxury. His mother had been a pill-head, who sometimes had not even recognised him, while his father, a scientist, had hardly ever been at home. I tingled with empathy as he described his former sterile environment: the ceaseless hum of domestic appliances, and the automata who kept the place running, while his mother lolled on the couch, living in some better world. He explained to me the phenomena of why people like us ran away. 'We know it is over. Society is dead, but some of us know we can still exist beyond it. It is like a sinking ship. We have to jump overboard with faith and hope, otherwise we'll just be dragged down with the wreck and drowned. This is the age of the individual; the age of the hive has passed. We are all floating in the sea, clinging to our bits of wreckage, but eventually we'll become sea creatures ourselves and learn how to breathe its element.'

How could I not love a person who spoke like that, with such passion and optimism? He did not know about my difference - especially the physical aspect. I did not want to tell him because he was my first real friend. If he knew, it would change things. He might be disgusted or, worse, full of pity.

Some girl he knew gave him a flask of alcohol. We flavoured it with the remains of a bag of sugar substitute we'd found in our basement, and one night sat across from one another and drank it. It felt shamanic, the rhythmic passing of the flask from one to the other. We both knew we wanted to be drunk, for there was business between us that the barriers of a sober mind inhibited. I was acutely aware that before the night was over he would know about me. I felt nauseous with nerves, eager for the intoxication that would free my tongue and allow me to speak the words that must be spoken.

He began to talk about the future again, rambling on about some faraway utopia that could be constructed from hopes and dreams.

Something about his vision made me uncomfortable, and I said, 'This is the end, not change. We are dying.'

He crawled over to me then and put an arm around me. 'No, no, you are wrong. This is not death at all. You are living in the past. Look forward, not back. Don't let the past become your future.'

I wanted to believe, and partly did, unaware of how he spoke the most ultimate of truths. He put his head against my hair and said, 'I have to ask you something. Don't answer if you don't want to but... are you really a girl?'

I laughed a little, more out of embarrassment than amusement. What could I say? The answer was neither yes nor no. 'What makes you think that?' I asked.

I could tell he wished he'd never spoken. 'I don't know. The way you walk and talk. Just body language, I guess. I'm sorry. You must think this is just an excuse to...'

I touched his arm to silence him. 'I am what you say.'

He grinned in relief. 'I knew it. You want people to think

you're a boy because people will leave you alone then.' He paused. 'I'm sorry. That sounded patronising.'

I shook my head. 'No, don't apologise. The thing is, I'm male too.'

He frowned. 'In your heart, your head?'

'No. In some ways, that would be more simple.'

'Then what *do* you mean?' The puzzlement had swept back; the tide of delight and anticipation had receded.

'It would be easier to show you,' I said and stood up.

The only light came in from outside, but then we of the wilderness rarely craved artificial light at night, other than a fire for protection. I peeled away all the layers of my tattered clothes, feeling as if each discarded item represented a year of my life. It was all being sloughed away. When finally I stood naked before him, he sat with his chin in his hands and said, 'You look male to me.'

I squatted before him and took one of his hands in mine, guiding him to the truth of the matter. He didn't say anything then, but kissed me. I felt his fingers digging into my shoulders like spikes. I could feel his heart racing. He'd wanted to do this for some time, and now felt he had been given sanction. I welcomed it too, but some part of me became annoyed that he looked upon me as a female and took it for granted that I must be dominated. Did women ever feel this way? It might sound like justification, but I feel that he was partly to blame for what happened to him. We should have come together as equals, but then I didn't know he was not equal to me. I was stronger than he was, and forced him into submission. It was only a game, I swear. I just wanted him to realise what we were, or could be.

It took him a day to die. I was helpless. I tried everything, but whatever mutant substance lived in me was poison to him. Not all the water in the world could wash away what I had done to him. My essence ate into him like acid, devoured his being. The only blessing was that he did not realise what was happening to him. With my hands, I was able to stroke away most of the pain. With my thoughts I willed his mind to a far place, that idyll he had spoken of, and there he died.

I set fire to our home and emerged from it into the night against a backdrop of flames. I had been right and he wrong. Humanity was dying and I was one of nature's weapons. I could never love, for to love me was to die. Could anything be crueler than that?

If only I had known the truth then. He could still be here now. The one who discovered that truth with me was but a pale spark to his radiant sun, but perhaps that was all part of it, the great lesson I had to learn.

For days, perhaps weeks, I roamed the wilderness, feeling more drunk than I had on that hideous night. I truly wanted to die, and sometimes climbed the high, broken towers to think about throwing myself over, but even in my grief I was too afraid of being broken, dying slowly. I kept seeing his face, hearing his laughter, and then an image of his death would come to me, the terrible writhing, the whimpers. I was more of a monster than even my mother had imagined.

I came to an area that had been inexpertly flattened; a plain of rubble, from which rusting spikes rose like the bones of dinosaurs. Here, I collapsed and stared up at the sky, watching the colours change and the stars reveal themselves. I could move no further. Here, it would end. I felt strangely at peace, and numb. I could not feel my body.

When I saw the stooped shadow gliding towards me over the stones, I barely raised my head. Death had come for me. It loomed over me, breathing heavily, and dark greasy hair brushed my face. I saw a glint of metal and heard muttered words. 'Be still, my pretty. Do not fear. I shall come to you without pain.'

I did not know he meant to eat me. I just thought of sex and murder, but he opened a vein in my arm and began to drink, nibbling the flesh at the edge of the cut. He was a modern vampire, human and reeking, not at all the romantic vision I'd seen in old movies. As I lay there, feeling the pull as my blood pulsed into his diseased mouth, I was not sickened or afraid, but amused. It is not easy to find food in the wilderness, and some will do anything to live. If my death meant the life of a debased creature like this, then so be it. There was some justice in it, I thought.

But I did not die. I found myself awake with raw morning light falling down upon me. Beside me was a wretched creature who squirmed upon the ground, clutching his belly. His hair had come out in clumps and lay upon the stones. I felt weak, but also vital. As I looked at him, I laughed. Not only was my touch death, but it seemed I was also very difficult to kill. Part of my new role, I decided, was to stay with my victims until they found peace in death. I would do what I could to ease their agony.

Unlike my beloved, this one did not die after the first day. Sometimes, he was raving and hallucinating and became violent with a preterhuman strength. At other times, he wept and mumbled about his childhood, his fingers over his face. His body was hot and bloated. He must be strong. How long would it take him to die?

After two days, it began to rain, and I dragged him into a ruined office block. The rain itself can be toxic. Here, I built a small fire, and then went foraging, killing four bedraggled pigeons. I came back with two birds, and some welfare rice I'd haggled for with a band of oldsters I'd come across. My attacker, my victim, could not eat, but I cooked the pigeons and watched him as I fed. There was no feeling within me, merely a faint sense of curiosity. His skin was peeling.

On the morning of the third day, I woke up and found myself alone. I thought my companion must have died in the night, and some scavenger had come in and taken the body. Then I heard the words, 'what am I?' and turned to see an angel in the doorway. As his skin had peeled, so had all the filth. He stood before me, holding out his arms, looking at his smooth flesh. I could not give him answers. There were none. I felt that I had made him into something more and above me. He shared my difference. I had birthed a daughter-son.

I had thought him the most degenerate of beings, yet I quickly learned that he blazed with vitality and intelligence. Perhaps this was just another aspect of the change he had undergone. He asked me questions constantly and experimented with the force of his being. Unlike me, he was curious about the way he could affect reality; make inanimate objects move, heal pain, hear the whisper of others' thoughts. He was proud of what he'd become, and did not hide it, but the shadow community to which he'd once belonged were now afraid of him. They did not want his healing power, his radiance. They saw not an angel, but a freak.

Unperturbed, he became almost evangelistic about our condition. 'We must make more like us,' he said.

I was appalled and shook my head. 'No. You are a fluke. It is not meant to be this way.'

'How do you know?'

We were not easy companions, yet our similarities, and the fact that I had made him the way he was, kept us together. He had changed so much from the wretch he'd been. We lived in the office block where he'd undergone his transformation. One evening, he made me climb a nearby hydro-tower with him, where the rusting shell harboured clear water. He took off his clothes and dived in, summoning me to join him. 'We are not part of the filth now.' He sluiced my hair and rubbed the grime from my skin. 'I want the grief to run from your body with this water. You must be renewed, like I am.'

I think the transformation had affected his mind. He needed a religion to run.

'How did you do it?' he asked. 'Tell me. Tell me.'

'I don't know. It just happened. You were trying to devour me.'

The light in his eyes was like that of the stars; cold and distant. 'Yes,' he murmured. 'Yes.'

I should have known he'd act independently. One day, he took me to a building near our lair, and here revealed to me his twisting litter of children. I was horrified, yet also amazed. Twelve people, both male and female, shivered and whimpered at my feet; all of them infected with his blood. I had seen myself as an avatar of death, but remote and accidental. Here was someone who was an active instrument of it, only he did not realise the fact. He thought he was a god, with a god's powers. If I'd done something to end it then, what would the world have been like now?

Of the twelve, only four survived, and all of them previously male. We tried to soothe the agony of the others with the healing power in our hands, but the experience was harrowing. 'I think this process cannot be conducted with females,' my companion said, with scientific detachment. 'But we must try it with others.'

'No!' My protest went unheard.

I would not help him, other than to attend to his victims as they suffered. I didn't even think about killing him, or trying to stop it any other way. At the time, it just didn't enter my mind, but now I think it was because part of me knew that what was happening was preordained. My companion saw it as a cleansing ritual for the world. He loved the creatures he made, marvelling at their beauty. I saw them as perverted homunculi; as lovely as the angels of hell. Yet, despite this, they were also part of me and I was part of them.

I under-estimated the regard my companion had for me. He did not set himself up as a leader of our developing clan of beautiful monsters. That privilege he reserved for me, even though I shunned it. 'It is your responsibility,' he told me. 'You began this.'

'Only because you were hungry,' I reminded him.

'Can't you see the potential here?' he demanded. 'This is the beginning of something. It is what comes next.'

I could only look down at the corpses of those who had not survived. The cost of the selection process was too high. 'This is murder,' I said.

He nodded. 'You are right. We should give people the choice.' As an inducement, he now had seven successful transformations to parade before the eyes of the desperate.

I never became involved in his recruitment drives, and for many years no other human tasted my blood. I cannot say that I wasn't affected by my companion's enthusiasm, and grudgingly I had to accept the benefits of being part of a community, something I had never previously enjoyed, other than those few weeks of running with the girl-pack. This was different though. With the girls, I had been a tolerated outsider. Now, I was part of a group of individuals who all shared the same attributes. It was both scary and exciting.

Although we could not effect the change in women, a few of them, through persistent entreaty, still joined us. In many ways, we had more in common with them than with men. From our sisters, we learned about the wildest excesses of adorning our bodies. We became tribal and developed our own rituals connected with the inception of newcomers, or the simple celebration of our estate. Sex became sacred, yet less taboo. There was so much to explore, and so many delights concealed in the labyrinth of our dual gender.

One night, we undertook a rite to name ourselves, opening up our minds with the effects of narcotic fungi. My companion became Orien; a name he felt held power. As for me, I wandered the star-gleam avenues of my mind, until I came to a place where a white shrine glimmered against a backdrop of stars. It stood upon the primal mound of creation, guarded by two pillars, and surrounded by the waters of life. Here, I learned my true name, the person I was to become. I am Thiede. The first of all. And the name we took for ourselves as a group was Wraeththu; a word that held all the anger and mystery of the world. The visions told us the truth: we were no longer human and must forget all that we had been before.

We were close-knit, and did not merely co-operate with one another. Laughter was spontaneous, and in our wild nights of dancing, as new recruits struggled with the process of transformation, I learned about the fulfilment that close friendship brings. I was intrigued by the way the different personalities within the group interacted with one another; the partnerships that developed, the enmities. We weren't above petty squabbling, but if anything from outside threatened our group, the ranks would close and seal as tight as a steel door. We were not afraid to kill to protect ourselves, and sometimes that was necessary.

Various human clans and groups heard about us, and some were afraid, and thought we should be eradicated. We were seen as vampires, as predators, who stole people away in the night. In fact, that was not true. We hadn't resorted to such measures since the first days of my companion's explorations. We had to keep on the move, but even so, humans would often sniff us out and come pouring over the ruins, holding flaming brands aloft, intent on burning us alive. Then we would rise up, howling, our wild hair flying, our faces striped with the colours of the night.

We never lost a single brother in our skirmishes. In our unity, we were immensely strong.

Everything that begins in the world starts small, be it a mighty tree from a seed, or a deluge from a single drop of rain. A cell becomes a child becomes a king or queen. The greatest concepts are based upon the most fleeting of ideas. Such it was with Wraeththu, the race that I spawned from my fear, my pain, my ignorance.

I stand upon the pillars of the world, and look down to see the carnage perpetrated by the human race that had been its guardian. I am amazed that humanity, with all its cruel selfishness, ever rose to prominence, and that the world itself allowed the situation to continue for so long. We are the exterminators, who will rid the palaces of the earth of all its vermin. We have no choice in this role; it has been decided for us. We are the true messengers of the gods. The howls of slaughtered innocents rise from the ruins, the whimpers of the bereaved, the snufflings of the betrayed. I stand as a colossus above it all, looking down. There is a star in the sky that is the soul of my lost love, and my own soul has fragmented into a thousand parts, into each of my children. But I do not grow weak from it, only estranged. There is much to explore about myself, and for this I need a real wilderness, where all the devils of the earth and the angels of the air can come to tempt me and teach me. I cannot make the inward journey here in the city debris.

Last night, Orien came to me, worried that some of our brethren had split off to form a separate group. I tried to assuage his fears. 'This is the way it will go,' I said. 'We were the catalysts, nothing more. We must not interfere with the growth of our child.'

He thought I was mad, or damaged, and spoke softly. 'The time will come, soon, for us to move toward the city core.'

I nodded. 'I know,' I said. 'You will.'

He touched my shoulder. '*We* will. You cannot deny us, Thiede.'

And I smiled at him to reassure him, knowing that already I had left them.

The Law of Being

*"To the House which none leave who have entered it
To the Road from which there is no way back..."*

From an Assyrio-Babylonian stone tablet recounting the myth of
Ishtar and Tammuz

It was the biggest Transmission of Future Light convention ever.
Held in Amsterdam, thousands of followers from all over Europe
had flocked to see its luminary, Emory Patrick, in person. The
diversions on offer included a week of rock concerts by over a
dozen well-known bands, theatrical productions with a spiritual
theme, and panel talks by eminent New Agers, occultists, writers
and media stars. There would be group rituals, workshops,
meditations and dances; night parties by communal fires.
Everyone had the intention to drink and dope themselves into
cheerful oblivion. To the many thousands of Future Lighters, as
members of the movement liked to call themselves, Emory
Patrick, rock star, philosopher and healer, was the new Messiah.

Patrick had risen to prominence two years before. TOFL
had been established round about the same time as the band,
which was also named Future Light. Patrick was the singer and
motivating force behind both the music and the movement,
although he was assisted by two close friends and business
partners, Linford Brown and Iliana Forsyth. Transmission of
Future Light attracted the young. It was a beacon which shone
relentlessly through the dusty, mildewed catacombs that orthodox
belief systems had become, being youth-orientated,
uncompromisingly modern, aggressively forward-thinking, and,
perhaps most potently, largely free from dogma.

Emory himself was the creed, simply by example: You can
live like me, be like me. He was incredibly successful, and did not
make any attempt to conceal the more commercial aspects of his
movement, boldly asserting that there was no shame in having
money or earning money, as long as you didn't attempt to rip
people off. Thus, the books, t-shirts, badges and magazines were
plentiful (the merchandise sheets alone were virtually a magazine),

but reasonably priced and made of quality materials. They were fun too. Future Light was not po-faced; its slogans sometimes included swear words and buzz words from youth culture. Its image was bright and vigorous, and its philosophy did not appear to carry any great threat to the establishment, even though the young flocked to Emory's camp in droves.

On the day before the convention started, Future Lighters from nearly a dozen European countries were setting up their stalls around the edge of the site. The high, razor-topped wire fences had already been erected, and TOFL security was patrolling with walky-talkies and dogs. Beyond the wire, as the following arrived in vans or on foot, brightly coloured tents were sprouting up into a sprawling and lively temporary community. There was an atmosphere of expectancy and excitement. Emory Patrick himself appeared around noon, in the kind of long black limo in which stars were expected to travel. He was accompanied by his band, their dancers and the inevitable presence of Iliana Forsyth and Linford Brown.

Leaving Emory to meditate in his bungalow-sized caravan, and Iliana to supervise the last details of the catering, Linford wandered off to inspect the enormous, canopied stage. It too was in the last stages of completion, only a few more adjustments being required to the lighting rig. Linford wandered onto the stage and stared out over the vast space that would, by tomorrow, be filled with adoring Patrick devotees. He was a spare, angular man in his late thirties, who had perhaps lived a little too hard, but who had found, in Future Light, a comfortable niche in which to exercise his talents, which had been forged in the music industry. Emory Patrick was an easy person to work with and for. He was genuine. Although Linford was not at all religious, and grinned at the most avid followers who declared Emory was undoubtedly the New Son of God, he believed in Emory's power as an individual. He believed Emory really did have the capacity to change the world in a positive way because, in loving people, he gave them courage and confidence in themselves. There were no tricks and no bullshit.

Linford was just in the act of reflecting how perfect his life was when something large and dark hurtled past the edge of his vision and hit the stage with a sickening, liquid crack. Immediately, there were shouts and the sound of running feet.

Linford blinked and stared at the object lying very close to his feet. It was the body of a man; very decidedly a body, rather than just a man, because the neck and limbs were all contorted into highly unusual angles and blood had begun to pool across the stage. Linford was stunned. He couldn't move. Someone was shouting, 'Get an ambulance, get an ambulance!' and someone else was shoving Linford out of the way.

'Fucking hell, he's dead, man, he's dead!'

People in Emory Patrick t-shirts were swarming all over the stage. The corpse was one of the lighting technicians, Linford realised. Must have fallen. Oh God! He turned away, collapsed onto his belly and vomited over the edge of the stage. Wiping his mouth, numb in the midst of confusion and panic, he looked up and saw Emory walking towards him, obviously having been disturbed from his trance by the shouting.

'What's going on?' Emory asked.

For a brief moment, Linford was filled with the blinding realisation that everything he had worked for was about to be demolished. He did not want to tell Emory what had happened, didn't want him to see the hideous broken flesh, which was screened by the frantic huddle of people on the stage. He wanted to lead Emory away, because then nothing would change. Linford, though imaginative, was also something of a sceptic. He rarely heeded his instincts. 'An accident,' he said. 'Terrible accident.'

Emory climbed nimbly up onto the stage. He looked vulnerable and fragile and young, his long hair tied back, his eyes wide and curious.

Struggling into a kneeling position, Linford put out his hand to grab hold of Emory's shirt. 'Leave it, Mori. There's nothing we can do...'

Emory looked down at him. He didn't say anything, but something in his almost vacant expression rekindled Linford's bone-deep apprehension.

'Mori...'

Emory was pushing through the crowd. Linford followed. People had instinctively drawn back as Emory approached, allowing him to squat beside the corpse. Emory's face was still expressionless. Squatting in the pool of blood, he methodically straightened the limbs and head of the dead man.

'Mori, don't,' Linford said in a soft voice. He couldn't bear to look at the corpse again, but rested a hand on Emory's shoulder. Surely, the body should be left alone until the proper authorities had arrived? Ignoring Linford's plea, Emory lightly placed both of his hands on the dead man's chest. His head drooped forward. Linford could see that Emory was shaking. He wished the ambulance would come. Emory himself would need treatment for shock. The onlookers were observing Emory's behaviour in wide-eyed silence. Some appeared awed, which was typical of TOFL people when Emory did *anything*, while others looked a little embarrassed. Seconds passed.

When the dead man twitched and uttered a groan, three of the people watching fainted immediately.

Linford swayed and stepped away from Emory Patrick. He felt bile rise in his throat again. *This isn't real. Can't be. No, the guy wasn't dead.* Stunned. *He was just stunned! Yes.* The rationalising thoughts gushed through Linford's mind. Around him, people were moaning or weeping, while others were muttering grateful prayers. Yet, beyond the circle of their bodies, the silence of the day was immaculate.

Ignoring the spectators, Emory helped the lighting technician to sit up. The two men embraced and Emory kissed the resurrectee on his bloodied mouth. Watching, Linford bit through the edge of his tongue.

Doctors, who would later examine the man who fell to his death, would find no trace of a fracture, not even a bruise.

Nina Vivian was a very disgruntled woman. Primarily because she could not believe the Department of Paranormal Resources was taking this business seriously, and secondly because she had bad feelings about getting involved in it. Call it guts, call it instinct, or good old Mother Goddess, she wasn't interested. The DPR unfortunately *were* interested, and as she was one of their Temps, and a very special one at that, their interests were inevitably hers to share.

'Of course, there is always the possibility this guy is not a fake, not even Talented, but exactly what his followers claim he is?' She only said it to provoke her companion, but still twisted the rather emotive statement into a question, before laying the printout she'd been given down on the desk in front of her. The high-ceilinged office was bathed in the muted light of a single desk lamp. Outside, rain patted at the windows. It was very late.

The man seated behind the desk in partial shadow was swivelling gently in his plush executive chair. With his fingers steepled against his chin, he raised one immaculately curved eyebrow. 'That cannot be ruled out completely yet, but personally I find it hard to convince myself it might be the explanation. My dear Nina, as an experienced member of the DPR yourself, I am sure you must feel, as I do, this man has to be one of ours.'

Nina grimaced. She didn't really believe Emory Patrick was a paranorm or a Messiah. 'It's a stunt,' she said. 'Has to be.'

The man's eyebrow lifted again. 'Well, whatever your opinion, because of the enormity of what Patrick *appears* to have done, coupled with his considerable influence, it is imperative we establish whether he's paranormal or simply a cheap magician. If it's the former, then we'll have to have a little chat with him.'

Nina wrinkled her nose and peered at the black and white digitised photograph on the polished mahogany. What looked back at her was a prime and immaculate specimen of masculinity. 'He looks like a rock star to me, nothing more.'

The man smiled tolerantly. 'The media seems to concur with you. However, some of the individuals who witnessed the event were not connected to the organisation – caterers and so on – and Patrick's people have been insisting they be given lie detection tests to prove their man's a miracle worker.' He rolled his eyes in exasperated scorn. 'Although Patrick himself has refused to discuss the subject, several of his staff have appeared on TV, earnestly insisting the resurrection was genuine.'

'Great media stuff!' Nina said.

'Quite.'

Nina grinned. 'Personally, I think it's a great stunt!' She gestured at the printout. 'Come on, Gervase, your initial research doesn't seem to have thrown up anything damning. This guy's clean. He's just a showman.'

The man shrugged. 'I don't believe anyone making that much money from such a project can possibly be clean, but then I am not a spiritual person. Perhaps I'm too cynical.'

Nina pushed her fingers through her hair. It felt lank. She'd been called from her bed in the middle of the night before what promised to be an excellent shoot in the morning. The DPR didn't call her out at any time unless something big was going down. Nina Vivian only did 'big stuff'. She leaned back in her chair, sending a hopeful message to the Receiver she knew was sitting out in the next office that yes, she was rather in need of a large coffee. 'So, spit it out Gervase, what d'you want, or expect, me to do with this?' She flicked her nails against the photograph.

He spread out his hands. 'Do what you do best, my dear, in your expert inimical way. Investigate... bring him in, if necessary.'

She sighed. 'I hope you're not going to say anything like I'm booked on a flight to Amsterdam in the morning, because that will annoy me intensely. I have Sable Grant up before my lenses first thing, and believe me, I can't and won't miss that.'

Gervase Allerby closed his eyes and laughed silently, throwing back his head. 'No, Ms Vivian, your flight is booked for early afternoon. That should give you enough time. I tuned in to your schedule before I woke you.'

'Efficient. So what was I dreaming?'

He grinned. 'My dear, I never pry.'

Sable Grant proved more tractable than Nina would dared have hoped for, which at one time would have been an unusual trait in an up and coming starlet. Not so nowadays. The image had changed. The New Age had bit deep into Hollywood flesh, and everything was mellow. Nina still couldn't help wondering how much of the girl's perfect bone structure and flawless configuration was indebted to the surgeon's cosmetic knife. Perhaps America bred these lissom creatures as a kind of sub-species, whose natural habitat was the film industry. Even though Nina was aware that all self-respecting stars made a point of discussing in their interviews how much they shunned the *prima donna* temperament nowadays, she still wouldn't have believed it until she'd met Sable. Everything was natural, everything was relaxed. Only desperately insecure people possessed painful egos to inflict on others. Sable was well at home in her skin. She was charming.

During a break, while Viennese coffee and wafer-thin Continental chocolate biscuits were handed round by attentive film company personnel, Sable Grant hunkered down beside Nina, who was sitting on a pile of packing cases, fiddling with her equipment. She didn't need to fiddle with her equipment, but it prevented her having to make conversation. There was nobody there Nina thought it was worth talking to. Just the girl and her entourage. She didn't imagine the girl would want to speak to her.

'You're good,' Sable said. 'You make me feel so tranquil.'

Nina smiled. She didn't think Ms Grant would ever be anything other than tranquil in front of a camera. 'That's kind of you. Thanks.' Was she supposed to deliver a compliment back now?

'I really wanted to come to England. I love it. I love the history.'

Don't they always, Nina thought. 'Yeah... there's plenty of that.'

'And you have Emory Patrick over here too. That's wild.'

Nina looked up sharply, far too sharply. It was her DPR persona look, not the habitual laid-back expression of Nina Vivian, photographer.

'What is it?' Sable asked quickly, eyes wide.

Nina shook her head. These New Age techniques the stars were getting into made them too damn sensitive for her liking. 'Oh, coincidence, you know. I was just thinking about him. I have to photograph him tomorrow.'

Sable's eyes widened. '*Really!* Wow, I mean, how lucky for you.' She laid a beautiful, long-fingered hand on Nina's knee and lowered her voice. 'Hey, I know this might be a heavy question, but is there any chance I could get to meet him? Could you, like, arrange that for me?'

Nina smiled. 'I'm sorry. The shoot's in Amsterdam, not London. I wish I could oblige but...' She gestured helplessly.

'That's OK. I understand. I would have liked to meet him though. Just to see whether he's on the level.'

Nina was surprised. 'Think he's a fake, then?' she asked.

'No, not exactly. I think I'm scared he might be all that his people claim he is. It's strange, but in a way I think that would be worse.'

'Yeah,' Nina said. 'I suppose it would.'

Linford Brown was worried. Since the incident at the convention, everyone had thought it best if Emory moved to a hotel, rather than stay in the caravan on site. The place was crawling with media scum. Emory had seemed dazed, as if he'd been severely drained of energy after the lighting guy had done the sit up and walk gig. Emory had passively submitted to Linford's and Iliana's suggestion of privacy, only now he wouldn't come out of the hotel room at all, and wasn't taking calls. He was still eating, but refused to see anyone other than hotel staff. Now, Linford was standing outside the door to room 223, trying to address the person inside, getting more and more wound up by the fact that people kept walking by and giving him strange looks. The TOFL Security man on duty outside Emory's door studiously ignored the proceedings.

The convention had been limping along since the incident at the site, but the atmosphere seemed flat without Emory there. People were understandably disappointed. After all, they'd paid a large fee for the privilege of seeing him. The band performances, sideshows and panel talks had continued as planned, but the audiences only wanted to talk and hear about Emory's healing miracle. All other subjects seemed to have lost their appeal. This obsession was beginning to frustrate the official convention guests. Several of them had left after the first day, mainly writers and scholars who claimed they found the publicity associated with the event somewhat distasteful. It was fortunate the musicians and actors had taken an opposite stance and were unashamedly lapping the publicity up. What worried Linford more than absconding guests was the amount of people who were turning up at the site gates demanding entrance. None of these newcomers had tickets – the event had sold out months ago– and they were either invalids or accompanied by invalids. They had come to see the master. They wanted his healing power. Despite being kept outside the site, they would not go away.

Linford himself was feeling dazed and drained of energy. He'd always been behind Emory a hundred per cent, had believed without reservation in the man's sincerity and convictions, had basked in the Apollo glow of Emory's charisma. Only he hadn't believed in miracles. This was spooky shit. Future Light was meant to be about finding yourself in a world gone crazy, and using that self-knowledge to enlighten others, thereby helping the world to heal. Now, the whole movement was poised on the brink of zipping back to the Dark Ages as fast as it could. Just as Emory did the one thing that perhaps proved his followers' claim that he was the New Son of God beyond all doubt, an immovable host of doubts was cast over the organisation. It was all too weird. It didn't fit into Linford's scheme. Now the man himself was acting crazy.

'Look, Mori, I have to talk to you. Don't do this to me, man. Let me in!' Normally, Linford would not raise his voice to Emory, but perhaps, he gambled, a little uncharacteristic aggression might produce results that habitual serenity would not. 'I'm not taking any more of this shit! If this door doesn't open right now, I'm out of here. For good. I mean it!' He thumped the door with a closed fist and then kicked it. He heard the lock rattle.

'They'll charge us for the paintwork,' Emory said, opening the door. 'You'd better come in.'

Linford felt embarrassed. He'd never behaved like that before, never threatened or used emotional blackmail. The feeling of powerlessness, of regression, was crippling. Emory was wearing a long dark-blue robe which hung open. He was naked beneath it. Some cans of beer were chilling in a bucket of ice. He tossed one to Linford. 'I expect you need this.'

Linford wondered whether Emory was drunk. He had never shunned alcohol but his intake was always moderate. 'I'm sorry. I...'

Emory waved a hand at him. He was standing at the window staring out through the floor length nets. ''S'OK. Forget it.'

'Are you all right?'

Emory looked at Linford over his shoulder. 'Fine. Why shouldn't I be?'

Because you were virtually catatonic when we brought you back from the site; because you've been incommunicado for nearly two days; because you've shut both Iliana and myself out, that's why, Linford thought, but said nothing. His burst of anger had passed. He shrugged. 'We were worried about you,' he said.

Emory turned away from the window and flung himself into a large, white overstuffed chair, one leg hung over the arm. 'I know what you and Iliana have been thinking. You're thinking I shouldn't have done it, right?'

Linford sighed and sat down on the edge of the bed, which appeared unslept in, but of course the maids came around regularly. He wondered whether Emory displayed himself to them so blatantly. 'You know I wouldn't judge you,' he said. 'You did what you felt, at the time.'

'Which was perhaps the wrong time. I know.' Emory closed his eyes and rested his head against the back of the chair.

'Mori,' Linford ventured timidly. 'What exactly *did* you do?'

Emory swallowed, the small convulsion shivering down his long throat. 'Something natural,' he said. 'That's all. It wasn't that guy's time to buy it. It was an accident.'

There are no accidents. There are no coincidences. Those were two of Emory's maxims. Linford felt uncomfortable. He couldn't quite rid himself of the suspicion that Emory had done what he'd done simply to display his power. Linford hadn't imagined that Emory's powers might encompass anything so potent.

'Was he really dead?' Linford asked. He had to. Even though he'd seen the body, that broken scrap so evidently vacated by anything resembling human life, and had spent the last two days trying to convince himself he hadn't.

Emory gave him a withering glance. 'You want me to say "no", don't you. You want me to come clean and admit it was all some kind of sick stunt. It wasn't. I'm sorry. You'll have to live with that.'

'Mori...'

Emory sat upright, suddenly animated by a spasm of emotion, which looked very like rage. 'Isn't this what you all wanted?' he asked. 'Haven't you marketed me as the great saviour of the world? I can't understand why you're so pissed off about this.'

'Emory,' Linford said, hands extended. 'I've said nothing. How could I? You've refused to see me since the incident.'

'You don't have to say anything.' Emory stared at him balefully.

He can't read my mind, Linford told himself firmly. 'All I'm worried about at the moment is the way this business has affected you,' he said, trying to sound calm and reasonable. 'It's obviously upset you, otherwise you wouldn't have hidden yourself away like this.'

'I'm not upset. I needed to think, that's all. I needed to think clearly. Much as I love you both, you and Iliana are distractions.' Emory got up out of the chair and wandered back to the window.

Linford cleared his throat. 'Well, anyway, I'll call the

promotion people and go over to the site today. We'll have to wind it down...'

'No!' Emory turned round in a whirl of blue cloth.

'What do you mean, "no"? The followers want you, Emory, nobody else. And you're here, shut in this damned room. The site is surrounded by weirdoes, who are also all crying for you. It's got out of hand. We have to fold the show.'

'You won't close the site, Linford. It's not finished.'

'What isn't?'

Emory threw up his hands. 'I don't know! I don't know!'

'Talk to me!' Linford cried. 'What is going on, Mori? Everything's changing, isn't it? What's happening?'

Emory curled his lips into a sneer. 'You don't want me to talk, you just want reassurance!'

This is like an argument, Linford thought. *This is like trouble.* He and Emory had never exchanged angry words before, or experienced an uncomfortable atmosphere between them.

Emory leaned against the wall, rubbing his face vigorously, as if to massage something away. Then he dropped his hands and laughed. 'Shit,' he said. 'I'm terrible for you, so much hassle... I know. Come here.' He opened his arms and Linford walked into the embrace, because he hadn't the will or desire to refuse. The blue robe enclosed him like a shroud. It felt like goodbye.

Nina read through her notes again on the plane. No flimsy print-out this time but a bound booklet of laser-printed information, complete with comprehensive illustrations and photographs. It was the biography of Emory Patrick's life. Her job was to fill in the blanks.

According to the DPR data, when he'd been only five, Patrick's parents had died in the famous Milton Keynes murders, gunned down by a psychotic member of the Pro-Life group, who'd freaked out in a hypermall. Following that undoubtedly traumatic incident, Emory had been entrusted into the care of his Aunt Mary, who had been a devout Christian of the Women's Institute persuasion. There was no evidence to suggest the woman had forced her own beliefs upon the boy, but Nina envisaged a childhood surrounded by garish representations of nearly naked crucified men and white-robed limpid saviours that might well have had some influence on Emory's development. He appeared to have enjoyed an unsurpassingly normal childhood in his aunt's care, although once he went to university, his personality had evidently blossomed. He'd studied psychology and had embraced the teachings of some of the wackiest gurus available to the student population at the time. As well as joining a student band, through which he could exercise a previously unglimpsed musical talent, Patrick had initiated consciousness-raising meetings. By the time he'd achieved his degree, with honours, he was a hero of the social scene and the hub of a thriving self-awareness group. Information had been collected from individuals who'd known Patrick at the time, who claimed he'd had a certain magic, that his touch was healing, that he could influence reality with a single thought.

After he left university, close friends had encouraged Patrick to expand his self-awareness group into the organisation now known as Transmission of Future Light, and he'd eventually met up with Brown and Forsyth, who'd since steered his career in an upwards direction. It had been Brown who'd brought the band to prominence, realising it was the ideal medium through which to reach the youth culture. Patrick's physical attractiveness obviously contributed to his success. Although his religious beliefs were fairly unstructured and subject to change, and certainly estranged from the established, patriarchal Church, many people believed he really was the New Son of God. Patrick did not publicly concur with this idea, but neither did he deny it.

After one last look at one of the photographs – Patrick on-stage, his shirt falling off one shoulder, hair all over the place, mmmm – Nina closed the binder. She felt a little dazed. That part about Patrick being brought up by his Aunt Mary was just too much, and what percentage of the anecdotes about his college years, gleaned from old friends and acquaintances, was reliable data? Not a great deal, Nina suspected. She was also sure most of the information had been gathered from the newspapers. Although they scanned the media and culture for potential paranorms, both directly and psychically, the DPR had probably thought Patrick was a money-making joke, like all the other New Age manias, until the Amsterdam gig. They hadn't thought him paranormal until now, because he hadn't really done anything to suggest that.

Nina took another look at the photographs: Emory Patrick talking to crowds of adoring devotees, Emory Patrick singing with his band, Emory Patrick holding group meditation sessions. His charisma shone from the frames; he was indisputably star material. People fell for that; they loved heroes, but only un-Talented ones. *So, Mr Patrick, what now?* she wondered.

The Dutch authorities were freaked – understandably so – and because Patrick was British, it had fallen to the DPR to investigate and presumably shuffle the New Son of God off the continent and back to the UK. And, she had to admit with a private smile, it would be kind of weird having the New Son of God on the Temps list. What would they call him in for? Divine retribution, when it was needed?

Nina still didn't believe Patrick was paranormal. Despite her earlier misgivings, she had become intrigued by the Amsterdam affair and was looking forward to delving into it, but somehow the thought that a Talent had been responsible seemed unreal. In her experience, paranorms spent their lives trying to live down their differences, hide them and apologise for them. They did not veer towards flamboyance. Still, if Patrick was a Talent, his days as guru were numbered. Once the public found out, his movement would be history. Paranorms had never been popular, a circumstance initiated by fear and ignorance more than anything. Nina herself never divulged her Talent. It was fortunately easy to conceal, and certainly in the DPR's interest to keep it under wraps. Even the DPR branch she worked for was a highly secret operation that only a very few people knew existed. Should she ever be unveiled, the DPR would probably deny all knowledge of her. Her name would not be found on any DPR file, and the office she was called to visit in the middle of the night would be as empty and dusty as if it hadn't been used for years.

Her camera case lay on the rack overhead. The camera was a prop for her Talent, but not essential. It disguised what she could do, just as much as it had revealed what she could do. The memory was mercifully fading with the years, but that time on the shoot in the Lake District still festered darkly in the depths of Nina's heart. They'd told her to confront it, wear it out by becoming familiar with it. *That bitch who tried to ruin my life! God, I have no regrets!* But she did. She had so many regrets that she'd nearly lost her sanity. It had been the DPR who'd picked up the pieces after the incident, called in by frantic onlookers who'd realised what was happening. Gervase Allerby had been the suave, dark angel who'd glued Nina back together. She felt he now held the keys to her soul, even though she sailed through her glitteringly successful professional and social life as if she hadn't a care in the world. In reality, she felt she belonged to the DPR alone, the unacknowledged underworld of the DPR that no one knew about, the truth beneath the bureaucracy and red tape above ground. She had no complaints. Without them, she'd be locked up in one institution or another. So, she did the job, and sometimes the job was tame. She hoped this one would be. Still, the DPR must be frightened of Emory Patrick, very frightened, to put Nina Vivian on his case.

Nina was due to meet a Dutch telepath at the airport, who'd been doing some preliminary work on the Patrick situation. The two of them would work in concert until they'd managed to ascertain whether Emory Patrick was Talented or not. Presumably, once that was established, the telepath would butt out and leave Nina to do what was necessary, if anything *was* necessary.

The telepath was named Chantal, a skinny, dark-haired gamine, who looked like a refugee from a Delacorta novel. Like most young Dutch people, she spoke flawless, idiomatic English.

'You're French?' Nina asked, as they shook hands.

The girl wrinkled her nose. 'Yah, sort of. Mother was. Lived here all my life, though.'

Chantal took Nina through the beautifully clean streets of the city to a cool, dark bar, where they sipped champagne, courtesy of Chantal's agency's expense account, and swapped gossip about other paranorms they knew. Nina was beginning to feel muzzily philanthropic by the time the subject of Emory Patrick was introduced. Chantal had lit a slim cigar and leaned conspiratorially over the table.

'I've been sniffing round the convention site,' she said, 'but the man has gone underground since the incident.'

Nina had lifted her camera out of its case and now peered through the viewfinder at her companion. 'I expect there are quite a few people sniffing about,' she said. 'I'm not surprised you didn't come up with anything. Patrick's people must be feeling very paranoid right now, and don't paranoid people have a tendency to erect their own unconscious mind blocks?'

'Oh, I found out enough,' Chantal said. 'Enough to tell me the Future Lighters are as stunned by Patrick's Jesus trick as much as everyone else. He's never pulled a stunt like this before.'

'There's mention of healing sessions in the briefing notes I've got,' Nina said.

'Yeah, but Patrick never claimed responsibility for that. Always said the people concerned had healed themselves through their belief. Nothing paranormal about that. Even your family doctor will prescribe a little positive thinking to kick out the blues nowadays.'

'That's true. It's crazy isn't it? Along comes someone who might genuinely have the most awesome Talent and the authorities are terrified of him. From what I've read, he seems a genuine guy, not even particularly power-hungry. I wonder why the DPR are so nervous about him? Why not just let him get on with what he's doing, which is basically cheering people up in this goddamned shit of a mess we call a world?'

Chantal shrugged and pulled a face. 'Perhaps it's because he's genuine and not power-hungry that makes your DPR nervous. My lot are the same. Let's face it, a religious leader who isn't a bone-deep self-aggrandising bastard and a Talent who isn't ashamed of his powers makes for one poky individual. Think about it. I reckon if we do find out Patrick is a paranorm and he decides to come out about it, he wouldn't lose any popularity at all.'

'Oh, he would! Certainly in the UK. anyway. I know what people are like about paranorms there.'

Chantal shook her head. 'No, Emory Patrick is different. You don't understand what he does to people. His followers really *love* him. Desperately. Wouldn't make any difference to them what he is. If he confessed he'd killed his parents or a thousand babies, they'd forgive him.'

'How can you be so sure?'

Grinning, Chantal turned the collar of her leather jacket around to display an Emory Patrick badge. 'I've been close, very close, to members of the Patrick following,' she said.

'Wow, paid up member!' Nina said. 'Hope your agency picked up the tab.'

'Naturally. Anyway, it's up to you to get us close to the man himself now.'

'Thought it might.'

'I picked up which hotel he's staying in from someone at the convention site. We're booked in there too now.'

Nina lifted her camera to her eye. 'I'm impressed!' Then she winked around the camera's body at Chantal. 'Take me to your leader,' she said.

Iliana, lying on one of the two beds in the hotel room she was sharing with Linford, bit through another of her lovingly manicured nails with an audible snap. Linford jerked in irritation, lying on the other bed. Air conditioning hummed into the summer afternoon. Everything was very still in the microcosm of the room. Outside the city buzzed faintly, as if the sounds came to them through a virtually impenetrable shield.

'Maybe we should go back to England,' Iliana said, and then spat, expelling a sliver of fingernail.

'We can't leave him!' Linford snapped.

'I meant we'd take him with us,' Iliana replied in a flat voice. 'That was your thoughts speaking, honey, not mine.'

She shifted restlessly onto her side, a shapely odalisque in turquoise leggings and an Emory Patrick t-shirt, silky blonde hair falling over her coquettishly frowning face. Appearances were deceptive, Linford thought. He'd always considered she looked like a mindless tart, but the brain inside that cover girl body was as sharp as a hypodermic and capable of injecting equally subcutaneous poisons. It was she who held the business side of the Future Light together; a cage around the men that kept predators away from their meat. Iliana: metal and sharpness. *You should listen to her,* Linford thought, and then remembered the promise he'd made to Emory earlier, a promise he'd been almost physically coerced into making.

'The convention's only half-way through,' he said. 'People have paid.'

'People can be refunded, for God's sake! We can mail them all a care package as well, if that's what it takes! This is a mess. I'm confused. I can't think. We need to lie low for a while, re-evaluate our set-up. Anyway, I can't see Mori coming out of his room to address the crowds in the near future, can you?'

Linford sighed. 'I don't know what he's thinking. His mood

is... strange. He's shut off from me.'

'Idiot!' Iliana exclaimed and thumped the duvet. 'Idiot! Idiot! Idiot! Why the hell did he have to go and do that?' She'd already asked this question about a hundred times over the last few days. Linford had run out of answers.

'I'm going to have to say something I've been putting off saying,' Iliana said into the silence that had followed her outburst.

'What?' Linford was apprehensive of her tone of voice.

Iliana sat up on the side of the bed, legs apart, hands dangling between her knees. Linford noticed, for the first time, how tired she looked. She almost looked her age, which was unusual. Although he was unsure what her true age was, she generally looked about twenty-five, and he'd known her too long for that to be the case. 'There's something I haven't been confronting in my head, Lin. Emory really did it, didn't he? He really brought someone back from the dead. What does that mean?'

'Something we've always believed. That he's no bullshitter.'

Iliana closed her eyes and shook her head. 'No, my darling, it does not. What it means is that our beloved Mori has... powers. Magical powers? Spiritual powers or even... paranormal powers?'

Linford sat up. 'No! You can't mean that! He's no freak!'

'Now don't get hysterical on me,' Iliana said in a low, deadly voice. 'We've no time for that. This is serious.'

'Yeah, I'd say so! It'd be the end of us!'

'That's not quite what I meant,' Iliana said. 'It's going to open a whole can of worms, don't you see? The implications are awesome. Tie in the religious aspect with paranormality, and you get a nasty mess of quandaries regarding faith healers, psychics, my god, perhaps even people like tarot readers, I don't know! Unwittingly, Emory Patrick might redefine the whole concept of what paranormality is and where its boundaries lie.'

'How can that affect us?' Linford regretted the question even before he'd finished speaking, aware of its selfish tone.

'The DPR will be interested in Emory, Lin. They might already be here.'

'So what? They're just a bunch of clerks!' Linford couldn't help laughing. *The DPR! Yeah, terrifying, really terrifying.*

'Don't be pathetic,' Iliana said. 'They'll be wondering what other little surprises Mori might have up his sleeve. They could just snatch him.'

'That's illegal.'

'Grow up, Linford!' Iliana stood up.

'Jesus, Illa, you've been watching too many spy movies,' Linford said. 'This is the real world, with formal procedures etc. No one can just snatch someone like that. Not officially.'

Iliana turned, one hand on her hip and sneered at him. 'Despite the vast experience you claim to have, you're really such a child, Linford! Emory has power, real power. Thousands belong to TOFL, every one of them prepared to stand by their Great Man. If that Great Man turns out to be a paranorm, things could get nasty. How will the great general public react, for example, knowing a paranorm has so much influence, that their sons and daughters flock to his concerts and talks? The DPR would *have* to do something. They'd have no choice.'

'But Emory might not be a paranorm,' Linford said.

Iliana snorted. 'Don't be ridiculous! What else could he be?'

'But...'

She threw her hands up over head in a dramatic gesture, stalking towards the window. 'Oh, Linford, face reality will you? There's no Messiah, no Second Coming, there's only Hope. That's what Emory is: Hope. Nothing more, in a spiritual sense.'

'Then what can we do?'

For a moment, the pair of them swapped the most naked glance that it is possible for two people to share. They knew that as survivors, which they undoubtedly were, they should leave Emory Patrick to his destiny. They should run while they still could.

Then Iliana visibly steeled herself. 'He's not losing it, Linford, he really isn't. I don't quite what he *is* doing at the moment, but Emory is no fool. All I have to suggest is that we go back to England. The rest is up to him. We'll have to trust him.'

'You mean, you think his powers are strong enough to protect him from... well, anything? Strong enough to protect us?'

Iliana grinned a crooked grin. 'Doesn't he say you only have to believe in something to make it real?'

'It's a risk, Illa.'

'Sure, and I'll be watching his back like a goddamned hawk lady until he's got his act together again.'

The hotel lobby was full of people, wearing Emory Patrick t-shirts and little identification clips. They all appeared to be scurrying around doing nothing very much except scurrying. Nina had brought only her camera case with her, plus a hold-all, with a change of jeans, cosmetics and a toothbrush. Chantal appeared to have brought nothing, but of course she would have checked in earlier. Nina noticed the Dutch girl nodding hello to quite a few of the Patrick people.

'Any of these the ones you got close to, like really close?' Nina teased.

Chantal pulled a face, and then pantomimed a demure voice. 'I believe you misunderstood my meaning, or perhaps my grasp of language was in error.'

'Your grasp of language seems sweetly accurate to me, lady!'

Chantal shrugged. 'Well, some of the guys are cute.'

They went into the lift. 'Our room is as close to Patrick's as I could get,' Chantal said. 'Fortunately, the hotel staff are not paranoid and therefore as easy to read as a cereal box.'

'Does he have security?'

'Course. They have a few heavies – you know, concerned *brothers*, to keep the hordes from the big man.'

'He's not doing interviews, I take it?'

Chantal rolled her eyes. 'No, not exactly. I reckon you should get to Forsyth or Brown to get to Patrick. If not directly, then through the merchandising staff or something.'

'You mean I might have to buy a t-shirt?'

'It may come to that. Can't your expense account take it?'

'You kidding! I'm a temp for the DPR. Whatever I buy on expenses has to have about six invoices, a signature in blood, ten good reasons why I bought it...'

Chantal groaned. 'Oh, grim! Well, here's our floor. We should make dinner if we hurry. Perhaps that'll give us our first contact.'

'Damn, I knew I should have brought a posh frock with me!' Nina said.

Chantal put a hand on her arm. 'Nina Vivian, this is Amsterdam. Anything goes here. Relax.'

Linford did not feel like eating. He felt hyped up, excited. Iliana glanced pointedly at his glass every time he summoned the waiter to refill it with Scotch, but she said nothing, eating her seafood like a cat, in a dainty yet macabre manner, and betraying no sign of unease other than her nibbled fingernails. She'd been to see Emory before coming down to dinner and had not yet divulged the outcome of the interview. Linford felt she was tormenting him deliberately by her silence, but he shrank from asking her outright.

'I shall miss this food,' she said, clawing the flesh from her last monster prawn. They'd eaten out at Indonesian restaurants every night before this, but tonight some instinct prevented them from straying into the city. Both of them wanted to stay near Emory. Iliana had said earlier she was sure Emory 'wasn't losing it', but just the fact she had spoken those words suggested she was worried he might be.

Eventually, Linford could stand it no longer and shouldered his pride aside. 'How did he seem tonight?' he asked.

Iliana licked her lips. 'Wired, I'd say. He's suffering, Lin, I know he is. Kicking himself, I think, but he won't talk about it.'

'I told you,' Linford replied.

Iliana ignored the remark. 'I suggested England and he was vague about committing himself. But I reckon if I just book the tickets and pack, he'll comply.'

'God, I do hope so. I've started getting really jumpy since you put that thought into my head about DPR creeps. I'm seeing men in grey everywhere! Do you know...' Linford noticed he no longer had the shred of Iliana's attention he'd had before. She was looking up expectantly, a welcoming smile spreading across her face. For a moment, before he followed the direction of her gaze, Linford thought Emory himself had shown up for dinner. But what he saw first was a large expensive camera, and then the tall, lanky woman who was holding it up to her face. He stood up, extending his arms, fingers spread. 'No pictures!'

'Oh sorry!' The woman lowered the camera, revealing a strong attractive face with little makeup. She pushed back her long, straight brown hair behind one ear.

Iliana put a restraining hand on Linford's arm and said, 'It's all right, quite all right.'

The woman came right up to their table, the camera dangling heavily against her chest. She wore a faded t-shirt with a badly-screened fractal print on it, her leather jacket was scuffed and her jeans were ripped, but something about her presence spoke comfortable affluence. 'I hope you don't mind,' she said, beaming at Iliana. 'I realise now who you are, but – you won't believe this – when I saw you sitting there I thought you were someone else, a Hollywood someone else as it happens. I do apologise. You must be going through hell with photographers at the moment. I was well out of order, pointing a lens at you like that. I *am* sorry.'

Iliana would normally crush such an approach with a blast of well-delivered verbal cruelty, but tonight she was obviously prepared to be magnanimous. 'Oh, as I said, it's quite all right. You staying here, or just passing through with your recording eye?'

God, she's flirting! Linford thought, aghast.

The photographer grinned. 'Staying here actually. I was just about to sample the cuisine of this establishment with my colleague.' She gestured towards another jeans and leather-clad female hanging back by the door with folded arms.

'Really? Well, please, join us!'

Linford was astonished.

Iliana extended a hand, which the photographer shook vigorously. 'I'm Iliana Forsyth and this is Linford Brown.'

'Pleased to meet you,' the woman said. 'I'm Hazel Rose.' She beamed at Linford and indicated the seat by him. 'Can I sit here?'

'Nina, you are brilliant, absolutely brilliant!' Chantal leaned against the side of the lift, her grinning, slightly intoxicated face reflected in the shiny doors opposite.

'Hazel, please, not Nina!' Nina said, giggling. They had spent a very pleasant evening in the company of Iliana and Linford, being heaped with delicacies both culinary and alcoholic, all of which had been paid for by the Transmission of Future Light.

'I could get into religion if it's this well-paid!' Nina had whispered to Chantal as they'd left the restaurant. Now they were on their way to a meeting with Emory Patrick himself.

'I don't know how you did it,' Chantal said. 'It looked so natural.'

Nina rearranged her hair, peering at the misty reflection of herself in the doors. 'It *was* natural,' she replied. 'Anyway, we've got a few minutes alone together, so tell me what was on their minds.'

Chantal wrinkled her nose. 'They're planning on leaving soon. Iliana couldn't stop thinking about it. She was also quite surprised at herself when she asked us up to meet Emory. As for Linford, he nearly had a cerebral haemorrhage when Iliana came out with the invitation. Still, they don't suspect we're anything but what we claimed to be.'

As far as the Future Lighters were concerned, Hazel Rose and her assistant were in the city to photograph a local rock star's wedding.

'Your Department certainly sent the right woman for the job,' Chantal said. 'You have one amazing Talent for coercion.'

'Yeah.' Nina didn't mention the rest of it. She already liked Chantal a lot and didn't want to lose her friendship. They'd just kind of clicked together, made a good team. If Chantal knew the rest, she'd back off. It didn't take telepathy to work that one out.

Linford and Iliana had gone back to their room and had arranged for Chantal and Nina to meet them there in ten minutes or so. Enough time for Nina to drop off her camera – Linford had insisted on that – and for Chantal to roll a joint of the excellent grass she'd insouciantly ordered from over the counter in the bar they'd visited earlier.

As they sat on Chantal's bed smoking together, Nina was aware of a certain tightness in the fibres of her body, and consciously regulated her breathing. Was that fear or excitement? 'Read me,' she said to Chantal.

Chantal frowned. 'Don't have to. It's radiating off you, like you're just about to go on your first date. Palpitations! He freaks you, this guy, doesn't he?'

Words flashed through Nina's brain, almost as if she could hear them, but she didn't recognise the voice. *Sometimes, it's like a premonition*. She stood up, swaying a little on her feet. 'Come on, let's get this over with.'

Iliana was putting down the phone after speaking to Emory, Linford hopping around uncomfortably behind her, between the beds. 'Well, what did he say, apart from "go to hell"? We don't know these women, Illa. What are you playing at?'

Iliana straightened up and turned round slowly. She looked like an ice goddess, all stretched white satin and glittering paste jewellery, statuesque neck and coiled hair. Her expression, however, was strangely vague. 'Linford, you know me as well as anyone. I don't know why I invited the Rose woman and her friend up here. I just felt compelled to. I still do. That's not like me, but in a way, I'm not worried about it.'

'What's going on, Illa? This sounds weird.'

'Gets weirder.' She sat down on the bed, leaning back on straight arms. 'Emory knows, Lin. I'm sure he does. He knew what I was going to say before I spoke. Oh, he let me say the words, but he could have stopped me at any time and finished my little speech. All he said was "I'll be ready". Just that. No argument. Nothing. There's something special about that woman...'

Linford's mouth dropped open. 'Oh my God!'

'What?'

'She couldn't be... well connected with what we spoke about earlier, could she? A woman in grey?'

Iliana laughed. 'Don't be ridiculous! No. I have a nose for officials and Hazel Rose doesn't have the right smell. She's poky in her own right, but I strongly feel she's independent. Good God, Linford, you really are seeing grey shadows in every corner, aren't you!'

'Remember you're the hawk lady.'

Iliana nodded. 'I know. But Hazel Rose isn't prey, isn't vermin. She's another hawk.'

'Jesus, she's really made an impression on you, hasn't she!'

Iliana shrugged. 'She picked me out. I'm not stupid.'

The atmosphere in Linford and Iliana's room was electric when Chantal and Nina arrived. Nina had to escape to the bathroom, where she sat on the toilet with her head in her hands, trying to collect her thoughts. Why did she feel like this? It was just a job like any other. Her stomach churned with pain as if her guts were twisting into knots. Was she genuinely ill or something? This was terrible. She'd have to be in peak form to handle the next stage of the operation. One moment of lost concentration and the whole fragile structure of coercion she'd erected around Iliana –

and hoped to extend to Patrick – could crumble.

Iliana came and knocked on the door. 'Are you ready? Emory's expecting us.' Nina flushed the chain and came out. Iliana put a hand on her arm. 'Are you all right, Hazel? You look very white.'

Nina raised a hand. 'Yeah, I'm fine. Had a busy, busy day, that's all and a little overindulgence. Got a bit of a headache.'

'Would you like something for that?'

Nina shook her head. 'No, really. I'll be fine. Just don't offer me another drink.'

Walking the short distance up the corridor to Emory's room, Nina felt as if she might faint at any time. Chantal, picking up the way she was feeling, linked her arm through Nina's to give her some support, both physical and emotional. Nina was thinking, *This is a gruesome parody of sociability. We all feel as if we're going to our deaths, yet we're still walking, still smiling at each other. It's a sham. Are you in control of this, Nina Vivian, are you?*

A tall, well-muscled individual, obviously a bodyguard, stood outside the door to Emory Patrick's room. Two young girls were sitting on the floor against the wall. They had a large ghetto-blaster between them, which filled the corridor with raucous music. The enormous, half-empty bottle of wine sitting on the carpet indicated the girls were entertaining the bodyguard during what must be the loneliest watch of the night. Both the girls wore identification clips which proclaimed they were Future Light merchandising staff. They peered curiously at Nina and Chantal as Iliana addressed the muscle-man.

'Hey, I've seen you,' one of the girls said to Nina. 'Weren't you in ID magazine last month? Aren't you that photographer... er... sorry, forgotten your name... what was it?'

Iliana glared frostily at the girls, as she opened the door. 'Come along Hazel.' Clearly she disapproved of mixing with the menial staff. As Nina went through the door, she heard the girl's lowered voice say, '*Sure* the name wasn't Hazel...'

Linford was relieved to see that Emory had dressed and shaved himself for the occasion. He was looking splendid in tight black leather with a loose red shirt, his hair hanging round his shoulders and back. Iliana busied herself with the introductions, as she poured everyone a drink.

'Emory, this is Hazel Rose, and her assistant Felice.'

Emory smiled at Nina. 'Ms.... *Rose*, pleased to meet you.' He held out his hand to be shaken. Nina hesitated, prompting Chantal to take hold of the hand herself.

'Hazel isn't feeling too well,' Iliana said brightly. 'Have you any Perrier, Mori?'

'No, but we could ring for some.'

Nina sat down in one of the white, overstuffed chairs. She flapped her hands at them. 'Oh, please don't make a fuss. I'll be OK in a minute.' Chantal sat down beside her on the arm of the chair. Nina was grateful for her support. The initial sensation of being in Emory Patrick's presence had been like standing too close to the lip of a volcano. One false step and she'd fall, to a death either by broken neck or incineration. Yet that feeling had only lasted brief seconds, and she felt it might have been self-induced. She'd hyped herself up for this meeting far too much.

'I'm very pleased to meet you Hazel Rose,' Emory said. 'I'm familiar with your work.'

The room bucked before Nina's eyes. 'Are you?' she managed to say. 'I'm surprised.'

'Why? You're fairly well-known aren't you? I've seen your stuff in all the glossy magazines.'

He knows who I am, she thought. *He knows everything about me.* And yet she was sure that, for whatever reason, he wasn't going to expose her to his colleagues. He probably thought she was a scheming little paparazzo, angling to get some sensational pictures, and had decided to play along for a while. The indignation she felt at that revelation cleared away some of her confusion. She sat upright. 'So, are you going to let me photograph you when you get back to England, then?'

He shrugged. 'Perhaps. *If* I go back.'

'I thought we'd decided that earlier,' Iliana said sharply.

Emory looked at her. 'Had we? The convention's only half-way through, Illa. I shall be returning to the site tomorrow.'

'What? Are you mad?' Iliana appeared to have forgotten there were strangers present. 'You can't! Your stupid stunt has probably drawn crazies from half the known world! It's too dangerous for you to go back there.'

'Iliana, there is no danger.'

'Well you might have had the decency to mention this earlier!'

'I hadn't decided earlier.'

Nina hoped Chantal was busy using her Talent on Patrick. She herself didn't feel it was the right time to bring hers into play. Not yet. Some part of her still believed it wouldn't be needed, and she hoped Chantal's probing would back that conviction up. Her initial impression was of a man who was clearly used to adulation, but nevertheless did not take himself too seriously. Like Sable Grant, he was comfortable in his skin. He had a confident performer's compelling eyes, but the charisma was just part of the act. This was a showman, not a messiah, she was sure of it. She could not imagine him raising somebody from the dead.

'How's your headache?' he asked her.

She shrugged. 'Manageable.'

'Give me your hand.'

Aha, it was show time. With a cynical smile, Nina extended her arm. He took her hand in his. The skin was warm and dry, but there was no electric jolt. *He's not Talented*, she thought. *He's not.* Emory closed his eyes briefly and squeezed her fingers.

'Stress,' he said.

'You don't say.'

He let her go and pulled a wry grin. 'I can tell you're not a believer.'

She shrugged again. 'Well...'

'It doesn't matter,' he said. 'You clearly have your own belief system that works for you pretty well.'

'Not as well as yours, I'm sure.'

He grimaced. 'Some people might say mine isn't working too well at the moment. Strange, isn't it? You give people what they want and it scares them.'

'Like raising the dead?'

Linford cleared his throat loudly and interjected. 'I don't think we should discuss that now, Emory.'

'Why not?' Emory asked in a reasonable voice. 'I'm not ashamed or embarrassed about it.'

'Look, neither am I...' Linford blathered. 'But...'

Emory turned away from him. 'You're sceptical about that, aren't you?' he said to Nina.

She nodded. 'Do it again in front of me, and I might not be.'

'Is that a challenge?' Emory laughed.

She raised her hands. 'If you want it to be.'

'Part of being what I am precludes rising to challenges.'

'Oh well, never mind.'

Emory smiled. 'Ms Rose, I might not be able to provide the hard evidence you so obviously want, but what do you say to accompanying me to the site tomorrow? You could get some good pictures there at least, and a ringside view.'

He was making it too easy for her. Nina felt edgy. 'Er... yeah, thanks.'

'That'd be marvellous!' Chantal said.

'I hope you're doing the right thing, Emory,' Iliana said.

'I'm just doing what comes next,' he answered.

On the way back to their room an hour or so later, Chantal said, 'Well, how's your headache? Did the Great Man heal you or what?'

Nina smiled. 'The headache – and the gut ache which I didn't mention – have gone, but they were caused by stress, being too tired and having drunk and smoked too much. I don't think Emory was responsible for getting rid of them. I just sobered up and relaxed, that's all.'

'You really are too sceptical, Ms Rose!'

'So enlighten me otherwise. What did you pick up?'

Chantal pulled a face. 'You won't like it.'

'What won't I like?'

'I couldn't read him at all. He'd protected himself.'

'Are you telling me he protected himself in a Talented way? Now that I really won't like!'

Chantal shrugged. 'Non-paranorms can't generally screen themselves, and when they do it's reflexive. Otherwise, it registers as a Talent, I'm afraid. Anyway, why are you so anxious to prove Patrick isn't a paranorm?'

Nina couldn't tell her, partly because she didn't know, and partly because once that fact had been proved, she would have to call the DPR for further instructions and she knew what they'd be. Since she'd become familiar with her Talent, she had never doubted it for an instant, but she still shrank from confronting Emory Patrick if he was Talented himself. It wasn't that she felt she'd fail, or that he'd be more powerful than her; it was

51

something else, something buried or undefined, something she didn't want to know. 'I suppose I don't want to spoil his party, in a way. He's not doing any harm.'

'Well,' Chantal said, 'I'm sorry, but tomorrow I've got to phone in my report, and it will have to include that fact that Emory managed to block me tonight.'

'We have no real proof yet. He might just be strong-minded. Can you delay reporting in until after we've been to the convention site?'

Chantal didn't look too happy about the request. 'OK, but this is thin ice, Nina. If anything happens, and things get out of control at the site, my withholding information might incur disciplinary penalties.'

'Look, I can use my Talent to make sure things don't get out of control. Trust me.'

Chantal sighed. 'Well, as the lady said to our friend Mr Patrick, I hope you know what you're doing.'

In the morning, Nina woke up with a tense headache. She knew the DPR would want evidence that Patrick's 'miracle' had been faked, and although she was sure it had been faked, she felt that Emory himself didn't realise it. She was honest with herself enough to realise she wanted his image of sincerity and concern to be a true one. Had she dreamed about him?

Chantal was a little surly with her. 'You fancy him, don't you!' she accused.

'He's a stunner,' Nina admitted, 'but my guts are telling me he's not Talented. That's all there is to it.'

'Yeah, course!'

The two women went down to the lobby in uncomfortable silence.

Accompanied by the triumvirate of Future Light, Nina and Chantal rode to the site in a hired limousine. Emory seemed calm and at ease, although his colleagues were rather antsy. Iliana flipped through a sheaf of schedule notes, while Linford fiddled with a pocket computer. Emory sat between them, hands comfortably laced, smiling gently to himself and not catching anybody's eye. Nina didn't want to look at him, but her eyes were continually drawn to his face. Wonderful bones! She chastised herself silently. *Remember, this is a job, a job.* The words became a mantra long before they approached the site.

Chantal sat beside Nina, staring out of a side window. She was sullen and twitchy because Nina had repeated her request about not phoning in the report that morning. 'I don't want to contravene the rules!' Chantal had said.

Nina had been surprised by that; she hadn't thought Chantal the sort of person to care about rules particularly.

The silence in the car was oppressive. Its cold, purified air was sickly with vehicle deodorant.

It was easy to tell when they were nearing the convention site, because there were so many people milling around wearing Emory Patrick T-shirts. Many of them wore back-packs. Even through the polarised, security windows of the limo, the pumping sound of loud music could be heard. The car glided forward, as noticeable as a hearse, but although people turned their heads to glance at it, no one appeared to realise it might contain the sacred presence of their Great Man. Nina wondered how Emory was feeling, knowing all these people were his, disciples of the pop Messiah. Her camera case felt heavy upon her knees. She noticed Emory looking at it. She smiled at him. He blinked at her, turned away.

'Thank God they haven't realised who's in this car,' Iliana said, shuffling her notes into a neat pile and inserting them into a briefcase. With her action, a sense of movement and communication came into the car. Linford put away his computer.

'What are you going to do today?' Nina asked Emory.

'Talk to them,' he replied. 'Perform. Do what I'm here to do.' His voice was almost cold. Nina felt as if he'd slapped her.

'I called the band,' Linford said. 'They're ready for you.'

Emory nodded, distracted.

He's worried, Nina thought. *He's trying to hide it, but he's worried.*

Having skirted the main entrance, they were now approaching a smaller gate in the high fence that led to the performers' enclosure. Here, the crowds were pressing up against the site boundary, and the TOFL security staff was augmented by local police. The day was going to be hot. The police looked cheerful in shirt sleeves. Then, Nina noticed Chantal press her fingers against the car window. 'Look at that. Shit, look at that.'

Nina looked. Hot glint of chrome against the fence. She saw wheelchairs, hundreds of them, people with other people carried in their arms, children lolling mindless and drooling against desperate breasts. She saw bodies without limbs, and limbs in plaster, atrophied, deformed.

'Oh... my... *God*!' Iliana looked disgusted. She turned away from the window.

'Aren't you used to this?' Nina asked. 'Isn't this part of the show?'

Emory gave her what she supposed amounted to a hard look.

Linford said, 'No, no it isn't.'

'You brought this to us,' Iliana said, not looking at Emory. 'By Christ, you brought this to us!'

People had stuck things to the wire fence; messages, entreaties, petitions, ribbons, babies' clothes, photographs. Overhead, helicopters whirred like carrion birds.

'They can't get in, those people,' Iliana said. 'It's tickets only.'

'Fortunate for you,' Nina said.

Emory Patrick said nothing.

The car swept round behind the enormous canopied stage and parked among a cluster of marquees and caravans. The flattened grass was damp underfoot, squeezed of its juice, and strewn with sand in places. The air smelled of hot rubber and electricity. People were milling everywhere, all wearing identification clips. Security was heavy. Dour men were marching around, speaking into walky-talkies. Photographers and video crews, who were either Future Light employees, or people who'd paid their way in somehow, were weighed down with equipment, the majority of which was pointed at the car. Everyone had been informed Emory Patrick was going to make an appearance. Getting out of the car, Nina sensed the atmosphere immediately, like that of a huge, hungry beast that, scenting meat nearby, was straining to be let out of its cage. The crowd beyond the stage, hidden from this area, was a gigantic muted roar, the buzz of the helicopters an almost insignificant guttural whine above it. Word was being passed around already, perhaps a wordless telepathic message: Emory Patrick is here. They must have *sensed* his presence.

'This is freaky,' Chantal whispered to Nina. 'Too powerful. I wish you'd have let me phone in.'

'I didn't physically stop you,' Nina hissed back waspishly. 'I only asked a favour. You didn't have to agree.'

Chantal shrugged and moved away.

Emory Patrick was last out of the car. As soon as he set foot on the ground, flanked by Linford and Iliana, the crowd of officials and Future Light personnel swooped on him in a twittering, sycophantic flock. He smiled affably, nodded and raised his hands, Linford and Iliana clearing a path ahead of him. Iliana, dressed in black leather, her hair piled high, her eyes hidden behind huge shades looked mean. People skittered out of her path. Nina and Chantal, already apart in feeling, were separated by the milling bodies, shunted away from the star.

Everyone converged in one of the marquees, where wine and beer were being served on trays. Nina, remaining near the entrance, helped herself to a beer and took her camera out of its case. Linford came over. 'He's going on stage in ten minutes to address the crowd,' he said.

'Doesn't waste any time, does he!'

'Er... no. You can follow us up. He's asked you to.'

Nina nodded. 'OK. Is this anything like you expected?'

Linford pulled a sour face. 'Emory's appearances are always a powerful event, but this is different. Kind of hysterical.' He shook his head. 'I wouldn't have asked you here, but Emory was insistent. Seems like he and Iliana have both taken a fancy to you.'

'Oh.' She'd certainly influenced Iliana, but was unconvinced her Talent had swayed Emory Patrick in her favour. Neither had she sensed any evidence of it.

'I don't think he should be doing this,' Linford said suddenly.

'I know. I think you're probably right.'

He smiled gratefully. 'The crowds at the fence are causing a problem. We've been told the riot control squads might have to be called in.'

'God! Didn't realise it was that bad. How awful.'

'It's worse at the main entrance, apparently. They're all sick. They've come from everywhere. Seems like thousands of them. Where have they come from?' Linford shook his head in despair. Nina felt an unexpected stab of sympathy.

'Riot squads to control sick people?' she asked. 'Seems a bit extreme.'

'There's so many of them. They're all trying to get in, to get at Emory. They want him to heal them.'

'Like Lourdes or something,' Nina said.

'No, not like that,' Linford replied. 'It's fevered, desperate... They're like animals. One of the video crews has been filming it all. I've seen the footage. They're running it on a VCR back there.' He gestured behind him and then shook his head again. 'I wish we could go back to England this minute. Perhaps you can use your influence on Emory. He likes you.'

How ironic, Nina thought. *That's probably exactly what I'm here to do.* 'I've hardly met him, Linford,' she said. 'I really don't think I can get involved.'

He shrugged. 'Oh well. You'd better come with me now. Where's your assistant?'

'Oh, she's around. It's OK. I can manage by myself for this.'

The view from the side of the stage was breathtaking. Before Emory or any of his musicians and dancers appeared, Nina climbed up the speaker stacks and took a few shots of the crowd, using her most powerful lens to take a look at the distant boundary fence, the thousands of desperate faces pressed up against it, the desperate fingers hooked through the wire. The audience itself was a swaying, colourful monster, arms rising and falling in some sort of cult dance. Voices ululated into the summer morning, a crooning chant that held an undeniable note of threat in its depths. Overhead, police helicopters were weaving their own frantic dance, back and forth, back and forth, as if they were concerned about what was happening, but unsure what to do. An enormous security man wearing an old ripped Emory Patrick t-shirt came and shouted at Nina to get down. Reluctantly, because although the crowd alarmed her slightly, she found the sight of it compelling, Nina scrambled down and allowed the man to direct her, none too gently to where Linford and Iliana, along with a group of Future Light satellites, were standing in a raised enclosure to the right of the stage.

Even before Nina reached them, the crowd began to scream. She turned around, fighting away from the security man's insistent hold on her arm. Everyone in the vast audience was rising to their feet. The colourful, hungry monster was flexing its spine. The hairs rose reflexively on Nina's neck and arms. She didn't even have to look to know that Emory Patrick had just walked on stage.

Iliana, nervous and tense, pulled Nina towards her. 'What do you think?' she asked in a desperate, brittle voice.

Nina shook her head. 'Awesome,' she said.

'I've never seen anything like this,' Iliana replied. 'Don't know if it's good or bad yet.'

Emory Patrick's voice came over the p.a., almost drowned out by the baying of his devotees. He greeted them, made a few jokes about remarks the media had printed recently, and then called for silence.

Never! Nina thought. *He's got to be kidding.*

The crowd fell silent.

'Now we shall breathe together!' Emory told them.

Nina's own breath was caught in her throat. She was aware of Iliana's fingers digging into her arm through her leather jacket. She was aware of many thousands of chests aligning themselves into a single organ. 'Oh God,' she said weakly.

If the planet itself could sigh, it would sound like this, she thought.

Tranquillity fell over the crowd like narcotic dust. Emory breathed. The crowd breathed. Emory's arms swayed. The crowd swayed.

Is this a Talent at work, Nina thought. *Is it?* She was unsure.

Then, the music started up, faintly and slowly at first, and a line of dancers whirled on to the stage. Emory dropped his arms, dropped his head onto his chest.

He's left us, Nina thought. *He's no longer here. He's somewhere else.*

The reality Emory Patrick inhabited was that of his own power, his own universe. A great crashing of drums came through the p.a.

Emory raised his head and roared.

The crowd went wild.

Nina lifted her camera and began to take shots automatically, her lens pointed at Emory Patrick. He was in her sights. She could act now, couldn't she? Somehow, she hadn't the will. She just kept firing the shutter, again and again. He turned his head. Had he sensed her? Had he seen her? No, his eyes were closed. The music swelled around her, a cushion for the power of Emory's voice as he hurled his philosophy at the crowd. The words meant nothing to her. Drained, Nina patted Iliana's hand and indicated she wanted to go and sit on the steps that led down to the ground. Iliana, thinking this was an invitation, followed. The steps were like a small pocket of no-time, where the sound of the music and the crowd was muted.

'He's really on form,' Iliana said. 'Brilliantly so. Perhaps this fiasco will turn out for the best after all.'

'I hope so,' Nina said.

I've seen nothing that indicates paranormal activity, she thought. *I've seen a star, a hero, nothing else.* No matter what Chantal thought, no matter what she said in her report, Nina intended to phone the DPR shortly and tell them Emory Patrick was clear. Powerful and charismatic as an individual, yes; a little crazy, quite possibly; but in all other respects completely normal. If he was a threat to the authorities because of his influence, it was not a problem that fell under the DPR's sphere of activity. Let someone else deal with it. Let someone else uncover the charade that had made a man appear to rise from the dead.

Then Linford Brown came charging towards them, and Nina's world tilted on its axis, never to right itself again.

'Illa, there's trouble!' he gasped.

'What? What trouble?' Iliana was high on the power Emory had invoked. She didn't stop smiling.

'The crowds at the fence. They're going berserk. Breaking down the wire. There're riot squads homing in. We've got to get Emory off-stage and out of here!'

Iliana seemed dazed. 'Are you sure?'

'*Yes!* For God's sake, prepare yourself. I'm going to get the power cut!'

He leapt off the steps and disappeared. Iliana and Nina stared at each other for a few moments.

'Is this real?' Nina asked.

Iliana stood up. 'Come on.'

They sprinted back up the steps and Iliana, with her official capacity, got them past the security men to the very edge of the stage. At that moment, the music stopped dead.

There was a moment's stasis. The band looked surprised,

confused, while the crowd poised open mouthed, arms raised, bodies contorted in mid-dervish chaos. In that moment of utter silence, horrendous sounds could be discerned coming from the boundary fence.

'Emory!' Iliana yelled.

He seemed dazed, and she had to shout twice more to get his attention.

'Come here!'

The crowd had now started to yell and jump around, still good-natured, because they believed this to be a temporary halt to the proceedings. Their ears were buzzing. They had not yet deciphered the sounds rising behind them.

Emory paused to adjust his mike stand and then sauntered over, ignoring Iliana's frantic gestures for him to hurry. 'What's happened?' he asked. 'Can they get it fixed?'

Iliana shook her head. 'No. It's not fixable. The people at the fence are rioting. It's all very ugly. You'll have to leave now.'

He smiled. 'No, Iliana.'

'Emory, I know you're enjoying yourself, but this is a dangerous situation.' She grabbed his arm. 'Come along. We'll go to the car quickly. We'll be out of here before anyone realises you've gone.'

Emory stared at her for a moment and then addressed Nina. 'What's happening?'

Nina shrugged helplessly. 'Exactly what she said.'

'Mori, please, let's go!' Iliana's voice had become desperate. She was afraid.

'I can't,' Emory said. He glanced back over his shoulder.

Linford Brown came hurrying towards them, his habitually pale face quite red. 'Water cannon!' he gasped. 'It's on the video monitors. It's like a fucking massacre!'

'What!' Emory roared.

Linford pointed at the distant fence. 'Police everywhere, shields, horses, the lot. And water cannon. They're firing on the cripples.'

'I don't believe it,' Iliana said in a restrained voice, as if to refute a small piece of scandal.

At that moment, the convention of Future Light transformed into pandemonium. Having broken through the fence, all the non-paying spectators, able-bodied and otherwise, poured into the site, followed by the riot squads, who'd been trying to drive them in the opposite direction. Even from this distance, Nina could see the high, razor-topped fences falling like the walls of Jericho. An ugly surge was spreading down towards the stage as panic was kindled among the crowd. Police horses were cantering into the melee. Nina's camera was to her face, the shutter firing, film winding, too slow to capture what she was seeing. It was so medieval, like a scene from hell. Terrified people were struggling to find safety, clawing at each other, trampling each other underfoot. Some were trying to break through the security barrier in front of the stage in an instinctive attempt to be on higher ground. Nina caught the image in her viewfinder of a lone wailing child, seconds before the child disappeared in a jumble of panicking bodies. She took another shot of two teenage girls, weeping and clutching each other, a senseless third lolling between them, blood on her face. They were tiny images, picked out and magnified by her camera, in a landscape of insanity too big to take in as a complete picture. Nina could hear the sound of cars, four-wheeled drive vehicles and limos, starting up from behind the stage as staff tried to make an exit.

'Emory, let's get of here,' Linford pleaded. 'Now!'

Emory did not answer.

He glanced coldly at Nina, who had lowered her camera. The glance went on too long, and there was certainly a message in it, but not an obvious one.

Emory tried to pull away from Iliana, failed, and was therefore obliged to drag her with him as he strode back to the microphone. The band and dancers, more sensible, had vanished.

'The mike's dead,' Linford said to Nina. 'What's he fucking playing at? They won't hear him.'

A high-pitched whistle filled the air.

'Enough!' roared Emory Patrick. 'Enough! Enough!' His arms were raised. His voice, amplified a thousand times, boomed out like the cry of a god.

Nina fell to her knees, as a sour wind knocked the breath from her belly. She felt Linford drop down and huddle against her. Her hair was whipping across her face, her eyes were stinging, but she could just see the statuesque shape of Emory Patrick looming on the stage, Iliana crumpled at his feet. The air was a seething mass of dust motes that writhed like a leviathan over the crowd.

Emory screamed.

The helicopters, careening overhead, were suddenly flung aside, not crashing, not falling, not bursting into flames, but simply blown away to new skies. Nina saw them go. Emory gestured wildly, as if he was throwing power outwards. Nina could hardly breathe. Everything was too confused. It was like a nightmare. And then time froze. Nina closed her eyes. She was alone in a desolate place, completely alone. A wind was blowing from far away, carrying memories, fragments of dreams. She had always been alone, for eternity. Alone with her purpose, her secret, shameful purpose.

Then a warm, living hand touched her face. 'Hazel!' She opened her eyes. Linford was staring at her, wide-eyed, strings of hair hanging over his eyes. 'Help me,' he said. 'Help me get him out of here.'

'Can we move?'

'Try!'

They could move, but only sluggishly.

Hanging on to each other, as if fighting against a gale, Nina and Linford stood up and struggled on to the stage. The crowd was, once again, held in stasis. Nina wanted to look, to understand, but Linford dragged her forward relentlessly. But in one glance, she had witnessed enough. What had she seen? Horses frozen in mid-air, people in mid-fall. Limbs tangled and rigid like the limbs of trees. A thousand expressions of dismay, terror and bewilderment caricatured in a complete lack of animation. A cataract of water turned into a shining bridge. Debris thrown into the air and caught there as if held in rock. A multitude of agonised individuals, the component parts of the hungry beast, were caught in freeze-frame. Reality had become a tableau, a single frame of a movie. It was a power that spread out from Emory Patrick's staring eyes, Emory Patrick's outflung arms. Everyone who'd been standing behind him had been unaffected, and the majority of them had fled the scene.

Iliana was kneeling on all fours, blinking through her dishevelled hair, a shunned handmaiden at the feet of a manic deity. Emory Patrick's body was rigid, his arms held above his head, his dark eyes round and wild.

Somehow, and later the memory would be incomplete and fragmented, Nina and Linford manhandled Emory Patrick towards the side of the stage. Iliana tried to assist, but was too shocked and confused to be of much help. Nina did remember, and would always remember, having the courage to look into Emory's eyes and say, 'You're coming with me.' She had projected her Talent, but only slightly, terrified that in some way it might rebound on her from the face of Emory Patrick. He returned her gaze, only half aware, only one foot in this world. Then, his body went limp and they could take him, drag him away. Simultaneously, a tide of movement and hysteria swept back over the crowd. Nina did not turn to see it.

Only one car was left back-stage. It might have been the one they arrived in, but there was no driver with it now. Everywhere was eerily deserted. Litter blew along the ground. Nina remembered Chantal, and with a twinge of guilt hoped she had got away all right. She shut off her mind to the sounds of terror and panic that had once again come to dominate the day.

Linford climbed behind the wheel of the car. Fortunately, the keys were still in the ignition. Future Lighters were trusting; they did not steal from one another. Iliana and Nina shoved Emory into the back seat and sat on either side of him, gripping his arms. He did not speak or move, did not even blink. Iliana was weeping. Her forehead was cut, but not badly. Blood had stained the ash blonde waves hanging over her eyes. Linford cursed as the car refused to start. Perhaps that was why it had been left behind, abandoned in favour of more reliable transport, like feet. Then, the vehicle roared into life and shot forward with a jolt, catching the guy ropes of a nearby marquee and nearly dragging it behind. Both women buried their faces against Emory's shoulders as Linford put his foot down and accelerated forward through what was left of the fence. Things bumped the car. Nina dared not look. Things were under the wheels. She dared not even think.

After a nightmare journey, as Linford tried in vain to remember the route, they eventually arrived back at the hotel, through sheer luck rather than strategy. They clambered dazedly out of the car, leaving the doors hanging open, and ran into the lobby, dragging

Emory between them. Nina was alert for the presence of police, but it seemed all efforts must still be concentrated on the convention site. Other Future Light personnel, who'd fled the site earlier, were hanging round the reception desk. Some appeared to be checking out hurriedly.

Linford wanted Nina to come up to their room. He implied they'd need help with Emory, who had still not spoken.

'I'll be there,' Nina said. 'I will. Soon. Just let me check to see if Chantal made it back. OK?' There was a call she had to make first.

Even before she'd unlocked the door, Nina knew Chantal would not be inside. The Dutch girl's clothes were still thrown over her bed, a pair of sneakers lay on their side in the middle of the floor. Nina did not look at them too long. She sat down on her own bed and picked up the phone, requesting the secure emergency line to the DPR. She stared at her hands while she waited for the connection, the phone jammed between shoulder and jaw. Her hands were shaking. They were bloodstained. She'd lost her camera, her purse. Oh God!

'Nina?'

'Gervase? Gervase?' She could only say his name.

'It's all right,' he said. His voice was low and soothing. 'We've seen the bulletins. Are you hurt?'

'No...' The sound of concern over the line seemed to burst the shield she'd constructed around her emotions. She began to cry, her chest convulsing in great heaving sobs. Allerby let her weep, making appropriate comforting sounds down the phone.

'You're so far away,' Nina said. 'So far.'

'Nina, remember the Dallywell shoot.'

She held her breath, even her sobs cut short. It was a code between them, a slap in the face.

'I'm sorry,' Allerby said. 'But it's imperative you regain control. You can regain control. You know you can.'

She laughed shakily. 'Thanks for the cold shower.'

'That's better. Now listen to me. Other personnel are already on their way. Loric himself will be with you shortly.'

'You want us to get Patrick out, right?' She wiped her face, wishing she could light a cigarette, even though she'd given up smoking three years previously.

'Nina... Events have progressed in a direction everyone

hoped they wouldn't. This is too big. Too... *awkward*. We're really concerned about it, Nina. Very concerned. Therefore, we feel it is necessary for you to bring us a picture of Mr Patrick.' He didn't say anything more, but she could feel him in her mind. Remember the Dallywell shoot. Remember your training. Now, you are machine. Nothing more. She glanced towards the chair under the window where her other camera lay, its lens reflecting the sun. Too hot for it there. Stupid. Should have moved it.

'OK,' she said, and hung up.

Iliana answered Nina's knock on the door. She enfolded Nina in a close embrace, pressing her wet bloodied face against Nina's cheek. Nina raised one arm half-heartedly.

'Oh, this is terrible, terrible,' Iliana said, dragging Nina into the room. It appeared to be packed out with a confused and terrified bunch of Future Light personnel. Some of them were suffering from minor injuries, patching each other up from a ridiculously small first aid case. 'We'll probably be thrown in jail!' Iliana cried. 'Linford is trying to make reservations on the next available flight. Oh Hazel, I'm scared, actually scared. I'm wondering if we'll ever get home.'

'How's Emory?'

Iliana shook her head. 'He's gone to his room to pack. Linford's with him. He's making the calls from there. I don't know how Emory's feeling. He's calm, but he hasn't said much. I'm just thankful he's doing what I tell him. Do you think we'll get out of here, Hazel?'

'I don't know.'

Iliana clutched at Nina's arm. 'Thank you for what you did. I'll never be able to repay you.'

'It's OK. Don't worry about it. Can I see Emory?'

Iliana shrugged. 'That's up to him.'

'Right. I'll go see, then.'

'I'll come with you.'

Nina looked into Iliana's eyes. 'No.' Iliana dropped her arms, flinched.

Then Nina walked out of the door.

Emory Patrick's room was full of peace. There was no other way to describe it. Linford Brown's voice was an insistent whisper against the phone, but had little effect on the atmosphere. Emory himself was carefully folding shirts and putting them into a case. Nina had simply knocked on the door and walked right in.

'I was waiting for you,' Emory said.

Nina shrugged and touched the camera hanging round her neck.

'Linford, could you conclude your business elsewhere?' Emory asked.

'I've finished,' Linford said, putting down the phone. 'If all goes well, we should be out of here by tonight. Took some doing, but...'

'Thank you Linford.' Emory's soft remark was a dismissal.

Linford fled.

Emory and Nina faced each other across a small space. He folded his arms. 'Why are you so afraid?' he asked.

Nina said nothing. She knew she shouldn't speak. She raised the camera to her eyes.

'So it's come to this,' Emory said. He turned his back on her, walked away, began packing again.

'Emory.' He did not look up. 'Emory, look at me.'

He paused, then did so. She began to raise the camera again.

'You don't need that,' he said. 'Or is that your shield, the shield across your perception. Can't you bear to see what you do? It's like shooting me in the back.'

Ignore it, she thought. *Don't listen.* She summoned her Talent, projected it into the viewfinder, felt it slide off the mirror inside the camera, slither into the lens itself.

'They made a monster of you,' Emory said, still packing. 'So much so, you don't even have the capacity to think about it anymore.'

She felt the power go, felt it sizzle like a laser from her mind. Emory looked up at her. She felt her power enter his body, felt the resistance of muscle and bone giving way. He walked towards her and tore the camera from her neck. She cried out and stumbled, momentarily stunned, the breath squeezed from her throat. Her neck was burning.

'At least have the decency to return the look you demand of me!' he said.

She shook her head to clear it, rubbing the skin of her neck.

Very well, if that was the way he wanted it. She raised her chin. If it was to be a contest, then so be it. He folded his arms and smiled. His eyes were as dark as infinity, unfathomable. And suddenly, she was not seeing him at all. She was peering through a long lens at a woman posturing for the camera. She hated that woman. It was the person who had tried to destroy her, undermine her career with lies, steal her lover. Simone Dallywell. As she pressed the shutter, she was thinking, *Die you bitch, die!* And then there was blood everywhere, blood from the eyes and nose, and a strangled croak. There was death. It had been the first time.

'Coercion,' said the voice of Emory Patrick, 'to the point where you can order a person's own nervous system to destroy the body it services. No trace of murder. That's some Talent, Nina Vivian.'

She blinked, and the image of Emory Patrick swam back into her field of vision.

'I just wanted you to know I'm aware of the truth,' he said, in a gentle voice. 'That's all. What happened with the Dallywell woman was an accident, Nina. Everyone has murderous thoughts like that sometimes. You were not to know you could make them real. Neither are you to blame for what you are now, but the people who fucked your head over after the Dallywell incident certainly are!'

Nina could not speak. The image of the Dallywell shoot was still too strong in her mind.

'I knew why you were here even before you did,' Emory said. 'But, I feel there is one thing you should know. Your instincts were right: I'm not one of your kind.'

'You are,' Nina said, speaking in spite of the unwritten rule she had created for herself never to converse with her subjects once the process had begun. 'I saw what happened at the site, and you've just proved you're a telepath. My instincts were wrong maybe, but I know a Talent at work when I see one.'

He shook his head. 'No. Not quite.'

'What are you, then? Really the Son of God?'

He smiled. 'There is no God, Nina, not in the sense people understand it, but then you know that, don't you. There are chances though, chances for the future. Sometimes the universe creates such chances, such hopes. But it is futile. People aren't conscious enough. I love them all, but I know they're not conscious.'

'Tell me,' she said. 'Tell me what you are.'

'I am shattered hope,' he said. 'And you must do what you came here to do. I realise now I've had my chance. You are my reward.'

'You're a liar,' Nina cried. 'You're a paranorm.'

'Then kill me like you've been ordered to!' he shouted. 'Go on, do it!'

She turned away. *Can't do it. Can't.* 'Get out of here, Emory Patrick. Get out now. Run anywhere. There's not much time.'

She heard him laughing. 'Beautiful,' he said. 'What a beautiful ending.'

'I mean it!'

'I know you do. You have fought against this so painfully, haven't you? You have been dreading it. But it's inevitable. Now.... turn around.'

She could not disobey the order. Even as she was turning, with agonising slowness, she was remembering the words of Sable Grant. *If he is what his people claim he is, it would be worse.* Yes. Worse because the world can't handle it, doesn't want it, not even the so-called enlightened New Agers, such as Sable herself. The world destroys things it can't understand. *Don't make me do this. Don't!*

She was facing him now, and he was holding her Talent in the depth of his eyes. He held her in stasis, as he'd held the entire convention site before him in stasis earlier. He directed her will.

'No,' she said, but the word never made a sound.

'I felt you coming yesterday,' he said. 'And some part of me welcomed it. I can't let you deny me now. It's over, Nina. I screwed up. Now it's time for me to go.' He grinned wearily. 'Let's just say I have better things to do. I'm sorry. I hope you'll forgive me one day.'

Inexorably, he drew her Talent out of her, focused it on himself. Her eyes were streaming. She could taste blood in her mouth. It was as if her hands were around his heart, crushing it to a pulp. He was too strong to resist. There was no contest. Her Talent was tiny in comparison to his. In the end, she let go, and let him have it all.

Soon, he was lying back on the bed, and a single fly was buzzing round the otherwise silent room. His eyes were open and he looked slightly surprised but not afraid. Nina stood over him swaying, one hand forced between her teeth. She was biting hard, but could feel no pain. She felt drained of all feeling. Ultimately, it had been just another job. She'd deceived herself believing the thing she'd become would have it any other way.

'You're so beautiful,' she said in a thick voice, mumbling around the obstruction of her hand. 'I don't have to forgive you, because there's nothing to forgive. This is just what I do. Sometimes.'

Then she sat down beside him to keep the vigil, until the others came.

The Green Calling

She feels she is losing her humanity, bleeding into the green and the damp. Her flesh is sprouting silvery, scaly fungus that has to be dabbed with ointment every night. She is never dry. And now, trapped and held by the vengeful green, the legends no longer seem implausible.

It was Canvey's notes that started it off.

'At night, the man-woman looked in through the screen door. It seemed to be naked, its skin covered in a green pigment.'

A man-woman? Could mean anything. An effeminate boy, a masculine girl. Some deranged dream of Canvey's. Perhaps only an illusion, kindled in the sputtering lamplight; a face beyond the screen. The green calling.

Silva wishes she'd never seen those words. It is too easy to believe in them when it's dark.

She dreamed of rain for three consecutive nights before she began the journey that led her inevitably to Canvey's Retreat, on the inner jungled slope of an extinct volcano, in the heart of the Neotropic cloud forest. Not gentle, soothing rain but furious hot downpours; unending and corroding. It was presentiment perhaps, or just an educated guess.

Now, bathed in a patina of her own sweat, she sits gazing at the gauze-covered window openings of the Retreat, wrapped in a steamy lamp-light haze, listening to the pitiless downpour beyond the mouldering walls. Dying insects convulse upon the page beneath her hands, poisoned by the odourless insecticide painted onto the inner walls. The desk she is sitting at groans as she shifts her position to glance at the place above her right wrist, where her dark-coloured shirt leaves the skin exposed. There is a strange discoloration of the flesh there, a strange consistency. Deliberately, Silva pulls down her sleeve. A rogue torturing thought meanders through her sluggish mind: I will never go home, never. I will stay here forever until the moulds and the lichens cover me and kill me. She stands up abruptly to stem the discouraging mantra. She opens the screen door and looks outside.

Beyond the meagre light of the lamp, the night is hot-breathed, pungent, saturated darkness. Silva feels the jungle's presence rather than sees it; she senses its voluptuous oppressiveness. She knows that somewhere out there her companion preservationist, Lal, is intruding into the brutal, deadly lushness, perhaps crouched beneath a drooping tree-fern, or squatting on the sodden walkway that cuts a perilous pathway through the foliage.

'Where are you?' Silva hisses into the night.

Lal is not human, but a multi-task biomech, laboratory bred, laboratory tested. To some degree, Silva shares this heritage, even though her specialities, her genetic nudges are widely different from Lal's. In many ways, the jungle is their mother, enveloping and vast: it spawned the plants that surrendered the magical elixirs which permeated the womblike fluids in which Lal was constructed by molecular computers and Silva floated as a foetus. Silva, like Lal, is an experiment. For the experiment to be successful, she will never age. She is the daughter of Longevity Program VI. The fate of daughters/sons one to five remains unknown to her.

Silva does not want to call out into the dark. She is afraid of what she might invoke; something other than the sleek wet form of Lal, something so very *other*. Then again, she hates to be alone here at night. It is too easy to succumb to the feeling that she is being watched. She has two human assistants, Luis and Jesus, who are locals, but they take one of the vehicles back down the trail to the village at the end of every afternoon. Silva is spending more and more time alone, poring over the documents and data-disks that are bursting from every damp wooden box and rusting crate in the Retreat. Most of them can be junked, but there are jewels to be found; Canvey was one of Virichem's best operatives. Now that he is dead, his notes and files are treated with reverence. They are to be preserved - the paper documents laminated, the magnetic media transferred to holocrystal. Canvey supervises these procedures from the walls. There are dozens of photographs of him as a young man pinned up around the desk. He was sixty-seven when he died; alone, uncared-for, malnourished. The victim of a stroke. There are no photographs of him as an older man. Only the memory of his youth kept him company. And who knows what wild ideas Canvey came up with, living alone up here in this wilderness? Who knows what he might have discovered?

'So much information is lost every day,' Silva's mentor Alcestis once said to her. 'Every day, priceless human knowledge crumbles to dust, data is corrupted, never to be regained.'

'But surely someone else will think of it one day,' Silva said, frowning. 'There are so many of us. Someone will think the same thing again.'

'That is not the point,' Alcestis replied stiffly. 'Each mind colours the information it generates with its own unique tone. There is no such thing as precise reproduction.'

It was Alcestis who'd encouraged Silva to specialise in information preservation. Alcestis had been a young research grad then. Now, she is a woman going grey who's discovered her metabolism is inexorably slowing down. Silva still looks like a teenager. She and Alcestis have maintained a close friendship via computer link for a long time, but never meet face to face any more. Alcestis resents growing old.

Thinking of Alcestis, Silva wonders whether she should go back indoors and call her via the laptop. The laptop will not last for much longer, she is sure. At this very moment, in this landscape of speedy adaptation, a new mould is bound to be developing that specialises in eating computers. Silva wants to tell Alcestis about the patch of strange skin on her arm; she wants reassurance. Alcestis has a medical background; she will know things the over-worked, not-too-informed local doctor will not. Silva has been putting this call off for several days.

She glances at her watch to try and work out what time it is where Alcestis lives. The watch has stopped. She notices its face is partly occluded by a yellowish stain. Tears of weary frustration gather in her eyes. A dear friend, years dead, had given her that watch. Now it is tainted, half eaten by the jungle. She removes it lovingly, saying under her breath, 'I hate this place.'

The laptop makes a disturbingly unfamiliar noise when Silva turns it on; a tired whine deep in its micro-depths. A moment of panic, the fear of being isolated is interrupted by a more sensible thought: *so, order another one! (But what if the roof-dish falls*

71

apart? What if... What if...?)

The computer utters a musical sequence. Silva squats down in front of it and turns off the video eye. Presently Alcestis' face will appear on the screen, while all Alcestis will see on her home monitor is Virichem's logo. It is better that way. Silva is worried that if Alcestis should see her, she'd be compelled to make some kind of light-hearted sarcastic comment. Silva doesn't want to hear anything like that, because the words will drip with pained bitterness. The two women haven't seen one another for years. People like Silva never feel comfortable speaking about what makes them different. There is a kind of unity in that. At least, Silva has never heard them speak. In the centre where she grew up, there were other genetic experiments; some more obviously so than others. They never fell for the spiel that they were 'special'. Some of them died too young, others simply fell apart: emotionally, psychologically and in a few sad cases, physically. Silva is one of the lucky ones. And yet, even now, at the age of 37, there is a danger Silva might begin to age dramatically, or develop a plague of cancers, become blind, lose her hair. She has seen some of those things happen to others. Bald children eaten from the inside; faulty flesh machines. The time that Silva lives through never really feels as if it belongs to her. Is that because of what she is, or simply part of feeling human, being a woman? Does Alcestis feel the same?

'Oh, you're going out.' It is obvious to Silva that Alcestis has dressed up for some occasion. Gems sparkle at the corner of each eye. The woman looks good; she's lost weight, although the lines on her face seem deeper.

'Silva! How are you? How's the jungle! Oh, God it's been so long! I feel awful... I'm just...' Alcestis pulls a comical face, and sits down before her video eye. 'What the hell! Five minutes? He can wait!'

'You look great!'

'Nonsense! You can only see me from the waist up. Gravity is winning the battle with my will-power, my love, never mind my muscles! I've got Researcher's Arse; comes from sitting at a monitor all day!'

'No really, you look...'

Alcestis interrupts. 'So, how's it going? Had Canvey discovered all the secrets of the universe as everyone thought?'

Silva shakes her head, even though Alcestis can't see her. 'If he did, I've yet to come across the evidence. I think he was off his head at the end. There's some very weird stuff.'

'Oh?'

'Yeah. I think he was seeing things! I've found these notes about, well, *creatures*.' Silva's laugh sounds a little embarrassed even to herself.

'Creatures, eh!' Alcestis grins and wipes a lock of hair from her brow. 'What kind?'

'He describes them as green men-women.'

Alcestis shakes her head. 'Hmm, perhaps you should lose that stuff! Sure he wasn't writing a novel?'

'Hadn't thought of that actually. He was looking into local legends, though I'm not sure whether he made them up or not. This place is a bit creepy.'

'Yeah, you sound... tense.'

Silva is sure that Alcestis is wondering whether she should ask her to turn on the video eye. Her concern would make her want to inspect her friend, but Silva knows Alcestis is afraid that what she would see might sicken her, anger her. She'd once said, 'the worst thing about growing old is that I can remember what it was like to be beautiful.' Silva respects that and yet she wants Alcestis to see her. She needs reassurance. 'It's bad for the health here, so damp.'

'How much longer have you got to stay?'

Silva shrugs. 'Until the job's done. I've got a biomech assistant, but Rodgers gave it some other task to do. It's always out collecting samples. Isn't much help. Al...'

'What?' The image suddenly shifts, blurs. Silva's heart jumps. *Don't fade, don't go...*

'I've got this patch on my arm. Think it's some kind of fungus, but it won't respond to treatment.'

Alcestis frowns. 'Is it spreading?'

'No... I don't think so. It doesn't hurt. I've tried a topical anti-fungal agent on it, which might be keeping it down, but it won't cure it. Everything gets eaten by mould and fungus here. I don't like it.'

'Can you get to a local doctor?'

'Yeah, it was she who gave me the ointment.'

'What was her prognosis?'

Silva sighs. 'She sees so much, so many diverse ailments. The jungle causes them. She says she often sees cases that she knows she'll never see again. She didn't seem that worried though.'

'But you are...'

'Well... I suppose I've got a touch of Cabin Fever.' She laughs. 'I'm scared I'll turn into a walking mushroom, like something out of an old Japanese movie!'

'Are there any other symptoms?' Alcestis asks, suddenly and sharply.

'What do you mean?' There is a moment of tense silence, during which Silva incubates a hot core of anger. 'It's not cancer!' she says at last, 'and no, there are no other symptoms.'

There is another moment of silence and then Alcestis says, 'Turn on the video, Silv.'

'No, there's no need. I'm fine.'

'We had a promise!'

'Now is not the time to honour it, Al. Really. I'm fine.'

Alcestis sighs. 'Look, I'm not going to mince words. Get back to that doctor and if she has the facilities in that godforsaken place, get her to check you for soft sores. You can't afford to play around, Silv.'

Silva is furious. She wants to say, 'You want me to die, you want me to fall apart. You're wishing it!' But it is not in her nature to confront people. 'OK,' she says.

'I mean it, Silv!'

'I said OK. Look, don't you have a date waiting? I'll call you back some time. Take care, Al.' Abruptly, Silva breaks the connection.

For several minutes she sits stiffly, paralysed by rage. How dare Alcestis say those things! She inspects the place on her arm where the discoloration stains her skin. It is not a soft sore, she is sure. It's something else, it has to be; something jungle-born. The face of Canvey, youthfully thin, grins down from the wall. He stares beyond her.

Silva lies sleepless on her bed, the Retreat grinding and flexing around her. The forest is chastened by a hurrying wind. Before dawn, Lal comes in and stands by the window processing information. Its hum is comforting, even though it lacks the human desire or sensitivity to utter a greeting to Silva. Its shape is vaguely human so that it can give public presentations without causing distress to children. It can speak in a computerised voice that sounds vaguely West Indian. Staring at it in the dark, Silva is convinced it has a personality, a soul; Lal just keeps itself to itself. Its work fascinates it, but nothing else is of interest. It is blessed with the ability never to feel lonely. Neither, Silva is sure, can it feel afraid.

Early morning. Mist hangs down from the forest canopy in shrouds. The air is not hot, but it is very humid. Silva is standing on the damp wooden walkway that has been constructed as a precarious safe route through the forest. The planks feel spongy underfoot; already the wood is rotting. Silva is playing a game with herself. In this game, the forest is the Garden of Eden, the primordial garden. In Eden, there was only one of every tree, shrub and fern. Here, it is the same - almost. Two tree ferns, remnants of a prehistoric age, grow close together in the lush foliage. Overhead, aerial gardens of orchids, ferns and mosses droop tendrils downwards. Everything is poisonous in Eden - plants, animals and insects - but Silva knows that natives to this land build up immunity to such things. Luis and Jesus are up at the Retreat transferring some data Silva has prepared onto holo-crystals. Today, Silva is trying to feel positive, actively fighting lethargic depression. *(There is nothing wrong with me.)* Standing here, on this narrow sanctuary, she has to fight the compulsion to step off the path. Potential death lies to either side. Luis has told her to watch out for the ajo vine; if someone steps on one they become irretrievably lost in the forest.

What would happen if I did that? Are there any foundations to their legends? Perhaps the vine gives off some kind of vapour if it's bruised that causes disorientation. There is an explanation for everything.

The forest canopy meets over her head and invisible animals and birds traverse the aerial pathways. Silva squints upwards, narrowing her eyes into the green.

What else lives here unseen?

The jungle is older than memory, and though partially ravished by the encroachment of humanity, still able to reserve a deep inner chastity that is both dangerous and inviolable. Silva wonders whether she can will something inexplicable to manifest before her eyes, whether she can fool the jungle into giving up one of its secrets. *Green men-women? The wistful fancies of a lonely madman. No such thing.* And yet, as she thinks that, the sensation of unseen eyes fixed upon her unguarded back sweeps over her like a wash of fetid, warm water. She can smell something that reminds her of vomit, or certain species of fungi; sweet carrion. Something is waiting to drop onto her from the whispering canopy; something is *thinking* of dropping down onto her. She looks over her shoulder, and there is a blur of green movement at the corner of her vision, but then there are always blurs of green movement in this place. Silva has yet to develop what Luis and Jesus call search image - a refined visual sensitivity to the teeming shadows of the jungle. There is nothing between me and the Retreat, she thinks. I can get back at any time. She can even see the walls of the place at the end of the walkway: a short run.

The noise of the forest seems to have fallen; it is like a song being sung in a lower key than usual. Silva's precise footsteps sound loud on the soaked boards. She turns her gaze back up towards the canopy overhead, strains to discern some camouflaged shape amid the green. Then, there is a sound which could have been a human laugh or the call of a bird, and a cascade of warm liquid splashes down onto Silva's upturned face. She splutters and stumbles, surrounded by a lemon ammonia reek. Urine! It has got into her eyes, her mouth. She is blind, fumbling along the hand-rail, retching uncontrollably. Luckily, Luis hears her curses and spittings, and comes out of the Retreat to investigate. He laughs as he hears her angry explanation, as she wrings her trembling wet hands and paws the front of her shirt.

Urine. Yes. Monkeys do that. Piss onto travellers. Monkeys.

Later, her hair and body washed in the primitive shower - luke-warm gritty water - her mouth well sluiced with mint mouthwash, Silva sits down at Canvey's desk to work. Her head is wrapped in a towel, her body in a robe. Lal lurks somewhere in the room behind her, though wrapped in its own thoughts as usual.

Earlier, Silva asked it what it thought about Canvey's notes on the subject of humanoid life-forms in the forest.

Lal was philosophical. 'I would rule nothing out in this place. So much of this territory is uncatalogued, but then one would suppose the natives would know more about it, if it existed.'

'Supposing they'd want to tell us,' Silva added. 'We are the despoilers, after all.'

'I doubt whether everyone holds that view,' Lal said, and then utilising its intuition banks, added, 'Have you discovered some more evidence to support Canvey's theory?'

Silva shrugged. 'I don't think so. Perhaps I'm looking too hard for evidence, and they do say that an obsessed seeker will inevitably find what they're looking for... in one way or another.'

'Whether they create it for themselves or not,' Lal added. 'Perhaps that explains Canvey's notes. He was searching for a dream.'

Silva laughed. It amused her to hear the machine speak in that way.

'I intend to work outdoors tonight,' Lal said. 'Will you be all right alone?'

It was the first time it had expressed concern for Silva's welfare. She immediately became suspicious, defensive. 'Of course I will! Why shouldn't I be?'

Lal was impervious to waspishness. 'Well, keep the bleeper by you anyway. I won't be too far away.'

As Lal ambled, in its strange gliding gait, towards the screen door, Silva grabbed a limb that, in a human, would be an arm. 'What do you know?' she said, eyes narrowed.

'Regarding what?'

'Why are you suddenly bothered about my well being?'

Lal gently pulled away from her hold. 'I am merely empathising with you. You are my close colleague. It is one of my utilities.'

Silva let it go.

The night presses down on Silva. She is trying to read some scrawling notes of Canvey's, which at some time must have got wet. It is a difficult, rather pointless task. She has her hands over her ears, because she keeps tuning in on strange noises outside. Of course, these noises will have been there ever since she arrived; only now her active mind insists on applying labels to them. She can hear what sounds like whispered conversation in high, clicking voices, or conversation that's coming from an old radio hidden just inside the forest. Occasionally, a howler monkey will roar like a drunken man. There are no lights outside.

Her arm is itching slightly. When she scratches the strange skin, some greasy, silver scales come off under her nails. Soft sores? No! Soft sores usually originate in the groin or armpits; moist areas. (*But everywhere is moist in this climate!*)

'Oh, stop scaring yourself!' Silva says out loud.

She turns a page. Canvey was writing in brown ink, a colour like dried blood. She realises she hasn't been reading the words for some time; only scanning the pages while paying acute attention to her own agonised thoughts. Now, a few sentences seem to leap at her from the page. Above them are some notes on forest biomass; below a list of provisions Canvey once required from the research station downtrail. But the words in between, like a bolt of inspiration, stand out alone. Curling script. A feeling of ancient times.

*"They come at night - though never seen. **Dawn** - they manifest, come through to me. Green dawn - time of the undying. Like water children; sleek as seals, or fish...'*

Silva reads the words several times. She cannot help feeling that Canvey must have woken up momentarily from a lethargic state, became truly alive, to write them.

Silva can feel her heart bumping. Sitting there alone in the modest halo of the hurricane lamp, there can be no question of disbelieving what Canvey wrote. He meant it. He'd seen what he wrote about.

At first light, a flock of birds known as the *guardabarrancas*, the guardians of the ravine, wake Silva with their tinkling song. It sounds as if a thousand wind chimes are being subtly excited by a tantalising breeze. The light, when Silva opens her eyes, is opalescent, glowing. Gold-green radiance falls in spears across her bed, shining motes held in the beams. The air is cool, caressing, and has a sparkling taste, like fern wine. Silva is caught in a transient moment of pure Earth beauty, those times when the planet unveils itself, when it does not realise it is being observed by a member of the hungry race it spawned. Silva stretches languorously, ignorant of the moment, simply *being* it, when she becomes aware of an unfamiliar shape in the room.

She realises someone is standing among the long coats - most of them Canvey's, one hers - that hang near the door.

'Lal,' Silva says, and props herself up on her elbows in the bed.

The shape moves forward a pace from the shadows. It is slim, green, alien; not Lal at all. Silva thinks: *Should I scream, jump up, find a weapon, or wake up?* These thoughts are quite lucid and calm.

Instead, she does nothing but observe.

The figure, though uncomfortably unfamiliar and impossible to categorise, has a sleek, streamlined beauty. There is a feeling about it of extreme age, yet vibrant youthfulness. It is hairless, and apparently sexless, though reminiscent of both genders. Muscular yet slight. Its eyes are a phosphorescent vivid green, like quetzal feathers. Despite its alien appearance, Silva is very much aware of its consummate Earthly origin. It is like the tinkling birdsong, the wild hazardous beauty of the forest, the magical light, made flesh. Like Silva, it is ageless.

We are kin... in a way, Silva thinks. There is no fear inside her, only a huge sense of expectancy.

Her visitor extends an arm; too long, out of proportion. It opens its mouth as if it is shaping words, but no sound comes out. It is encased by the ancient gold light of the cloud forest.

Then, the moment of pure beauty is ended, and the light changes, the birds lift from the trees in a ravening crowd, their song disordered.

Silva blinks into the shadows that are left behind. There is no one in the room with her.

Alcestis calls midmorning.

'Can you believe it? Rod's going to be working just a hundred or so clicks away from you. Isn't that a coincidence?' Alcestis laughs. Today, she is very much 'at home', her hair tied up in a girlish knot on top of her head, peacock blue silk kimono hanging open to reveal the upper curves of a chest that is deeply tanned, but the skin is beginning to crinkle, like the most delicate tissue paper.

'Who's Rod?' Silva asks. She cannot help sounding cold because she hasn't forgiven Alcestis for the previous conversation they had.

'I've been seeing him.... Oh, he's inconsequential! The important thing is that I've invited myself out there with him! Silva, I'll be able to visit you!'

Silva is stunned by these words. Alcestis sounds like an excited teenager. She has not suggested a meeting since... since Silva hit twenty-five and Alcestis hit thirty. A parting of the ways. Tacit veil drawn over their association, the friendship mutating into whispers through the veil.

'Here?' Silva's voice sounds choked.

'There!'

'When?'

Alcestis pulls a face, shrugs. 'Oh, a few days' time. Can't specify exactly when. I'll have a look around... I'm interested in Rod's field, after all. Maybe I'll play the entertaining companion for a while before scrounging some company transport and heading up to see you.'

'It's not an easy journey,' Silva says.

'No, it isn't,' Alcestis agrees blithely.

'It's really very boring here...'

'You're trying to put me off, aren't you?' Alcestis utters another laugh, almost convincingly.

'We haven't seen one another for so long.'

'I *want* to see you, Sil.'

Silva is thrown into a panic by the threat of Alcestis' impending visit. She gets Luis to drive her down to the doctor's surgery in the village again. The doctor is a small Spanish woman, who to Silva looks as if she should be the heroine of a romantic novel.

Silva grins as she extends her arm for examination. 'Can't you just scrape this stuff off?'

The doctor ignores the suggestion. 'Any pain?'

'No.'

'Itching?'

'A little.'

'Try this ointment.'

'Haven't I tried this before?'

'No.'

Silva sighs. 'What is it? You must have some idea.'

The doctor shakes her small, perfect head. 'I've seen nothing like it. At least it isn't spreading.'

Silva clears her throat and utters the words she hates. 'Could it be... cancerous?'

The doctor glances at her sharply. She knows nothing of Silva's background. 'If it is, I've never seen cancer like it before. I'm fairly sure it's a simple fungal infection.' She hesitates. 'I could send a tissue sample down to the research station, if you're worried.'

Silva stares at her arm for a moment, sucking her upper lip. 'Perhaps... Yes. Do.' She wonders whether she should mention what she saw that morning standing in her room, but decides against it. It could have been a hallucination, another terrifying symptom of an unspecified decline bubbling through, but she doesn't think it was. She doesn't *feel* it was. But then, of course, she'd make herself think that. The alternative is too horrible. She doesn't want to discuss it.

On the way back to the Retreat, partially comforted by having been touched by medical hands, Silva carefully interrogates Luis about Canvey. Luis manoeuvres the four-wheel drive vehicle with the panache of a rebellious teenager in his first car. Silva hangs on grimly to the roll bar.

'Canvey had some pretty weird ideas about what lived in the jungle,' she says, as introduction. 'Have you bothered to read any of his stuff while you've worked with it?'

Luis curls his lip and shakes his head. 'No. He was a strange man. But these genius types often are, aren't they?'

Luis was educated in the city. Although born in a local village, his manners are very urbane, his speech barely accented. Now he works for Virichem, flitting between isolated research retreats. He has many skills in advanced technology, but is still essentially just a handyman.

'Perhaps it drove Canvey mad, living here alone,' Silva says.

'He wasn't mad,' Luis answers shortly. 'He just didn't want to be an old man.'

'Did you know him well?'

'He was a very nice person.'

Silva realises this avenue of enquiry is going to be unproductive. 'I wonder where he got these ideas about green-skinned people that live hidden in the forest...' There is no response. 'Is that a well-known legend?'

'This land is alive with legends,' Luis answers, with the pride of a man who has secrets the interloper can never penetrate. 'There are whole cities buried beneath the vines. Deserted now, of course, but who knows what race once lived in them.'

'Any of these ruins near here?'

'No. Not that have been uncovered anyway.'

'Do you believe the green-skinned people exist, Luis?'

He grins at her as he savagely changes gear. Silva's head makes abrupt and painful contact with the roll bar. 'Now what kind of question is that?' Luis says, grinning, and shakes his head.

She wonders what he'd say if she told him she thought she'd seen one of these people. She wants to believe that, because of his vague answers, Luis knows more than he lets on, but perhaps she is deluding herself, seeing evidence where there is none. Already her memory of the visitation is dimming. It's hard to believe she didn't dream it.

In the dawn, they come to her again - three of them this time. Silva slips from her bed and follows them out of the Retreat, acquiescing to, rather than obeying, their soft, insistent beckoning. Outside the air is radiant and the song of the *guardabarrancas* is a fountain of sound. Silva can see a golden walkway, a mist of gleaming rays, leading into the forest. She can walk upon it. It vanishes down through the thick foliage, down the side of the ravine. *I am dreaming*, Silva thinks, and keeps on walking. She passes the still form of a great sloth hanging from a low branch. She has never seen one this close before. Its fur is green with algae, and inhabited by silver moths. A ribbon of data, remembered from Canvey's notes, which she read the day before, passes across her mind. *'The majority of animals survive in this landscape by specialising... sometimes they are invisible to the casual observer...'*

'I have the search image,' Silva murmurs. 'Now I can see.'

The people of the green lead her downwards, to the heart of the dead volcano.

She stands upon a wide grey slab, gilded by lichens. A crowd of Canvey's dream people sway around her like blades of grass or stripes of viridian water; insubstantial. They reach out to touch her skin, nodding their small heads to one another, but she cannot feel their touch. One of them fingers her patch of scaly skin and recoils, as if burned. It flushes a deeper green, and communicates without speech, in an agitated way to its companions.

'They believe I am the future of humanity,' Silva thinks. 'And I am not.' She feels they are pleased, even excited, by the phenomenon of her. How long have they been here? Are they recent blossomings of the humid, breathing green or the last remnants of an ancient breed? Silva does not know how to reach them. She feels too dazed to think rationally, too tired to lift an arm.

Alcestis takes charge as soon as she arrives, striding into the Retreat, throwing down her travelling bag, standing with hands on hips to address the two men, who look up at her with resentful suspicion.

'It stinks in here!' she announces, by way of greeting. 'Where's Silva?'

Jesus resumes his work with deliberate slowness, leaving Luis, whom he knows can handle these city types, to answer the woman's question.

'She's not here.'

'Then where can I find her?'

Luis shrugs. 'She's probably outside.'

'You're not being very helpful,' Alcestis growls.

'I don't know where Ms Merin is,' Luis responds politely. 'She is under no obligation to report her movements to us. Can I be of assistance to you, Ms… ?'

'I'm here to see Silva.' Alcestis turns a complete circle on the spot, appraising the Retreat. 'This place is falling apart. It smells like old mushrooms. How could anyone live here voluntarily?'

Luis is aware the question is rhetorical. 'The job is nearly done,' he says.

Alcestis raises her brows. 'So quickly? When I spoke to Silva a week ago, she implied there was quite some ground to cover yet.'

Luis clears his throat, and pointedly drops his eyes from Alcestis' stare. 'It appears Ms Merin has discarded a large amount of material she felt was superfluous.' He shrugs. 'There was little here worth saving anyway.'

Luis and Jesus do not know when Silva will be back. They

say they haven't seen much of her for the past few days. Alcestis makes direct enquiries about her friend's health, but all the men will say is that Silva made two visits to the doctor downtrail. She does not, in their opinion, look ill.

When Lal makes an appearance soon afterwards, Alcestis does not find it at all helpful. The biomech is intent only on telling her about the research it has been conducting. 'The evolutionary thrust in this area is towards a vast variety of species, with a wide area of dispersal. There is no spring protein pulse in the neotropics, therefore...'

'Excuse me,' Alcestis interrupts. 'This is no doubt very interesting, but I'm more concerned about Silva. Where is she and how is she?'

'Some varieties of species have yet to be discovered by us,' Lal finishes. 'Silva will be back at sunfall. She has adopted this habit recently. As to her physical condition, I would say this locality causes her stress. She is not sleeping well.'

As it is early in the day, Alcestis decides to drive down to the village and speak to the doctor there. Before making this visit, before badgering her casual lover Rod into letting her come over here with him, she had wheedled her way into getting her hands on the case notes of previous longevity experiment subjects. Deterioration of their condition had begun with skin cancer; rapid aging had followed, accompanied by dementia, and paranoid hallucination. To her mind, Silva is very much in danger of going the same way. Alcestis has remained alert to the nuances of Silva's voice, even though she has refused to see her. The woman she spoke to recently was not the Silva she remembered. There had been a vagueness about her, which Alcestis felt camouflaged a kind of panic.

As she sends her vehicle screaming and bouncing down the outer skin of the volcano, she mutters to herself. 'Would this be worth a few more years of youth? I don't think so! Who are they kidding! Why don't they give up?'

At the surgery, she claims to be Silva Merin's physician and friend, and demands information. The small, Spanish woman clearly objects to Alcestis' hectoring manner, and makes soft remarks about confidentiality.

'Don't you know anything about Silva Merin?' Alcestis

demands, or rather accuses, and when no answer is forthcoming, replies to her question herself. 'No! For your information, she is the product of genetic engineering. She is thirty-seven years old.'

The doctor's eyes widen in surprise.

'Yes!' Alcestis says triumphantly. 'And there is a possibility she is prone to sarcoma, oat-cell cancer in particular. I know she consulted you for a skin disorder. Didn't you bother to have samples analysed?'

'As a matter of fact, yes,' the woman answers stiffly. 'They are currently being processed. I only took the sample a week ago.'

Alcestis rolls her eyes almost gleefully. 'You should have taken a sample when you first saw her! Was there evidence of any other disorders? What about her mental state?'

'She seemed like a very self-possessed young woman. The sore she showed me did not resemble oat-cell. It was a fungal infection.'

'I hope you're right!' Alcestis snaps. 'Let me know the minute you get those results. I'm staying up at Canvey's Retreat.'

As soon as she walks into the Retreat, Alcestis knows the men have been talking about her. The thick silence contained by the rotting walls is gravid with recently-uttered criticism. Lal too has a furtive air, hovering in the background.

'You!' Alcestis says, pointing at the biomech. 'Am I wrong, or is one of your functions to monitor the condition of your colleagues in remote employment locations?'

'You are not wrong,' Lal answers silkily, gliding forward. 'Might I be of assistance?'

'Have you monitored Silva recently?'

'I monitor her constantly, as a background utility.'

'And you have computed no conclusions as to her condition.'

'She is under stress. She worries.'

'And the skin problem?'

'She has a fungal infection.'

Alcestis makes a growling noise to signify her exasperation. 'You took samples?'

'No. She has not asked me to.'

Alcestis narrows her eyes and jerkily nods her head. 'Well,

you're certainly fulfilling all your functions, aren't you, lovey! Have you noticed no evidence of disorientation, absent-mindedness?'

'Unfortunately, I'm not that familiar with Ms Merin's personality to ascertain whether or not she is behaving abnormally.' The biomech sounds frosty. 'Now, if you will excuse me...' It attempts to pass by the woman, who is blocking the door.

'Fetch her,' Alcestis says firmly. 'I need to see Silva now. Although none of you *appear* to have noticed, she needs attention. Urgently.'

Lal answers politely. 'I would comply with your request if I could, but regret I don't know where Ms Merin is at this present time.'

Another growl. 'Don't give me that! Of course you know where she is, or else you're an inferior model in a Meg6 skin! What are you playing at?'

The men have remained silent, almost as if they hope their lack of noise will make them invisible to this storming female. Now, Luis clears his throat and says, 'She strays off the trail. She could be anywhere. Only the walkways are monitored.'

'And you haven't tried to stop her!' Alcestis explodes. 'Doesn't her behaviour strike you as irrational? She is not a person to take unnecessary risks.'

Luis' eyes drop back to his work.

'This is outrageous!' Alcestis shouts. She flexes her shoulders. 'Well, if none of you will go out and bring Silva back, I will! Tell me where to start looking at least!'

For a tense moment, there is only silence and then Jesus mumbles. 'You could try the path down to the crater.' He cringes beneath Luis' sudden warning glance.

'There is no path,' Luis says in a low voice.

Jesus shrugs. 'There is now. She's made one.' He points through the window screen. 'That way: down.'

Silva is lying in a pool of green radiance, surrounded by the swaying, lustrous forms of the forest-born. Their eyes glow fondly, mirroring the flashing feathers of the flock of *quetzals* that wheel about their heads. The rarest birds. Never more than one sighted at a time. A flock of the rarest birds. Silva sighs. She can feel her limbs melting into the green, into the moist earth. She is enveloped by the scent of unstoppable growth, enwombed by it. It all seems so clear to her now.

Canvey knew. He knew what these people were. Now, she cannot believe the emaciated husk that was found lying on the bed in the Retreat was really him. She feels he is close to her, one of them. He is watching her now, just a few feet away. She does not dispute his body died, but the spirit of him, the spirit... Another sigh escapes her like a breath of dawn mist. Canvey knew. He had the search image. He learned to see the immortals, to become part of the miracle that is unfurling here amid the green. And she is becoming part of it too. The forest spawned her; a miracle spore helped unravel the braids of her DNA and reformed them in a secret image. Sentience. Green sentience. And now she is home, unravelling once more, transforming.

The figures lean over her, spinning round in her sight, and ribbons of her essence spill out to be taken by their hands. They will dance these ribbons into a new shape. And she welcomes it.

Alcestis can see at once that degeneration is taking place. She can see Silva lying on her back in a clearing in the forest that looks as if it has been torn out by human hands. Alcestis has no doubt that, should she examine Silva's hands, they will be cut and abraded by vines and tough stems. Insects will have burrowed into her unprotected skin, laid their eggs there, liquefied her flesh to feed. Uttering a cry of heartfelt anguish, Alcestis pushes her body frantically through the resistant green. In the emerald light of the forest, Silva's damp skin looks greenish, terminally sick. There is hardly any flesh to her at all. She appears at once mummified and putrescent.

'No, no, no...' Alcestis murmurs a prayer of denial as she stumbles over the short remaining distance that separates her from her friend. She falls to her knees and scoops Silva up in her arms, horror and an unfamiliar sense of helplessness bringing equally unfamiliar tears to her eyes. She hugs the flimsy body to her. 'No, no, no...' But even as she tries to deny the terror of what is happening, and fights an inevitable, desperate grief, there is a sickening part of her that thinks, 'She is not beautiful any more. She is not young.' The sly inner voice that utters these words is almost too soft to be heard. It can easily be silenced, or ignored.

Suddenly, Silva twitches in Alcestis' arms. 'Sil! It's me!' Alcestis croons. 'I'm here. I'll take you back... God, why didn't any of those ass-holes do anything about this?'

Silva moans and turns her head slowly from side to side. Then she opens her eyes, and Alcestis can see that they are filmed, unfocussed, the eyes of a dead woman, or someone so old their sight is obscured by cataracts. She realises then that taking Silva anywhere would be futile. It is too late. The experiment, though undoubtedly useful, has failed.

'Al,' Silva murmurs. 'What are you doing?'

'Doing? Doing? I'm gonna have Virichem by the balls, that's what! That goddamned biomech must have known this was happening, must have been monitoring... God, it's sick! They knew! They did nothing!'

'No,' Silva murmurs. 'They don't know... They don't have...' She manages a weak smile, a grim parody that resembles the grin of a fleshless skull. 'It's all right, Al, don't be scared. This is all part of it...'

'Oh, my baby!' Alcestis grips Silva's body firmly, as if trying to keep her spirit earthbound. 'I'm with you. Of course it's all right.'

'No.' Summoning what must be the dregs of her strength, Silva tries to raise herself. 'Can't you see? Can't you see *them?*

'Who, honey?'

'The forest-born. They're all around us. Look, Al, look at them. This is why you don't have to worry. They're taking care of me, taking care of me during my change...'

Alcestis feels a finger of fear claw her spine. For a moment, she feels Silva is talking sense. But all she has to do is raise her head to see that they are alone in the forest.

'There's no one here,' she says.

Silva frowns and then stretches her papery lips back into a ghastly smile. 'Oh, of course. You don't have the search image. But you will Al, if you stay here long enough. You will. And then we can be together always.' She sighs weakly and her head drops back against Alcestis' arm. Her hair is coming out on the sleeve of Alcestis' jacket. Her body is a decaying husk holding the soul of a vibrant girl. So cruel.

This is what life does to us, Alcestis thinks. *This will come to me also, but in my case the stalking is slow and measured. It takes a little away, bit by bit, but at the end it will be the same.*

'Oh God!' she says aloud, and throws back her head. It seems the forest, the interminable, wretched, burning green, is spinning round her head. Birds shriek and the mocking howls of monkeys fill her head. It seems they are jeering at the puny women below them. Squatting there amid the ageless green, Alcestis is painfully aware of her own mortality. It is lying in her arms. Her worst fear made manifest. Decay. Age. The bitter memory of youth. Death.

Silva's voice is little more than a grating whisper. 'Don't worry,' she says, as her rebellious meat corrupts. 'We can be together here always, face to face. Stay awhile. Rest awhile. We can be young together always.'

In the Retreat, Jesus raises his head from his work. His eyes reflect the green-glowing light as the rain-clouds gather outside. 'She is blessed!' he says, in his native tongue. 'It doesn't matter about that other woman.'

Luis is systematically destroying data, unsure of in which world his feet are rooted: the past, the present or the future. Grim-faced, he ignores his colleague's remarks. Later, he will get drunk.

Lal mutters to itself, unheard.

Somewhere, a long way away, the daughter of Longevity Program VII draws breath. Her name is Hope, the secret name of all of who came before her.

Angel of the Hate Wind

My friend Jericho was taken by the Angel of the Hate Wind. At least that's what I think, and though people might not like to share my view of the world, or of the angels, I know it's a deep-seated fear within everyone. Taken by the wind.

We were rolling down the Fear Coast road in a land-dinghy when the seeds of the Taking were sown and took root. It was one of those hot, red evenings when you just feel it in your gut that anything is possible. We had stopped for the night and lit a fire within the skeletal shelter of a petrified spinney. Branches clacked like bones, bleached white in daylight, but black against the sun, sinking lovewards. The road plaited to each horizon. Mountains smudged the fear sky. We looked for spirit lights, but there were none, only wisps of cloud.

Jericho said, 'I have to do something before we get there. Do something *now*.'

We were on our way to Jasper's Fayre, on the Hate Coast. By profession, Jericho and I were tregetours, did a few juggling sketches with plasma spheres and firefly bhajis. The fayre meant income to us, but more than that for Jericho. He was sure he had tripped into a passion. I wasn't so sure, but he got hot and angry when I tried to reason with him, so it was easier to humour him. The object of his affection was Dendria, and she was a variant, not even completely human. What grew on her head was like feathers or ferns; her eyes were yellow, with vertical pupils, like a cat's; her skin a strange, bluey-white colour, which showed disturbing hints of bone and internal organs if the light caught her right. I suppose she was beautiful, in an aesthetic sense, but I would not have wanted to touch her, and deplored the fact that Jericho had spent the last sennight mooning around, undoubtedly composing bad poetry in his head to the Beloved. She was a cidaris; a created species, wrought for pleasure in the nutrient vats of hatish Amalgamators. Some had bred. There were hybrids. Nowadays, with everything boiling over as it is, there are no regulations to control the incubi and succubi of our wildest dreams. Some learned to be tumblers; Dendria was one of those.

She belonged to a troupe called Excoriasts, who as well as flipping and flapping in all manner of contortions, could insert sharpened rods through their skin and hang from hooks, recreating all the fakir stuff from an earlier time. Dendria was the only cidaris with the troupe, although some of her colleagues represented other sub-species: admerveyelles, with their spangled eyes and multiple breasts, erminee boys, softly furred; spine-haired errinys, with their vestigial facial features and muscular limbs. I enjoyed looking at the variants, with their unexpected surprises, but no way could I desire one. Like called to like, I thought. Jericho was mad.

True, he sucked too many stalks of the erigeron, and saw visions I could not see. Sometimes, I had caught him inserting guidon thorns beneath his flesh; invoking a hallucinatory experience which would hover on the edge of his perception, but last for sennights. My disapproval of his habits provoked only outrage. I had hardened my heart. As long as he could pilot the dinghy, service its capricious sails and wheels, I could put up with his behaviour. If it eventually killed him, or sent him plummeting down a psychological abyss I could not fathom, then I would find a new partner. Perhaps even a variant. No doubt they could juggle too.

So, I was squatting in the dust, reconstituting a protein slab, listening to Jericho raving. 'It is the future,' he said, 'for us all to become one, all the differences and specialisations to meld into one unique template.'

By that, I realised his fascination for Dendria had escalated into the desire to breed with her. This was too much. I said nothing, stirred my pot. Jericho's face was demonic in the jumping light of our fire, but he still seemed wild and stunning to me. I thought, sadly, that our association must eventually end, and sooner rather than later. At first, I'd imagined our friendship would develop into something physical, but it seemed, as merely human, I was too common to ignite his libido, or perhaps he just regarded me as a sister. I rarely thought to primp and preen, and I knew I should pay more attention to personal hygiene, even though there is little point when travelling the roads between the fayres.

The end of the millennium approached. Humanity had grown careless and torpid, too lazy to make war, too idle to invent. Our technology fed and governed us; we had little to do but play. Anyone with any fire, zeal or curiosity about the universe had moved off-world to the spiralling colonies. I had often suspected we had out-lived our purpose, but because our knowledge protected us from extinction, we were doomed to linger on, wraiths of what was, without particular promise. Perhaps Jericho was right. For the variants, life was new and exciting. They lacked seriousness of mind, but that might come eventually. Then what? Would they want to own land, claim territory, fight for it? Would they turn their attention to the skies, covet the silent leviathans that circled our world, fly to make war with the remnants of humanity? I wondered about it, even though it seemed unlikely. Variants were frivolous; they had learnt this from us. All that Jericho thought of was indulging his desires.

We had met the Excoriasts only four sennights back at Cackerel Festival. It had been prestigious to earn a stage there, as the most superlative of performers had shoaled to the area. I suppose it was my fault Jericho got to meet Dendria, as I became friendly with Intempera, the troupe-leader. She was a tall, weighty woman, who oozed sex appeal, despite her size, and had the best sense of humour I'd ever come across. Also, I envied her collection of wigs. My hair, forever unwashed, I hid beneath a caul of metal feathers whenever I performed. Intempera had glorious hanks of hair hanging up in her caravan; scalps of azure, viridian, cyclamen, daffodil, the longest of which trailed behind her on the ground as she stalked across the festival ground. Intempera taught me to drink Lizard's Tail liqueur, which is best imbibed without breathing. She had a lover/son, Loadstar, who was seven feet tall, with a beautiful sad face, and plaits to his waist. She said he was an angel hybrid, because she had got pregnant during the Rites of Ecstasy sixteen years before, and Loadstar had been born as a miniature adult, rather than a baby. I wondered how many of her recollections were coloured by Lizard's Tail, but the story was fascinating, and I wanted to believe it.

I took Jericho with me to Intempera's caravan one night, to play livers, and the cidaris was there. It was obvious the game bored her, because she wouldn't join in, but neither would she let the rest of us get on with it. Personally, I found Dendria's behaviour very irritating. She insisted on leaping around us, upsetting the liver-stones whenever anyone was near to winning, and giggling, extending her head fronds and widening her pupils in Jericho's face. I expected he'd find her a nuisance as well, but men's reactions can never be predicted. Intempera occasionally picked up a rug-beater and smacked Dendria with it, which elicited raucous cries, but it didn't stop her gadding about us.

'What a simpo!' I confided to Jericho later, on the short walk back to our wickyup.

He sighed. 'I have seen a creature of aether, a denizen of love.' His hands described cidaris-shaped outlines in the air before him. 'Made flesh, but of a less common substance.'

True, he had been quaffing Lizard's Tail, but I hardly expected such a sodden response. 'Are you all right, Jericho?'

'She is divine,' he answered, blinking.

I presumed the condition would evaporate by day, but it didn't. Dendria, I think, was aware immediately of Jericho's sudden and intense obsession. She flirted cruelly, forever wafting by the stage when we were performing, or else just standing to one side, in prominent view, biting into hunks of barbecued meat that dripped with spiced grease, or else sucking long fruits. Me, she ignored, all her attention being riveted on wretched Jericho. To his credit, my partner never fouled the act, even when the paramour was present. I know that, at least on one occasion, she let him have sex with her, because I happened to stumble across them while they were doing it. Perhaps that was intentional. I believe Dendria knew all about the way I felt for Jericho, and enjoyed pricking my feelings as much as tweaking Jericho's strings. I remember finding them in the wickyup, she on all fours, he taking her from behind. She was making a sound like a donkey, some kind of bray, which I supposed was of pleasure. Her buttocks were turquoise, as if bruised. When Jericho saw me, he could not stop, merely closed his eyes. Out of pique, I went in and made myself a sandwich while they finished. She cleaned herself up without modesty afterwards, even using some of my tissues, which I employed for removing stage makeup. I couldn't help but sneak glances. Her genitals were swollen, and dark blue, nothing like mine in shape or size. As if for my benefit, she spread her legs and twitched her muscles, and the lips of her vulva moved like a mouth. No wonder cidaris' are so popular with men. Still, she had very little breast.

Poor Jericho. His torment lasted a mere four days. One morning, the Excoriasts had left the site, with no message from Dendria left behind. At first, I was glad, but when it became obvious that Jericho wasn't going to get over his obsession, I relented and gave him what comfort I could. Intempera had told me we would be able to get together again at Jasper's Fayre. Jericho's joy at this news made me miserable: it was feverish, a cacoethes of passion. I felt it could kill him.

Now, he sat in the dust before me, shredding a dried grass stalk, his eyes watering with anticipation and longing. 'I won't be denied, Saralan,' he said, not really seeing me. 'At Jasper's, I will have her.' He paused then, as if becoming aware of my existence, and the fact that I could hear, and make deductions for myself. 'Of course, this will not affect our partnership. Maybe we could work Dendria into the routine.'

I smiled thinly, hoping he could see it was thin, but knowing he would see only the upward curve of a mouth and read it as approbation.

'What can you do?' I asked perfunctorily. 'A cidaris is a flighty creature. What if she does not want to come with us?'

Jericho was clearly annoyed with these remarks. 'I will make her my wife,' he said. As if that solved everything.

Part of me hoped he would make a fool of himself, but then I remembered I'd have to deal with the emotional debris. 'What if she doesn't want to be a wife?'

Jericho shook his head abruptly, as if assailed by insects. 'I know, I know,' he said. 'I've thought of that.' His body language did not align with his words.

'So what are you going to do?'

He rested his chin on his clenched fists, staring at the flames. 'Obstacles will have to be removed. Namely, her ignorance. With clear sight, she will know for herself that we are meant to be as a pair.' He fixed me with a frightening glare. 'I shall call upon the powers of hate to aid me.'

I couldn't help sniggering a little. 'So, you are a worker of magic now!'

He bridled. 'You know hardly anything about me.'

Something snapped inside me and let a feeling of defeat slide in. Jericho and I had never argued before, or sniped at one another. How things had changed. How cruel the powers of passion, ruled by the lords of love. I glanced at the sky of their direction, where still the sinking sun stained the threads of clouds, and thought how pitiless they were. As some were moved to deeper feeling, others were swamped and drowned.

While some might call upon the lords of ecstasy, with their weapons of fire to charge the will, and others invoke the mighty lords of fear to subdue the object of desire with their shrouds of midnight darkness, and yet more still would obviously, and dreamily, petition the lords of love, with their flowing vases of desire and harmony, Jericho went for hate. He had a very logical mind most of the time, which might explain his choice. Hate for clear sight, for sharp things, the sky of the rising sun, the morning, potential there but unfulfilled. He would call upon Amaritude, the Angel of Hate, Lord of the Swords, Prince of the Morning, White Eagle of the Dawn, Rider of the Hate Wind. Still, as we all know, Hate has its other side, that of the bloodied weapon, of breakings and endings, of discord and cruelty. I would not have made that choice.

There was a ridge on the other side of the road. During the day, it looked yellow, at night was black. It was here that Jericho decided his ritual would be performed. I had no wish to participate, but Jericho asked stiffly for my assistance; he needed someone to operate the perfume-squeezers. 'I have to speak my mind,' I told him. 'This is folly.' I wished I hadn't mentioned that the Excoriasts would be present at Jasper's Fayre. It had been a moment of weakness to reveal that. Now what would happen?

'I know what you think,' he answered. 'But I'm asking you as a friend, to help me.' Behind his words, but in his eyes, were the unspoken reminders of times when he'd give me support over emotional dilemmas.

'Oh all right,' I said. 'But don't blame me if things go wrong.'

The sun was merely a slit-eyed sliver of red on the hateward horizon as we built a spiral fire of skinned sticks. The sky above us was black, unpricked by stars, yet it looked so clear, so translucent. There were greedy fogs around us, unseen, but sucking up the light.

Jericho's long toes gripped the dirt as he wove the shape of the fire. His hands shook. Occasionally, he cursed as a fumbling movement spoiled the pattern. The twig spiral wove outwards, deosil. I hid within it some shells I had picked up from the gape of a vanished sea, back lovewards. This I did for tenderness, as a protection. The Lords of Love drank salt liquors from shells, the tears of the infatuated. Their faint influence might temper the passions of the Angel of Hate.

Then it was time, and I was squatting outside the circle that Jericho had marked with small white stones. He walked deosil within it, sprinkling self-igniting Grains of Cloud upon the unlit fire, a powder we had bought from another fayre, far distant in time and space, when there had been a clear road between us, and no fog. I held a perfume squeezer in my hand, my toes ready on the foot-pump. Amaritude, as with all angels, was a cantankerous, capricious spirit. His requirements were precise. If I squeezed too much, he would not come, if I squeezed too little, he would not come, or worse, he might decide to put in an appearance anyway, and then do something dreadful. He might crack our bones and suck the marrow, or make us die of desire. I'd heard it could happen.

The Grains of Cloud began to smoke, exuding their own aroma of seas and rain and wet grass. Presently, the fire was crackling, and I risked a hesitant puff on the perfume squeezer. The essence vapoured forth in a couple of restrained coughs, little puffs upon the night air, round and friendly. Jericho stood with legs apart, his arms thrown high, his head thrown back, long, tangled hair falling down his back. My heart ached, and tears blurred my eyes. It was the fumes. Perhaps the squeezer was leaking. Jericho faced the direction of hate, his back to me. He began an invocation, a heart-felt plea to Amaritude's brethren, who preened and guarded him. 'Brothers of Hate, of the Blue Morning, bring forth to me, your Father and Lover, Amaritude!'

A breeze stole furtively past me, shivered across the circle, influencing the flames, so that they leaned in the direction of hate. I applied my feet and fingers to the squeezing of perfume; careful exudations. The scent slapped my head before it flowed towards the circle; the smell of dawn, of fresh light and grass, but with the suggestion burning faint within it of the embers of someone's home.

It is the fumes that bring the visions to us. We are familiar with the archetypal forms of the angels, because we have lived with them since we were children, when we were told about such things. We know what they should look like, so when we invoke them, we see what we expect to see. That is what I believe. I know there is power in the universe, and that it can be wrought into forms. Intention fashions our desires into shapes that we can see, and will-power charges them with intelligence. We can control these forms if we can control our desires, but hectic passion engenders hectic forms, and that can be troublesome. That night, as I sat hunched upon the dry dirt outside Jericho's circle, I pushed, with all my will, some kind of temperance towards my friend. If he was frenzied, I would be tranquil. I was not afraid for myself, but for him.

They came, the shivering reeds of radiance; seven of them. The Lesser Angels of Hate. They twisted like smoke, made of smoke, some feet above the lungeing tongues of the fire. My eyes were stinging. I could see the smudge of their faces, the smoking blue luminance of their eyes. Jericho was a black silhouette before them, frozen in position, with his arms thrown up. Sparks swirled around him in a circling, dervish dance. 'Bring forth to me, Amaritude!'

Slowly, the forms drew apart and there was a stair of light leading up to the infinite dark of our imagination, the sky. Amaritude came down this stair, robed in ferocious rays of blue-white effulgence. His hair was a smoulder of stars. I wondered if he had captured them all that night, to wear. Was that why the sky was so black? I squeezed out some more perfume, trembling. I had seen angels before, naturally. Everyone did. But in the past, they had been invoked, in my presence, for gentler purposes; a healing, a plea for security, a lessening of anguish. Never had I witnessed an invocation of this Lord of Hate to bend the will of another. It was frowned upon, and for that reason, I believed the essence of Amaritude, a creature formed from the dreams and desires of generations of people, would hunger for it.

Jericho looked so small and fragile, with the immense shape of the angel hanging over him. His words seemed like tiny, dry leaves falling to the ground. 'Mighty Lord of the Morning, I entreat thee to hear my petition. Ignite the passion of the cidaris, Dendria, that she might adore me. Open her eyes to me, open her heart, open her mind to me, open her body.'

The angel-form seemed to listen. Jericho versed his request in several different ways, over several minutes, presumably so that Amaritude would be in no doubt as to what he required. When Jericho had finished speaking, the angel raised his hands, each the size of a small tree, and shook his fingers so that grains of light fell down. Something occurred to me as I performed another discrete squeeze on the perfume. What was Jericho offering to the angel? Angels disliked doing things for nothing, and some small sacrifice was required, if only a pinch of incense. Surely Jericho could not have forgotten this important obligation? As I thought this, it seemed to me that Amaritude's giant hands swooped down and cupped Jericho in their blinding radiance. Jericho uttered a distressing sound, as if he was being crushed. His back arched. I heard him gasp, 'I thank you Lord of the Hate Wind, for your presence, for your benevolence. Please accept my humble gratitude.'

Would that be enough? I laid off the perfume-squeezing, thinking it was about time that Amaritude took objection to the taste of the air and departed. He had deigned to take notice of Jericho's invocation, so I had to believe my friend's petition would be granted. The giant hands lifted, the burning countenance grew dimmer, and Amaritude retreated swiftly up his heavenly stair. As he diminished, his brethren closed ranks, until the smoke of their essence expanded into a roiling cloud and abruptly evaporated with a sound like someone opening a hundred air-tight lids all at once.

Jericho sank to the ground, half kneeling, half squatting, his head hanging forward.

I kicked aside the white stones and went to him, took him in my arms. His skin was cold, crackling with frost. The fire burned blue, an effect of the Grains of Cloud. Hurriedly, I dragged Jericho from the circle and took him back to our homely fire down the ridge, on the other side of the road. Here, I wrapped him in a blanket, and gave him a tin cup of liquor, from which he sipped in silence, staring at the flames. There were spots of blue on his face. I feared frost-bite. 'It is done,' he said.

I shuddered. Above us, stars had begun to blink on and off, a binary language. Amaritude had released them.

It took us another two days to reach Jasper's Fayre. Poor

Jericho. He was so ill, yet fired by a manic fever of emotion. I myself found it hard to keep warm. I dreamed of the Angel of Hate, the enormity of him hanging over me, his grains of burning cold light raining down on my face, freezing out my eyes, scorching my tongue. What had we done? I asked myself that question too many times a day, hoping that as my memory of that night receded, so would my unease. I thought that the impact of the Lord of Hate upon my mind was too great, too surreal, and that was what caused the nightmares and the physical discomfort. Jericho and I were doing these things to ourselves, because we believed we had seen something beyond belief.

We could see the flimsy pagodas of Jasper's Fayre several clicks down the road, as we approached at sundown. The tiers of the pagodas were spangled with winking lights; green and gold and white. Jericho seemed preoccupied, which did not surprise me, and we spoke little as the dinghy coasted easily towards the sinking sun. Soon, we heard music; a sad melancholy sound, as thin as the memories of childhood. The only other noise was the creak of the dinghy and then the hum of a dirigible hanging overhead, its gondola packed, no doubt, with the children of the rich, high on the rites of ecstasy performed in clear air. A pale silk ribbon came twisting down and landed on our mast, a trophy from someone's hair. I looked at it clinging there, so limply, and felt the spider hands of anguish flex within me, squeeze my guts.

Jericho left me securing the dinghy with hexes, while he went in search of the Excoriasts, or more precisely, Dendria. Furiously, I beat back the desire to follow him. I adored him as he walked away from me; the pain was total, almost as if Amaritude had inflicted me with the cankers of baleful desire. I refused to think about Dendria, how she might be waiting with fluttering heart and eyes, her blue-palmed hands scored with persistent itches to wrap themselves around Jericho. If he succeeded in his advances, I would leave him. There was no way I could stand putting up with Dendria's sly eyes sliding off me all day, every day. I knew she would be lazy and cruel, and that I would never like her.

To ease my heart, I wandered off alone among the stalls and carousels, the houses of death, the tunnels of enchantment, in search of liquor or philtres of forgetfulness. Every time I caught sight of someone vaguely cidarissy, I flung myself into the hectic crowds, drawing bodies around me like a cloak of invisibility. At an apothecary's booth, I bought a small, dark fruit that tasted of carrion meat: I was assured by the vendor that swift oblivion would follow its ingestion. Shortly, staggering from blaring sound to blaring sound, I bumped into a man I knew vaguely and elected to spend the night with him. We found a Folly of Dreams, built from stick-like bones of spun sugar and polymers, paid our entrance to the masked admerveyelle at the portal and threw ourselves into the marshmallow clouds of the dreams. When I woke up the folly had evaporated into the dawn mist, and had apparently taken my transient lover with it. I did not care. Today I must taste the most bitter of reality's liquors.

Jericho was sitting on the edge of the dinghy, with his back to me, as I approached through the mist. All around me, unseen, the entertainers of Jasper's Fayre, and the sodden revellers who had fallen asleep or unconscious in the muddy sawdust between the booths, were making faint noises of wakefulness. Sounds were muted but forlorn. I stepped over a slim, discarded arm which lay, half-submerged in the mud. The fingers were curled, beckoning. I hoped it had come from an automaton or a doll, and did not look too closely at its ragged stump. As the dinghy loomed nearer, my heart began to panic. The silk ribbon still hung, damp, from the dinghy's mast. Jericho's posture was unreadable, but it did not speak to me in loud tones of success and euphoria.

He has failed, I thought, emotions of different types swelling within me. *He forgot to make sacrifice to Amaritude, and the petition failed.*

Jericho's grief would be terrible, but I felt I could cope with it. Eventually, his sad obsession must fade and we could coast on to new roads until his grief became melancholy, and finally a wistful memory to be discussed over camp-fires and liquor, late at night. Already, optimism was blooming within me, and I increased my pace. I said, 'Jericho,' expecting him to ignore me, but he turned at once.

I stopped walking, almost falling, as the huge headache carried in my brain sluggishly failed to respond to the change in pace. *His face!* Even now, I cannot find words to describe his expression. It was as if the history of the world, with all its atrocities and tragedies, had been etched into his features. His skin looked colourless, all the muscles beneath it dragged downwards. Was this the face of loss, of passion unrequited?

'Saralan,' he said, in a flat tone. 'I wondered where you were.'

I laughed uneasily, pressing with numb fingers the throbbing node of pain in my left temple. 'Oh, I've been around... How did your night go?'

He grimaced. 'I wish I could say it was indescribable, but it wasn't.'

At that, I hastened forward, arms outstretched to embrace. 'Oh Jericho, I'm so sorry! Still, we should have known! What sacrifice did you give to Amaritude? None! And now he has spurned your petition!'

Jericho flinched away from me, forcing me to clutch the painted sides of the dinghy instead. 'Sacrifice? Oh, the sacrifice was taken, and the petition was granted.'

'I don't understand.' After climbing up over the slick boards, I sat down beside him. Now, I was shaking, and my teeth had begun to chatter.

'How foolish we are!' said Jericho, staring darkly into the mists. 'We can't understand *their* ways, no matter how we delude ourselves into thinking otherwise!'

I presumed, wrongly, that he meant the ways of the variants. In a suitably hushed voice, I enquired, 'What did she do?'

Jericho jerked his head around to stare at me. His eyes appeared unfamiliar and I had to glance away. I did not look at him directly once during the time he told me what had happened, and his voice was painful to my ears, ringing with a new harsh note.

So, he had found the caravans of the Excoriasts, his heart full of dreams and scared hope. Dendria had been sitting on the steps of Intempera's wagon, playing cat's cradle with a red string, almost as if she'd been waiting for someone. Jericho described his approach to her, the dreadful nervousness and anticipation that had flowered in his heart. She had caught sight of him, and for a moment, seemed surprised and afraid. Then she had leapt nimbly to her feet and had come towards him, her sharp face filled with welcome. Jericho had known then that his petition had been granted and the fires of passion roared brightly in Dendria's body and mind.

It was at this moment, I think, that Amaritude, with a certain mordant humour, had taken his sacrifice. Even as Dendria had reached for Jericho with her long-fingered hands, his heart had turned to a muscle of stone. Her face, alight with desire, had filled him with repugnance. The scent of her body, reaching out to him in yearning, had made him gag. He no longer cared for her. She had become an object of disgust and embarrassment. Dendria, however, had clearly never felt more drawn to Jericho. Her obsession was evidently unique and total, which was only to be expected if Amaritude had infected her heart.

Jericho, alarmed and sickened, had attempted to flee the scene. He talked incoherently of how he'd thought of running back to me for my support, but Dendria, since the object of her desire had manifested before her, intended not to be denied. Her lamentations had been loud, her finger-nails sharp. An awkward scuffle had taken place, quelled only when Intempera herself, roused from a snooze by the din, had come billowing out of the caravan and separated them.

'I had to hide from her all night,' Jericho said, adding accusingly, 'Where *were* you?'

I swallowed the sharp retort that came like bile to my lips. Inside, my spirits were singing like a heavenly choir. This was triumph, but I sensed that the smoke of battle hid vile carnage, and when it cleared the victory might not be as sweet. 'If I had known, Jericho, I would have been here for you, but how *could* I know? The purpose of our being here was your pursuit of the cidaris, after all.'

Jericho made a harrumping sound. 'We must leave at once,' he said.

Dendria trailed us for several sennights. She was a sick wraith at our heels, and the strength of her obsession was as painful to Jericho as her indifference and aloofness had been before. I realised very soon that he feared her, to the point of phobia. He dreaded her touch as much as some dread the touch of spiders or snakes. Of course, his dreams were full of her. The most regular nightmare involved Dendria creeping up over the sides of the dinghy and stealing to Jericho's cabin, where she smothered him with her body. In this dream, he could neither call out nor move. Eventually, to assuage his night terrors, I began to keep watch until dawn, and sleep during the day, while he piloted the dinghy alone.

The end was horrible.

I was awoken at mid-day, by a hair-raising, womanly scream from Jericho. Pulling on my jacket, I threw myself from the cabin, still half asleep as I stumbled up the deck. The road was long and straight, running between dead, yellow fields, where nothing grew. A thin drizzle hazed down from a grey-green sky. It looked as if the land was in mourning.

Dendria must have overtaken us somehow, perhaps hitching a ride in a dirigible or hanging onto the runners of a train. Now, she ran towards us down the road; a hag, Jericho's nemesis. In her disarray and wretchedness, it seemed she had become more alien: she was stick-thing, gnarled and knobbled, that might have squeezed out from a child's worst dream into the waking world. Her colour was dreadful; dark and contused, and her head fronds were torn and ragged. For a moment, I felt pity. Jericho had made her into this.

I hurled myself forward, shouting out at Jericho to trigger the anchors, for Dendria was directly in our path. My voice was blown away from me, gathered up by the cold, cruel hands of the winds of hate, sweeping like blades across the empty fields.

I do not know whether he meant to run her down, or whether, in his panic, he lost control, but before I could reach him, she had disappeared beneath our runners and wheels, with a thin scream like that of a tortured bird and some other, more stomach-churning noises of breaking flesh and bone.

Cursing, slipping, I smacked Jericho away from the controls and brought the dinghy to a shuddering, bumpy halt. There was a sound of liquids spattering onto the road, and I jumped quickly over the side of the dinghy, worried our fuel-lines had been damaged. But the sounds came from what was entangled in the undercarriage: cidaris remains that jetted dark ichors like fluids that might come from a squid. I stood for a while, hands on hips, staring at the repulsive mess. Her head, mostly intact, was wedged between two moving parts and stared at me with expressionless eyes. Then, I became angry and yelled up at Jericho. I would not clean the bits of Dendria from the dinghy: it was unfair! I'd put up with so much, but this!

Jericho moaned and whimpered above me, hunched down, rocking to and fro. He seemed not to hear me, although I heard him say clearly, 'Now, she has won. Now, she will haunt me. Forever.'

Eventually, I poked what I could away from the dinghy with a long stick, and later coasted it through a shallow stream, which seemed to do the trick.

Jericho was inconsolable, and I was forced to give him an overdose of erigeron to shut him up and stop him seeing things. I reckoned that if we sailed swiftly enough, I would reach the settlement of Migalissin within a day, where therapists might be able to do something with him. The winds of hate worked against me, tugging at the dinghy with unseasonable rage, their shrieking whistles turning to laughter in my head. Jericho's ravings annoyed me to the point where it seemed Amaritude's mean trick had affected me too. My passion was dying, or mutating into despising. 'Fool!' I told Jericho as he twitched in a rug at my feet while I piloted the dinghy through the dry storm. 'What did you hope to achieve?' I had to stop myself from kicking him.

Migalissin was in sight ahead when, without any warning, Jericho leapt up, threw himself from the side of the dinghy and ran like a rat up a lovewards hill, bleating fragmented invocations and scattering dry incense around him. He was gone before I could trigger the anchors.

I jumped down and stood in the road for while, feeling tired. Abruptly, the winds dropped. I was not surprised. I waited, straining my ears for a scream or a cry, but there was only silence. The branches of a petrified forest, which blanketed the hill, were unnaturally without creak or whisper. Occasionally, a feeling would eddy up inside me, and I nearly ran after Jericho, but the urges were fleet, purling away from me before I could act on them. I knew that I had lost him, and even should I find the body that had his name, the persona I cared for had long fled from it.

Evening came in a gentle blaze and I climbed back up onto the dinghy. It felt empty and strange to be there alone. I wanted to be sad or sickened, but could only be numb. Drizzle began to fall in a veil around me, making the deck greasy. Wide-winged black birds came out of the wood, uttering mad cries. I could only leave the area, go on. Jericho had gone to the angels, of this I was convinced. I hoped Amaritude would be kind to him, now that he had Jericho's sanity closed in his shining fist.

In Migalissin, I paid for lodgings in a shack of a bar with the story of what I had experienced. An oily fire sputtered and hissed, offering the only light in the low-ceilinged saloon. I described Jericho as a fool, and felt angry about it. Only later, would I find the strength to weep.

When I had finished the story, I sat back to sip a mug of wine in the apparently awed silence of my audience. Then an old woman in a red kimono spoke up. 'That is an astounding tale, although I have heard worse or stranger in my time. Still, if I were you, I'd seek Amaritude's favour quickly, in case any residue of his displeasure of your partner's stupidity lingers around your vessel.'

I shuddered: the thought of addressing the Angel of Hate, for any reason, made me feel ill.

However, after two days of thinking about it, I performed a small, respectful ritual on and around the dinghy, even though I felt no liking for the Lord of the Hate Wind, and resented having to petition him myself. He made no appearance as I squeezed his favoured perfumes into the air, for which I was thankful. Hopefully, he has forgotten me now.

In the winter-time, I met Intempera at a festival. I had a new partner by then; a young girl with a great talent and a greater amount of impertinence, but her rather abrasive presence served to keep any lingering ghosts of Jericho at bay. I felt an unpleasant wrench in my heart when I recognised the voluptuous, statuesque shape strutting through the booths towards me, Loadstar in tow, but Intempera seemed delighted to see me. She told me she had disbanded the Excoriasts, in favour of a new troupe, comprising only sets of identical twins. 'The variants were too unpredictable,' she confided, grimacing. 'Also, they would persist in contracting strange illnesses that I couldn't treat. Often, they died.'

Later, over the familiar, lethal cocktails in Intempera's

wagon, I told her what had happened to Jericho. She expressed surprise, clearly having no idea that he had harboured a passion for the cidaris.

'Well,' she said, wrinkling up her nose and flapping a hand at me, 'I should not be amazed! It is a pity you did not speak to me at Jasper's about this.'

I sensed a profound meaning behind her words. 'Why? Would it have made any difference?'

She shrugged. 'It is hard to say, of course, and I'm even wary of telling you...'

'Telling me what?'

'They are famed for it!' Intempera declared. 'Variants, and the cidaris strain in particular, flirt and frolic around us human folk, and pretend arrogance, but it is known that having once shared a human bed, they are entrapped! They do not show it, of course, because they don't see the need. But I have seen before what happens when a man - and it is generally men - falls for one of these creatures. Men cannot understand the ways of variants, and always feel rebuffed and used. Some even take sick on it. Whenever I come across a wretch in this condition, I always tell him that all he has to do is turn away from the object of his passion. Then, in almost all cases, the variant will develop a peculiar obsession and throw themselves at the feet of what they perceive to be a cold heart. If I had known about Jericho, I could have told you this. Your poor friend didn't need to go invoking the Cruel and Shining Ones. He paid so dearly! What a waste.'

I don't know how I felt after I'd heard her words. Perhaps my system was too shocked to organise itself to feel things. Instead, I took a sip of the evil liqueur, smiled and shrugged. 'No matter. I could not have won, either way.'

Intempera raised her glass to me. 'True. I hope you are now recovered from the incident.'

I nodded. 'Yes, but I will never forget him,' adding, 'as he was at the beginning.'

And it is true.

The Feet, They Dance

It was the hands of the dead boy that first intrigued Grigor; slender, attenuated, lying in repose. They had not held anything in their long fingers for thousands of years. There was a hole in the rib cage beneath where they lay, as if in his last moments, the boy had sought to stem the life blood that had flowed away from him. Now, his face had sealed itself against the bones. He would not have been as gaunt as this in life, and yet, despite its desiccation, his face was still beautiful.

Grigor was the curator of the Middle Eastern section of the Museum of Man, an establishment full of death. Displayed in a glass case, beneath revealing lights, an Inca child was curled eternally into the position in which the frost had found her on a high South American mountain; in another section, blackened Egyptian mummies lay stretched in various stages of decomposition; in another, a misshapen male body, preserved by a peat bog, was curled up stiffly with his hands tied behind his back, his stone-like face still screaming. In these rooms were the rings and seals of long dead kings, the sandals of a martyred queen; the crabbed dismembered hand of a faithless concubine. Poison lay dried in fatal dishes, confined behind glass, and rusting weapons that had changed the destiny of forgotten kingdoms were held tight against display boards with metal and plastic. It was called the Museum of Man, but in truth it was the Museum of Greater Forces, and Man was rendered tiny as grubs before its power.

The mummy of the boy had arrived only the day before, and would provide the centre-piece for a themed exhibition, before Grigor and other physical anthropologists attempted to unravel the boy's secrets. It was remarkable how well-preserved the body was. Grigor marvelled at the precise eyelashes, still lying against the polished cheek. The fingernails were perfect, as was the coppery hair, caught in a coil at the nape of the neck. Hoops of gold still adorned the boy's ears, his throat collared by a necklace of golden leaves, his body swathed in the remnants of a dark blue robe, fringed and pleated. How could he look so peaceful when the cavern of his dreadful wound still screamed its evidence of violent death? Had he been a sacrifice or a victim of murder?

The boy had been named Nezzar, which was an approximation of the fragmented glyphs, found on a strip of linen laced between his hands. Nothing like this had ever been found before. His dating had proved difficult, the resulting data conflicting. All that was certain was that he'd lived between three and four thousand years ago, in the hot land where once Babylonia had spread its pageant over history. Some cynical voices had already been raised to suggest the mummy was a hoax, because mummification was not a process that had been favoured by the Mesopotamians, although the conditions under which it had been found had contributed to its preservation. A *tell* in Armenia had been excavated, and beneath it, a warren of tunnels and chambers, scoured by strange, subterranean winds that were hot and dry. Some said the chambers constituted an underground city, others that they were merely storage rooms for food, perhaps even catacombs. No other bodies had been found, however.

Nezzar was unique and mysterious, found alone in an unadorned sarcophagus in an empty room. For over two years, his existence had remained a closely-guarded secret, while anthropologists from around the world had worked to decipher the secrets of his parchment flesh. Then, the Museum of Man had secured the privilege of undertaking further tests. The Armenian authorities seemed to have surrendered him almost too readily. Were there rumours surrounding him? Had those who'd uncovered his remains been cursed, driven mad, killed, or had inexplicable events taken place in the establishments that housed the corpse? Grigor had not uncovered any rumours. He himself was not a superstitious creature, but he was charmed by the quaintness of its lore. He would not be afraid to undertake a midnight vigil with a cursed artefact, and would expect nothing to happen, but would still be disappointed if it didn't.

As Grigor prowled around his dead prize, strange images came into his mind. He thought of dusty vaults, where splendid butterflies were arranged on pins and no-one came to view them. He thought of the distant lilt of female voices raised in ululating song. He thought of incense, fierce and potent, and fire-flies blinking against a sky, diminished by stars. He thought of dancing, stamping feet.

That evening, Grigor went back to his apartment late, as everyone had worked overtime to complete the new installation in the Middle Eastern rooms, where Nezzar was the central motif in a collection of ancient artefacts, all creatively arranged with discrete lighting. Grigor's staff had gone out together for a celebratory drink, and his assistant, Nell, had tried to persuade him to join them. She was an acerbic young woman, who had cropped hair and chewed gum continually, her body forever slouching in chairs or shuffling through the lofty corridors of the museum. Her ragamuffin appearance, however, belied her firm academic background. She looked like a boy and had the body language of a boy. Grigor admired her greatly, although deferred to her sharp moods and was always a little frightened of her. He was grateful for her invitation to the staff gathering, but had intuited the sense of duty behind the words. He and Nell might spar together comfortably, but he knew that conversation would not flow so easily between the staff if he were part of the group. No, he was content to go home alone. He did not consider himself to be lonely; work consumed him. He was writing a book on the mysteries of ancient cultures, and any time not spent on jobs for the museum was donated to this task.

At home, Grigor collected his electronic mail - messages from physical anthropologists around the world - and then browsed through various internet forums on anthropology and archaeology to read the latest pronouncements about the mummy. Opinion was still divided. Grigor chuckled aloud to himself as he read them. No-one could explain Nezzar, he confounded all efforts to pin down his origins, as his tissues were capricious, refusing to obey the laws of nature. As yet, not even exposure to the poison-soaked air of the late twentieth century had succeeded in altering his composition. He was inviolate.

After consuming a modest supper, Grigor opened a bottle of red wine, put a CD of Turkish music on the stereo system in his living room and sat down with his two cats on the oversized sofa, which smelled musty and had clearly once belonged in a much larger room. This was true, because five years earlier, Grigor's wife, Marigold, had told him their marriage of fifteen years was over, and that he would be leaving their home. They had both reached their mid-thirties, and Marigold was experiencing a rekindling of youthful vitality. Grigor, though handsome in a gaunt, cadaverous sort of way, was now too ascetic for her tastes. She had already found for him an apartment on the other side of town; not too far away to be inconvenient should she require something of him, but distant enough so as not to bump into him in the corner store. She had used the excuse of the division of spoils to refurnish the house, and Grigor had been allowed to take his pick of the remains. He'd submitted to his wife's decrees in the same manner he'd dealt with every situation in their marriage; with quiet acquiescence, almost distraction. Marigold was annoyed he didn't seem upset, but then he wasn't. Grigor missed neither his home nor his wife. He'd brought his cats with him, and that was enough. In fact, he far preferred the solitude of the apartment, where he could play his favourite CDs of eastern music undisturbed. Marigold had detested them.

Grigor sipped his wine, and laid out on the low table before him some of the colour shots of Nezzar's mummy. The music provided a haunting back-drop to his scrutiny of the pictures. In the dim light, Nezzar looked like a beautiful carving. He had been spared the ravages of age or famine or sickness. When the exhibition had its opening in two days' time, Grigor would have to make a speech. Now he began to make notes and colourful sentences composed themselves in his head. He didn't want the lecture to be too dry, as the majority of the guests would not be exactly scholarly, but at the same time, he'd have to impress his colleagues and the other academics who'd been invited.

The following day, Grigor went into work early, keen to examine the mummy once more. He found Nell in their shared office, drinking coffee with her feet up on his desk, browsing through a sheaf of drawings. Art was another of her accomplishments.

'Hi,' she said desultorily without looking up.

'Good morning,' Grigor said, carefully arranging his coat on the stand by the door. 'Did you have a nice evening?'

'Yeah.' Nell threw down the drawings and swung her feet in an arc to the floor. Without further words, she went to the coffee machine and poured some for Grigor into a plastic cup. He took it from her with a warm smile, hoping she wasn't in too sour a temper today. Nell mothered him in a very detached sort of way, which he appreciated. Neither of them ever stepped over the boundaries, and they'd never look upon one another as friends, but there was a strong mutual respect between them. As he sipped the scalding, bitter liquid, Grigor glanced down at the papers scattered on his desk. A shock vibrated through his body. A face looked up at him, as if through time. The shadowed eyes, the sculpted cheek-bones, the enigmatic smile. He put down the cup and lifted one of the drawings. 'This is... this is incredible, Nell.'

'Huh?' She never liked to admit she enjoyed compliments. 'Oh, that.'

'But it's... how did you do it?'

Nell grinned at him quizzically. 'I went out at dawn, ripped down a tree, then mulched some of it to make the paper. Then I stared at it for over an hour until an image formed on it.'

Grigor chuckled. He'd learned long ago not to gulp down her bait in a single bite. 'What I meant was it's a brilliant likeness of what Nezzar must have looked like in life. That's some feat.'

Nell frowned and came to take the paper from his hands. 'What? Oh, no, you've got it wrong, Papa G. That's not the mummy, although...' she wrinkled her nose as she examined her work, '...I suppose it could be. Yeah, does look like the old fossil a bit. Weird!' She threw the drawing down onto the desk.

Grigor still felt a shade light-headed from the initial shock. 'Then who is it?'

'Just a friend of mine. I've done some sketches for a portrait.' Her eyes took on a wicked gleam. 'Why, fancy him, do you?'

Grigor spluttered. 'Really, Nell!'

She wagged a finger at him. 'Ah, now I understand what you get up to lurking around this old ruin night after night. You're conducting affairs with dead boys! Their lamenting spirits look upon you as the master. You are the towering magician in their midst, uttering horrible spells of resurrection!'

Grigor wondered whether he should feel offended by Nell's remarks, but experienced only an odd thrill. Perhaps it was because she thought him more interesting than he was. 'My curiosity is merely academic,' he said, smiling mildly.

The opening night was attended by the usual throng; local

professors, writers and celebrities, a few government officials and journalists and the friends and families of museum employees who never turned down the chance of free drink. A few students hung sulkily around the fringes of the gathering.

In the privacy of the office before the event, Nell had dressed herself in silver jeans and jacket and had applied false eye-lashes. She had not mentioned her drawings again, and Grigor felt shy of questioning her, although he had thought about them a lot over the last couple of days. Something about this particular exhibit had affected him deeply, but he did not give credence to Nell's salacious suggestions. It wasn't that kind of interest, but something more. Now, sipping the appalling, vinegary wine typical of museum opening nights, Grigor rehearsed his speech beneath his breath, though he knew it by heart already.

In the centre of the room, people filed past the glass case where Nezzar was displayed in splendour, high-lighted by the tasteful lighting that managed to plunge the vast room into interesting shadow, while ensuring that all the exhibits lay in concentrated pools of radiance. Emily, the director of the Museum, flitted busily from clique to clique, talking wildly, no doubt attempting to secure future funding from whatever direction possible. The exhibition itself seemed inconsequential to her. A money woman: that was Emily, an essential evil in these corporate-minded times. It was doubtful Nezzar had cast any spell over her. Grigor watched other people's reactions to the mummy with interest. They would see him as a fairy-tale creature, entombed in glass, perhaps ready to awake.

Grigor realised, by the way he was unconsciously scanning the twittering crowd, that he was looking for the motley band of Nell's friends, who normally showed up at openings. He admitted to himself that he hoped the model for Nell's pictures might put in an appearance. Nell was wrong about his interest in the boy; he did not succumb to the pangs of physical attraction, and never had. It was a language spoken by other people that he had no desire to learn.

A batrachian-looking anthropologist cornered Grigor by the canapés and began to drone on about the academic debate over the mummy. Normally, Grigor enjoyed these discourses with colleagues, but tonight was special, different. Nezzar kindled excitement and magic. Grigor did not want to discuss the science of Nezzar, but the enchantment of his physical presence. He knew that Nell's crowd were more likely to empathise with him, for hardly any of them shared Nell's working interests - they belonged to the more artistic side of her nature.

The party, such as it was, was in full swing when Grigor noticed someone peering into Nezzar's glass case. There was an intense air of concentration about this person, who at first Grigor couldn't tell was male or female. Long, red hair, escaping from loose bindings, fell down onto the glass. Grigor noted the ravaged leather jacket, the ripped jeans. He was slightly affronted. Breath would cloud the polished surfaced, pollute it. Perhaps sticky finger-marks would follow. He was about to make his excuses to his companion and march over to confront the infidel, when Nell loped out of the crowd by the door and sauntered over to the display case. Here, she flung a proprietorial arm about the interloper's shoulders. Grigor experienced a clenching in his belly. It was the model; he knew it. Not because the young man now raising his face to Nell looked like the drawing, or even physically like what was left of Nezzar. It was something else - an otherworldly mien. Nell had succeeded in capturing his essence, if not his physical appearance. He looked Hispanic - beautiful at first glance, but with some displeasing rough edges to his features that further scrutiny revealed in detail. The nose was a little too flat, the brow too low. His hair was dyed; a harsh coppery red, its blackness no doubt stripped by bleach. Grigor felt absurdly disappointed, but still found he had edged away from the group he was with, in order for Nell to catch his eye. She did, perhaps by telepathy. The smile she gave him was knowing, slightly irritating, and she had the audacity to whisper something to her companion, which Grigor dared not conjecture about, although it caused the youth to grin. Best to retreat now, Grigor thought, although Nell clearly had other ideas. She called to him, and in order to silence any unfortunate remarks, Grigor hurried over to her. 'My boss,' Nell said.

Grigor gave her a stare. 'It's going well, isn't it.'

She laughed. 'Yeah, great. Until you begin to orate. Then everyone will go home.'

'Don't deny me my minutes of fame,' Grigor said, dryly. 'You know how much it means to me.'

Nell smirked at the sarcasm. 'Well, this is Gez, who you wanted to meet.'

Grigor dared to examine the youth. 'Did I?'

'I told him what you said about the drawing. What do you think, Gez? Is the stiff like you?'

The youth wriggled his shoulders in what Grigor presumed was a shrug. 'After a long, bad night, maybe. It's creepy. Probably a fake.'

Grigor felt nettled by the youth's tone. 'Did Nell tell you that?'

The dark eyes met Grigor head on. 'No. It just seems too good to be true, too well-preserved.'

'I agree the mummy is phenomenal,' Grigor said, which made Nell laugh. He regretted the remark at once.

'You think it's real, then?' Gez asked.

'Would I have it on display if I didn't?'

'What proof have you...'

'Shut up, shut up,' Nell interjected. 'We can talk about this later. Grigor, someone's signalling you over there. Better get your notes together. Wake me up when you've finished.'

Grigor knew that Nell thought he gave very accomplished speeches, but would never say so. He left her with her friend, and prepared himself to speak. Once he positioned himself behind the lectern near the central display case, the room quickly fell to a hush. He knew he'd have to convince a lot of people here, who believed the museum was risking making a fool of itself over such a controversial exhibition. He began to speak, informally, relating a few anecdotes about the problems they'd had with the installation. 'No-one, as far as we're aware, has yet been cursed,' he said, conjuring a ripple of subdued laughter.

As the lecture progressed, Grigor became aware he felt quite light-headed. The spot-lights burned into him, yet seemed unable to dispel a pressing darkness. He thought he heard a deep rasping of breath and for a moment paused. Everyone looked at him expectantly and he realised he'd stopped in the middle of a sentence. He'd been speaking for half an hour, yet his mind had been working independently. He couldn't remember what he'd said. He saw Nell frowning at him, sending a silent question: Are you OK? He laughed nervously and carried on. It was because he'd forgotten to eat earlier. Two glasses of cheap wine had gone straight to his head and now churned acidly in his stomach. He wished he could get to the end of the speech, but it seemed interminable. His mouth worked automatically, reciting what he'd written over the last couple of days. Still, it seemed to impress the crowd. Eyes were round. Nobody was drinking. They were all transfixed, listening to him. He was conscious of one of the museum technicians aiming a camcorder at him. It seemed like a gloating eye.

Finally, Grigor's mouth ran out of words, and after a moment of what seemed to be stunned silence, Nell raised her hands above her head and began to applaud. Presently, the rest of the room joined in. Nell uttered a piercing whistle and all her friends cheered. Was I that good? Grigor wondered.

He stepped away from the lectern and Nell came over to him, holding out with a glass of wine. 'I think I need something to eat first,' Grigor said, taking a handkerchief from his pocket and pressing it to his damp upper lip. 'Felt a bit odd there for a moment.'

'Papa G, that was something else,' Nell said appreciatively. 'All that stuff... it was like Lovecraft, or something.' She shook her head. 'Daring, but clearly a great success. These people didn't know what hit 'em.'

Grigor gazed at her numbly. 'Lovecraft?' he said icily, picking up on that single word.

'Well, yeah.' Nell looked puzzled for a moment, then her face grew uncharacteristically expressionless. 'The description of what Nezzar's life might have been like and all that weird stuff about forgotten gods and lost temples. You know...'

Grigor wiped his brow. He looked down at his notes as if he'd never seen them before. 'I can't... I can't remember,' he said.

Nell stared at him speculatively for a moment, then took his arm. 'The office. Come on. I'll pick up the video tape.'

Grigor went to sit in his darkened office, and waited while Nell busied herself dragging the VCR through from another room. He felt removed from reality, not afraid, not even surprised. Something unusual had happened. Of course it had. But why? He sensed a presence in the door-way and knew immediately it wasn't Nell. A cold finger of dread stroked his heart as he looked up. He didn't know who or what he expected to see, but it was only Nell's friend, Gez, who now seemed ordinary in the extreme, unimportant. Grigor was mildly irritated the boy was there, and did not speak.

Gez lounged insolently in the doorway for a few moments, and then slowly drew himself erect, taking his hands from his pockets. He seemed to change, as if he cast off a mask or a cloak, a disguise; confidence, and a strange, comfortable arrogance emanated from his body like an invisible aura. Grigor sensed this was a new persona, and it had a definite purpose. What had Nell said to him?

'You didn't write that speech,' Gez said.

Grigor stared at him. He couldn't answer for a moment, and then muttered, 'Over-tired.' He laughed nervously, wondering why he felt so intimidated. 'Got carried away.'

Gez came out of the shadow of the threshold and walked slowly to where Grigor sat drooping in a chair. He exuded a strange odour, which Grigor couldn't help thinking was almost reptilian. So many perfumes nowadays smelled strange; not like perfumes at all, but reeks and stenches. Gez stood in front of him, a looming shadow, with red metallic flashes in his hair where it caught the meagre light. Without warning, he reached down swiftly and took Grigor's chin in a strong grip. His face was very close, the eyes gleaming like dark jewels; utterly black. 'I could pour into you the dust of centuries,' he murmured, 'and the ashes of cities, and the fumes of death. Cadaver beetles could fall from my lips into your body, and the desiccated tongue of forgetfulness. I am death and I am life.' With these words, he lunged and covered Grigor's mouth with his own.

It might have been a kiss, or something else. Grigor didn't know. His arms scrabbled around in the air like those of a stricken insect; his feet scraped uselessly against the floor. A calm part of his mind told him that a strange young man had just made an unmistakable advance to him, while another whirled in a vortex of history, back into the past. He caught a glimpse in his mind of some of the things he'd said in his lecture, but strangely there was no sense of familiarity.

Gez released him, breathing heavily. 'I am not as beautiful as you think,' he said.

Grigor stared at the boy's shadow, unable to speak.

Then Nell wheeled a trolley into the room, and turned on

the light. 'What's up?' she asked.

Grigor shook his head. 'Nothing.' His lips were still wet. He could taste something; sour and perfumed, like frankincense or funerary balm.

Gez had turned away and now seemed threatening and strange no longer. His body had adopted the sloping posture of youth, the slouch, the shiftiness. If anything, he seemed bewildered, even shocked.

While Nell had enjoyed Grigor's lecture, he could only cringe as he watched the video. What had impelled him to say those things? It was fantasy, but where had it come from? He saw himself speaking vehemently of Nezzar's calling as a temple dancer of the Stamping God, Sin-na'el. Grigor had not heard of this name before, but in the film he went on to describe with apparent authority the shadowed Temple of Transcendence, where Nezzar had served his deity, dancing in the moonlight to an unheard music; a lone figure in an empty court, partnered only by his swooping shadow.

As he listened, Grigor saw the pictures in his mind. They did seem faintly familiar now, but it was like recalling an experience of *déjà vu*. He could not remember when or if he'd thought or read of these images before. How could he have spoken so confidently of Nezzar being not quite human, how the royal blood of the Shining Ones ran in his veins? What possible evidence could he have that Nezzar's mother had been locked in a high tower, where a god had visited her and made love to her? However, on the video, Grigor seemed sure that the woman had conceived, but had died giving birth, for Nezzar had torn himself from her body. He had also eloquently described Nezzar's adolescent beauty as strange and disturbing - alien - and how he had moved with a feminine grace that was also feline and ophidian. Nezzar had danced with the broken wings of carrion birds around his shoulders, bowing to the Stamping God, who could be heard dancing deep within the earth, all the time bellowing out his eternal pain, for he was banished from the light.

Grigor turned away from the video, reaching for one of Nell's cigarettes from the packet that lay on the desk, even though he had given up smoking three years previously. Nell watched him, frowning. 'That wasn't me,' Grigor said at last. He felt light-headed from the first draw. 'I don't know where all that stuff came from.'

Nell laughed abruptly, shook her head. 'Are you possessed, Papa G?'

Gez fidgeted uncomfortably in the doorway, gradually edging himself into the corridor beyond.

Grigor rubbed his forehead. He shrugged. 'I've been working too hard, thinking about the exhibit too much.' He glanced up. 'This is real life, Nell. Tell me neither of us believe in that sort of rubbish.'

She paused, then nodded. 'Yeah, you're right. This is real life. Everything's ordinary and in its place. You're gonna have some explaining to do, however. What's Emily going to say?'

'I'll have some days off, tell her I'm stressed.'

'Yeah, do that.'

Gez, Grigor noticed, had vanished.

Emily, however, did not react in the way either Nell or Grigor anticipated. As Grigor attempted to make a furtive exit from the museum, she spotted him in the lobby and swooped down on him. Grigor fought an urge to run away from her.

'Grigor, you were marvellous tonight!' she bellowed. 'That's the sort of PR stuff we need for the museum. A bit of colour and excitement! Much more effective than all that tedious sermonising. Let's get the spirit of entertainment into this musty old place!' She laughed loudly.

Grigor winced. 'Let's hope all our guests feel the same.' He smiled ruefully. 'I suppose I was playing them up, making a point about their scepticism. None of what I said could be authenticated, Emily; it was fiction. I'm sorry if I caused you any embarrassment.'

Emily's face seemed unsure whether to fall or not. 'Well... I enjoyed it and so did the journalist from the Herald.'

'I bet!'

Grigor mumbled a few phrases about feeling ill, and Emily seemed almost relieved to learn he wouldn't be around for a few days. He could tell she thought it would give her the freedom to capitalise on his unwise and sensational lecture.

At home, Grigor lay restless on his bed. Outside the night was warm and sultry, reminiscent of some far eastern summer. He felt feverish, and after a bottle of wine and a couple of pain-killers, drifted on the edge of sleep, unable to succumb because his mind was so busy. He saw crosswords solving themselves before his inner eye, resolving into chequered roads that snaked through a black background. Then he was walking one of those roads, not dreaming, but visualising freely. The landscape around him was in negative; black trees on a white sky, even though he knew it was night. The path beneath his feet was of black and white slabs and they led to a tall building in the distance; a temple like a great cube of stone, its walls decorated with cyclopean bas-reliefs of striding gods so large he could discern their shape even this far away. He thought: I must go back, but continued to walk. Coloured smoke rose into the air above the temple from a tall, narrow chimney that was intersected by circular slates. The smoke was reddish brown - the only colour in the landscape - and he could smell it now: musty, resinous, bloody. He could hear a regular, heavy thumping sound coming from deep within the earth.

Then he was at the temple gates. They were over thirty feet high; dense satiny wood adorned with pictograms like none he'd seen before: an array of dots, spirals and lines. He could hear music now; staccato yet rhythmic, a whining flute backed by hiccupping drums. Colour had bled back into the world. The stones of the temple were massive, a polished tawny brown. He could not recognise their origin. The carvings loomed over him; an army of giants all facing towards the gates. They were inhumanly beautiful, with attenuated bodies and faces, swathed in cloaks of feathers and attended by monstrosities; lolloping foetuses tentacled and clawed, with the beaks of squids; deformed animals; women who tore their breasts with hooked finger-nails, whose mouths and eyes were gaping holes, whose hair was snakes and feathers.

Grigor put one hand against the door and a vibration shuddered through him. He was paralysed by it, his body rising onto tip-toe, his head thrown back, gasping. Then he was inside the temple, in a courtyard roofed with amber glass. The flag-stones beneath his feet were dusted with sand, and a hot breeze cut around his ankles. The atmosphere was intense, watchful. He felt as if he was under great pressure. Looking down, he saw he was dressed in a long robe, grey with dust. He was supporting himself upon an elaborately carved staff, for he was tired, having travelled a long way. Before him, the inner precincts of the temple were hidden in darkness. Through the tawny gloom, he caught a glimpse of columns, rank upon rank, and thick smoke oozed out heavily between them, hugging the ground. From far within, the music still called to him and he went towards it.

As he entered the shadows, a tall man dressed in the robes of a priest appeared beside him and bowed respectfully. 'Welcome master. You have come for the dance of invocation and the hour is nearly upon us.'

'Yes,' Grigor replied. 'But first, refresh me.' He spoke with a casual authority that shocked him and sat down on a stone bench between the columns.

The priest glided away, but presently returned, bearing a flagon of cold water, which tasted intensely pure and poured through Grigor's body like a reviving drug. He wiped his mouth and handed the flagon back to the priest. 'Take me to the inner place.'

The priest bowed again, and gestured for Grigor to follow him. They walked between innumerable columns and down what seemed like miles of triangular corridors. All the walls were of a strange, soapy green stone, highly polished and mostly unadorned, except for occasional sections where the alien script was cut into the surface. Grigor wanted to pause and examine his surroundings in detail, but his body felt full of urgency, and the priest's steps were swift ahead of him.

Eventually, they mounted a flight of glassy stone steps that led up to a shadowed gallery. Here dark red drapery swayed in the hot breeze and the air was difficult to breathe. There was a dampness to it, and the incense failed to mask a wet, earthy odour.

Grigor sat down and found himself looking over a balcony into a vast chamber below, clearly the heart of the temple. Its floor was slabbed with stones of different sizes and shapes like the board to an unknown game. They were dark brownish red and purple, and occasionally, gold. The middle of the room was dominated by an immense but slender pillar, fashioned from polished black basalt, and crowned by a large crystal stone, which Grigor knew represented the foundation and was called the Eye of Anu. His mind felt as if it was disintegrating, for while part of him gawped in astonishment, another part knew the history of this place and had walked there often. It was the Temple of Transcendence, which he had mentioned in his lecture earlier, and in this place the dance was sacred. The temple was dedicated to the Watchers, the fallen Sons of God, who were Anu's rebel sons, reviled and scorned. On the glazed green wall opposite, Grigor saw a gargantuan ochre-coloured pictogram of the sole of a foot, in whose centre burned the symbol of an unblinking eye. The feet of the dancers were holy here; they who saw the gods through the sorcery of their sacred steps. To left and right, six black columns reared down either side of the chamber. Grigor knew that each of them resonated a particular tone. When they vibrated in harmony they called the Watchers into the temple.

A slim figure glided out from between the left hand columns into the centre of the room. Grigor knew at once that it was Nezzar. He was clad in a short, peacock-blue tunic decorated in metallic thread with the same unusual symbols that were carved upon the outer gates. The tunic was belted with silver; long, delicate chains, strung with wafer-like disks, hung down around Nezzar's waist. His hair was bound up in a copper fillet, coiled tendrils, clattering with beads and shells, escaping down his back. His arms, his neck, even his face were decorated with curling tattoos, and his wrists and ankles were adorned with bangles hung with more bells and rattling beads. When he shook his head, long earrings tinkled like wind-chimes. He would provide his own music for the dance. His feet were painted red, and Grigor knew that upon each sole was a tattoo of the unblinking eye.

Grigor could see that his fantasies of Nezzar did not match the reality, if this was reality. His face was not perfect and in fact resembled Gez more than Grigor had believed. Perhaps it was Gez down there, invading his dreams. If I am dreaming, Grigor thought, then let it happen. I will enjoy it.

Nezzar stamped abruptly and filled the echoing hall with chimes. He began to move, slowly at first, invoking his body music. He stamped lightly, his hips rotating sensually, his sinuous arms held high, the fingers splayed out; rigid yet graceful. Conjuring a percussion from his beads and chains, he began to enact what looked like a primal flamenco dance. Gradually, his movements became faster; his hair and the chains about his waist swung out.

Grigor felt the air around him stir. It was stifling now. Each breath was an agony. Below him, Nezzar stamped and spun, and it seemed that the air was sparkling with jewelled dust around his body, as if he'd summoned it up to accompany the dance. The whirling motes slowly eclipsed his form, until he was a spinning maelstrom of glittering particles, each of which were pulsing and continually enlarging. Concurrently, the atmosphere in the temple became charged.

Grigor's heart had begun to race. Something was coming, moving swiftly towards the temple like rolling thunder. Grigor could sense the vibration of its approach through the walls, through the floor beneath his feet, and more deeply, within the sinews of his tensed muscles. A presence had been attracted by the dance and was now driven to manifest.

The Grigor who belonged in the waking world was terrified, and did not want to see what might happen next, but the other side of him was stronger and would not tear his eyes away.

Shadows rose like curling smoke from between the cracks in the flagstones of the temple floor, while the darkness at the edge of the room had become denser. The shadows brought with them the pungent, metallic aroma of carrion and reached out with waving filaments to touch the dancer, withdrawing as if scalded when they made contact with his shimmering nimbus.

Abruptly, Nezzar came panting to a stand-still, his body running with sweat. The sparkling mist still spun around him. Within it, he was a glowing being who raised his arms and saluted all four quarters of the compass. Then, he turned to his audience of one and raised his head. 'Master, He is summoned, and yours to command!'

Grigor stared down at the boy, perplexed. What had been summoned, and why? He could not speak now, but even as he thought this his body had involuntarily risen to its feet. He pointed down at Nezzar. 'You have done well. Go now to the Tower of Silence and await my presence.'

Nezzar inclined his head. 'As you wish, master.' He ran nimbly from the hall.

Grigor saw that the boy had left the swirling mist behind him. Shadows massed around it inquisitively. He sensed a sentience within them, that reached out to him. Its presence affected him deeply on an emotional and physical level; he felt both lustful and immensely strong.

'Sin-na'el!' he uttered in a rasping voice, then again, more loudly, 'Sin-na'el!'

The shadows and the glittering mist conjoined, condensed. Grigor saw Him then, complete and clear, in a single second. He was monstrous; ten feet high, a man yet not a man. His eyes burned with crimson fire in his dark face; long hair hung matted to his bony hips. His hands were clawed, and his obsidian skin was caked with dry blood and ashes. He wore a cloak of tattered feathers, decorated with bones and hanks of hair. His feet were splayed talons, like those of a gigantic vulture, and were bandaged at the ankles with bloodied rags. His cloak was adorned, like Nezzar's costume, with artefacts that conjured sound, but these were grisly instruments; bones of children, vipers and lizards. His beauty was terrible, almost repulsive, for while his features were refined they were twisted into a bestial leer. The sight made Grigor's eyes ache and burn, yet conjured a fire in his loins; such was the way the Watchers affected any human who dared to confront them.

'Nephilim!' Grigor called and the creature folded into a crouch, snarling up at him. A terrible cacophony started up, as if a thousand prisoners confined in dungeons below the temple had all started to panic and lament at once. Grigor heard screams and thumpings and draggings, the tortured sounds of metal against metal. His throat was dry, his eyes seared and tearless in his head. Yet he dared not look away.

'Sin-na'el,' he said, in a low yet ringing voice. 'You who were fourth avatar of the High Lord, and for your blood-lust cast out of Paradisa, the High Place. You who taught the children of men to dance for ecstasy, and who seduced the son of King Shusin, King of Ur. You whose eyes were plucked out for the sin of gazing upon a prince of the royal line, and whose feet were sundered from your body for the sin of profane dance, hear me now. Blinded Nephilim, whose corrupted flesh has lain for a thousand years, beneath a thousand rocks, below this sacred place, witness the desires of my soul with the life-blood which is your sight, for I have a boon to ask of you.'

The entity below straightened up, and a fearsome intelligence seemed to fill the burning, scarlet pits that had once been eyes of flesh. 'I may not see your form, priest, but your spirit I perceive well, for its light betrays to me your intent. I will grant you any boon, Ashur, if you can meet the cost.'

Grigor nodded once. 'I know this. My apprentice has applied himself diligently to learning the art of your conjuration. We have worked long years to invoke your presence, mighty lord. We are your servants and your worshippers, and will do your bidding. We ask in return the sacred contract; knowledge of longevity and passage through the sacred flame to the stars.'

The Watcher laughed; a hollow sound. 'Do not place faith in what you'll reap from me, Ashur. You say you worship me, yet the cold light of reason burns in your eyes.' Sin-na'el folded His long, sinuous arms. 'I know you are of my heart, my making, priest. You are my creature, but must prove it. Show me that your reasoning is worthy, by placing it higher than that which is most dear to you. Give this to me and we have the contract you desire.'

Grigor hesitated. He was conscious of being a passenger in a cruel, hard brain. His own instincts wanted to force himself to back off - he sensed a trick - but his voice said, 'You already have what you ask.'

'Then give it to me in a manner that will please me, but do not conjure me once more in regret, should the light of the flame burn your reason from you.'

Grigor bowed. 'As you wish, mighty lord.'

The dank, intense atmosphere and the vision of the Watcher vanished instantly.

Grigor awoke abruptly, as if someone had slapped him. He sat up in bed, terrified, gasping for air, and groped for the switch to his bed-side light. Vile, vile! His flesh was crawling. What was happening to him? He was in half a mind to call Nell, but forced himself not to. She already thought he was going slightly mad; this would only confirm her suspicions.

Grigor lay back down again, blinking at the ceiling. He still felt obscenely aroused, yet sick with horror, as if a lingering presence of the creature haunted the shadows of his room. Nightmare. It was best that he was going to stay away from work for a while. He must forget the exhibit, throw himself into mundane, ordinary things.

In the morning, Nell called him. Her voice sounded troubled. 'Grigor, I hate to bother you like this, but I think you'll have to come in.'

'Why? What's happened?'

'It's... it's the mummy. It's been damaged.'

'Damaged? How?'

He heard her sigh. 'Look, will you just come over for an hour or so?'

Grigor found Emily, the curator, prowling round the Eastern rooms in a foul temper. Several police were in evidence. She asked Grigor how he was, in a manner hardly indicative of concern, and then launched into complaints about how her demands for more security had been ignored, and now this had happened. 'It's your baby, Grigor, take a look.'

Grigor went reluctantly over to the mummy case. The glass shield appeared unmarked, and initially he couldn't see what the problem was.

The director came over and sighed. 'How the hell they did it, I've no idea! Bloody ghouls!'

It was then Grigor noticed the feet, or rather the lack of feet. Nezzar's attenuated legs ended in neatly-shored stumps at the ankles. He uttered a shocked sound. 'My god! The case is alarmed. How could anyone get into it?'

Emily sighed, her arms stiffly folded. 'You tell me. Probably some nutty group after gruesome relics for unhealthy practices or whatever. Perhaps they cast a spell on the security systems! Who the hell knows!'

Nell was standing some feet back, chewing the inside of her mouth. Grigor had the distinct impression she was more worried about this than Emily. She knew something.

'I don't like this thing,' Emily said, grimacing down at the mummy. 'First your funny turn last night, now this...'

The staff must have been gossiping about him to her. 'It was not a funny...'

She would not let him continue. 'Grigor, I know what I said last night, but I've had time to think about it since. I've worked with you for nearly ten years now, and I've never seen you like that. I realise now you weren't just ill. This thing is trouble. I'll be glad when the exhibition's over and the anthropologists have finished raking over the bones.'

So Emily had a superstitious streak. Grigor had to restrain a smile. 'What do the police think?'

'There's no sign of a break-in,' she replied. 'I don't want to think this is an inside job, but...'

Grigor couldn't help raising his eyes to meet Nell's glance. She shook her head at him slightly, looked away. 'I hardly think that's likely,' Grigor said, mildly, 'unless you believe my funny turn, as you put it, might have been a precursor to mutilation.'

Emily uttered a shocked snort. 'Grigor, I was not implying any such thing! I was thinking more about some of the students who come in.'

After speaking to the police, Grigor went to his office with Nell. 'OK, madam' he said, once the door was shut behind them. 'What's on your mind about this?'

Nell sighed and flopped into a chair. 'Oh, this will sound so loopy. I don't know. It was Gez last night.'

Grigor froze. 'What?'

Nell shook her head. 'He was very weird when we left here. We went to the club where he works and he was talking strange. Asked a lot about you - I mean, *a lot*. But it spooked me. Didn't seem like him. He seemed as obsessed with the mummy as you are. I didn't like it. It sounds weird, but I kept thinking he was - well - using me in some way, that he had an agenda about you *and* the mummy.'

Grigor sat down. 'Nell, we're both over-reacting now! I refuse to believe we can be affected by an exhibit like this - any of us. We can't give these fancies credence. That's dangerous territory.'

'I know that.' She leaned back in her chair. 'It was just what happened to you last night and then at the club...'

'What does Gez do there?' Grigor enquired.

She rolled her eyes. 'He's a dancer.'

Grigor's shoulders slumped. 'Oh dear.'

'What?'

'I want to see him.'

Gez was nowhere to be found. Nell called his home, and there was no reply. She and Grigor went out looking in his usual haunts, but there was no sign of him. 'What's this about?' Nell asked. 'It isn't just a fancying situation, is it?'

Grigor wondered whether he should tell her about the dream, then decided against it. 'No, it's just that he was a bit odd with me too last night, before you came in with the VCR. I think he has got something to do with the mutilation.'

'Perhaps we should just tell the police.'

'No, I just want to know why. Something tells me that if the police are involved, Gez will never be found.'

They left messages at various places for Gez to get in touch with Nell. 'It won't work,' she said. 'If he really did do it, he'll know I'm on to him. I never chase him around. I think this is just going to be an unsolved mystery.'

She and Grigor went back to Grigor's apartment - the first time Nell had been there. They drank coffee and Grigor questioned Nell about how she'd met Gez. 'It was at the club. We got on well. I liked him. He's a great dancer...' She paused. 'It was about three weeks ago.'

'Are you...?' Grigor enquired delicately.

Nell rolled her eyes. 'Get real! You think I'm interested? You think he is?' She grinned. 'Grigor, you're so innocent. The place where he works, it's a gay club. My girl-friend and I go there. I thought you knew that part of my *resumé*.'

'Oh.' Grigor couldn't think of anything else to say.

Nell jumped to her feet. 'Well, I'd better get back, otherwise the Dragon might think I'm off hawking stolen feet somewhere.' She leaned down and kissed Grigor on the forehead. 'Don't worry, Papa G. It'll all be fine. Call me if you want to. I'll look in on you later, after work. That, OK?'

'Yes, thanks. I'd appreciate it.' He'd already decided that later, after a bottle of good wine, he'd tell her everything.

Left alone, Grigor paced around his rooms, full of a strange energy. He felt he should be doing something, but didn't know what.

At six o'clock, his doorbell rang. Grigor thought it must be Nell and opened it without checking through the spy-hole. But it was Gez standing there. Grigor felt instantly surprised and pleased, feelings which were soon eclipsed by doubt and a tremor of fear. 'What are you doing here?'

Gez's dark eyes bored into him. 'Invite me in.'

'I don't think so.'

'Don't be afraid of me. There's no need.' He took a step forward.

Grigor felt as if he knew the boy, had known him for a long time. All because of the activities of a single day and the strange dream. It didn't make sense and yet it did. Feeling as if something had snapped inside him, something that had been causing discomfort without him knowing it, Grigor stepped aside and gestured for Gez to come into the apartment.

In the living room, Gez sat down on the sofa and lit a cigarette. His bony knees showed through rips in his tattered jeans. He looked starved and furtive like a runaway.

Grigor stood over him with folded arms. 'Did you damage the mummy?'

'What?' Gez appeared genuinely surprised, so Grigor explained what had happened.

'You think I did this? Why?'

Grigor shrugged. 'Your behaviour last night.'

Gez frowned. 'I gave you something you wanted and now you think I desecrate the dead? That's kind of you, very kind.'

'You said things - strange things.'

'So did you.' Gez leaned back on the sofa, spread out his arms along the back. 'That mummy is weird. It affects people. I don't think anybody cut its feet off. They're just walking.'

Grigor couldn't repress a shudder. He laughed nervously. 'Drink?'

'OK.' Gez took off his leather jacket. 'So that was why you and Nell were looking for me today - because you think I'm a grave-robber. I thought it was because you wanted to see me - for yourself. What a shame.'

Grigor handed him a glass of red wine, watched him drink it. 'Your world is not my world - er - Gez. What *is* your name - your real name?'

Gez smiled disarmingly. 'Angelo, but call me Nezzar, if you like.'

I don't know what to do with you, Grigor thought. *You are here because of me, and absurdly I don't feel worried about it, but I still have no idea what to do with you.*

Gez patted the seat beside him. 'Sit down. I have something to say.'

Warily, Grigor did so.

'I think we've known each other before,' Gez announced in a grave tone.

Grigor laughed. 'I don't remember.'

'Not in this life, stupid. Another.' He put his head on one side. 'You don't believe, do you.'

Grigor turned his wine-glass between his palms. 'At this moment, I don't know what I believe. It's been a very strange couple of days.'

Gez punctuated his speech with emphatic hand gestures. 'I had to kiss you last night, because it felt as if I'd waited a long time to do so. You know this too.' He let his head fall back against the sofa and blinked at the ceiling. 'You are a good, upright man from a good neighbourhood, and look at me, but I feel I can speak to you like this. We know each other - that's why.'

Grigor wondered if things were getting out of hand. Where was Nell? He wished she'd arrive. In a silence, Grigor rose and went to his stereo, inserting one of his favourite CDs into the player. Strains of eastern music twisted into the room. 'You want me to dance for you?' Gez asked.

Grigor opened his mouth, but nothing came out. He shrugged and nodded, sat down again.

There was hardly any room to dance, but Gez insinuated himself around the cramped furniture, his expression distant with concentration. Grigor sat on the sofa watching him, knowing that at some point the music would stop. Nell was right - the boy was a good dancer. He seemed made for it, moulding his body to the sound. Grigor remembered the dream and felt a stirring within him. It was another voice that said, 'Come to me'; a voice low and measured. Gez paused, then did so, kneeling at Grigor's feet. He put his hands on Grigor's knees, pushed them apart, then reared up between them. They embraced.

Grigor thought that he heard the door-bell ring, but ignored it. He was wrapped in a caul of exotic music and ophidian limbs. Their passion was claws and heat, demanding, almost angry and impatient. Finally, they went into the bedroom, and there fell asleep, with the window open and the CD player on repeat.

Grigor walked the path to the temple again, but this time went directly to the Tower of Silence. Nezzar was waiting for him there. He jumped up and ran over to Grigor, threw his arms around him. 'We have triumphed!' he cried. 'The work is over.'

'Yes,' Grigor said, and pushed the boy away from him a little. He traced the line of Nezzar's jaw with his thumbs, wondering.

Nezzar seemed puzzled. 'Is something wrong, master?'

'No,' Grigor said. 'Nothing's wrong. You are most dear to me.'

Nezzar smiled and rested his head against Grigor's chest. 'I love you. You are my lord.'

'You have worked hard for me,' Grigor said. 'I'll not forget that.'

Perhaps Nezzar sensed some finality in the remark, for his body stiffened in Grigor's arms, but Grigor wouldn't let him pull away. He kissed the boy, plunged his hands into the thick coppery hair, bit his lips, his neck. Responding, Nezzar purred like a cat and sank down to the floor of the shrine.

Grigor's consciousness partly left the body it inhabited. He felt himself being drawn away, down the labyrinthine corridors, into darkness. Another part of him was animal lust, grunting and thrusting into compliant flesh, but it was fading away.

When the screams began, he was tugged back into his dream body, instantly and shockingly. Blood everywhere, flailing hands, terrible cries. Nezzar jerked beneath him in the throes of death, his heart ripped out. 'Most dear to me,' Grigor murmured, the long-bladed knife slick in his hands. 'Most dear.'

Nezzar's eyes were filmed with blood, but for a moment, before they clouded for eternity, their expression was fierce and clear. He was already dead, but his arcane art permitted him to speak. 'You can't throw me away. Not now. Not ever. My spirit leaves this world, but I will find you! I shall always dance. You have killed my body, but in memory of our love, do not take from me that which is my true spirit.' His face fell slack, his lips silent, yet still his voice echoed around the walls of the tower. 'Ah, Sinna'el, hear me! This is forever!'

Grigor, who was Ashur, adept of the inner temple of the Stamping God, knelt alone with a dead boy in a veiled shrine. He had fulfilled his part of the contract, as far as he was able.

When he awoke, Grigor opened his eyes to find Gez leaning over him, his hair hanging down. It was all so clear now. Not dream, but memory, long buried. 'Will you kill me now?' he asked.

'You believe?' Gez whispered.

Grigor nodded. 'Yes.'

Gez plunged his hands between his thighs, hung his head. 'I came a long way to find you.'

'I know. Some part of Nezzar - some part of you? - influenced events so that the mummy ended up where I worked. This, I believe now. We have unfinished business from the past.' Grigor's voice was weak. He didn't know how he could believe such things. The world he knew had fragmented and blown away from him.

'I should kill you,' Gez murmured, 'but for the fact that in our other life, you granted my last wish. That means something.' He glanced up. 'You did what you felt you had to do. Neither of us went into that business without knowing the risks, the possible cost. And...' he paused, 'I still love you, Ashur.'

Grigor closed his eyes, his chest filled with an ancient pain. For some moments, there were no words between them.

Circles of time, ever repeating. Outside, sirens wailed and traffic growled. Hot summer air twisted the drapes. Gez's body began to move, his legs and feet trembled, vibrating upon the bed. He threw back his head and howled. 'What's happening to me?'

Grigor reached out and gripped one of the boy's wrists, unable to still the tremors in his body. In the living room, beyond the bedroom, shadows stirred and a reek of carrion polluted the air.

Gez expelled a sobbing sigh, as if he could barely draw breath. 'The moment we met the other night, just that one moment, He found us. We called to Him like a song. And He comes for what we denied him.'

Grigor's grip intensified around Gez's wrist. He sensed something swirling in the living-room beyond the reach of his bedside light. Something forming; hungry. 'What do you mean?'

'The feet,' Gez hissed. 'The heart and the feet.' His eyes were round and dark, full of terror. 'You fulfilled only half of the deal back then. I begged you to honour my feet, the house of my spirit, and you were weak. You obliged me. But it was never finished. Now, the Stamping Good has found us and taken the feet from the mummy.' He paused, expelled another sobbing breath. 'But will that be enough?'

From the living-room came the sound of something breaking; an ornament or a glass. *I should know the right words to protect us,* Grigor thought. *Ashur would have known, but I can't remember.*

Furniture scraped across the carpet, more things were broken. Grigor and Gez clung to each other in the bed, protected only by a small pool of electric light. Presently, that too was denied them and the room plunged into darkness. There was breathing at the threshold, a sense of something huge and unseen looming there, exhaling the stench of carrion.

'The feet,' Gez breathed, and began to ease himself slowly from Grigor's hold. 'They dance.'

Return to Gehenna

She didn't know how she'd caught the awareness. Perhaps she'd walked through an infected area one night, when she'd been drunk, and hadn't felt its presence. Or, it could have been coughed onto her by someone. Maybe. Perhaps its spore had impregnated itself into a piece of paper she'd handled at work. She hated work. Wouldn't it have come for her there? Work was hell.

It was hard to pinpoint exactly when the awareness had started, and whether the incident that occurred on the dead-skied Tuesday had actually been the first or not, but it was the first that Lucy could remember.

'Hell is not a place, it is a state of mind.' So said Dolores, who occupied the desk opposite Lucy's.

Lucy had just kicked herself backwards across the floor on her swivel chair, having announced, 'This place is hell.' Her work bored her rigid; the company sold insurance.

Dolores, with her long pink nails, which Lucy suspected were false, liked work. She had double chins, and a strangely slow tongue that reminded Lucy of a parrot's. It was pointed and narrow, and peered out without speed to lick the sticky parts of envelopes like a questing blind worm. Dolores disapproved of what she saw as Lucy's lazy temperament and streak of rebellion. Everyone had to work, so why not do your best? To help fulfil this urge, Dolores made copious cups of tea for the boss - a mangy non-entity, who smelled salty - and grovelled before the boss's wife whenever she called into the office. The boss's wife was vague and always seemed slightly surprised, unnerved by the obsequious Dolores. Lucy could not imagine that all of these drab people had a life beyond the office walls.

Lucy hated Dolores' smug piety more than she hated the job, but if she didn't get on with the woman, life there would be unendurable, since there were only the two of them and the boss didn't count. She also suspected that Dolores was quite capable of losing her her job, if she felt riled enough, but fortunately the woman made an effort to excel at being kind. Dolores was just too good; perhaps it was why she looked so poisoned and bloated.

'You make life so hard for yourself,' Dolores said. She was filled to the brim with platitudes and sayings that advised on how to exist nicely and properly. Niceness and properness were concepts that filled Lucy with dread. She felt she had somehow been cut adrift from the life she was supposed to have had and become marooned here, eking out a living in a nine-to-five job that barely paid for her small apartment. It wasn't as if she could get a better job, with her lack of qualifications. Sometimes, she wished she'd done something with herself at school, or perhaps later, but in her early twenties, all she'd wanted to do was party. Now, on the cusp of thirty, all her wild friends had turned suspiciously into people who wanted children and normality. Somehow, without Lucy noticing, they had acquired degrees or training that ended in certificates. They had deceived her; they were not the people she'd believed them to be. If they did come out for an evening, they talked about what their kids did, or joked about wall-paper. Lucy's horror had reached its height when she'd spotted a set of golf clubs in the boot of a car belonging to a man who had once sold drugs in the shadowed corner of the local student bar and whose hair had been long. Lucy's old friends were all sailing away from her and she could only wave sadly at their departure. Recently, she had half-heartedly made newer, younger friends, who were happy to go out whenever they could afford it, but they seemed shallow in comparison to the memories of her youth; they had no opinions and no fire. They were too interested in money.

'I've woken up in the wrong life,' Lucy told Dolores. 'But I can't remember when it happened.'

Dolores smiled in gentle disbelief and shook her head. 'Really, Lucy, I think you enjoy being miserable. You're an attractive girl. What's the matter with you?'

'I'm not a *girl*,' Lucy said, slouching backwards in her seat like a relaxing puppet, arms hanging down to either side. 'If I was, it might not be so bad. I'd have time to change things.' She could see from Dolores' quick, bright glance that the woman was longing to tell her to sit up straight.

'Have you done the filing?' she said instead.

It was dark at five o'clock when Lucy left the office, leaving Dolores to fuss around (unpaid) for an extra fifteen minutes, before locking up. Outside, the air was cold and damp with invisible rain, and sound seemed muted. Soon, the nights would be drawing out; Lucy looked forward to spring. This year, the winter seemed to have been going on forever. In the mornings, she hated leaving for work in the dark and then having to come home in it again at night. Lucy preferred heat, raging heat and blistering light. Was it feasible to emigrate to a warmer country when she had no money and no training?

Lucy hurried to the bus stop, intent only on getting home, where she could shut out the night. Just as she was rounding the corner, she saw the bus coming toward her, having already drawn away from the stop.

'Damn!' She threw up her arms and waved frantically at the driver, but he ignored her. Greenish faces peered down at her in mild curiosity through the passengers' windows.

'Damn!' Lucy glanced at her watch. Since when had the bus been early? It was supposed to leave at ten past five, and she could see it was still only five past. Usually, she had to stand there waiting, getting progressively more annoyed. Living on the outskirts of town as she did, she wouldn't be able to catch another direct route bus for at least half an hour. Half an hour of standing in the depressing drizzle of a late January evening. She didn't have enough money for a cab; it was too near the end of the month when her bank account tended to dry up, or rather her overdraft did. She considered approaching a cash dispenser in the hope of invoking money, but knew her prospects of success were bleak, and it would take her at least five minutes to reach the machine in the square. She might as well walk home. If she walked briskly, it would take only twenty-five minutes.

Her shoes weren't made for walking; they leaked. Lucy cursed the fact she had forgotten about that before she'd started off. As she walked, it seemed the dreary town shimmered in a mist, but the effect was not beautiful. Cars and buses hissed along the main road, throwing up dirty spray. People hurried along with their heads down through the garish gouts of radiance thrown out by shop-fronts. The puddles of light on the floor seemed muzzy at the edges, as if Lucy's vision were blurring. She blinked, cleared her eyes. *Perhaps I am crying*, she thought, subsequently wondering why she felt so numb.

She turned into the narrow street, Victoria Terrace, which provided a short-cut back to Carlisle Avenue, where she lived. Normally, she would take the long way round, as the terrace led to silent, dim-lit areas, where her heart would beat faster and her ears strain to detect threatening sounds. Tonight, she assured herself that at this time of day, there could be little danger, and there wasn't. The danger came from inside her.

Lucy knew the area well. On the boss's birthday, she and Dolores would accompany him to one of the many, small Chinese restaurants that lined the street, where he would pay magnanimously for a very mediocre meal. Further down, was the sandwich shop where Lucy went to buy her lunch. Acknowledging the landmarks of restaurant and shop, Lucy considered that her life had become narrow and its horizons were contracting all the time. Atoms of herself must be left on this street that she traversed so regularly. When she died, her ghost might haunt it.

Reaching the end of the Victoria Terrace, Lucy turned left. The street-lights here were few and far between, and high, narrow three-storied terraced houses of gray stone huddled together on either side of the road.

Lucy hesitated at the corner. She had walked down this street hundreds of times before, yet this time, on this cold, dark Tuesday, it was not the same. Normally, Lucy would see a row of terraced cottages - once cream, now soot-drenched, on one side of the road - while on the other, a line of shops, most of which were boarded up and abandoned, with litter in their porches. This street of tall, gray houses she had never seen before.

I have been day-dreaming, she reasoned, *I have taken a wrong turn*. Looking back up Victoria Terrace, she realised the thought itself was folly. The only intersection was halfway up and she could see it from where she stood.

Lucy's first instinct was to retreat, take the long way home, even return to the main road and wait for a bus, because this couldn't be happening. She must have gone mad, but in a moment of total disorientation, she found herself wondering if the street had always looked this way, and it was her memory that was faulty. Now that she thought about it, could she really swear the street had been lined with shops and dirty cream houses? Perhaps she was thinking of another street.

But I have never been here before...

The scene before her was utterly still; no lights burned in the tall, crowded buildings. At the far end of the road a massive edifice reared up, like an ancient factory or a prison. Its severe outline spoke of despair.

Without thinking, Lucy began to walk up the centre of the road. Looking up, she could see the sky was no more than a narrow, gray-orange band between the looming roofs. She did not feel afraid, only rather insubstantial, as if she too could blink out of existence at any time.

Her feet made a dull sound upon the tarmac, and the sounds of traffic seemed to fade away. *I should turn back,* Lucy thought. *Where am I going?* She thought she could hear faint music, lively and staccato, but when she strained to hear it properly, it died away. Perhaps the sound existed only in her mind.

The huge building at the end of street was growing larger before her. It might be a mental institution or a temple to a dark god. No, it was a factory. People toiled there.

A movement on the road ahead of her caught her attention. She saw what appeared to be a thin skein of smoke twisting in the air, close to the ground. As she approached, this perplexity resolved itself into a crumpled piece of paper, fretted by ground-level breezes. Closer still, and Lucy saw, with surprised disbelief, that the paper was in fact a fifty pound note. After looking around herself to check for owners of the note, and finding none, she picked it up.

Strangely enough, the note was dry. Someone must have dropped it very recently. Lucy looked up. Perhaps it had fallen from an open window, or even from an aircraft. She had heard of how human waste, and even dogs, had been known to plummet from the sky to splatter unsuspecting victims below. She did not object to being the victim of such a relatively large amount of money.

A noise now caught her attention, and she moved her perception from the magical note to the side of the road. Dim, crimson beams of light spilled from an open doorway, illuminating the wet sidewalk. The door apparently led into a bar of some kind; above its lintel a bottle shaped from pink neon tubes glowed and buzzed, two cocktail glasses winking in and out of existence beside it. Lucy was sure that moments earlier there had been no crimson light, no neon display and no bar. She smiled to herself as a foolish thought came to her: it was almost as if finding the money had somehow prompted the doorway to spring into being. Didn't she crave for excitement in her life? What further nudging did she need? Lucy approached the open doorway, the money still held in her hand.

Inside, the bar was very dark, its air filled with what sounded like live, jazzy piano music, although she could see no piano. Its decor was shabby but somehow alluring; shredding red plush and pink and red lamp-light. At first glance, she could perceive no patrons other than herself. There was a smell of stale beer and tobacco smoke, beneath which lurked an odour of hamburger and onions. Lucy approached the bar itself, although there did not appear to be anyone on duty there. A tall, oblong spill of yellow light, which interrupted the gleaming shelves and mirrors behind the bar, indicated an open doorway, which perhaps led to a kitchen. Lucy leaned on the polished counter. She could buy anything she fancied; the thought of a whole bottle of wine was attractive. Then she could sit at one of the shadowy tables, alone with a bottle and a glass, kick off her wet shoes and drink for an hour or so. Normally, Lucy would not feel comfortable doing any such thing, but she felt she had somehow stepped into an enchanted pocket of time and space, and the opportunity should not be wasted.

As a woman came through from the brightly lit area, it seemed a shadow was conjured into being at the end of the bar. Lucy could see now that she was not the only patron, for a thin-faced man in a heavy, dark coat sat hunch-shouldered on a stool, half turned toward her. He did not look up, but stared into a tumbler of amber liquid around which he had cupped his hands, although his fingers did not touch the glass. The bar-tender, who wore a bright red blouse of shiny material came to stand in front of Lucy. Lucy looked up at her. The woman had a tired face, yet her eyes were unusually bright, almost as if a more vivacious creature were trapped within the listless flesh. 'A bottle of wine, house red will do,' said Lucy.

'We don't serve wine.' The woman's mouth barely moved,

although her eyes darted quickly to left and right; it seemed to be a tic.

'Beer?'

'No beer.'

Lucy peered past the woman at the shelves behind her. They were filled with a startling array of weirdly-shaped bottles, which all looked as if they contained liqueurs. 'What do you recommend?' Lucy asked. She did not recognise the names on any of the bottles: Ogerond, Betwixtit, Tegammera.

The woman shrugged. 'What's your favourite colour?'

'Black,' Lucy responded, to be awkward.

Without changing her expression, the woman reached behind herself and produced a tall, dark bottle. From this, she measured a small amount of what appeared to be black ink into a glass that resembled a miniature champagne flute. 'Two pounds.'

'I've only this. Sorry.' Lucy handed over the fifty pound note, eyeing the strange little glass before her with caution.

The woman took the note from her, but did not hold it up to the light for inspection, as most people would. She sniffed it. Perhaps there were many ways to check for forgeries.

While she busied herself with sorting out change at the till, Lucy lifted the little glass and sniffed its contents 'What is this?' It smelled highly alcoholic and faintly of coffee, but also of molasses, and perhaps spoiled milk.

'A drop of black, as you asked for.' The woman handed her a bundle of notes and coins.

Lucy did not bother to check her change. She stuffed it all into her bag. 'But what's it called?'

'Axings,' replied the woman. She went back toward the oblong of yellow light, and was swallowed by it.

At this point, Lucy considered that she might actually be dreaming, and would soon be awoken by her alarm clock, nagging her into another pointless day's boredom at the office. She knew it was possible to be aware that you were dreaming while you were doing it. If that was so, she would enjoy it. Anything was possible, surely, in a dream? She took a sip from the tiny glass. It was difficult. She felt like Alice in Wonderland; a giant of a girl trying to drink from a doll's glass. Perhaps the liquid in it *was* ink. The liquor stung her tongue, but its taste was that of fear of the dark, of untravelled roads, of seduction. Astonished,

Lucy put down the glass. How could such things have tastes? 'Surreal!' she said aloud.

'A distillation of feeling.' The voice came from further down the bar, from the mouth of the thin-faced man.

Lucy looked at him. He was handsome in a gaunt sort of way. 'What?'

He raised his glass to her. 'Curiosity or fear?' The words sounded like a toast.

Lucy suddenly became uneasy. She felt the bar had filled up behind her, for she could sense pressing bodies, but when she looked around, it was still empty. Nervously, she took another sip of the drink, braced herself against the strange sensations its taste conjured in her mind. She felt the thin-faced man's scrutiny, the oppression of invisible bodies behind her. Whatever she looked at appeared stretched, as if it might break apart at any time. She glanced down at the diminutive glass held between in the fingers of her left hand. It seemed she had made no impression on the contents. *I must not finish what I started...*

Not knowing why she thought that, Lucy found herself at the door. She could not remember having walked away from the bar. Looking back once as she stepped out into the night, she saw the bar-tender had come back into the room and was standing next to the thin-faced man. Both of them were looking at her with expressionless faces. Her glass stood where she had left it, only something small and scurrying seemed to be moving swiftly away from it. Lucy went out into the street.

She felt disorientated, not frightened but confused, and staggered down the street for a few yards. *Where am I going? I should go back the way I came.* Her head was swimming. As she looked up, the world spun before her eyes. *Can I be drunk from one sip of the black?* Her vision cleared, and when it did, she fell back against the wall of a house behind her.

The street appeared as it always had; drab little cottages, once clean, now soot-drenched; a row of worn-out shops. The sound of traffic murmured distantly from the main road hidden by a huddle of decaying buildings. She heard a siren and the hoot of an angry horn.

'No!' Nausea came suddenly, and she had to double-up to vomit onto the sidewalk. It looked like blood; black in the street-light, but immediately after the spasm had passed, she felt better, normal.

At home, Lucy turned on all the lights, and emptied the contents of her bag onto the tiny Formica-topped table in her kitchenette. A tide of paper scraps came out. Lucy pawed through it with shaking fingers. Receipts, faded with age and like felt to the touch for being kept in the bottom of a coat pocket; an extortionate electricity bill addressed to 'the occupier' at an address she didn't know; a letter from a bank advising of an abused overdraft facility, written to 'whomever it may concern'; an eviction order for non-payment of rent. A catalogue of tears and woe - financial distress in all its forms - but anonymous; evidence only of universal, urban misery. Lucy stared at this drift of cruelty for over a minute, the fingers of one hand pressed against her mouth. Then she began to laugh. *Fairy gold; of course...*

The following day, when Lucy arrived at work, Dolores remarked upon her appearance, which she said was 'peaky'. Lucy considered, for a minute, telling her colleague about what had happened last night on the way home, but then remembered she had enjoyed discomforting Dolores a few weeks previously by describing her eventful drug-taking experiments of some years back. It was easy to imagine Dolores' private inferences, if not her overt responses, to Lucy's story. Perhaps acid flashback *had* been the cause of the episode. It was comforting now to think that.

At lunchtime, Lucy slouched through a slicing rain to investigate the street of transformation. By day, it was its mundane self; a thin, lank-haired woman came out of one of the houses with a push-chair, one of the few active shops remaining had a stock of exotic vegetable produce displayed outside its window. Lucy went to stand in the road. For a few moments, she closed her eyes, willing some bizarre image to manifest before her. When she looked upon the world once more, it seemed the scene before her shimmered, as if another place existed there, waiting to be focused upon, brought into being. Lucy blinked. A headache was starting. She had tried too hard to recapture a dream. It hadn't happened.

Nothing too remarkable occurred for several days after that, although in retrospect Lucy did wonder whether she'd just missed the awareness when it crept across her. Then, one lunchtime, as she strolled along the main street, looking into shop windows, she suddenly had the distinct impression she was walking through a movie set; nothing she saw was real, but a facade. It seemed she only had to half-close her eyes to become aware of something beneath the skin of the city; another place at once more exotic yet decayed. Her flesh shuddered in a thrill of anticipation, excitement and fear. There was something she wanted so badly, yet she had no name for it. Merely the thought of its existence filled her with an unexpected hope. A noise swooped towards her like a wind, a great whine, a buzzing, trailing a jet-stream of suffocating perfume, redolent of vanilla and ashes. Lucy gasped, threw back her head, trembling and vulnerable.

The feeling soon passed, and collecting herself, Lucy noticed that several passers-by were taking a wide detour around her and pointedly looking in a direction other than hers. She wondered whether she was starting to experience some mild form of epileptic seizure. Could there be some weird condition of the brain that caused sensory hallucinations? Thoughts of making an appointment with her doctor began to form in her mind, but before she could make any firm decision, a man walked close by her, brushing her arm with his coat. Lucy opened her mouth to complain - he had plenty of room to pass without jostling her, after all - but when she saw him, no sound came out of her. It was the man she had seen in the red-lit bar several nights before.

Their eyes met.

He did not slow his pace, yet they seemed to be within close proximity for several seconds. He said. 'Curiosity or fear?' And then was gone, swallowed by the lunch-time crowds.

Something is happening to me, Lucy thought, and for a while she dared to hope that it was something that could show her the door to the life she had misplaced somehow, the life she was supposed to live.

Back at the office, the weird sensations pulsed in and out of her awareness. At one point, sitting opposite Dolores as they drank tea during their break, Lucy felt she possessed tunnel vision, and that only the area in her line of sight appeared normal. If she could but turn her head quickly enough, she would see the room that existed beneath, or alongside, the office that was so familiar to her. She sensed it was a darker place of crumbling decadence, its appointments baroque. Dolores herself, would be seen as she really was; a large, colourfully-plumed bird with limited intelligence but able to be trained to perform certain routines.

'Are you all right?' Dolores asked, her face creased in concern. 'Are you eating properly, Lucy? Do you sleep enough?' She laughed in mild censure. 'I'm sure you spend too much time burning the candle at both ends.'

'I burn my candles from the middle,' Lucy answered.

Dolores shook her head. 'You should look after yourself. None of us is getting any younger.'

Lucy was not disposed to thank Dolores for that reminder.

From then on, the awareness came upon Lucy more frequently. It could strike at any time, in any place, teasing her because it did not reveal any secrets, only hint that they were there. Sometimes, when she was out in the open, she thought she caught glimpses of the thin-faced man, although he did not speak to her again. Once, she tried to follow him, but without success. Several times, desperate for answers, or a conclusion, she walked home the short way, hoping that one evening she would come across the tall, gray buildings again, but the narrow street at the end of Victoria Terrace appeared as it always had. She got the impression that the special conditions that had allowed the 'other place' to materialise had moved on to somewhere else in the city, like a cloud. She would just have to find it.

During these weeks, Lucy confided in no-one about what was happening to her. She stopped going out with friends, but spent her nights either sitting in her apartment willing the awareness to steal across her or else walking the streets, searching for an area of magic. She soon realised that concerted effort provided the least success. It seemed that only when she wasn't thinking of the awareness would it come upon her, and then, because she now hungered for it, with annoying brevity. She noticed, without experiencing any particular emotion, that none of her friends had bothered to call her to discover why she had dropped out of circulation. Obviously, she meant little to them, but this did not surprise her. She felt little for them in return. No-one was concerned about her, but for Dolores, whose concern she could well do without.

As March tried vainly to transform the dirty streets of the city, Lucy's boss and his wife celebrated their silver wedding anniversary. Wanting to share their happiness and provide a treat for their two employees, the couple offered to take Lucy and Dolores out for a meal on Friday night. In the office, Dolores agonised about a suitable present, which she felt she and Lucy should buy for the couple. Lucy, disinterested, donated ten pounds, which she could tell Dolores didn't think was enough. Neither could she be bothered to discuss what should be bought. 'I'll leave it up to you,' she told Dolores, who would probably top up the fund to at least forty pounds with her own cash.

'They're very good to us,' Dolores said, her voice full of hurt disappointment. No doubt she often wished she had a colleague more like herself.

Lucy experienced a pang, which began as a warm kind of feeling, but quickly hardened to resentment. 'They keep you comfortably on your perch,' she said, 'but you could be flying free.'

Dolores stared owlishly at Lucy, clearly attempting to decipher this cryptic statement. Lucy saw her *truly* then. She was not a bird, but certainly bird-like, dressed in disintegrating rags of red, yellow and blue, her hands scaled like the claws of an eagle, her face drooping with pendulous jowls that were very similar to the wattles on a chicken. Lucy stared at Dolores, who had now dropped her attention back to what lay on her desk. The desk itself was different: an ancient, carved table, covered in leather-bound ledgers and dusty, glass candlesticks, coated with thick wads of colourless stale wax. Long, yellow flames burned steadily up from the mess. Lucy lifted her eyes. Around her, the office had transformed from beige and cream tidiness to a high, cavernous room of grey and brown. It was enormous - Lucy could not see its nether end - and filled with huge, shadowy, metal machinery. She was sure these machines were the photocopier, computers, printers and coffee machine, all evolved from some kind of alternative technology, which was massive where modern technology was small. The scene before her was horrifying and beautiful, alien and endless. Tilting back her head, she could see that far above, cracked sky-lights provided a dim illumination, augmented only by the sputtering candle-light. The ancient panes were occluded by the dust and grime of centuries. Lucy became aware that beyond the office walls, there was a thumping sound, as of vast machinery churning and grinding.

The boss came out of his office, which was now a yellow-paned booth, reached by a flight of wooden steps. He looked like a corpse, clad in a robe of rotting brown sacking, his hands bound with flaking bandages. Lucy stood up and walked slowly across the room. She saw a small window frame, covered by fraying brown fabric, which she lifted with one hand. Outside, a limitless horizon of unfamiliar buildings reared up in Gothic spires, or spread low in curling labyrinths. Dominating all was the huge dark factory she had seen near the phantom bar. Tiny figures moved in and out of it in regular lines and sometimes an orange glow would ignite behind its myriad windows. Steam issued from rusting conduits in its walls, while behind it roiled a yellow-black sky, punctuated by the reaching limbs of metal cranes, so gigantic they disappeared into dirty cloud. Lucy's eyes ached for the scene before her. She wanted to drink it all in.

Only when she had opened the window, to let in the unsmelled odours of the true city, did she realise Dolores had her hand upon her arm and was repeating her name. Time and space jerked, with a feeling like a cricked neck, sudden and sharp. The awareness had gone.

'What were you doing?' Dolores sounded panicked.

Lucy shook her head. 'I saw something.'

'That was obvious!'

'Take the rest of the day off,' said her boss, clearly discomforted by what he perceived as women's strange behaviour, perhaps connected to hormones.

'No,' Lucy said. 'I'm fine.'

Friday evening, Lucy dressed with care, faintly depressed that this riskless gathering was going to be the high-light of her month. Her apartment, she felt, was a bubble of normality within a plasmic mass of uncertainty outside. Soon she would enter into it, step out into the dark and potential.

As she'd anticipated, her walk to the appointed restaurant was surreal. Sometimes, it seemed as if there were more than two realities pulsing in and out of her perception, but none of them gained a hold. Realities overlapped. Along the normal city street, a troupe of women dressed in black feathers stalked, wearing grimacing masks, their hands sheathed in scales of dull metal. A shining dark vehicle streaked by like an instrument of torture; barbed and sickled. Lucy saw an old woman, dressed in a sensible camel-hair coat and flat brown shoes, gazing into the window of a shop where a naked, shaved-headed boy pirouetted on a plinth. His limbs were oiled and gleaming in a ruddy light, his chest and arms laced with cuts that leaked dark liquid, which did not look exactly like blood. Lucy laughed out loud at this particular tableau, which caused the old woman to glance around in fear. The shop before her sold tasteless clothes, Lucy could see that now, and the window display was only of stiff, tired mannequins from an earlier age that gestured blindly at one another in the dark.

As she strolled, almost drunkenly, toward her destination, Lucy realised her life had become interesting again. She might be going mad, and this indeed seemed the most likely explanation, but if so, she welcomed it. Anything was better than the non-life she had slipped into. Perhaps this acceptance was part of the madness, and soon she'd be found, mindless and drooling, lost to the 'other place' that tantalised her senses. She tried to imagine how Dolores and the boss would cope if this should happen at work. She'd be carted off to the funny farm. *And would that mean that, one day, she'd wake up, in a bare white room, cured of her delusions and thus sentenced to eternal tedium in a world she had grown to despise?* The thought of that frightened her more than anything her mind might be doing to her now. She must learn to control her episodes of awareness, or hide them. Incidents like that which had occurred in the office today must not be repeated. If the awareness came to her, no-one must know it but herself.

The meal, surprisingly, took place entirely in the realm of the ordinary. Lucy, though deprived of weird sensations, felt utterly dislocated from her companions. Strangely, this made her feel unexpectedly warm towards them. Her boss and his wife were absurdly happy celebrating this anniversary of perpetual dullness. Their innocence and ignorance touched Lucy's soul. And sad Dolores, manless and childless, caring so much about others, when no-one was prepared to care about her.

After the meal, Dolores suggested that she and Lucy might share a cab home, even though they lived fairly widely apart. Lucy, however, liked to walk everywhere nowadays. The awareness never came to her in cabs or on buses. She could see the disappointment in Dolores' face as she refused the invitation; the woman did not want the evening to finish. For Lucy, it was yet to begin.

Out on the street, she somehow guessed that tonight something was scheduled to happen. Desperate for revelation, she forgot about going home, and ventured down any narrow, dark street that yawned before her. Instinctively, she sensed that these places were the most likely gateways to the 'other place', among the trash-cans, beneath fire escapes where desperate measures had been taken in lives devoid of all hope. Walking down unfamiliar alleys, where the buildings pressed close together in damp darkness, it would be difficult to tell when she crossed over. She must not strain for it. She must just walk.

She heard the music first: jangly piano. Then the red light spilled across her shoes, and she looked up. There was the bar almost directly beside her. Victory crashed through her body in a hot wave. She virtually ran into the building, determined to ensnare it in her senses before it vanished.

Inside, the bar was full of people, and Lucy realised it was not the same one she had stumbled across the first time. This place was more brightly lit, and less shabby. Huge fans turned slowly in the low ceiling, carving the smoky air into amorphous lumps that caught the light - red and green - and became twisting vaporous creatures, alive only for a minute. Bloody light glinted off crystal and gold; the carpet beneath her feet was like red velvet. The clientele all looked as if they were on their way to somewhere else. All wore coats, drank rapidly from glasses of every shape and size, talking animatedly, making sharp, thrusting gestures with their hands. Lucy was slightly disappointed that they all appeared so ordinary. She would have expected to see a collection of people like those you'd find in a fetish club; leather and straps and spikes. But then, she reasoned, such fads and fashions were the trimmings of her own, hated city. Here, it would have to be different. When she looked closer at the people around her, she realised they were not ordinary at all, but the difference was in their eyes and in their movements; a sense of danger and threat and promise.

I am home, Lucy thought, and then, *Am I home?*

She walked up to the bar and a thin, sallow-skinned girl in a black, halter-neck dress came to take her order.

'Do you have wine?' Lucy asked.

The girl shook her head, and behind her Lucy saw an array of ornate bottles come sharply into focus, dream bottles that had perhaps not existed a moment before.

'Give me something red,' she said.

The girl said nothing, but swung away to plunge her arms in among the sparkling bottles, delving for something too far back to be reached.

Lucy looked around herself. For a moment, she thought she saw Dolores sitting on a stool a short distance away from her, then realised it was only a very similar woman; large and fading, with her hair tumbling out of confinement around her neck and shoulders. Dolores' hair, Lucy realised, was created to tumble, but she always pinned it up severely, so that it had to strain to escape. Perhaps this stranger *was* Dolores, but a Dolores who had never allowed herself to exist. The woman before her sensed Lucy's attention and directed a smile at her. Something in the expression, which was not exactly predatory, but very akin to it, made Lucy shudder and turn away.

The bar-tender was putting a glass down before her - a small globe of crystal on a twisted stem, its bowl blistered with vitreous crusts of gold and green.

'How much?' Lucy asked.

The girl jerked her head. 'Paid for. By him.'

Lucy glanced down the bar and saw the thin-faced man raise his glass to her. Two coils of long, black hair framed his face. He was grinning. She knew then that she had to go to him. It was time, at least, for that.

'Thank you for the drink,' she said.

'Taste it.' His voice was low, and balanced on the edge of laughter.

Lucy was afraid it would taste of blood, but it didn't, not entirely. This was a taste of ecstasy, of passion, of intense hatred, a road accident, a field of burning poppies. 'Different,' she said, and waited for him to respond with the words, 'Curiosity or fear?'

but he didn't.

'You were waiting for the taste,' he said.

'Tell me,' Lucy said, 'I need to know where I am.' She felt he knew she was a stranger to this reality, a visitor.

The man shrugged. 'There are many junctions.'

'That is not an answer.' She sighed, fixed him with a stare. 'I wonder whether, one day, I'll be able to stay here, and not go back.'

Again, a shrug. 'That is your choice.'

'Who are you?'

He smiled more widely, showing very white teeth. 'A catcher of dreams. And you?'

'Perhaps a spinner of dreams.' She laughed uneasily. 'This is all so weird. I can't believe I'm accepting it.'

'*Are* you accepting it?'

Lucy looked into his face. It was like looking down a long tunnel. 'Yes. Anything is better than nothing.' She paused. 'Were you waiting for me?'

He put his head on one side. 'I have suspicions about you, that's all. A hunch. There's no pressure.'

'I want to see this world,' Lucy said. 'I don't want to hover on the edge. I want to be in it. I know that it exists.' She faltered. 'I don't want to go back.'

'Why not?'

'My life is hell back there. It is nothing. I might as well be dead.'

The man raised his brows. 'Oh!' He turned toward the bar, signalled the skinny girl, before glancing back at Lucy. 'Another drink?'

'I haven't finished this one yet,' Lucy said, and then realised that she had. 'Oh, all right.'

He put a glass into her hand, and this one was the size of a normal wine-glass and filled with a rich green liquid. When she tasted it, summer fields soared over her like a wave. It was an innocent drink and tinged only faintly with the fever heat of tortured jealousy.

The Dream-Catcher led her out of the bar, onto a terrace at the back of the building. Here, the city spread before them, an impossible jumble of tormented shapes and sounds and smells. Lucy breathed it all in, through every pore. It was ugly, yet entrancing; a fantasy world, where anything was possible. The people here would not be dull or obsessed with trivia. She sensed they all led dangerous lives, were tragic and fey, cruel and mysterious. Like the man beside her. She looked at him.

'Tell me I'm not mad,' she said.

'You're not mad.' He leaned upon the rusting railings, which were entwined with dead stalks of a plant that looked like the bodies of desiccated serpents. Fragile, withered blooms rustled like paper among the fibrous coils. 'One day, you became aware of the worlds beyond the narrow imagination of the ordinary, that's all.'

She sensed he could tell her much more, but perhaps she had to ask the right questions to invoke the information. 'But why me? I'm not that imaginative. Does this happen to many people?'

The Dream-Catcher looked at her askance. 'Only the hungry,' he answered, 'the *very* hungry.'

Lucy turned round and leaned back against the railings, her arms spread out to either side. 'I feel like I'm being given a second chance.' She shook her head. 'I really don't think I could bear to go back. That is... only if I can't come here again.'

'You come here often,' the Dream-Catcher said. 'You see this world all the time.'

Lucy shook her head. 'I see *glimpses* of it. That's not enough. I want more. I want to meet people, talk to them. I want to explore every corner. Just an evening a week would do. I could put up with my ordinary life then, I'm sure.' She didn't know whether the Dream-Catcher was a powerful figure in this world, but she suspected he had the ability to grant her request if he wanted to. What must she do to convince him? She asked him this.

'You do not have to convince me of anything,' he replied, 'but you do have to be sure, for once you decide there is no going back. You cannot exist wholly in two worlds. You have become aware of this one, and the gate is open, but you are just sampling the place at the moment.'

Lucy uttered a scornful laugh. 'I have nothing to go back for. My life is empty. Here...' She gestured widely to encompass her surroundings. 'Here, there is life and adventure and purpose.'

'How do you know that?'

Shrugging, she turned away, feeling embarrassed. 'OK, I got

carried away. But you just have no idea what my life has become.' She glanced at him. 'Then maybe you do.'

He shook his head. 'I do not know you,' he said. 'There are far too many people to know.'

'Are you happy here?' Lucy asked him sharply.

He smiled. 'There is a colour for happiness, and it resides in a pearly bottle. It may be drunk. There are an infinite number of colours.'

'I think I want to go back now,' Lucy said.

'So much for exploring.'

She gave him an arch glance. 'I only need to think.'

Everyone had moved on; the bar was empty, but for the skinny girl, who was wiping the counter with a rag in lazy, circular movements. She did not look up as Lucy passed her. A clock was ticking loudly and the music was silenced. *Do I want to leave?* Lucy wondered. When she stepped outside, it was probable she'd walk back into her mundane life. What if she couldn't find the gateway again? Did she really need to think? There was no fear inside her. She wasn't really sure why she was hesitating over the decision. Tomorrow, being Saturday, she'd have to go to the supermarket and stock up on her meagre supplies. Then, she'd spend the evening walking around again, perhaps without success, looking for a way into this other world, a place where she could hold onto it. What was the point in that?

She walked back out onto the terrace, half expecting the Dream-Catcher to have vanished, but he hadn't. He was still leaning against the rail, staring out over the city.

'I've made up my mind,' Lucy said. 'What do I do?'

He turned round slowly. 'Are you sure?'

She walked toward him, and rested her forearms upon the rail. Out there, she heard the echoes of screaming, and a gout of flame spurted up, followed by muffled thunder. There were gun-shots, and the crack of leather against flesh. There was hysterical music and crazy laughter. Below, on the street, a young, pale girl danced by in the arms of a tall, dark man. They were followed by a grotesque child, banging a tambourine, and a monkey in a waist-coat, strewing petals from a little basket. Behind them, soaring high, was the great dark building Lucy had thought was a factory. She could see now that it was a palace. Enormous black statues of winged men flanked its yawning, dark entrance. Fire burned within, flickering behind panes of crystal.

Lucy surveyed this scene for a few moments, then said, 'I am sure.'

The Dream-Catcher nodded. Now, he wasn't smiling, and appeared tense. Was he afraid she'd change her mind again? 'Then take off your coat, for you are home.'

It was only a light over-coat, insubstantial against the winter chill of the streets she knew and wanted to forget; a garment bought cheap in a sale because she could afford nothing better. Lucy undid the buttons and, with a feeling of abhorrence, wriggled out of the coat, letting it fall to the ground. As she did so, it seemed something larger than a mere garment fell from her shoulders. She felt taller, and already the tide of memory was turning, reeling in the life of Lucy, going back and back, to the time she had entered the gray world of the mundane. The Dream-Catcher handed her a glass. This was filled with a purple liquid. When she tasted it, it was the essence of kings.

'Well?' said the Dream-Catcher.

Slowly, Lucy felt herself settling into a persona who had been sleeping. It felt slightly uncomfortable and unused, but familiar. Not all of what she had experienced was clear yet, but she knew what the Dream-Catcher wanted to hear. 'I was right,' she said. 'But I had to see for myself. They claim to avoid the unspeakable, yet in their greed and ignorance, they have created all the worst possible forms of what they perceive as hell.' She shook her head, smiled quizzically. 'Famine, slaughter - they are some of the faces - but there are others too, the gray faces of conformity and dead minds and hearts. It is bizarre, but the process must work in reverse now. Hell's torments are torments no longer. In that world, I have seen people attempting to emulate the extremes of the inferno in an attempt to escape the horror of their predicament, which is nullity. They have created a void for themselves. It is terrible.' She reached out for the Dream-Catcher with one long, sinuous, bronze-skinned arm. How beautiful her flesh felt to her soul. He nestled to her side, and she kissed him. 'Dark angel, I have missed you!' she said.

'Welcome home,' said the Dream-Catcher.

A Change of Season

He only ever saw the seasons change from the inside of trains. Now, the summer was fading into that frowzy, tired sort of interim period - the Earth masquerading as overdressed and sadly declining middle-aged woman - before a brief spurt of harsh colour led the unforgiving winter in by the nose. The land rushed by beyond the dust-veiled window, and he rested his head against the glass. The urge to travel, to devour the miles, was fading inside him, as the colour faded from the land. Soon, he knew, it would diminish beyond recognition and he could settle down for a while. But first, a final roaming into unfamiliar territory; a time to step down from the train, vacate the arteries of the body, investigate the organs themselves.

The station was small, air cold and ripe against his skin. It seemed the summer had left the north already. He was the only person to get off the train in that place, and was given a sour up-and-down glance as he surrendered his ticket, by a gaunt, inbred-looking individual skulking in the inspector's booth beside the station gateway. The traveller did not bother to smile or speak. As he sauntered out into the empty street beyond, adjusting his backpack for comfort, a familiar sense of unreality stole across his senses. These are cardboard buildings, cardboard props for a second-rate drama. He walked towards the sun where it was high in the sky, a solitary figure in an uncluttered scene. He felt as if this was the ending of something, not the beginning. He would walk away out of existence. Yet his boots made a solid, satisfactory sound against the road and his flesh felt real and comfortable about his bones. He was a good performer.

It was not really a town, more a village, and a forgotten one at that. The sense of history was faint, although he was aware that people had lived in this place for many centuries. It had never witnessed any events of importance, he was sure, being no more than a receptacle for a few mundane souls who sped from womb to grave with less purpose than animals, or perhaps, he thought charitably, the *same* purpose as animals. The place looked empty, but he knew that, had he walked in the other direction, he would have come across the heart of it: the lone, under-stocked supermarket, the row of pubs, a small cinema showing films considerably out of date. This conviction was not the product of some psychometric skill, but merely a familiarity with towns of this type. You had to look hard for the romance in this country. Abroad, little towns seemed to possess a bustling other-life, like insects below the grass; there were often mysteries to uncover, mysteries that could be cherished like gems unexpectedly discovered in a rock that had seemed uniformly grey. Here, the social structure demanded a different kind of behaviour - upright, polite, mannered - but that usually meant the mysteries, when they were coaxed from hiding, were all the more delightful and perverse.

He wanted to walk out on the moors - there was little to interest him in the town - and sniff the air for exciting perfumes. There might be a solitary stone manor squatting in the furze, where deranged family members feuded with sanity. There might be a cottage where a love-sick desertee mulled over the painful intricacies of their past. There might be a farm, with buxom daughters and leery sons, where a traveller might weave a little mischief for a while. The moors seemed the proper setting for such scenarios. If he walked, he was sure to find something to pass the time. The richness and variety of the human race enchanted him; he was not repelled by weaknesses or failings and was tolerant of most behaviours, even the least endearing. In fact, difficult people interested him far more than those whose conversations and ideas inspired the spirit, or whose physical beauty constricted breath in the throat. He sought out the unusual, observing behaviour with cool, yet committed interest.

He had been travelling for many years, and had lost count of the exact figure. He had visited most countries where it was easy to gain access, and several where it wasn't. He wore a wide-brimmed hat that shadowed his eyes, shutting out the history of the world, if not his own history, to the casual observer. Sometimes he would play the role of enigmatic stranger, dark and impenetrable; at other times, he would be the world's fool, the travelling jester, and at these times, he might play an instrument or tell stories. Some countries reacted more favourably to this persona than others. In England, he observed the code of reticence and became the withdrawn one, the stranger on a train. Few people sat next to him on his travels, but those that did he generally wanted to communicate with. Now, at least for a while, he wanted to feel the bones of the planet beneath his feet. He would walk the moors and see what the future exposed to him, or exposed him to. He was never frightened.

It was a moist country, rich with the fecund smells of earth. Hills swelled towards the horizon, punctuated by the moving pale dots that were sheep. The sky was a high, bleached blue, and once out of the town, a waspish wind scoured the land. The traveller walked in an appreciative daze. He had a feeling in the sinews of his flesh that something intriguing would soon be offered to his senses. He saw some people with dogs striding through the heather; he heard the pixie call of excited children. The polished hides of parked cars burned in the distance, winking glares where they caught the sun. These things did not call to him. He was aware of the timeless ambience of this land. Perhaps the things he saw and heard were simply ghosts, or echoes, of high summer that would fade into the approaching cold.

He found a cluster of houses nestling in the cupped hands of a valley. The road that led to it was hewn into the land itself, its high banks thick with seeding grasses. There was a deep, loamy smell, as if some elemental creature was breathing hard beneath the soil. He came to a crossroads where a black and white sign pointed towards the houses and said, 'Little Moor'. Little more than what? wondered the traveller, smiling to himself. The other roads, it would seem, led to nowhere.

The houses of Little Moor surrounded a small post office and general shop, as if they had been drawn against their will to this lone node of communication with the world. Nearby, a white building protected the rise of a hill, and there was a sign to proclaim it a boarding house and inn. Shiny cars were parked outside, beneath an ancient monkey puzzle tree. Whenever possible, the traveller avoided the comforts of official hostelries, preferring to inveigle his way into private homes where there was more to enjoy. He liked a captive audience. Still, it was sometimes necessary to patronise the gathering spots of any community he visited, in order to strike up acquaintances. Picking his benefactors wisely, he seldom had any difficulty in securing lodgings. Women were intrigued by him, although the most subtle often hid this, and men considered him a 'character' who was *interesting* to talk to. Children, he resonated with on a completely different level - their own - so he was also popular as an avuncular entertainer. His personality was entirely unthreatening, despite his air of mystery.

As a preliminary investigation, the traveller went into the post office to purchase a soft drink. The interior of the shop was stuffed with merchandise of the most unlikely variety. A mature female in powder and cardigan held court behind the old glass-topped counter, and there was a squinting crone sitting on a stool next to a bead curtain that obviously led to the living quarters. The silence caused by his entrance suggested these two had recently been involved in dispute; it was more than the cautious silence reserved for strangers. The post mistress looked at him hard, ready to purse her mouth into disapproval, so he took off his hat and smiled. She visibly smoothed herself.

'Shut the door!' said the crone. 'Open doors let the air in.'

'Mother!' said the post mistress, in tolerant embarrassment as the traveller shut the door more firmly. 'What can I do for you, sir?'

The traveller voiced his requirements in his most velvety tone. He was charmed by the fact that the thick green bottles of sweet refreshment were stored in the cellar to keep them cool.

'Won't keep you a moment,' said the post mistress, dodging through the bead curtain, with an owlish backward glance that he guessed was meant to be sultry.

A stillness descended into the shop and the traveller could hear the low buzz of a motor-bike far away. 'Don't get paid for this!' said the old woman unexpectedly. The traveller smiled at her enquiringly. 'I count the post,' continued the woman, 'count it all, every one. No pay for it.'

'Oh.' The stillness became rather stiff. Did it really take this long to fetch a bottle from the cellar, he wondered? Perhaps the post mistress was applying a further layer of powder to her nose for his benefit.

'Here she comes,' said the old woman. The traveller thought she meant her daughter, but the door opened behind him and another customer came in. 'Hello dear!' said the old woman, in a tone of some affection.

It was a girl, maybe seventeen or eighteen years old. She carried a large wicker basket which was hung over one arm and pressed tightly against her body. She wore a long dress in a faded floral print and scuffed sandals. Her arms were bare and, he could see, rather scratched, as if she'd been playing with a boisterous kitten.

'Hi, Mrs E,' she said, and put her basket on the counter. She gave the traveller only the shortest of inspections. *Here she comes, indeed!* he was thinking. This was the lure, the gem in the heart of the rock, he was sure of it. After years of practice he could sniff out items of interest very quickly. Her long, abundant hair was the most beautiful shade of dark red; probably dyed, but enchanting nonetheless. Her face, admittedly, was plain, but her eyes were wide and contained the hidden shred of 'otherness' he had trained himself to spot.

The post mistress breezed through the curtain, clutching the bottle the traveller had ordered, her mouth pasted with a fresh gout of thick red lipstick. She smiled airily at the girl. 'Hello, Lily, love,' she said, and then redirected her attention to the traveller. 'Staying in Lil'moor, are you?' she enquired brightly, as he counted out his change.

He couldn't help smiling at the unintentional pun and was tempted to answer, 'Well, I will if she's amenable,' but opted for, 'It's a lovely spot. I hope to stay here, yes.'

'We get a lot of tourists,' said the post mistress. 'Where are you staying? At the White House?'

'I haven't decided yet.'

'There's no decision to it,' said the girl, quite coldly. 'It's the only place for tourists around here.'

'In that case, my mind is made up,' said the traveller, putting the bottle into one of the pockets of his long coat.

'Want me to open that for you?' asked the post mistress.

He shook his head. 'No thank you.'

'You're not one of those people that use their teeth, are you?' The post mistress touched her throat provocatively.

The traveller put on his hat. 'I always carry a bottle opener with me,' he said. 'Good day to you.'

Outside, he waited for the girl, Lily, to emerge. Of course, she spent considerable time chatting to the post mistress and her mother. He sat down on a convenient boulder and opened up the bottle, swigging idly as he waited. He never wasted an opportunity. He knew, through past encounters, that it was best to act on impulse or else regret at leisure. It was his duty, while roaming the world, to cram as much experience into his life as possible. He wanted to taste every fruit there was on offer, even if it was sour. More than anything, he liked to experience the effect he had on other people.

Eventually, the bell above the post office door made a muffled 'ting!' and the Lily maid walked out into the sunlight. She paused for a moment, and squinted up at the sky. Her basket was laden with tins and she had bought a couple of oranges that had the wizened appearance typical of small store produce kept long on the shelf. When she realised she was being observed, she assumed an almost guilty expression as if she had been seen doing something shameful. She nodded curtly, hesitated with a half open mouth, as if about to speak, and then began to walk away up the road. Once, she looked back. Satisfied, the traveller stood up, threw the empty bottle into a waste bin outside the shop and headed for the White House.

He would take a room there for a night at least. The interior of the place was all polished dark wood and horse brasses, with a token grandfather clock ticking in the hallway. A noticeboard advertised church activities in the area. He could not remember having seen a church nearby. It was necessary to ring a counter bell for service; clearly the White House was not crammed with business at the moment. A man, ex-military in type, came through from a room at the back. The traveller assessed him swiftly; retired, wife somewhere else in the building, hearty group of local friends, perhaps the father of a difficult child who had grown into a difficult adult. He did not fall prey to the traveller's charms at all, however well directed they were, and maintained a stiff, unwelcoming mien as his new guest signed the register. The traveller's appearance was perhaps not typical of the usual White House clientele, and it was likely he'd only been permitted to stay there because trade was slack. The proprietor would undoubtedly prefer to fill his inn with family holiday-makers and respectable moor-walkers. The traveller's attire and long hair probably suggested untold dissipations to this conventional creature, who would also scorn all males who had not enjoyed army life at some time. Enchanting delusion! The traveller envisaged many interesting encounters would be had with the landlord; his name was Mr Eager.

'Dinner at six thirty!' he said. The traveller imagined a peremptory gong would be rung at that time, and woe betide the listless guest who ignored its summons.

His room was comfortable, if not a little too flouncy. Mrs Eager would also be flouncy, of course, for the decor was her signature. The traveller would strike up a friendship with her, to the disgust of her husband. The traveller wondered whether the Lily maid ever came to the White House. His first impression of her suggested she was not the type to drink out in pubs. Once he'd made the acquaintance of Mrs Eager, he might be able to find out.

At six-thirty, he presented himself downstairs just as Mr Eager was about to bang the anticipated gong with a little felt-covered hammer. He nodded cheerily to the landlord who, surprisingly, went quite red about the neck and face. The traveller wore new black jeans and an open-necked black shirt, which revealed the white hollow of his throat, the place where it looked as if someone had gouged a hole in the soft, bloodless flesh with a knuckle. His long hair was tied firmly back at the neck and he had willed himself into a pleasing state of suave, groomed, aristocratic vagueness. He defied the landlord to call his appearance disreputable; he would be faintly patronising with the man tonight, as a lesson.

After dinner, during which he had made a point of ingratiating himself with Mrs Eager, (who was all that he had decided she should be), the traveller took a pint of beer out into the White House garden, and sat against a wall where a late-blooming lilac hybrid exuded its scent behind him. Gradually, as the evening thickened, other guests drifted outside to sit at the wooden picnic tables, and locals also began to arrive. Car doors slammed, a few children made an appearance. Then, there was a glimmer of white, and the Lily maid herself walked into the garden, dressed in pale cotton and wrapped in a fringed, woollen shawl. She sat down alone at one of the tables, and self-consciously fiddled with her hair, kicking the bench with her feet.

Delightful! thought the traveller, *how unbelievably*

opportune! He had not imagined she would come this close to him so soon, although he knew the seeds of interest he'd planted must have taken root, and wondered whether he should approach her right away. No, perhaps a minute of two of observation first... He watched her, savouring the moments before contact was made. She seemed so fey, so fragile, almost awkward. Once or twice she nodded and smiled at people she knew, but no-one made a move to join her. A moth fluttered above her head, and, for a moment, landed on her hair. The traveller shivered with anticipation.

Presently, a young man came out of the White House, carrying two full glasses. He sat down beside the girl and placed a drink in front of her. They did not speak, but simply sat there, side by side, looking into the dusk. The traveller suppressed a frisson of annoyance, even though he'd known it was unlikely the girl would be alone. Her partner was hardly more than a boy, pallid and scrawny, his hair unkempt and the starved curve of his jaw like a blade. He wore old, frayed jeans and a huge, shapeless jumper full of holes. He and the exquisite girl lifted their glasses in unison, drank, did not speak.

The traveller had finished his beer. He stood up, cradling the empty glass, and walked towards the lit garden door of the pub as if to purchase another. Just as he was within reasonable speaking distance of the Lily maid and her companion, the girl began to say something. He could not hear the words, but the boy nodded distractedly.

'Hello there,' said the traveller, and they both turned their heads in his direction. He smiled and gestured towards the pub with his glass. 'We meet again!'

At this point, if there was no sign of welcome, he could carry on walking without loss of dignity. The girl frowned at him, and then smiled wanly. She leaned towards her companion and began murmuring in his ear, dismissing the traveller from her attention.

The traveller walked past without pausing and went into the bar. He did not feel annoyed, only mystified. He employed a careful choreography when intruding into people's lives and yet, on this occasion, it appeared his first movements, which were often the most devastating, had somehow failed to arouse. He was puzzled by this, and checked his appearance in the mirror behind the bar. Mrs Eager, oblivious of his mood, was happily chatting into the air around his body as she filled his glass.

He had obviously made a mistake. Some people were immune to his allure because of an innate lack of imagination. It was pointless to bother with individuals like that; too much work. He'd simply made an error of judgement. He looked around the bar. Perhaps someone else? What he saw did not inspire him. Tomorrow, then, he would be moving on. A pity. His pique was destined to last no more than a few minutes.

'Don't you?' Mrs Eager said.

The traveller shook himself into the present. 'I beg your pardon?'

'I said how much I love this time of year, the smells, the feelings, don't you?' She waved dangerous, lacquered claws in the air. She smelled of heavy, Oriental scent, which failed to conceal the clinging aroma of flesh past its prime.

The traveller nodded. 'Yes,' he said. Mrs Eager, he was sure, would also be an amateur poet, and perhaps ran a small writing circle in the village. She would have been easy prey, if he'd been interested. 'Could I ask you something?'

She puffed up with pleasure. 'Of course!'

'The young couple out there; a girl with red hair and a shawl, the pale boy: do you know them?'

The question was obviously not the one Mrs Eager had anticipated. Her face had fallen a little. 'Oh, you mean the Winter twins?'

'Twins? I don't think so.' Even as he said it, he realised he was wrong. Of course they were twins.

'Well, they're the only people who fit that description,' said Mrs Eager. 'Why?'

'I met the girl - Lily? - earlier today.'

'Mmm.' Mrs Eager leaned conspiratorially over the bar. 'They...'

He wouldn't let her say what she wanted to say. 'What are they drinking?'

Mrs Eager jumped back abruptly. Later, she might wonder, with her poet's mind, why his softly spoken words had made her feel as if she'd been slapped across the face. 'They usually drink cider,' she said. 'Are you buying for them?'

He nodded. Mrs Eager worked the pump with a pursed

mouth. 'What's that scent you're wearing?' he asked her, smiling.

He wasn't normally so obvious in his manoeuvres, but realised there was little point in trying to deny how deeply Lily Winter had aroused his interest. Her resistance called for dramatic measures. Carrying the drinks on a metal tray, the traveller went back out into the garden. He would not have been surprised if the twins had already left, but they were still sitting together at the table. Lily was leaning down to fuss a mongrel dog with a madly wagging tail that had come to sniff around her ankles.

'Mind if I join you?' he asked, sitting down. The twins looked at him with some surprise and the dog slunk away. He put the drinks down in front of them. 'I hope you don't mind. I feel like a bit of company and I'm afraid you ' - he wagged a finger at the girl - 'are the only person I've met around here.'

She laughed without reserve, a reaction he hadn't expected. 'Hardly met!' she said. Perhaps she felt safer with her brother there. The evening light suited her. How could he have thought her plain?

The traveller shrugged and grinned sheepishly. 'I know, but everyone else in this place is...' He pulled a face.

'We call it a pre-graveyard,' Lily said, nodding. 'I know what you mean.'

'You're Lily Winter, right?' So far, he hadn't yet looked at the boy.

She didn't seem too pleased he'd found that much out about her; perhaps because there were other things to discover, which she feared he'd also picked up. 'And you are...?' she asked, a little coldly.

He told her.

'Are you foreign?' she asked. 'No, of course not. Are you a Gypsy, then, or something? What an unusual name.'

He shrugged again, offering no further explanation.

'This is my brother, Owen,' she said, gesturing to her companion, 'or did you know that too?'

The traveller shook his head. 'No. Pleased to meet you.' He met the boy's eyes for the first time, expecting territorial surliness, and found, to his relief, he was merely looking at Lily's eyes again. Uncanny: a mixture of caution, amusement, and a certain cynical awareness of his purpose. He realised, half unpleasantly, that these two somehow *knew* him. Was this a disadvantage or not? The boy was more presentable than he'd first thought as well. How fortunate to find these creatures here; their acquaintance might provide more experience than he could have hoped for.

'He *lurked* outside the post office for me,' Lily said to her brother, flapping a hand at the traveller. She did not deceive him. She and Owen had undoubtedly discussed the matter already.

Owen smiled.

'I do not deny it,' said the traveller. 'As a contrast to the hags in there, you were like a goddess!'

The twins exchanged a secret glance, but it did not altogether exclude him. They were willing to play, he felt. He experienced a delirious moment of weakness, as if the performance was not his, but theirs. It was a strange and unfamiliar sensation, but not unpleasant.

'Are you on holiday?' Lily asked him, drinking from the glass he had given her, but keeping it low to the table. Her eyes smiled at him over its rim.

'A travelling holiday,' he said. The twins both made noises of interest, so he began to relate some stories about his experiences, a few of which were fabrications and distinctly less interesting than the truth.

'So, are you lost now?' asked the boy. 'This is nowhere. How did you end up here?'

'I never know how I end up anywhere. I just keep moving. It's the best way, I find. Sometimes, I discover wonderful things. I don't look for them, I just make myself receptive. How did you end up here?'

'We live here,' Lily said.

'You don't seem typical of the natives.'

She made a careless gesture. 'Well...'

'Our mother was an outsider. We inherited the house,' Owen said.

It was perhaps rather an odd way to put it, but at least implied they lived alone and might have spacious accommodation. The traveller had the distinct impression that Owen was thinking the words: 'wasn't that what you wanted to know?' but was aware he might be projecting his own desires onto these people, reading more into their behaviour than was actually there.

'So, what is there to see around here?' he asked, taking a drink.

'Nothing!' the twins said, in unison. They laughed.

'There is always something,' the traveller said, 'anywhere. Always something.'

'Don't count on it,' Lily said. 'What sort of thing are you looking for?'

He shrugged. 'Just places of interest.'

'Monuments, ruins, that sort of thing?'

'Yes, that sort of thing. I like history.'

'Oh, there's plenty of that here,' Lily said. 'History. No present though, and certainly no future. Nothing changes.'

'Sounds idyllic.'

'Depends on what you like, I suppose,' she said. 'Living here gets very boring.'

'If you don't like it, why stay?' he asked. 'Couldn't you sell your house?'

'We could,' Owen said, 'but if we went to a bigger town, we'd have to work. Our income is enough for Lil'moor. We don't want to work for anyone.'

'I can't say I blame you,' the traveller said. It was a sentiment he shared.

'You're staying here, then?' Lily asked.

'For the time being. I acted on your recommendation.'

'It was hardly that!' she said. 'What do you think of the Eagers?'

'I don't think Mister likes me. She seems all right.'

Lily nodded. 'They've only been here five years. Now, they think they own the place!'

'They do a lot,' Owen said, which implied criticism rather than praise.

'She started all this church business. Fetes and things,' Lily said. 'It's absurd. Lil'moor doesn't even have a vicar of its own, but this man comes out from Patterham now and again. More regularly, since Mrs Eager took him in hand, I think. The old dears like it.'

'I didn't see a church,' the traveller said.

'Oh, it's a way out of the village,' Lily told him. 'Almost as if Lil'moor was bigger at one time, and has just shrunk away from it. You'd like it; it's very old.'

'We could show it to you,' Owen said. Lily looked at him sharply and then smiled.

'Yes, we could. Do you want us to?'

'It's very kind of you.'

'It's just something to do!' she said, and stood up. 'Well, come on then.'

'What? Now?' The traveller was taken aback.

'Better by moonlight,' Lily said. 'Come on.'

There was no moon, but the clear sky lent a ghostly radiance to the land. As they walked together up the middle of the road, the traveller again experienced a feeling of being helplessly overwhelmed. Lily appeared to have undergone a dramatic personality change. Gone was the reticent, innocent reserve of their encounter in the post office. She chattered the entire time they walked, mainly about other people in the village.

'They don't think much of us,' she said.

'Why drink in the pub, then?' he asked.

'Because they hide the fact they don't think much of us,' Owen said, 'but we still *know*. They might think they don't want us around, but they'd be disappointed if we weren't. We're part of this place.'

'I don't care what they think,' Lily said.

'You must get lonely sometimes,' the traveller said. The thought of them living alone together in isolation suddenly made him feel uneasy.

'Oh no,' Lily said. 'Never.'

'We have a car,' Owen said. 'We drive to places, don't we, Lily.'

'We drive to places,' she said. The traveller was beginning to wonder if they were not rather simple in the head.

The church was really quite unremarkable, and not as old as the twins had suggested. Its most significant feature was that it had been built in such a bleak spot. It was surrounded by gravestones that were kept in check by a dilapidated fence. Several tired-looking yew trees provided the traditional vigilance for the dead. It was a place where lone spectres might walk, but there were none in evidence tonight.

'It's locked up,' Lily said. She was wearing her shawl low on her arms, and the traveller could see her skin was pimpled with cold.

The three of them stood against the fence, looking at the graveyard. It seemed they had made rather a pointless journey.

'Let's show him the ringstone,' Owen said to his sister.

'That's a good idea.'

It seemed rather staged. The traveller was unsure what to expect, but wondered whether he was about to be on the receiving end of a joke.

They went through a lych-gate that seemed unnecessarily imposing, or part of an older structure. A straight gravel path ran up to the church doors, and appeared to circle the building. The traveller was bemused to see there was a TV aerial sticking out from the church roof.

'It's round the back,' Lily said, running into the shadow of the church.

'We often come here at night,' Owen said.

'I thought you might,' the traveller replied. They were just children.

The ringstone was nothing more than a listing gravestone, its engraving long weathered into nonsense. 'This is it,' Lily said. She was leaning on the stone, her white hands gripping it at the top.

'And what is it, exactly?' asked the traveller.

Lily and her brother started laughing. The traveller felt decidedly uncomfortable. 'We must join hands around it,' Lily said.

'How pagan,' the traveller observed, unimpressed.

'Oh, probably,' Lily agreed, 'but it's a custom.' She held out her hands and waggled the fingers. 'Join hands.'

Reluctantly, the traveller complied. Lily's fingers were icy cold, Owen's warm and dry. 'Do we have to make a wish, or something?' the traveller asked. He felt absurdly awkward.

'No, we circle,' Lily replied. She pulled on his arm.

I can't believe I'm doing this, the traveller thought, stumbling round the stone. I *have no control over these people. They are wild.* 'Whose grave is this?' he asked.

'Don't know,' Lily said. 'It's not important.'

He suspected that circling the ringstone was a custom traditional only to the Winter twins, and strongly hoped no stray dog-walkers from the village would come along to observe this ridiculous ritual. 'That's enough,' he said, after a few minutes, pulling away from their hands. They did not object.

'Tomorrow, we could take you somewhere else,' Owen said.

They escorted him back to the White House and cheerily waved goodbye, promising further entertainment the following day. The traveller was not sure of his feelings about Owen and Lily Winter. In some ways, they annoyed him, and Lily was not at all like he had imagined her to be. She should have been a shy virgin whom he could have gently initiated into the ways of the world. He suspected now she was not a virgin at all. How disappointing. There would be no scholar's bedroom, with bookcases full of slim volumes. There would be no delicate watercolours on the wall, painted by her own untutored hand. The scratches on her arms, which he'd fondly thought she might have incurred playing with a favourite cat in some secluded, scented garden, had probably happened while she'd been fixing her car, or something equally mundane. Still, she and her brother were unusual people, even if not in the direction he'd hoped.

Mrs Eager was still hovering around the bar cleaning glasses; it was not as late as he'd thought. She offered to make him some meat sandwiches, which he gladly accepted and sat down in the guests' lounge to read a local paper while she made them up. Mr Eager sauntered in, pushing out his belly, and attempted to be sociable. He asked the traveller whether he played golf.

'I'm afraid not.'

'Hrrm, hrrrh.' The landlord was either clearing his throat or playing for time. 'Sitting with the Winters, were you?' he said eventually. 'Rum pair, rum pair.' Mr Eager shook his head in perplexity. The traveller made no comment. 'Bit of square-bashing wouldn't harm the lad...'

'They seem very young to live alone,' the traveller said.

'Tch, yes!' said Mr Eager. 'The mother died two years ago, but they keep the old place up. They're looked out for around here.' He glanced at the traveller in a knowing, and slightly threatening, manner.

Mrs Eager had come into the room, carrying a tray. She had obviously overheard her husband's remarks. 'Mrs Winter was a very private person,' she said, offering the traveller a plate of sandwiches. 'She came here when the twins were babies. Had a little money, I think. She always kept herself to herself, and never mentioned what had happened to her husband, but she was a good woman. The twins have run a little wild perhaps, since she died, but grief can do funny things to people, can't it. You spent the evening with Lily and Owen?'

The traveller nodded. 'Yes, they're very quaint, but I enjoyed their company.'

'We look out for them here in Lil'moor,' Mrs Eager said. 'We have a close community.' Her concern explained why she'd seemed a little frosty with the traveller earlier on, (perhaps she'd imagined he'd had sinister designs on the Winters), but it was certainly at odds with the way the twins thought they were regarded in the village. Poor waifs. They lived in a fantasy world. How would his intrusion affect it? He hoped to find out very soon.

At lunchtime, the following day, the traveller had a visitor. He had been hanging around the White House in the hope that Lily and Owen would turn up and was therefore surprised, and even a little disappointed, when Owen arrived alone. The boy was wearing the same tatty clothes he'd worn the previous evening, but had apparently brushed his hair. His flawless skin looked shockingly clean against the oily wool of his jumper.

'Lily's busy,' he said. 'I've got the car outside. I'll show you around.'

The Winter car was a big, rounded vehicle upholstered in aromatic leather, with walnut interior trim. It smelled of age, and Owen was quite dwarfed by it, sitting behind the steering wheel like a child. He drove, however, with the habitual terrifying confidence of the young.

'Lily's making a meal,' he said, as the car bowled along one of the lanes leading from Little Moor. 'A meal for you. For tonight.' He grinned at the traveller.

'That's nice. Where are you taking me?'

'A ruin. That's what you want, isn't it?'

'Drive on!' The traveller poked his hand out of the car window, letting his fingers run through the whipping grass of the steep hedgerows.

'You could cut yourself,' said Owen, 'Lose a finger. Are you afraid of blood?'

The ruin, like the church, lacked the antiquity the traveller enjoyed sensing in old buildings. It was simply a small house on the moors, a crofter's cottage, set back from the road, gutted and forlorn. He tried to hide his disappointment from Owen who appeared quite proud of the place.

'Wait till you see it properly,' he said. 'It's quite remarkable.'

The traveller followed the boy from the road, and a few sheep bustled away from the empty house as they approached it.

'Is this a place you and Lily visit often too?' the traveller asked.

Owen wrinkled his nose, his hands deep in his trouser pockets. 'Not really. It doesn't have the mood for regular visitors. You have to respect the feelings of these places, you know.'

'I see.' It was becoming clear to the traveller that these two children, deprived of stimuli, had invested their landscape with a rich personal symbology. He wasn't sure whether this was endearing or exasperating; he would have to wait and see.

The door to the house was missing, leaving only a black hole. 'Look at this,' Owen said. The traveller looked inside. All of the floors had gone, even the ground floor, so that the whole building had become a kind of dark well, littered with rubbish and pale plants. 'It's bigger inside than outside, you see,' Owen said. 'That's very unusual. Come round the back. There's a way in. I'll show you. You must feel it inside.'

The ground around the house was swampy and strewn with animal droppings. The traveller picked his way through the mulch without much enthusiasm. The house appeared taller from the back than at the front; the basement was at ground level. Owen ducked into a hole which seemed to have been frenziedly torn into the wall; bricks covered a wide area of ground nearby. The traveller wondered whether Owen and Lily were responsible for it. Hesitating only for a moment, he followed the boy inside.

The traveller had to concede that Owen was right about the place; it did seem larger than it had appeared from outside, but he knew that was an illusion. Pigeons were roosting in what remained of the attic rafters and the moist, peaty ground was white with their guano. There were signs that people came here regularly. Crates were bunched together to form a makeshift table, their surfaces marked with candle wax. It was as if occult rituals had been conducted there. The traveller swallowed thickly, and the taste was sour. He hoped he was wrong.

'Feel the atmosphere,' Owen said, in a whisper. 'Just be still, and feel it.'

The traveller felt nothing. If this was the Winter twins' temple, its ambience left him untouched, but then it would.

'What am I supposed to feel?' he asked.

The boy looked at him sharply. 'We thought you were like us,' he said, and then shrugged. 'Close your eyes. Wait.'

Sighing, the traveller did so, and then opened them again quickly. By his side, Owen Winter was standing with his head thrown back, his eyes peacefully closed, his lips slightly parted. The traveller realised the boy was really quite beautiful. He looked like a dying saint, or someone inviting a kiss. Not realising he was being observed, Owen reached out and took the traveller's hand in his own. 'You will feel it through me,' he said. The traveller felt nothing, nothing other than the warm pressure of living fingers. That, at least, was not unpleasant.

My dalliance with these waifs will be short, he thought, *but not without refreshment.*

Owen sighed and released the traveller's hand. 'Well,' he said, blinking. 'Did you feel it?'

'I felt only you,' the traveller replied.

Owen smiled. 'I think you are too old, or something. Let's go.'

They spent the afternoon tramping around the moors, visiting several other empty cottages and farm buildings, but none of these were treated with the bizarre reverence Owen Winter had displayed for the first house. Some of the places were indeed interesting, and the weight of the centuries there pressed down upon the traveller like a welcome blanket in the thick of winter. Owen's behaviour was erratic. At one moment, he appeared almost scholarly, talking about the history of the moors, while at another he might sound positively deranged, alluding to ghosts and unexplained phenomena. The traveller was genuinely confused as to whether the boy was slightly mentally ill or just deliberately contrary. It was impossible to tell. He could not believe this innocent was involved in any occult practice; he was simply an immature romantic, looking for mystery. *And don't I do that myself, in a way?* thought the traveller. Owen did not attempt to touch him again.

In the late afternoon, they got back into the car, and Owen drove them home. The traveller was intrigued by what the Winter house might be like. It could be large and look haunted, with ivy over the eaves, or small and cottagey, hugged by climbing roses. He dismissed the possibility of it being nothing more than a grey semi-detached house, bought by the mother from a district council. The reality, however, was none of these options.

It was a detached house, though not large, situated on a winding lane, where family homes were widely spaced. It was surrounded by tall evergreens, but had no name. It had rather a raddled appearance. Owen parked the car in a muddy drive at the side of the house, and when the traveller got out, he could see a distorted, wire chicken-run behind the house, where a few ragged birds were scampering up and down. There was a kennel and a chain, but no dog, and a bare clematis hugged one of the walls. The back door was painted in an unsightly flaking turquoise colour.

Owen scraped mud from the soles of his pumps on a piece of metal by the door and, out of politeness, the traveller did likewise. Then, they went inside.

The back door led straight to the kitchen which was steamy with the smells of cooking food. Pots bubbled on an old gas stove. The traveller took off his hat and put it down on the large, farmhouse table. He looked around himself with interest. The walls were bare brick, except for one that had been inexpertly whitewashed; splashes of white marked the brown tiled floor. Bunches of herbs hung from one of the roof beams, but were so dusty, it did not look as if they were used for anything. Three crates of apples under the table gave off an over-ripe smell, one of them occupied by an elderly cat, asleep among the fruit. A group of new kitchen units against one of the walls were the sole concession to modernity but, white as they were among so much dark and earth, they looked absurd and out of place. Their formica surfaces were already scored by cutting knives, and the scratches had been stained brown by tea. At one time, someone had begun to turn this dilapidated house into a home, but the job had never been finished, and there was no sign of recent work. Strange. The twins' mother must have lived here for about fifteen years.

'Hope you don't mind the mess,' Owen said and went to open a door, calling 'Lily!' into the space beyond.

The traveller stood in the middle of the kitchen, bombarded by the images before him. His home, when he returned to it, would never be allowed to sink into such disarray. How could a person be comfortable within such chaos? It mystified him. He was beginning to think of home more often now. He sat down on a wooden chair by the table an Owen said, 'No, don't sit there. Go into the parlour.' He gestured to show the way.

The parlour was surprisingly comfortable; a woman had made her mark here. Perhaps the mother had begun renovations in this room. The walls were covered in framed embroidered samplers and a large, welcoming fire was burning in the huge stone hearth. Again, the walls were of bare brick, but in this room, it was simply rustic; a decorative effect. A beautiful old Persian rug covered most of the floor, but around its edges the boards gleamed with honey-coloured varnish. The traveller threw himself into a well-padded chair and Owen offered him some wine. 'Home made,' he said. 'But you'll like it.'

The traveller was not prepared to disagree, although he had a refined palate which objected to brutality. Owen poured out a glass of pale liquid from what appeared to be a crystal decanter. 'We make it from apples,' he said. The traveller was pleased to find the wine tasted of fairly well-bred sherry.

Then, Lily came into the room. She looked enchanting, wearing a simple, long black dress, her hair held back with a silky scarf. She had painted her lips with a smudge of pale lipstick and her lashes were spiky with mascara. The traveller's heart warmed. He wished she had been with them for the afternoon.

'Did you have a good time?' she asked, sitting down on the arm of the traveller's chair. He burned with the proximity of her body. She smelled of soap and floral scent.

'Yes, it was very interesting,' he said.

'Did you show him the house, Owen?' she said.

Owen sat down on the rug at their feet. He nodded.

'What did you think of it?' Lily asked the traveller.

'I suppose you mean your little church,' he said.

Lily laughed. 'Well, it's not exactly that!'

'I think I disappointed your brother. I wasn't sure how I was supposed to react.'

'I wasn't disappointed,' Owen said. 'We only wanted you to go there. You weren't supposed to react.'

'Why did you want me to go there?' the traveller asked. He thought he might as well enter into the spirit of their game.

'We wanted to show you to the land,' Lily said.

'Oh.' A dark misgiving touched the traveller's heart. He did not approve of the implications in those words.

'Anyway, the food's ready now,' Lily said, jumping up. 'We'll eat in here, shall we?'

The meal was wholesome, if rather sloppy. Lily and Owen kept up an inane chatter the whole time, plates balanced on their knees. When everyone had finished eating, Lily piled up the plates in the hearth, and refilled the wine glasses. Her cheeks had become slightly flushed. She curled up on the floor by the traveller's feet and, twirling her glass in her hands, said, 'When are you going home?'

He smiled down at her. 'Soon,' he said.

'Where do you live?'

'My family have a place further south.'

'And you're going back there?'

'Yes.'

Owen was lying on his stomach in front of them, his chin in his hands. 'What do you do? Do you work?'

The traveller paused. 'I will do, I expect.'

'You're rich, aren't you!' Lily said, pleased with her deduction.

The traveller shrugged. 'My family have money, but that's no excuse for being lazy. Besides, I will have a family to help support eventually.' He wondered why he was telling them even this much. Why? It was the first occasion he had ever opened up to anybody during his travels, including those times he'd spent with distant kin. Perhaps he was satisfying a need because the journey time was nearly over. Perhaps he was throwing coins at destiny. Perhaps.

'Oh,' Lily said, having digested this information. 'You have... a girlfriend, or a wife, then?'

The traveller leaned back in his chair and blinked at the ceiling. 'I will enter into a marriage when I return home.'

Lily giggled. 'What a funny way of putting it.' A silence came into the room.

'I'm not married yet, though,' the traveller said, and sat up straight again, with a sigh. He held out his empty glass to Owen. The boy gave him a studied, calculating look that went on for a few seconds too long before he got up and refilled the glass.

Lily extended a cautious hand and traced a pattern on one of the traveller's boots. 'You are a very strange man,' she said.

'How strange?' he asked.

'Well, we don't like people much, but you are different. We like you, don't we, Owen.'

'That's why we showed you things, invited you here,' Owen said. 'We like you.'

'I'm flattered.'

'Do you like us?' Lily asked him shyly. She did not look up at him, but the traveller could see her colour had deepened around the face. Her little ears had gone scarlet. He reached out and put a hand on her shoulder.

'I think you know the answer to that,' he said.

'We have many secrets,' Lily said. 'We think we can trust you.'

'People here think we're witches,' Owen said, 'but we're not.'

'We are very close,' Lily said. 'We always have been.'

The traveller got out of his chair and sat down on the rug between them. He gently pulled Lily against him with one hand and reached out to stroke Owen's hair with the other. 'Don't tell me,' he said. 'It's not necessary.'

The traveller woke up alone beside the fire. He lay for a few moments reliving the delicious experience of Owen and Lily Winter: their hands, their young eyes, the impossible slimness of their bodies, their utter submission to his pleasure. They had obviously experimented together for a long time. Where were they now? Had they stolen away to indulge in a more private communion? The traveller considered that, for tonight at least, it would be best if he returned to the White House. The clock on the wall told him it was not yet midnight. He sat up and pulled on his clothes, noticing that Lily and Owen's garments were still mixed up with his own. Wherever they had gone to, they had gone there naked. Strange and lovely children. He wondered how long he should stay with them. He did not want to encourage a dependence, which he suspected was a risk, but neither did he want to leave this abundant orchard right away. All too soon, the time for travelling would be over. He would be given new responsibilities and commitments. There could be no more sampling of the world's fruit then.

The smell of apples, very strong, slightly sickly, drifted in from the kitchen. The traveller went out there, stretching, looking for his coat and hat. The lights were all off and he did not know where the switches were. It was very dark, and the house was making comfortable, sleepy sounds, wrapping him in its perfume of apples and cooking. It no longer seemed unhomely to him; its mess was comfort. His coat was lying over the back of a chair. As he shrugged himself into it, he looked out of the window at the dark garden. He saw pale shapes moving about, and heard a sharp, high-pitched giggle. The twins were out in the garden; naked in the chill, naked beneath the stars. The traveller stood by the window to watch them, an affectionate smile on his face. They were so beautiful, like sprites, slim and white. They ran around a sundial, around and around. He wished he could scoop them up, put them into his pocket, and carry them home. He would like to have such wonders in his own garden, one day.

You have your secrets little wild things, he thought, *and I have mine, but tonight mine are heavy, heavy.*

He sighed and thought of his mother's face, one straight finger pressed against her pale lips. 'Never speak, never speak of what you are. Trust only your kin, for the kin stay together, and those beyond the community are a danger to all.' Her words echoed through his mind, words that had been with him since childhood, so long ago. He forced himself to look away from the window, but just as his head turned, an odd movement caught the edge of his vision. He pressed his face against the glass, his mouth open. His fingers were flat against the panes.

Twirling, dancing, long-limbed sprites, they were attenuating even as he looked, their muscles flexing outwards. They were blurs upon the dewy grass, reaching out for one another with fingers like blades of frost. Changing shape.

We thought you were like us...

He could not believe what he was seeing, and the gristle cracked in his own face as he stared.

We have secrets...

Yes. Yes! You shouldn't exist, not here, not alone.

Our mother was an outsider...

The traveller ground his forehead against the glass with a groan of pain. Look away, look away. Forget!

Impulsively, he smacked the flat of his hands against the window, and the sharp, sudden noise of cracking glass splintered the night air.

The twins froze, caught like animals in a glare of light, looking, with the startled eyes of feral animals, in at the house. Loners are not tolerated. Loners unwittingly betray. They must be culled!

Lily walked up to the window, and put her fingers to the glass, touching the place where his brow pressed the other side. Her small breasts nudged the panes. She looked very brave. She could not guess what was on his mind. She thought he was afraid. 'It's all right,' she said. 'Really. It's all right.'

'It is not!' the traveller said, through clenched teeth.

She looked puzzled, throwing a glance behind her to where her brother stood uncertainly by the sundial.

The traveller's throat had filled with fluid. He blinked at the pale wraith outside. 'Keep moving,' he said thickly. 'Sell the house! Go away! Keep moving!'

Lily frowned. 'It's all right,' she repeated. 'We often dance outside like this. There's a wall round the garden. No-one can see we're undressed.'

Perhaps he was wrong. Perhaps he'd seen nothing but a pair of children enacting a private rite of their own. The glass was old, warped. He backed away from the cracked window.

'No,' Lily said, her brow puckering, 'don't go. Please don't go.'

He knew he had to leave. If he left now, he could convince himself his sight had deceived him. If he stayed, they would show him their secrets, all of them. They had promised as much. Now, he was afraid of what he might find out. He did not want to be the keeper of unwanted knowledge, for the keeper defers to a higher authority eventually, and then the time would come when a stranger would arrive in Little Moor, someone whose function was to eliminate dangers from the world. The traveller could not bear to think of that. If they *were* like him, the Winters did not know what they were; they were innocent. The people in this village looked out for them. They might be safe, unless another of his kind came by.

'We want you to stay with us,' Lily said urgently, patting the glass with her fingers. 'Stay for a while. We will make you happy.'

'I know,' the traveller said, standing in the shadows. 'You already have.' He backed slowly towards the door, feeling behind him for the handle. Outside the air was sharp with the promise of frost. He inhaled deeply, feeling the needles in his lungs. Then, he walked briskly away towards the White House. Nobody followed him.

The train sped south, casting a flickery shadow over the yellow cornfields, recently harvested. The traveller stared out at the dying season, his cheek pressed against glass. The winter was coming now, coming fast. Up north, in the hidden valleys, on the bare moors, in the timeless pockets of life where very little ever changed, the secret people thrived. They could be very different these people - outcasts from the human race, eccentrics, grievers, loners - an infinite variety of separate souls. The hard season would come to Little Moor, and in the moonlight, wraiths might dance in the snow, pale as the winter element, timeless creatures. He remembered the warmth of their hearth, the warmth of their flesh. He remembered nothing more.

How Enlightenment Came to the Tower

He lived within a tower of white stone, in a part of the forest where the light was greenest and the trees dwindled to a furry, sighing sward. The tower was crowned by sparkling marble, which could be seen from the nearby mountainside town of Tooreal, poking up above the trees, golden radiant upon sunny days and shining with the pallor of a sad, sick face at night.

He had been within the tower for so long that most people no longer knew the reason for his lonely exile, and those that did remember never spoke of it. The people liked to make up legends concerning his existence, for that is the wondrous thing about forgetting the truth; it is possible for the realm of fantasy to blossom. He within the tower lived by fantasy. He knew these things. Some said that he was walled within the stone because of some mysterious misdemeanour he'd committed as a child (rumours of death, poisoning, darkness abounded), whilst others claimed that it was because he was a sorcerer who had no control over his visions, who was dangerous and fey and to be shunned. Those who were wisest thought to themselves that the reasons for his imprisonment were infinitely more complex than that, and it may be said that those folk were the most accurate in their musings.

There was no door to the tower, the stone was skin smooth, and its narrow windows began halfway up its height. No briars grew against the poreless walls, no lichens formed, no lizards scaled the hot mid-day stone; it was inviolate and pure, a pristine symbol within the earthy confines of the forest, whose equally earthy activities daily affronted the aura of the tower. In the morning, rays from the rising sun would fall across the exile's bed to wake him with the lightest of touches. He would rise, stretching like a cat, and his shadow on the bedroom wall would be that of a great cat. Then he would dress himself in dull, black silk and put his feet into worn, silk slippers, go through the long windows open to the dawn air, onto the balcony and lean upon the parapet to let his hair fall forward over the stone. Then he would sigh. Every morning began this way; the days were endless.

Sometimes, he found himself wondering why he did not vary the routine by going to bed at different times or waking up at different times, when the colour of the light would be different. He never did. The mirror in his bedroom was veiled. Each morning, he would look at the veil, but be too afraid to lift it. His reflection was within the walls anyway; he could not escape it, but there it was a soft and harmless thing. Mirrors were too harsh and he feared their cruelty, their passionless honesty. Perhaps too he feared being turned to stone, but in reality he should have worried more about being turned to ice.

He could not remember his life before the tower, the term of his imprisonment. He felt he never aged and it was rare that the melancholy or the boredom became too much to bear. Sometimes, if his guard was lowered, a small voice inside him would speak of loneliness, but he had learned long ago how to silence it quickly. Contemplating the walls of the tower and what they meant was painful and he was most happy when he forgot they were there. Few things could remind him now. He could take up a quill and draw the destinies of men with red ink, but he had covered all the mirrors because he could not bear to look upon loveliness.

Of course, it was inevitable that he should acquire within the neighbouring towns, the reputation of a seer, and inevitable too that people in aspects of distress and confusion should come to the base of the tower and call out to him for guidance. Sometimes he wanted to speak to them, but he knew the dangers of walking out onto the balcony, for then they would see and his privacy could no longer be ensured. Out of the shadows of swaying curtains he would tell them that he could not help them, for he truly couldn't, and then maybe they would wait a while, sitting down on the velvet grass, gazing up at the empty window and the curtains, where the hint of jewels might coruscate and the ghost of a white hand waver in the folds.

Sometimes at night, or in the dewy, breathless time before the darkness came, demons would alight upon the balcony, folding their glossy wings and speaking in voices of intense allure. Once, long ago, the exile had protested against their mockery, but experience had taught him that this was only wearying and futile. Now, he could draw the curtains and think to himself, *No, you cannot touch me, not through words, not though anything...* and turn away into the dim lamplight and take up the quill. Inside himself, he was drawn to the parchment, for within it he could truly live and breathe; physical life was just an illusion that he scorned and resented.

Yet some part of him, some unquenched, adventurous spark, spoke out against the seclusion, the half-life, so that occasionally he would find himself upon the lip of the tower stairs, gazing down into the dusty shadows where the stairs disappeared, towards the door that should be, but was not, there. It was like a dream and, on waking, he would feel feverish and unnerved, his icy calm laced with cracks that leaked uncomfortable heat.

Outside, the demons clawed at the curtains and shook them, mocking his grace and coolness. It angered him that he could not yet make himself utterly deaf to their chatter, yet it was only to himself that he spoke the response: *I exist, in simplicity, without artifice. My soul is me; there is no other.* At these times, he would be standing at one of the veiled mirrors, a trembling hand resting upon the shroud.

Voices asked him, 'Don't you want to know why you are here?'

But he knew inside himself that only the intelligence behind the voices wanted the answer to that. Why they should care what he thought about himself was beyond him. Was it important? The same voices told him he was selfish, that his exile was selfish, and he could not find the words to explain sufficiently how the silence was safe and aloneness was safe. They thought he lived in fear, but he did not see it as that.

At various times during the long days, he would find himself walking into the pale dining room and there would be simple food laid out upon the great, whitewood table. He could still sense the life within it, and because of that its taste would be as ashes in his throat. There was little life within the tower. Its visions were sterile and without warmth; he knew them utterly.

One day, when he awoke, the sunlight seemed more golden than usual and the heavy warmth of the forest was invading his room more than usual, so that when he stood up and stretched, his body seemed to sing like a plucked string. As he walked to the window, the veil fell from the mirror, and for a moment, he was facing a stranger. He no longer felt alone. His reflection filled the room with radiance.

'It is you, you alone,' he said to the glass and for a time his spirit soared in a magnificent fountain of sad, sweet pain. He could have walked to the mirror and put his lips against the coolness, but he did not. Instead, he went as usual to the balcony and gazed out at the forest. All was still, but from the darkness of the foliage, lambent eyes stared up at him; jets of light like ruby fire. A great cat, crouching, life shivering in its sleek muscles. He gasped and put his hands against his face, conscious of a hurt within him, deep inside. When his hands fell back against the stone of the balcony, they twitched and the nails were red. The forest trilled with life as warmth crept from his skin, from his brow, and fell in dark droplets onto the stone, where they hissed like acid. The eyes were gone.

He turned away, dizzy, seeking the sanctuary of the tower, but a threnody of sound came out from the trees below, so that he paused and looked down once more. From the moving leaves, he saw a white horse emerge with bowed neck, a golden bit making flashes of fire around its chewing mouth, its pelt shining like sun on snow. Its rider let it walk right out onto the sward, gazing upwards all the time, shading his eyes with one hand, which was gloved in black.

The eyes met. Other eyes. The cornered prey. Birds flying upwards, whirring, clattering. Shards of light glancing off the marble, brief spears of light. Reality shimmering within a breath of bright light.

The exile panicked. Now he was no longer He; there was another. The walls of the tower had to speak his name to make him real again. His hands were against his eyes again. He said, 'I am Saphariel, angel of the bow, the hoof, the two in one.' He blinked. Strangely, he had thought to find himself crouched against the floor of the balcony, cheek against stone, knees against throat, but instead he found he was standing upright holding his robes about him, staring down.

The visitor called, 'You are Darkness?'

And he answered, 'No, I am Sephariel.'

'As you wish,' the stranger said.

It seemed so far away, the floor of the forest, that Saphariel felt disorientated looking down. He hardly ever did that.

'Do not look down on me,' the stranger said and Saphariel shook his head.

Now the stranger was beside him on the balcony and the balcony did indeed seem a lot closer to the ground. Looking over the stone, Sepharial could see the definite blades of the grass and hear the animal sounds coming from the trees.

'What do you want of me?' Saphariel asked, and his voice felt so strange; he realised he could not have spoken aloud for quite some time.

'Your beauty is legendary.'

'And is that what you want of me? Beauty?' Saphariel's voice was cold.

'No. What I want is for you to come out of the tower. You must return to Tooreal.'

'Impossible,' the exile replied, but without particular emphasis. He knew the simple facts of his estate.

'How did I get here?' the stranger teased.

'I don't know. I suppose you are a sorcerer. They speak of me that way. Perhaps they hope that you are stronger than I.'

'And how do you know what they say of you?'

Saphariel did not answer. He looked away and found that a sparkling decanter of wine had appeared upon a fragile table beside them and that they were now sitting in wicker chairs softened by cushions. Birds with amethyst plumage sang in cages, heavy ferns drooped against the stone and there was a soft, brown aroma of sandalwood in the air.

'Do you see me?' the stranger asked.

'Of course I see you!'

'Describe me then.'

'I don't want to.'

'Then you don't really see me, do you!'

'I don't want to!' Saphariel stood up and gazed longingly at the dark interior of the tower. 'You must go,' he said.

'You cannot make me, nor do you want to,' the stranger asserted.

'I wish only to be left alone! I am inviolate. That is the way it should be. Inescapable. You must go!'

Then he was alone, his face against the smooth stone, and

the birds and the ferns and the chairs had gone, and shadows fell across the sward, a long, long way below. He was surprised to find his cheeks were wet, and that it was not blood.

That night, inside the tower, he started to walk down the winding stairs, but soon he was lost in the darkness and could only feel the wall beneath his hand, no longer sure of solid stone beneath his feet. He crouched down and stared into the shadows, but they did not move.

Upstairs, the last of the evening light glowed in blues and greys into his favourite room, where the long curtains were white and the walls and floor were white. He sat at a table and visualised a mirror and visualised himself going into that mirror, and from there out into the world beyond the tower. He thought that only his reflection was real. In the shadow world, he sought out an oracle, hoping for wisdom, but all he got were questions, questions, which he did not want to answer. He said, 'I believe I know myself,' and the oracle answered, 'You are blind!' and then laughed at him. Stung, he returned to the tower. A voice in the air said to him, 'Look into the mirror!' but he was afraid to. He covered it with the veil once more.

In the morning, he found his visitor of the day before sitting by his bed, looking down on him. The stranger threw down a divining card and Saphariel saw the picture. It was one he knew.

'Eight of swords,' he said, 'for bondage.'

'Quite so,' the stranger answered. 'You are bound by your own hair and tendrils of your own heart.'

'This is not true! I deny you!' Saphariel insisted and closed his eyes tightly, but the stranger was still there when he opened them again.

'You are such a liar,' the stranger said.

'How can I be? I rarely speak.' Saphariel wanted to get up out of the bed for he felt at a disadvantage lying down, but he was concerned for his modesty.

'How long have you been waiting for me?' the stranger asked him.

'Never, that I know of.'

'You see? I told you; you lie!'

The stranger laughed and walked out of the room.

Saphariel scrambled, shaking, from the bedcovers and struggled into his clothes. He found his visitor waiting for him in the dining room. The food upon the table was sumptuous, tempting smells and savoury steams. The stranger was eating and whilst he was in the room, the curtains there were no longer white, but deep blue, and the floor was carpeted in deep, dark crimson. Saphariel walked silently to the window and put his hand upon the glass, for it was comfortably cold, despite the warmth of the sun upon it. He could hear the chink of metal against china and then the sound of a chair being pushed back along the carpet, and he knew that now the stranger stood close behind him. A physical presence; their auras touching, but their bodies miles distant. Saphariel felt the sun shine through him. He felt transparent.

'Your neck is lovely. Your hair caresses it. Your bones shine through like pearl through finest silk.'

'No!'

'The gracious curve of flesh between shoulder and jaw is constructed expressly for the accommodation of an adoring human hand.'

Saphariel put his forehead against the glass. He did not want to hear this. 'If you are right, then I am mine alone,' he said, and if a hand had been extended towards him, it was withdrawn, and the room was empty around him. The back of his neck prickled with damp. He reached up and rubbed the skin slowly, and pulled out straight one long, curling lock of hair.

The veils fell from all the mirrors in the tower. His reflection, like a bright star, sizzled with colours off the glass. White as milk, black as night.

In the middle of the night, he woke up screaming, beating stone with his fists and found himself at the base of the tower, in utter blackness, clawing at the walls. All was smooth. Cold as a tomb – and no door. After a while, he pushed back his hair, turned away and climbed back into the dim light of the world he knew.

Now sleep became a terrifying thing, for it was full of dreams and the dreams were of hands and eyes and warmth. He screamed, 'NO! NO! NO!' endlessly. He would awake with aching limbs and tangled hair and suffered in full the terror of feeling alone.

The stranger did not visit him again for weeks, and he found himself thinking of a demon face that was both wickedness and desire and also kindness, that had no name for he was afraid of naming it. He could not even draw it, for beauty was repellent to him. Everything was ugly!

In his room, Saphariel threw things at the wall, helplessly, impotently, shrieking inside at the truth he feared and the inevitability of Fate. For weeks, he struggled feverishly with his control and sometimes had the strangest feeling that he was out in the open air, rushing breezes against his skin. He closed all the shutters in the tower. His body, white as marble and slim as a reed, was hidden from the mirrors once more. He wanted to twist himself with pain, but that was impossible.

When the stranger came again, he carried a single, black rose which was symbolic of many things. Saphariel, dishevelled and gaunt, threw himself onto the floor, near the stranger's feet. 'Why must you torment me?' he cried.

'You torment only yourself,' was the answer. 'You must speak the truth. How did I get here? Tell me!'

Saphariel could not do that. Never. He curled into a tangle of limbs upon the cold, unresisting floor, and wept.

It was then that a star came out of the sky, white-hot and burning. It was a Presence, and the Presence was Truth. It entered into the heart of Saphariel. A rare thing, but the gods are merciful sometimes.

Saphariel saw a shining figure that was himself, wrapped in thorns. As beauty is only in the eye of the beholder, so too is ugliness. Eyes deceive and the eyes are the sentinels of the heart. Saphariel was blind. He could feel but he could not see. In blindness, he offered up his throat to the blade, for he anticipated the pain and terror, but found herself touched only by cloud, the lightest of touches, like sunlight, like fur. Without sight, there is only sensation, neither could there be guilt. In the light of dawn, Saphariel opened his eyes and reached out. What he found within his reach was without darkness or crudity or fear. It was merely light.

When he walked down the tower stairs, there was no shadow

waiting to claim him. The door stood open and he walked out onto the grass where a lean, enigmatic man waited for him on a white horse. Saphariel looked back at the tower, but already it was half hidden by ivy. He said, 'You came because I wanted you to come, didn't you?' And, behind him, he heard a great crack splinter the roof of the tower. Gleaming tiles fell around him like scales of pearl. When Saphariel smiled, the whole forest was lit by his radiance.

The stranger (who was no longer that) spoke. He said, 'I have always been here for you Saphariel, if only you'd known where to look...'

In that part of the world, people speak of a legend. It is of a beautiful sorcerer whose soul could only look inwards, who chained himself within a tower for he was afraid of life. They speak of a ruin in the forest where a miracle happened, where the Unattainable, the Chimaera, made flesh and came to him and broke the chains. It is only a legend, of course, and one that I first heard a long time ago, but even now, I've heard it rumoured, that in the forest near the town of Tooreal, on the nights of the full moon, travellers may still see the vision of Saphariel walk through the air like a ghost, and his glance fills the soul with Light.

By the River of If Only, in the Land of Might Have Been

There were no questions in the wilderness.

The debris of our camp was lit by a cold glow that came down from the sky. How? I don't know. We couldn't see the stars from there, and the sun and moon wore shrouds of impenetrable cloud, shining unseen above. We knew of these heavenly guardians, for they were in our legends and rituals. We spoke to them often, but we never looked into their faces. Our tribe was Obliviata, the Forgotten, aimlessly treading the Wheel of Life, around and around.

We were hardly ever cold in the wilderness, but never too warm either, never starving, never sated; existing in a tenuous state, between comfort and discomfort. To the East, the empty grey towers of a wasteland town poke at the sky; a place where lichens thrive. We gathered the lichens. Some could be used for healing, some for enabling the eyes to see beyond the edge of the world, some for poisons. The most toxic has the name of Sweetbreath, because its perfume makes you weep with poignant joy before the dreams of death begin. It was said, among the hara of my tribe, that people craved death from the Sweetbreath because the visions in its exhalations made our fragile lives seem too wearing and pointless an experience to endure. The victims of this candid fragrance gather handfuls of the lichen, filling their mouths and eyes and noses with its taste, its seductive aroma. Death might not come fast, but it is without pain, without regret; the dream becomes reality, becomes the final sinking that we all crave, all seek, becomes the numbing kiss that leaves only the lips sensitive to heat and pain. I have seen them, those hara, as they died. They were all smiling.

To the South lie the plains, the canyons, where flames grow

from the earth like flowers; red flowers. Gangarad the shaman told us that it was possible to pick those flowers, the sweet, hot fruit of fire. You could walk right in and take them in your arms. Somebody asked him, 'But do they burn?' He smiled and said the caress of fire must necessarily always burn. 'Then why do it?'

'Because, for a moment, you can be at one with that element. You can take it and taste it, the heat of it touches your soul. Though it will scorch your body black, you can pick the blossoms of fire, that are the tears of the Great Lion, the dew of the Rising Sun beyond the veil.'

These are the words of Gangarad, whose left hand was almost transparent from the scalding embrace of Fire. He was cautious. There are some that never came back from the South.

To the West lay the wide, sluggish river we called the Torrent of If Only. Perhaps this was because nobody ever followed it far enough to discover where it ended. 'If only we could go with the river,' hara would say as they sat on the sulphurous banks. It disappeared into a haze, sometimes with a gleam like gunmetal, sometimes green and slick as the undulating spine of a great serpent. If you drank the waters from the river of If Only you could live your dreams, but from a distance. I and my friend Omarel did so, just once. I saw the wilderness fade away. Around me grass sprang like living wires from a fertile soil. Across the field, a slow figure moved towards me that had no face - for I faced the West, which is the direction of the twilight - but, all the same, I knew it to be myself; a self that was strong and free. I held out my arms for the uniting, the melding of flesh that could make me whole and spirit me away from the wilderness, but my body remained cold. I looked down. I stood in a circle of ash, where nothing grew, and I knew that wherever I trod that ash would be with me, binding me to reality. The figure glided past me; blind, wandering, searching. I roared with despair and found myself beside the Torrent of If Only once again, my chest constricted with a grief too great to be contained by flesh, that had to be screamed and screamed away.

The North was hidden from us. Nobody knew what lay that way. All we could see, far away, was a black wall that the shamans said was smooth as glass, and poisonous to the flesh. We were also told that the wilderness was so large, it could never have been traversed in one lifetime, on foot.

Sometimes, travellers came in from the east, because hara lived in the old cities there. They treated us with contempt, because they had Old Things The Men Had Left Behind which, they said, made life easier for them. We tolerated this behaviour so that we could choose from the goods they brought for trade. Ananke, with the seeking eyes, once bargained for a silver net for me that I could wear around my neck. I wore it all the time for there were stars within it and stories of the past, where the wildernesses were but earth's own secrets and not a violent testimony bequeathed by humanity. I had known for a while that Ananke liked me, and I liked him, although he had a reputation for eccentricity. When he gave me the silver, I lay in the dust and opened myself to him. Afterwards, I found I needed to do that again and again. Ananke did not seem to mind. He liked to speak about the stars to me because they were important to him. I just wanted to inhale him so that his scent was with me even when he wasn't there.

'I am a star,' he said, 'and at the end of each of my glowing points, there is a different feeling for you.'

I didn't know whether I was supposed to laugh at that, but I did. We used to laugh a lot, but sometimes I felt it was only a superficial thing, like the gleam on water that hides the dark currents beneath. I wondered what it could be that was hidden within the laughter and whether I would like it. Ananke spoke to me with his eyes, trusting that I understood his silent language. I don't think I ever really did. And I never found out what lay within the laughter.

Then there was the time when Isatar went mad from the pull of the hidden moon and attacked me in the dark, by the river. I don't know why he chose me, but he tore my skin, and the silver net that Ananke had given me was lost in the dust forever. Poor Isatar. I had to hold him close for a whole day until he could see properly again.

Ananke went strange as a red eye. He no longer laughed and, soon afterwards, gave himself up for sacrifice at the Doon Tower in the east, so there were no more gifts for me. I gathered the special mushroom for him that weeps indigo blood and performed a ritual all by myself in his memory.

I wish that could have been a turn of the Wheel in my life, but it wasn't. Days came and went, as always. We gathered the lichens, charmed dew into our metal troughs, and fought those who came to steal our land. At night, I stared at the sky, as I always did, remembering the feel of Ananke's hands on my waist, his breath against my neck, his scent in my throat. I couldn't understand why I felt so strange, so sad, so empty, why all I could think about was him. Before he left, he'd said to me, 'I'm going to Doon.' It had surprised me. Nohar went there unless they wanted to die, and Ananke was a respected figure in our tribe. As far as I could see, he had everything to live for.

'Why?' I'd asked, truly puzzled.

He'd sighed and looked around him and then at me. 'Because I can remember.'

'Remember what?'

'When things were pure. When I believed in the stars.'

I couldn't understand him. It seemed nonsense. 'And that makes you seek Doon? You won't be able to think about those things again after that!'

He'd given me an odd, almost fearful look, and had touched my shoulders with his long hands. 'No,' he'd said and put his lips against my mouth.

So strange. He did not give me breath at all, just his touch. And then he left me.

Sometimes, I went to sing and dance in the ruins, behind the low-slung canopies and tents of the tribe. In my head, the sky was a different colour and the air full of rich scents. There, my confusing thoughts of Ananke could express themselves in movement, which I found more comfortable. Once, as I danced, a mad nomad came upon me and said, 'You are lost! You are all lost!'

I asked him what he meant and he shook his head, muttering words I could not hear. I wanted to understand because I believe that all insane hara must be incredibly wise, but he'd said all he wanted to say and only slapped at my hands when I tried to approach him.

After that, I walked alone to the foot of the Tower of Doon, expecting to see blood upon the stones outside, but there was nothing there. It was silent and lifeless, and I was too afraid to go inside in case it thought I had come for death. I sat and leaned against its smooth side and thought of Ananke's hair and eyes for a while. Then a strange thing happened. I stood up and walked towards the east; just kept on going. There was no conscious thought that initiated this action, no decision that I could recognise. I just found myself walking.

This is senseless! I thought, because I had no water or food with me, and it would be very easy to get lost among the fallen towers and skeleton stones of the dead towns. There would be hostile creatures and hostile tribes living there too but, even knowing these things, I did not want to turn back. I *could* not turn back.

For a long time, I hardly saw a living creature, just the odd stray cur that whined and winced when it saw me, before darting away. Later, as the sun began to sink, a troupe of young harlings emerged from a grating at my feet, and pelted me with stinking mud and sharp stones. I ran, and they did not follow.

When the dark came, I happened across a palm-stroker sitting in the dirt by the side of an old road, in the shadow of a tumbled house. By that time I was feeling hungry and thirsty. Corroding dust had shredded my sandals and had started work on my feet. I had kept walking for hours, my mind a fierce star of confusing light, leading me to only the gods know where. The palm-stroker, clearly taking pity on me, offered his hand out of the darkness, and told me he could change my future for the price of a pitcher of sweet juice. I looked around the desolate, empty landscape and replied that he would be hard-pressed to find somewhere to buy such a luxury, even if I could afford it. 'You have seeking eyes,' he told me. 'Maybe for your breath I will change your future anyway.'

I squatted down beside him. He had a small fire of twigs and moss, and I noticed a grey loaf of bread, half-eaten, protruding from a worn, leather bag at his feet. He caught the direction of my gaze. 'Is it only Hunger's Haunt, then, that brings me your company, rather than a need for my art?'

I had to tell him. 'I walked to the tower of Doon and it made me keep on walking. Perhaps that is my death. Perhaps I need your talents more than I realise, more than I need to quiet the beast gnawing my belly.'

The palm-stroker laughed and offered me some of what he had. 'Where do you come from, little seeker?' he asked as he watched me eat.

'From the west. I belong to a tribe that lives beside the Torrent of If Only.'

'Ah, the Obliviata, the Forgotten Ones. You see, I have heard of you. Maybe, you are not as lost as you imagine. I know too that you sprang from the ruins of the tribe of Uigenna, from their blood upon the ground, in fact. You are far from the territory of your parent tribe here, you know, or perhaps I should say, the memory of your parent tribe.'

'I didn't know we had a parent tribe.' I was more interested in what was in my mouth than what my ancestry might be.

'Didn't your hostling, or your father, tell you the tales that are carried by mind, the Speaking tradition?'

'I never knew my father. He could be anyhar. My hostling died from a toxic wound when the Grey-Limbs came and attacked us. I was very small then. I can only remember his hands - not his voice, his eyes or anything else.'

The palm-stroker nodded, though I doubt if he was interested in details of my personal history. He was looking at my mouth and asked me to unbraid my hair, which I did. 'So hidden from the sun and moon are we, yet they live on in the hair of our children,' he said, stroking it. 'Where will you walk to, little seeker? Will you walk until you die?'

'If that is my fate perhaps you can change it,' I suggested.

He lifted my hands in his own and looked at them keenly. 'You have lost a lover.'

It started as a statement then somehow changed into a question when he looked at me. I knew he meant to confuse me, for love is one of the words used in the past to cover untruths of feeling. We, being more evolved, called this thing aruna, which was the connection of bodies, and much more truthful.

'I have heard talk of this,' I replied. 'I know what you mean. If aruna is love, then what you say is true. The har who touched me most went to Doon. I never saw him again.'

'And what is this *Doon* you speak of?'

'The tower, as I told you. The one that made me walk. Those who seek death go there to find it, I suppose. I only went there to remember Ananke. I had no intention of seeking death, or at least I'm not conscious of doing so.'

'There are no towers that bring death in this city.'

'This is no longer a city, and how can you know about the towers? Many strange things can be found here. Anything is possible. This much I know for sure.'

The palm-stroker raised his brows, but said nothing. He resumed his scrutiny of my destiny. I watched him wrinkle his nose and shake his head. After a while, this discomforted me so much that I snatched away my hands. 'Clearly, you don't find much joy in what you see,' I said.

'Nothing is permanent,' he replied. 'That's what I do - change the future.'

'Then change it.'

'First I must have my silver - in this case the molten metal of your loins, the priceless currency of your breath. The future for you as I see it is this: very shortly we shall be part of each other, which I shall enjoy. Then we shall see about the rest.'

He had about him the heady aroma of desire, which filled the dull night air with flowers. When he removed his robes, I could see the marks of old scars upon his chest and arms, the marks of deprivation which were the revelation of his ribs and hips. I lay down in the dust and ashes and he said, 'You are far too passive.' It was not a comment I felt the need to respond to. He gave me visions of crimson skies, a sweet smell of smoke that brought the dawn with it and a single bird high in the light grey sky, dipping and soaring. We had taken aruna through the night, yet it had not seemed that long. I held out my hands. 'You promised,' I said.

The palm-stroker smiled. He rubbed my fingers with his thumbs and pushed hard against the skin of my palms.

'Little need,' he said. 'You will find what you seek in the Tower of Doon. Go back and climb it. Face the direction of what is hidden and - perhaps - something may be revealed.'

I looked over my shoulder. To the west, I could see the crooked finger of Doon against the sky. Climb it? Clearly, this har was insane and I had wasted my essence on him. My palms tingled. 'You doubt my words,' said the palm-stroker.

'Is death my only future then? Did you do this to me?'

He shook his head. 'A long time ago, your people were cursed into the wilderness. As time goes on, it may be that the curse fades and some of you may escape it.'

'What curse? Why?'

The palm-stroker got to his feet and slung his bag over his shoulder. 'It may be that your fate was to wander eastwards until some calamity befell you or you were adopted into some other lost tribe. I changed your future for you, as I promised. Now I must go. Take my advice, do what I say.' He bowed and expressed a sweeping farewell with his free arm.

I watched him clamber over the rubble, robes flapping, towards another spire of smoke, where others might wait for his art.

For a while I felt quite alone and kicked at the ashes of his fire. There seemed little to do. Life was beginning to creep around me; the suggestion of hidden hara, furtive animals or curious spirits. I turned around and walked back the way I had come.

There was luck for me on the return. A small group of traders, attracted by my loose hair, which in their body language signalled an invitation of some kind, encouraged me to share their fire. I spent most of the day with them, listening to their tales of the city circuits. They spoke of places where hara had set themselves up as kings, like men, and gave orders in loud voices, clawing back the ruins into some kind of order. They told me of other places, where everyhar lives alone, shunning all contact except on certain nights, when wild, orgiastic rituals take place for the conception of harlings. And there were places too, at the end of all tales, where life and death have become inseparable, and strange creatures of light and dark walk the shattered stone. I wasn't sure how much to believe of what the traders told me.

Halfway through the night a pull from the west dragged me from under the blanket I was sharing and to my feet. The har whose arms had held me muttered in his sleep, no doubt feeling the cold, but I was already off into the night, shivering like prey, determined as a hunter.

In the grey predawn, I reached the steps of the listing spire that is the Tower of Doon. The cracked glass and crumbling, granular stone were close enough for me to touch, should I want to do so. I paused on the threshold and tried to peer through the dark glass. There was nothing to see. It was all too dim. Knowing I could only go forward, I took a great lungful of air and stepped through the door.

It was disappointing. I had expected arcane and terrible things, but all that faced me was merely rubbish; faded writing on the walls, old strips of cloth and paper hanging down from the walls and ceiling. *Well*, I thought, *then I must go up. And up and up and up.*

There was no sound in the tower of Doon, other than that of my own bare feet against the greasy stone. I could smell damp though, and in places the walls were moist and rotten. It was almost completely dark in there. Had Ananke trodden these steps before me? What had been in his mind? It occurred to me, for the first time, that he could not have felt much true liking for me, to leave me so abruptly and so finally. If it had been me in his place, would he have wandered into the ruins in his grief? Would he now be climbing these steps? Somehow, I thought not. Questions filled my head, and just a faint whisper of anger. Was it really Ananke I was looking for? Was it he who'd dragged my feet to the east, or something else? I paused in the dim light and it was so far to go back down, so far to carry on up. I had no weapons with me. This was senseless. I kept on climbing.

I came to a floor with glass walls all around. Most of them were cracked, all of them were dirty, so it meant that a strange light came into the building there. The sun was beginning to rise. Tired of climbing, I decided to investigate the rooms. I must have been virtually at the summit of Doon for the glass-walled place was really a sort of path that curled round the edge of the tower, with rooms leading off it. I walked along the path, around and around, peering into the rooms. They all seemed empty. Looking out through the glass, I could see for such a long way. I had never seen so far. It made the world look so small. In the distance, I could even see dark dots that I thought might be the tents of my tribe, and there was a glinting, sulky stripe that just had to be the Torrent. A heat haze to the south proclaimed the boundary to the realm of fire. And to the north... Nothing could have prepared me for what I saw in that direction.

There was a great tumble of stones, each one bigger than the sky itself; grey and black and brown. Paler ribbons threaded through them that looked like deep walkways through the rock, some of them coruscating slightly as if water flowed there. Ragged birds hung over the sharp peaks of the stones, screaming in the new day. The north; of all the directions of the world, it was the most fascinating, because we knew so little about it. From the territory of the Obliviata, all that could be seen of it were black cliffs in the distance, but here... I was awed by the size and splendour of the bare rock. How many hara had stood as I stood now, gazing out through the glass, perhaps waiting for death, and unsure how to claim it for their own? Was Doon the shrine of self-destruction - the dark cup, the razor knife? I had seen no sign of life or death here. Doon was empty. I was sure of it.

And then the sun lifted himself from the bed of dawn, rising up behind the Tower of Doon, up over the cracked and fallen city, up above the broken needles of other, lesser towers, to stretch out the sleepy limbs of his muted light over the mountains before me. It happened suddenly, as if there had been a crack in the enveloping clouds - which I knew was impossible - but the grey and the brown and the black of the hidden north absorbed the light and threw it back to me in a splash of colour; green and purple, dark blue and yellow. I blinked against this unbelievable vision, this hallucination of exploding light and life. There before me, yet far away, I could see the sparkling foam of water falling, the placid gleam of a great lake, the moving black motes that became, as I stared, a slow-moving herd of beasts loping to the water. There were great forests that swept down onto lawns of flashing green, starred with acid-bright blooms. The Tower of Doon took the sun, impaled upon its crown, and showed me this: *this* that existed, unseen by the Forgotten hara, above the black cliffs, the gateways of impenetrable, vertical stone. This. If I'd known the word then, I'd have called it Paradise.

In those moments, as I blinked at the hills, I thought of my tribe scrubbing, banished, exiled in the wilderness and how they never questioned what might lie beyond the boundaries. All we needed was courage to investigate. We could follow the Torrent to its end. We could run across the plains of fire. There had to be another side to the ruined towns - they couldn't go on forever - and above the black cliffs, there was life.

Whatever we had done to be imprisoned within the wilderness, within the city, within ourselves meant nothing. There were no real barriers to cross other than those erected by our own lassitude, our idle acceptance of the very least because it required effort to attain the very most. Some hara must have known the truth because they'd come from far away and yet they never told us. The palm-stroker had known - obviously. This was the secret of the Tower of Doon. Death, yes, maybe, but not extinction of the flesh. Ananke must have seen this. Did his bones still lie here or...?

I looked towards the north once more. I felt hot tears gather in my eyes. It was a strange experience and oddly cleansing. I wept aloud, as a harling might, as the harling I'd once been probably had, at the time his hostling had become cold forever. I could not remember. To me, the release was the first of its kind. I had not wept for Ananke.

'You did not come back for me,' I said, and punched the thick glass with my hand. 'Why didn't you come back? Why?'

There was grief, hot and hard, around me on every side, that I could not escape. There was anger too, but it would not stop me following him. We might never meet again, but my future had been changed for me. I would follow. I would find a way through the black cliffs and soon my feet would be trampling grass, not ash, and my vision self would have a face, and it would embrace me, and I would be whole.

There are no questions in the wilderness...

Fireborn

You can waste a lot of time being in love with people. Or so said my friend, Maqite, as she lay dying of a broken heart. Perhaps it was her calm resignation which kindled the final, fatal anger inside me. That, or my helplessness, as I watched this woman sink and fade like a sunset before my eyes. Sunset colours: that was Maqite. Even as her skin paled and shrank, her hair was the colour of evening across the shawls of her bed. She handed me a bead necklace, said 'Take it'. It hung limp from my outstretched hand; limp and so cold, splashing colours over my knees as the light passed through the beads.

'Is there anything I can do for you?' I asked her.

She looked at me long and wonderingly. Perhaps there was.

She could not speak the words, because she doubted whether she should or could, but I saw them in her eyes; flickering glyphs that spoke of an unacceptable hope. She was a good woman, and had suffered much in silence. Now, a shivering candle of resentment burned dim against her goodness.

Some months back, a sashaying, slant-eyed travelling-girl had come to our settlement. Her name was Kamaara. She had surveyed our community and attached herself to Maqite at once. She clearly did not intend to waste her time with anyone who did not sit upon the highest boughs of the community's social tree. Maqite was a woman of status. Her lover ruled our settlement with an inflexible will. Everyone adored him, which I suppose made him despise them.

For a while, Maqite's friendship with Kamaara offended me, for hitherto we had been inseparable. Then, extending her questing awareness further, the interloper used her clever eyes and a basket of exotic promises to lure Maqite's lover into her canopy of indigo folds. Maqite had been devastated. I had been furious, and secretly glad, for hadn't Maqite at first been as bewitched by the stranger as her lover now was? I was shocked too, for the strange, beautiful creature who was Maqite's man had seemed immune to feminine wiles. It had always amazed me he had remained by Maqite's side, but I was relieved he had, for otherwise I might have had to do something about him myself. It was a prospect that filled me with feverish excitement, but also a sense of dread. He was like no-one I had ever met; inscrutable as a cat, and just as deadly. Better he remained safe in the arms of my friend.

'Banish her!' I told Maqite, when she finally admitted her suspicions to me about Kamaara.

She shook her head. 'No. It will fade. He is only interested in the dazzle. It is nothing. I should have kept silent.'

I knew she still entertained Kamaara in her canopy, and kept her anger under control. But, despite this outer calm, knowledge of the affair only weakened Maqite. It infuriated me that she would not fight. Now, all the life was draining from her. It was hard for her, so hard that they had brought her to this. Hard for me too with my black, bound feelings.

I replenished Maqite's incense bowl, and went outside, the beads clutched tight in my hand. Her daughter, Mivien, was playing in the dust. Around me, the awnings and canopies of the settlement looked tired in the late afternoon, flapping listlessly. Maqite's tent was seamed with dust; testament to her inability to shake the fabric recently. Mivien looked up and asked me how her mother was.

'Tired,' I said. It was then I decided I could not let her kill herself. Not for this. As for me, I doubted there was anything to do with this matter that could kill me. I had developed an immunity, sipping the poison continually over the six years I had been a member of the community.

At that precise moment, a shape came out of the heat-haze, wreathed in dust. This phantom pranced to a halt before me; a nervous, over-bred horse, betasselled and steaming. Its rider dismounted, conjuring running, crouching boys, who competed with one another to lead the animal to shelter. He stood there, desert-dusted, with only his eyes flaming out from the scarf around his face. Whenever he was near me, I could smell burning.

Mivien leapt up and danced past me, crying 'Dadda!'

Her joy at his advent made me feel nauseous. I began to walk away, towards my own dwelling.

'Pashti.' He said my name. To me, a violation, at that time.

I did not turn but said, 'Yes?'

'How is she?'

I knew he would have picked up the child. I could hear her babbling excitedly. How dare he ask me that? 'She is resting.' I am supposed to bow, to manifest my supplication to this man. He has the power to crush me, exile me, perhaps worse. I should guard my words. Still, he let it rest, and I heard him go into the tent, followed by the low murmur of voices, the sharper remarks of the child, who craved his attention. I wrapped the necklace around my wrist. Maqite would not want me to act, but I had to. There was no choice, come ill or good. I waited until sundown, before I blanketed my pony and rode away.

A woman gives her life to a man. Her expectations of life are, in the main part, modest: shelter for herself and her children, continued support on an emotional level. She is quite prepared to fight her own fights to secure nourishment, and will defend her family more fiercely than any man. Her inner ways are unknown to men, as they should be. Something had attacked Maqite so fundamentally her sense of survival had fled. In her place, I would have struck out, exchanged snarl with snarl, cunning with cunning. The thorn, when it had stabbed my friend, had been poisoned. She now lacked the strength to defend herself. I, possessed of sanity, and an ability to concoct strategies, must become *her*, fight this battle for her, as she would, if she had the stamina. There must be some way to rekindle her energy, so that the war-flag could be passed back. Ultimately, she must be the one to inflict defeat. I could not do this alone, for I lacked the power of persuasion. She sickened, as if cursed, yet could not look with clear eyes upon the cause of it.

Besides, it was also my battle.

To ride to this place, it is essential to perceive the world in a different way; we ride into a dream reality. Nothing but the most severe need would propel any of us in this direction, between the standing stones of The Hovering and The Backward-Looking. There is no trail to follow as such, just a feeling of intense aversion, a prickling of the skin, a grinding of the joints, which signals a person is heading in the right way. I had to blindfold the pony, but wrapped around his eyes a layer of palm fronds soaked in the juice of the desert violet pod, which brings visions of a pleasant land to human or beast; a place where the hawks hover in flocks: an unusual and impossible image. Thus, I tricked him into trotting towards the unthinkable, but still I dismounted at the place where the red scrub becomes glistening black stones, and tied him to a shrub beside a mud pool, where he could nuzzle the gloop and believe himself supping nectar. If the palm fronds dried out before I could return, he would come to his senses and rid himself of the blindfold, before galloping in terror back to the settlement. I hoped this would not happen, for I had ridden, by then, for two hours.

I walked into the shunned territories. People lived there, we knew that, and they were feared, for they were not like us. It was said they were exiles from a far, high place, where they had grown tall in the rarefied air. I had never seen any of these people, and sometimes doubted their existence, but for the tales that were brought to us, and the garbled, fevered rantings of those who travelled towards them, desperate and numb to fear, seeking answers and favours. The tall people were known by many names, but we called them *Yazatas,* the adorable ones, out of wary respect, for we lived too close to their lands. In the holy books of our people were the commandments which forbade us to build in stone or wood. This rule was said to have come from a Yazata mystic, who had come to our people when we lived in a town of obsidian glass. He had shaken his staff and the town had shattered. Now we lived under fabric and hung charms at the swaying portals to ward off eyes of evil, which were the eyes of a bird, hungry and yellow. The holy books said many things about the Yazatas, although only the seers and scryers had read them all. We knew that the adorable ones understood true sorcery, and that they worshipped the demons of fire. They were known as a dangerous and capricious race, to be avoided. Why then was I walking towards them, when I had laughed at the desperate fools who had gone this way before?

The answer is simple. The Yazatas were powerful, and could proffer solutions to any problem, for those who were brave enough to ask.

I walked down into a valley, following a path scoured, as if by running water in some far-distant time, through the bleached yellow rocks. The crags here were lumpy and twisted, as if wrung by the hands of giants into tortured shapes. That, or they were petrified titans, frozen in anguished poses, shying away from a divine lightning blast, or a vision of ultimate truth. I began to feel uneasy. My teeth ached, and I was sure I could hear sounds that were not there at all.

At last, the path led me out into the open. It was a place that looked as if a god had punched the earth; an uneven oval hole in the rocks that it might take an hour to cross. All around me the stone reared high, while the flat centre of the valley was marked by strange monoliths; twisted red and ochre stone catching the light.

My heart was beating fast. As I approached, I realised that among the bulbous towers of stone, there was a village, or rather the stones *were* the village. The nearer I came, the more the scene before me seemed to solidify. Between the dwellings, I could see the smoking remains of many fires, dying in wide, shallow pits. The ground beneath my feet changed from yellow dust to black and grey cinders. Each crunching footfall threw up a reek of ashes. The air smelled strongly of smoke, which was acrid as if weeds had been burned. From the sentinel towers, I sensed watching, waiting eyes, although I could see no sign of human life. Only a few skinny dogs were nosing among the embers, and they did not appear to notice me.

For a moment, I halted in the shadows of the towers, and considered turning back. An instinct within me warned I should go no further, that to carry on I risked death, or something more damaging. Yet would I be allowed to escape, now that I had come this far?

My flesh tight against my bones, I walked between the silent, watching towers. Daring to look up, I could see that each one comprised layers of rooms - which I presumed were living quarters. Each tower had only one entrance, at ground level, but dull rags flapped before rough-hewn holes that punctuated the towers' height. Strings of tiny bells hung from these openings, chiming thinly in the wind, wound around what looked like long hanks of hair or combed hemp. I sensed a thousand watching eyes, and kept on walking, simply because I was too afraid to stop.

She stood, as if waiting for me, at the edge of the settlement. It seemed to take an age to reach her. Her unnaturally tall, angular body was swathed in dark cloth and she leaned into the wind. When the distance of only two or three strides separated us, I halted and said, 'I have come.' I had no doubt she had expected me. She wore a ragged shawl of charcoal grey fabric around her head, which she held closed at the neck with a long-fingered, dark brown hand. Tails of grey-black hair whipped around the edges of her shawl. Her face looked very different to those of the ancient desert peoples I had encountered before. The cheek-bones were high, the nose aquiline, giving her a haughty appearance. She seemed to be unthinkably ancient, yet her black eyes were bright, and her skin strangely smooth. Her lips worked in rhythmic chewing, and whatever she had in her mouth exuded a thin stream of black liquid, which ran over her chin. She did not seem concerned about this. I could hear her muttering faintly to herself, but the words meant nothing to me.

'Will you help me?' I asked her. Simply by looking at this strange woman, I understood the danger I was in, and the folly of having come to this place. Still, it was too late to regret that now.

She nodded to me, and bade me follow her, away from the settlement, up into the rocks. A path was cut there, worn smooth beneath the passage of countless feet. My heart beat painfully like the dull throbbing of a bruise. My vision became dark. Above me yawned the entrance to a cave; shocking yellow rock against the lilac sky, framing a core of black. Throwing back my head, I watched the shimmering image of the woman enter into the darkness, but I could not follow. She must have sensed my reticence, for she turned back, looked at me for a few moments, then beckoned for me to come to her. I detected a sense of impatience in her gesture. Wasn't this what I had come for? Why now did I balk at the very threshold of understanding?

Then, I saw his face hanging before my eyes; a mirage of deceit. The image retreated before me, mocking, and I walked after it. Thus, I entered into the dry darkness of the cave. I said aloud, 'He is the most beautiful thing alive.' But the only response was the soft sifting of desert dust, duned by the restless winds, and the threading plash of water. I knew that I had surrendered myself willingly to the caprices of a place of power. The air hummed with it. Deep within my ears rustled the crackle of flames and my nostrils were filled with smoke and the perfume of clear water.

As my eyes opened up to the darkness, I could see that the far wall of the cave was curtained by a waterfall, which frothed into a wide, shallow basin. I thought to myself, *'Why, the water is powerful here, yet they worship fire.'*

My guide stood beside the spuming basin. I could see her bare arms now, scored with ancient black tattoos. She was grinning at me still, her jaws working as she chewed. Then she spat onto the sandy floor, expelling a black, greasy wad of something, and wiped her mouth. She spoke to me, but her words were harsh explosions of sound, which I could not understand. Pulling a grimacing face, she gestured towards me, and laughed.

'You know why I am here?' I asked her.

She grinned more widely still, and turned in a whirl of ashen cloth, to duck beneath the waterfall. I did not want to be left alone in this place. Anything could come. Anything could happen. One wrong move and I would be dead. Perhaps that what why she left me there. These thoughts were part of the ritual I had begun when I had made my decision outside Maqite's canopy.

I waited as patiently as I could, although my heart still hammered with the desire to flee. The busy water, the walls themselves, seemed imbued with spiritual presences, none of which felt benign. I began to wonder whether I would escape this place alive and even moved back towards the mouth of the cave. But just as my toes nudged the bar of sunlight across the threshold, I heard a movement behind me. Turning, I saw my guide had returned. In her hands she held what appeared to be a bottle of green glass.

'Come,' she said, the first word she had spoken that I understood.

I hesitated.

'The weak are afraid,' she said, 'and the selfish, and the ignorant. Are you any of these?'

I summoned my courage and went to her. Her hands were awash with viridian light, and at that moment I realised the bottle itself was not green, but filled with a brilliant emerald liquid. She held the vessel out to me. 'This is black gold.'

I wanted to ask why, in that case, it was green, but shrank from doing so. I nodded.

'Do you know what it is?'

I shook my head. 'No, madam.'

She laughed. 'Oh, but I thought this was what you had come for.'

'Perhaps it is,' I answered.

She teased me with the bottle; holding it out to me, then withdrawing it. 'Do you have the right currency to trade with us?'

It occurred to me then that I had brought nothing with me but myself, and I grew cold to think that my body and soul might be currency enough. 'Name your price,' I said, but my teeth had begun to chatter.

The woman narrowed her eyes at me. Still holding my watering gaze, she withdrew the stopper from the bottle and held its lip to her mouth. I watched as her long, brown throat worked, swallowing. My own mouth had become dry. When she withdrew the vessel, her lips glowed vivid green, until she wiped the stuff away with the back of her hand. Her black stare held me, but as I blinked at her, helpless, her eyes filled up with green fire. It was the gaze of a serpent goddess. Her nostrils flared and she took in a great lungful of breath, held it within her, then gasped it out, shuddering. I could sense power pouring from her in invisible flames. She held out the fatal bottle to me, and said, 'Drink, then.'

I took it from her, and the glass was cold against my palms. Serpent light sickened my flesh. A strange aroma curled from the lip of the vessel; acrid and sweet. Sorcery lived within the bottle, a witchery that could be drunk. What would it give me? Knowledge, power? Then I thought of the many costumes of Lady Death, the many masks she wore. One of her gowns was a livid green, and she shook its skirts in the faces of those who craved life.

I shook my head and handed the bottle back to the Yazata woman. 'Thank you, but no.'

She grinned, took the bottle and re-stoppered it. 'You are wise,' she said. 'Come.' She placed a dry hand upon my shoulder and turned me towards the entrance and the brilliant light of the afternoon sun, which scorched the cinder paths of the settlement below. We stood there, upon the lip of rock, looking down upon the towered dwellings.

'You see,' she said, gesturing with the hand that held the bottle, 'that is my home there.'

I followed her gesture with my eyes, but could not discern which bulbous tower she indicated. 'Yes, madam, I see.'

'How many layers can you count?'

I guessed. 'Six?'

She grinned. 'Seven. You cannot count very well. My great great grandmother went to live in that dwelling when it was but a single layer. When her son came of age, he took a wife, and built another layer to live in. My dwelling is on the fifth layer, and my great grandson is already building the eighth.'

'Does no-one live at the bottom now, then?' I asked.

'I told you,' she answered. 'My great great grandmother lives there.'

'She must be very old,' I said.

The woman nodded. 'True. She is very old.' She held up the glass bottle. 'This is our elixir, what people come here for. The elixir of life or the potion of death. It depends upon your heart, and your reasons for using it.'

'Longevity,' I said. 'It gives you that.'

'Among other things.' She smiled. 'You are not here looking for a long life.'

I shook my head. 'No.'

She squeezed my shoulder. 'Come then, come back into this sacred place, and tell me of your desires.'

I was reluctant to do so, having hoped our business could have been concluded there and then, but she had still not named a price.

We went to sit beside the bubbling pool, which the Yazata stirred with a long, brown finger. There were flashes of silver beneath the water's surface, which might have been fish or thoughts. The Yazata drew her curving brows together. 'Your heart beats with black blood.'

I squirmed upon the rocky floor. 'There is a man.'

'Of course.'

I pushed back my hair. This was not easy for me. 'He has abused my friend. She loves him and has given him her life, her body, yet he has committed an act of betrayal with another woman, a stranger. Maqite, my friend, is dying because of it. She is a good woman. It is not right that she should suffer. I have come here looking for justice.'

'Ah, death,' said the woman, and turned her bottle of black gold in her hands.

I shivered as I looked at it. 'Yes!' The word came like a flame from my lips. I wanted him dead so badly. I hated him. It was strange that I did not think of Kamaara, who might have been easier to dispose of. 'He cares nothing for the feelings of others. He is as cold as the night-wind, and as cutting. I swear his glance can strip flesh from bone. But he has a cold, cold beauty, and people love him because of it. He has a strong spirit.'

'Born of fire,' interrupted the woman.

I shook my head. 'No, no. Nothingness, that is all.'

She sighed tolerantly. 'We can smell the smoke of his kind, even here, so far from your home. In his veins runs a liquid flame and his thoughts are smoke. If you did not love him so much...'

'I do not!' I interrupted.

She ignored me and continued, 'Or if you did not hurt so much, you would see that he is born of fire.' She lifted the vessel of black gold before her face and looked into it. 'Caught in a bottle, he is, like a captive djinn.'

I looked up into her eyes. The green glow had faded from them a little now; they were a mysterious mossy-black. 'Does it matter that he's born of fire?'

She nodded. 'Of course. It is the most important thing. Perhaps the real reason you are here.'

I closed my eyes, as if being unable to see would prevent me from considering her words. It did not occur to me that she might have some interest of her own in this man, or even wish to influence the outcome of my visit. 'I am here to find a means to dispose of him. I will buy the black gold to kill him, if you would tell me how to use it.'

She put her head on one side. 'You must have heard, of course, that to attempt to use our elixir for the wrong reasons could kill you.'

'I will not drink it,' I said.

'I did not say you would.'

I felt my face grow hot. 'My reasons are right and just. He has abused too many people, and perhaps you are right in saying that I love him, but if I do, I am the victim of his enchantment, and love against my own will. It must end.'

'As you like,' she said, grinning, and stood up. 'First, the price.'

I remained seated, looking up at her. There were no words to say that I could think of.

'You must give a little life for death,' she said. 'That is the price.'

'Life is precious to me.'

'As it should be. We shall take only a sweet drop of it.'

When we came out of the cave, the sky had turned the black of panther hide, lacquered with stars. Now the firepits of the Yazata settlement were alive with brilliant flame, and around each one, a group of people sat. I felt disorientated. Had time passed so quickly? When we had entered the cave, it had been around mid-day.

We paused beside one of the fires. The people scared me. Like my guide, they were dressed in dusty black, and their faces were grey with ashes. Lustrous black eyes shone out at me. All the figures were seated, but for one, a mature male. Everyone's attention was centred upon him and he muttered an incomprehensible incantation at the flames. His hair hung down his back and his face was gaunt. I could see his skinny body through the gaps in his loosely hanging robe.

My guide leaned down and put her mouth close to my ear. 'He is our priest, the favoured one of our family. What he forges in flame is neither life nor death, but elemental force. He has kindled armies of the dead for great kings. He has summoned sand-storms to choke a man's enemy. He has birthed djinn and deva from the cauldron of fire, and corked them into a bottle. You could buy one to release upon your enemy.'

'No,' I whispered back. 'It must not be that.'

'As you like.' We stood silently as the priest finished his incantation. Women scattered powdered substances into the flames, their long brown arms flashing out like serpents from their dark robes. Sweet, stinging fumes rose like spirits from the flames.

Now my guide stepped forward, pushing me before her. Her long hands curled upon my shoulders like the claws of a vulture. 'Here is one who would buy,' she said. 'She will trade a drop of life's liquor for black gold.'

The priest looked at me then. What I saw within his eyes

had no name, but it instilled within me the greatest fear I have ever known. I could not look away from him. He was fierce, with his long, wild hair and his ashen face, and his eyes glowed like polished beryl with the elixir of life. I had no idea how old he was; he could have been eighteen or eight hundred. My mouth and throat had become utterly parched. I wished I could faint, for I was sure I was about to endure something unspeakably terrible.

The priest made an abrupt gesture and another tall, sinuous male figure rose from beside the fire. Reluctantly, with the most gripping terror, I looked at him. He was completely robed; just a suggestion of an ashen face visible beneath his draped hood. Then two exquisite hands snaked out from the folds of cloth and tweaked back the cowl. I realised what stood before me was the most beautiful man I had ever beheld, more beautiful, even, than my hated beloved. It is amazing what the sight of such loveliness can do. I am ashamed to admit it, but my fear abated somewhat. His enormous eyes were lined crudely with charcoal, which also accentuated the hollows of his ashen cheeks. His hair was like the wing-feathers of the black griffin, softly falling over his shoulders. In his lovely gaze resided the knowledge of all the aeons. He held out his strong, slender hands to me and I took them in my own.

At that point, everything around me faded into oblivion. His finely-drawn lips were expressionless, but his eyes smiled at me; flecked with hints of scorn and pity, yet otherwise quite gentle. He pulled me down to sit opposite him beside the fire.

'What must I do?' I asked him, but he merely blinked slowly and shook his head.

He squeezed my hands, and then widened his eyes. A shock coursed through me as if a bolt of lightning had pierced my mind. He held me in his stare like a snake holds the eyes of its prey, and I remembered how dangerous these people were, how unpredictable and how unknown. My body began to shake, and his grip upon my hands grew stronger. My crossed knees hammered against the dusty ground. My throat corded. I could not breathe. I wanted to scream, but could summon no sound from my arid throat. Then, I felt a wrenching inside my head, my heart, my belly. Something tore within me. Through the power of his eyes alone, he sucked part of myself away from me, drew it out through my own startled stare, took it into himself. Then, he thrust away my hands and threw back his head, gasping, his mouth wide in a smile of pleasure and satisfaction.

I exhaled with a groan and slumped forward, my vision spinning. I felt as if I was extremely drunk, to the point of sickness, but my body could not vomit. My flesh was held in the vice of the most excruciating numbness and cramp. I curled up and writhed upon the cindery dirt, tears squeezing between my tightly-clenched eyelids. Was I dying?

Then, I felt hands upon me. Someone dragged my limbs out straight and forced something cold and hard between my teeth. Icy liquid, which burned like fire, ran down my throat. As it hit my stomach, the pain that gripped me melted away. I found myself blinking up at the bright stars.

I knew then: demons were not worshipped in this place. They were created here.

My guide, the ancient woman, took me out to the edge of the settlement. 'What will you use my essence for?' I asked her.

'Don't worry,' she answered. 'When the time comes for us to use it, you will not know about it, in any way. It has gone from you. No longer yours.'

I shuddered.

We had reached the shadow of the rock, where my path would lead back to my pony and the world I knew. Strangely, I was reluctant to leave. I looked back at the tall dwellings, black against the stars, and the crimson fires, greedy in their pits. I realised I had seen no children among the Yazatas, but perhaps they could risk breeding only rarely, if their lives were so long. I knew I would never come here again.

The woman withdrew something wrapped in a scrap of hide from her robe, which she pressed into my hands. I felt the hardness of glass between my fingers. 'Use it wisely,' she said. 'It is the intention which counts. Some things are destined to die, others to thrive. Only your heart knows which.'

'Thank you, madam,' I said, and obeying an instinctive impulse, reached out to embrace her. She returned this importunate gesture rather stiffly, then pushed me away to arm's length.

'Make haste,' she said. 'Those born of fire are alert for lone travellers beneath the stars' white flames. Smoke-men and djinn alike.'

I knew she watched me until the path turned a corner and the rocks hid me from view, because I looked back at the last minute, and saw her tall shape standing there, dark against the sand.

I reached the settlement of my people at dawn, my body racked with pain and exhaustion. For a day, I slept, and without dreams. In the evening, the call of the stars woke me and I went to bathe in their icy fire. Had I been changed? I wondered about it. I felt tired yet energetic, melancholic yet hopeful.

The bottle lay where I had cast it beside my cushions that morning. Its verdigris glow filled my canopy with emerald fire. I picked up the bottle and held it to my breast. I closed my eyes and thought about the one I wanted to punish, whom I might never have. Not because of Maqite, or my feelings for her, but because I feared he had no feelings for me. None that I could understand anyway. Born of fire. A desert creature, dry and hard and quick. He had been forged in a fire-pit and contained in a bottle. Someone had released him upon us, this djinn, whose fire was cold and who did not glow with flame, but was smoky, arid and caustic. Kneeling there among my cushions, with the star-fire coming in through the entrance, and the green glow battling with it upon my fevered skin, I accepted certain truths. I was proud and vain and fierce. I would love him until I died, beyond his own death, if necessary.

I walked out into the night. There was music; the chime of bells, the lament of a flute, the shrill warble of a girl's high voice and the beat of drums. I went to Maqite's canopy. It was full of weeping women. Kamaara stood among the curtains, her skin white as death's hand, her eyes dull. I knew she too was expiring, and would vanish by the morning, gone the way she came, a phantom. I did not have to do anything about her. She was irrelevant.

The women kneeling around the bed muttered prayers through their tears. 'Maqite is dying,' they told me, and I requested that they leave us together for a while. This, they were happy to do, because I was her dearest friend. I knelt beside her.

'Pashti, where have you been?' she asked weakly, smiling to see me. 'Would you leave me to depart this world alone?'

I put my right hand behind her head and lifted it, held the

unstoppered glass vessel to her lips. 'Drink,' I said.

Her lips quivered. 'What is it, Pashti?'

I swallowed. 'Please, just drink.'

Trusting me, she did so. I saw her eyes fill up with green fire. They blazed out at me, and she laughed. Her upper body reared up from the cushions and she held out her arms to the sky beyond the entrance to her dwelling. It was as if a beloved voice were calling out to her from the stars.

I watched and waited. All of my future hung upon these moments.

Presently, Maqite sank back down to her cushions with a rapturous sigh, and died there, smiling. I had not anticipated the outcome, only trusted my own heart.

I went back out into the night and summoned the women who, obeying custom, began to wail and keen.

I found him out beyond the peaked canopies, alone beside the water of the spring, sitting beneath a leaning tree. He glanced at me, his eyes hard, and I said, 'She is dead.'

He nodded, his hair hanging over his breast. 'It was expected.'

'Don't die from grief yourself, will you!' I threw myself down beside him, and he seemed surprised I had done so. Normally, I ran from him, and would not endure his company or the touch of his eyes.

'You blame me,' he said.

I nodded. 'Yes. And no. Certain of your actions are unforgivable.'

He sighed and leaned against the tree. 'I did not ask to be born,' he said.

It seemed, to me, an easy statement. I took the bottle from my pocket and tossed it into his lap. He stared at it, the green glow reflected in his eyes. 'What is it?'

'Yazata elixir,' I said. 'I went yesterday to fetch it for Maqite.'

He touched the glass with his artist's fingers and glanced at me. 'You were too late. How... pitiful.'

'Yes.' I stood up.

'You took a great risk.'

'Yes.' I looked down at him. 'Still, why waste it? You drink it instead.'

'I'm not dying.'

'It will give you longevity. I've seen it.'

He laughed, and I turned away painfully from his terrible loveliness. 'Drink with me, then,' he said.

I looked back at him and forced myself to suffer his eyes for a while. 'I don't know what will happen.' I watched him take the stopper from the bottle and drink.

Born of fire. *It will kill him, and I will be glad,* I thought. He blazed before me and it seemed to me as if dark, smoky wisps fled away from his body. Djinn! I must have made an astonished noise, for he frowned at me.

'Well, will you drink or not? I was brave enough to.'

I squatted beside him. 'You are not sad at all, are you?'

He was very still. 'A little,' he admitted, 'but what is a sanctuary to some is a prison to others.'

'Not that much of a prison,' I reminded him scathingly.

'Some people were trapped inside with me. Now I am free.'

He held the bottle out to me, and I drank.

I tipped back my head and swallowed a taste of chalk and velvet in a sauce of flame. I opened my eyes wide and the universe spun before me. Born of fire. We are. Desert creatures; kin to the djinn, to the deva.

I laughed at the spiralling sky.

When I had calmed down, he reached for my hand. I did not look at him, but we both stared out upon the night, thinking of our days to come.

Heir to a Tendency

It was the pressure of our fingers more than the application of the make-up itself that caused our cousin Lathorne's nose to go back into its proper shape. The indiscretion had first been perceived at breakfast by our matriarch, Letitia, when Lathorne's nose had seemed to stretch forth from her face to examine the steaming contents of the cup before her. Letitia had directed a significant glance at my older sister, Clarine, who quickly whisked Lathorne away from sight, before any of our menfolk noticed her aberration. Lathorne was a weak creature. She was elderly, true, but this did not excuse her tendency for spontaneous change.

Clarine had elected myself, along with two other female relatives, to assist her with Lathorne's cosmetics. The application of make-up to her seasoned features seemed to soothe their waywardness; we used it often. Now, long past the hour for lunch, we were still in Lathorne's chamber, shaping tranquillity within her as much as taming her capricious nose. This was a special day for us, a day to dress in our finest gowns. Lathorne had wanted to wear yellow. A good choice I suppose; it went well with her skin, which she took few pains to keep neat.

'I want to wear my favourite dress,' she'd said, trying to pull out of our arms and stagger across her bedroom towards the wardrobe. 'Like in the old days. The yellow one. I wore it with gold you know, gold at the throat and wrist. One poor boy wasted quite away with love for me when I wore that gown.'

It was hard to imagine this now, seeing her so withered and neglected, scrawny as a plucked hen in her underwear.

'But it is such a very old dress, dearest,' said Abisarah, another cousin, who was almost as old as Lathorne, though not nearly so peculiar. 'Quite out of fashion, and I dare say the *animals* have nibbled right through it. I shouldn't wear that one, my dear.' She laid a tough, uncompromising grip upon Lathorne's right arm.

'Nibbled through my yellow?' Lathorne's lips began to tremble as she struggled fruitlessly against Abisarah's hold. She spoke in a querulous voice. 'But what can I wear then for the

Homecoming? What?'

I was finding the whole procedure quite oppressive and went to the windows to fight with the nets and seek some air. The atmosphere in Lathorne's boudoir was hot and dry, spiced with a reptilian musk. She kept a long, thick snake in a glass tank by the door, which we'd all realised was a strategic placement to cover a certain aged, snaky odour emanating from Lathorne's own flesh. Naturally, because my people are forced to share this world with the little people, whose shapes are miserably unmalleable, and who age at an alarming rate, we have to adapt our appearances to mimic their life-spans to some degree. However, this does not mean we cannot appear to grow old *gracefully*. Lathorne, because of madness, stupidity or sloth, had simply allowed her shape to sag around her. It repulsed me having to pander to her defect, but I was aware that it must be kept secret. Letitia did not want the males to know about it. She did not want them thinking the females were somehow more insipid than themselves. The fact an aberration had occurred on this, our special family day, was just an added trial - though perhaps invoked by the stress of the situation. For today, Great Uncle Gerhard was returning to the family stronghold. Long absent from the bosom of his throng, long having wandered the world beyond our gates, he had sent word that his travels were over. For him, it was time to seek once more the protection and succour of his relatives - at least for a while.

Whether Gerhard actually *was* my great uncle is open to conjecture, if not lengthy scrutiny of the family archives. From what I could gather - and I must confess I had faint interest in the subject at the time - Gerhard and his immediate kin were somewhat apart from the main family; related in blood, but distantly. They were a wandering kind, producing no children in living record, and prone to fleeing the family demesne whenever possible. Indeed, none of Gerhard's consorts remained in the house, and sad to tell, there was cheerless news to divulge to him. Seven years previously, a fatal accident had abruptly stripped my Great Uncle of all his male lovers who had still been in residence at Gravewell Park. I hoped these tidings would not cause too much of an upset. Hopefully, Gerhard would have forgotten most of his consorts. After all, he was a very ancient individual; I had never met him.

Eventually, I was able to retire from Lathorne's room, leaving Abisarah alone to cope with any remaining afflictions. Bored, annoyed and a little sickened, I felt in no mood to celebrate. The afternoon was coming down towards evening, and shadows were lengthening over the lawns in front of the house. Lamps were being lit and soon the curtains would be drawn against the rustling darkness that braided the long driveway down to the gates. Soon, great uncle Gerhard would venture upon that rough stone. He would come by horse or carriage to the steps of the house. We would all see him.

Downstairs, in the shadowy hallway, I came upon my brothers, Valentine and Wylie, adjusting each other's neckties before joining the rest of the family in the drawing room. We are very much alike, my brothers and I, in temperament as well as appearance. Consequently, we don't always get along well together, especially at those times when a mirror is the last thing you want to face. This evening, however, we were in accord. I acknowledged their russet-haired, fine-boned beauty as I silently approached them. Great Uncle Gerhard would surely be proud of us.

'Celestine,' Valentine said, when he finally noticed me on the stairs. 'You look enchanting tonight.'

'I haven't even begun preparing myself yet,' I replied. 'Why should I bother at this early hour? Our relative will not arrive until after midnight. Our mother said so.'

'And is Lathorne prepared?' Wylie asked.

I ignored the implication in his words. The males might suspect Lathorne's unhappy nasal tendency, but they would never find tangible evidence.

'Indeed, she is ready and quite aglow with the prospect of a family celebration.' I glided past the pair of them, chin high.

Nearly all the family, my parents and their consorts among them, had already gathered in the drawing room, which was lit solely by dozens of tall candles. All the best jewels were out, winking wetly in the candle-light, and also the best perfumes. The atmosphere was quite intoxicating. Lesser kindred, who were not so well placed upon the family tree, were handing out aperitifs. Conversation was low, but an air of excitement filled the room. My mother, Delilah, looked radiant, her amber silk gown

221

complementing the autumn bronze of her coiled hair.

'Homecomings!' she said, opening out her arms to me. 'Oh Celestine, how poignant this must seem to you, close as you are to your first leavetaking. Ah, the travelling times are the most enthralling for a young girl!'

She was a well-meaning creature, but it always irked me that she felt compelled to emphasise my youth whenever possible. After all, I was nearly forty-two, which might be infantile in Grigori terms, but fairly advanced by human standards.

'Travel?' I withdrew from her embrace. 'Mother, I hardly think a lengthy incarceration in the stronghold of throng Yaling, counts as travel!'

'Nonsense, my dear,' my mother said brusquely, casting quick glances at those who overheard our conversation. 'You'll have to travel to get there. It's quite a distance.'

Valentine and Wylie had followed me into the room and were smirking at this exchange. For them, the threshold of our home opened up into a wide world of possibilities. Their travels would be far more interesting than mine, I felt. I cursed the fact that the Yalings had put in an offer for me, which would probably be the precursor to another offer - that of a strategic mating to enhance the bloodlines of the Gravewell and Yaling throngs. I hoped to escape Yaling hospitality as soon as possible in order to explore the world. Human women were so restricted by their culture, and to hide among them, we are obliged to mimic their behaviour. However, relative youth or not, it was not beyond my shaping skills to wear a form that superficially resembled a man. Then I could walk the countries of the world without fear.

'My darling, I thought you would be wearing the dove-grey gown I had made for you,' my mother said, perceiving a shortening of my temper. 'You'll look so lovely in it. Gerhard will be astonished to see what treasures have been born into the throng in his absence.'

'I will take a small aperitif before I begin my toilette,' I said. A certain measure of good humour was restored.

My nephew and confidant, Bayard, accompanied me to my boudoir, in order to assist me with the fastening of corsets. I suppose he is my closest friend, although sometimes he annoys me so much I could kill him. Pretty thing, Bayard, as deceitful as he is attractive, although I believed he feared me too much ever to betray me. We were the same age, and he too would soon be leaving Gravewell Park, unprotected by Grigori of experience, in order to sniff the wild lands beyond our gates. Apart from our dependent servants, humans were mostly an unknown quantity to us. Our elders had encouraged a reclusive reputation for the family. Only older, more trusted members of the throng interacted with the outside world, and no human in the county was aware of exactly how many Grigori huddled within the walls of Gravewell Park. Bayard looked forward to breaking human hearts out there in the world, whereas I was more intent upon examining their depths. Perhaps we would work well as a team.

At half past ten, Bayard escorted me back to the drawing room. 'Not long now,' he said.

'No. I wonder what he will be like, this antique great uncle of ours. Somewhat hideous, do you think?' I had never seen anyone thousands of years old, but there were rumours such creatures found it difficult to retain a corporeal shape of any great beauty.

Bayard pulled a sour face. 'If he is as old as people say, I wouldn't be surprised. It is a shame. Personally, I would prefer something appealing to land on our doorstep this evening.'

I squeezed his arm. 'Bayard, you are perverse.'

He grinned. 'No, I itch for freedom, for sensation. Is that so bad? Nothing - nobody - here excites me. It is like being hungry, yearning for the most exquisite and forbidden ichors, yet being offered only the juice of a dog as sustenance.'

'Perhaps you scratch your itches and sate your hunger too often to take pleasure in it anymore,' I observed.

He smiled ruefully, pushing his dark hair from his eyes. 'I want to be scarred by life,' he said.

Sometimes I worry about him.

As the clocks in the house were all preparing to strike eleven, we were disturbed from our polite revels by the sound of urgent knocking at the front door. The echo of it reverberated throughout the hallway like the booming of a monstrous drum; some pagan drum, summoning terrors. It brought quite a chill to my blood. Several of my relatives, whom I suspect had been harbouring desires to repair to their bedrooms for some time, perked up considerably. Did the knocking herald the arrival of Great Uncle Gerhard, earlier than expected?

All eyes turned towards our matriarch, Letitia, who rose up from her couch like a splendid queen of some ancient, forgotten city. She was dressed in a gown of eastern design, its hem decorated with embroidered eyes. Without a word or a glance to anyone, she cleared a path through the relatives by will-power alone, threw open the drawing-room doors, and advanced with stately tread into the hall. Here, without looking round, she raised a hand to stem the flow of relatives streaming behind her. Before she had finished unbolting the front door, the knocking came again; this time even more sonorously and impatiently.

'Gravewells,' Letitia said, addressing her family. 'I fear we have a man in need here!'

We all laughed a little, and the front door was opened.

'Oh,' said Letitia.

We all proceeded cautiously into the hall. There was a dreadful draught blowing through the doorway. What had been a clement day had rustled up a stiff wind in its passing into night, and a great deal of that wind was now coming into the house. It curled around the gaunt form of a tall man on its way inside; it blew his cloak out in front of him. His face was shadowed by his hat, but even at first glance, there was no indication that this was an aged individual. Indeed, my first impression was of a person young, vital and powerful. I had expected something - someone - quite different. This was a sentiment which I believe Letitia shared. I could tell her first instinct had been to embrace the traveller, but instead she stepped backwards, as if confused. The man on the doorstep bowed.

'Madam Gravewell?' he said.

'Come in,' said Letitia.

Letitia led the new arrival into the drawing room, leaving his single battered luggage bag in the hall. It was not raining outside, but his thick black cloak was damp with sparkling droplets. He wore a wide-brimmed hat, beneath which he concealed a grin and a clean-shaven chin that looked somehow raw. Not that the chin was without pleasing shape, or indeed the mouth above it. I chided myself for believing Great Uncle Gerhard would favour an ancient form. He looked young, but then, why not? Because of his long absence, he was a stranger in these parts. He could wear whatever shape he liked, supposing he still had a deft capability for it. Poor Lathorne, with her forgetfulness and her dreadful dim brain, did not possess the concentration or energy required to maintain a comely shape, but hers was an unusual condition. Perhaps I had come to judge all ancients like her, even though Letitia and Abisarah were very nearly her equal in years, and they were both glamorous creatures in their maturity.

Our visitor did not speak but, at Letitia's request, sat obediently upon a sofa. She summoned a relative to pour him brandy, which he sipped from with obvious pleasure. In the middle of a throng of family members, Bayard slipped his arm through mine and whispered, 'Well, well!'

'He does not seem overcome with emotion to be home,' I hissed back.

'I don't blame him!' was Bayard's last hushed retort.

'The wind is terrible outside,' Letitia said into the silence of the room.

'Indeed terrible!' added my uncle Everill.

'The like not seen this season,' trilled my mother.

The traveller shrugged. 'I have seen worse,' he said.

Surely the Homecoming should have been a joyous event with embraces, kisses and exclamations of delight all round? I could not understand this dour silence and awkwardness, where the loudest sound was the crackling of the fire. I wanted to leave the room with Bayard in order to discuss the situation. In that silence, I was reluctant to speak aloud. What a strange person Great Uncle Gerhard was.

'It seems,' he said, putting down the empty brandy glass upon the carpet, 'that I have intruded upon a family party.'

Everybody looked at one another. The man took off his hat, and a wealth of white-gold hair tumbled around his shoulders. His face was handsomely hewn, though raw-boned. I saw he wore an earring in the shape of silver sphinx in one ear. He smiled at Letitia, who was standing in front of him, the fingers of one hand pressed against her throat. Her mouth was open in astonishment; an expression I had never seen upon her face before. Her thin nostrils were pinched and white. I think it was at that point that I - and probably everybody else present - realised the man we had let into our house was not Great Uncle Gerhard at all.

The porters had let this stranger in at the gates. *They had let him in*! This meant he must be Grigori from some other family, because no-one human would ever cross the shadow of the gates, at least not without due preparation. Unless... unless he had entered our estate by clandestine means and *scaled the walls*! Was that possible?

'Who are you?' Letitia demanded. She looked very frightening and tall, but this did not appear to bother our visitor very much.

'Who were you expecting?' he rejoined, putting his hat upon his knees.

Letitia had folded her arms; always a fearsome sign. Her fingers tapped an anthem upon her sleeves. 'I entreat you, for the sake of politeness, to answer my question. I have offered you hospitality, after all.'

He shrugged. 'Forgive me, my lady.' He burrowed beneath his cloak and retrieved an envelope, quite battered and stained. 'If you will indulge me by examining these documents, you will see I am here in good faith. These are my credentials.'

Letitia snatched the envelope from him, and scanned the contents with raised brows. 'Peverel Othman,' she said, and stuffed the papers back into their envelope. 'Your family are a throng with whom I am unfamiliar.'

The man inclined his head. 'We are a small, yet distinguished line,' he said. 'As such, we are private people, and do not engage in social activities. I am not surprised you have not heard of us.'

'Yet the family Boonspill deems fit to grant your their endorsement,' Letitia said, with suspicion in her voice.

'Are the documents genuine?' queried one of her male consorts.

She shrugged. 'I find little to suggest otherwise. However, I admit to a certain discomfiture concerning your advent, Peverel Othman. Perhaps it is just the shock of your unannounced arrival.'

Our guest made a gesture of apology. 'You are right. Under normal circumstances, I would have attempted to contact you beforehand. Unfortunately, I found myself in this part of the country temporarily without accommodation. Having a full inventory of throngs in my possession, I made haste to the nearest haven.' He smiled sweetly, apparently attempting to flirt with the stony countenance of Letitia. 'I generally find that all Grigori are sympathetic to stranded individuals such as myself. That is, I have found such to be the case until this moment.'

Letitia narrowed her eyes at the gentle rebuke. 'I do not mean to appear ungracious,' she said, visibly relaxing a little, 'but this is not a common circumstance for us. However, you have crossed our threshold now so, please, take off your coat.'

Bayard had dragged me forward, so that we stood close to Letitia. She turned and fixed us with a commanding stare. 'Celestine, Bayard, enough of your whisperings! Seeing as you are obviously so fascinated by our visitor, perhaps you could conduct Peverel Othman to one of the guest chambers; the Peacock Room, I think.' She pointed an imperious finger at a lesser relative. 'Bradley, fetch kindling and fuel to light a fire in there.' Then, the situation resolved, she fixed the rest of the family with a steely eye. 'Noses into your wine, my dears. Please do not forget that we have an elder to welcome home soon!'

Well, as can be imagined, the actual arrival of Great Uncle Gerhard was quite eclipsed by the sudden and glamorous manifestation of Peverel Othman. Following his unusual introduction into our midst, Othman collected his bag from the hall and obligingly accompanied Bayard and myself up the great staircase, making affable remarks about the surrounding countryside, the weather and the interior of our house. In response, Bayard was outwardly flirtatious, while I maintained a cool yet courtly mien; sure my approach would be far more fascinating than Bayard's obvious manoeuvres. We took Othman to the Peacock Room, which despite its opulent appointments held little to do with peacocks, either spiritually or decoratively; it was named, I believe, after some member of our family with a leaning towards the non-essential.

Peverel Othman nodded in appreciation as I lit the lamps beside the mantle. Although it was one of our best rooms, it was not often used, and the air was chill. But a fire would soon invoke a more congenial atmosphere. After a short examination of his surroundings, Othman put his bag upon the ottoman at the foot of the bed. His friendly overtures had dwindled. I suggested he might like to rejoin the company downstairs, while his bedroom heated up. This he seemed inclined to do, although I must confess he had a preoccupied air about him, and scarcely seemed to notice either Bayard or myself. He intimated he would like to change his clothing, which we took as a request for us to leave the room. Somewhat nettled, Bayard and I went back downstairs.

'He wears a handsome shape,' Bayard said.

'No great feat,' I snapped. 'Behold, I wear myself most beautifully.' Whereupon, we both started giggling and swept back into the drawing room arm in arm.

Shortly, Othman reappeared, neatly dressed in dark clothing and with his hair tied back. He was adopted by a clutch of our menfolk and seemed quite happy in their company. Bayard couldn't keep his eyes off the man, whereas I, more mindful of my dignity, confined my curious scrutiny to glancing at the mirror opposite where Othman stood.

At a quarter hour to midnight, we heard the sound of a carriage crunching over the drive outside the house. We heard the driver call out to his beasts as they stamped to a halt. Letitia went to the front door, opened it, and let the light of the house spill out into the night. Again, we clustered behind her, although this time our anticipation was somewhat dulled. Outside, the carriage door opened, and Great Uncle Gerhard stepped down. He wore the aspect of a trim middle-aged man, not ugly but fairly plain, who spoke in a fussy manner to the driver's man about unloading his luggage, who rubbed his hands together in the cold, even though they were mittened, who said, 'Letitia, you are wondrous as ever!' and who came into our house in a very ordinary way; a relative returning home after a long absence. Still, his congenial character definitely had a beneficial influence on the rest of us. There was positive merriment in the drawing room as Great Uncle Gerhard sat upon one of the couches, surrounded by smiling faces, to recount tales of his travels. More wine was brought from the cellar and a selection of sandwiches from the kitchens. All those who but an hour ago had been looking fatigued brightened up and joined in the conversation. Predictably perhaps, there were a few minutes of glumness following Letitia's tactful description of the fatal accident concerning Great Uncle Gerhard's lovers, but it did not seem to upset him for long.

Only our gaunt visitor, Peverel Othman, did not appear delighted and enchanted by the mundane yet friendly presence of Great Uncle Gerhard. He stood some distance away from the family group, a globe of brandy nursed against his dark-clad chest. He appeared bored, only occasionally directing his glance towards Aunt Lathorne, who had become quite silly with liquor, but whose nose, I was pleased to note, retained its proper shape. It occurred to me then that it was perhaps imprudent to let Lathorne run riot with the decanter when strangers were present. I had little fear her shape would become indiscreet, for we women of the Gravewells took great pains to invigilate Lathorne, and were alert for the earliest signs of impropriety.

I was introduced to Uncle Gerhard by my mother. He was polite and avuncular, as one would expect. With a roguish twinkle in his eye, he spoke of having presents in his luggage for all of us. I smiled and batted my eyelashes, as I anticipated would please him. But on the whole, I found very little to stimulate me in his character. Bayard, I knew, shared this sentiment. Often, our eyes would meet, and stray in unison towards the sombre figure of Peverel Othman. I planned eventually to glide across the room and engage him in conversation, but just as I thought a judicious time had come, Othman left our presence, no doubt to retire for the night. I surmised he'd found our family reunion just as tiresome as I had.

In the morning, I dressed myself in my best dark silk, and arranged my hair loosely about my shoulders. I did not deceive myself this effort was employed for anyone other than our mysterious guest. I was disappointed to find that he had risen early and was therefore not present at breakfast, but I tracked him down later in the library, where he was perusing our collection of books.

'Are you refreshed?' I asked him, skirting the library table with a swish of silk.

He turned and looked me up and down, a book held open in his hand. 'Thank you, yes,' he said. It became immediately obvious to me that he considered me silly. In fact, I suspected he found all of my family somewhat trivial and uninspiring. The Gravewells are traditionalists and preservers of custom. Perhaps Peverel Othman espoused more revolutionary convictions. On the rare occasions I had met Grigori of a more progressive outlook, I had found their rebellious zeal, their desire to tread forbidden paths and rediscover the ancient, forbidden knowledge, annoying and wearisome traits, but in Peverel Othman, the suggestion of unorthodoxy only increased his appeal.

'Have you any plans for the day?' I enquired.

He shook his head. 'No.'

'Ah, then perhaps you would allow my nephew, Bayard, and myself to escort you around the grounds. There is much to see; the ornamental lake and its shore-line folly temples, the greenhouses - oh, such orchids! - and...'

'I said I had no plans for the day,' Peverel Othman said, replacing the book on its shelf. 'Neither do I anticipate making any.' He smiled at me; I felt stunned at the abuse. 'Excuse me, Miss Gravewell, but I am in a mood for relaxing and my greatest deeps of tranquillity are never realised in the company of others.'

'In that case, forgive me for intruding upon your solitude!' I said, in the crispest tone I could manage. Whereupon, I turned and marched to the door.

'You are forgiven,' he said. I suspected he was smiling, but I did not look round.

'He is attractive but rude,' I said to Bayard, as we took our morning constitutional among the yew trees behind the kitchen garden.

Bayard linked his arm through mine. 'He is travelling, isn't he? I expect he's had many adventures. It's only natural he would find the company of Gravewells dull.'

'You think yourself dull?' I asked, surprised. 'Personally, I believe us to be dashing and companionable creatures, even though we've yet to experience the outside world.'

'Perhaps he is a solitary creature, someone who is older than we imagine.'

'Make excuses for his impropriety, if you must, Bay,' I said haughtily, disengaging myself from his arm, 'but I feel your sympathy is misplaced.'

This altercation brought a disagreeable atmosphere to our walk, and we finished it quickly, in awkward silence.

I had no idea how long Peverel Othman planned to remain a

guest of my family. In fact, I don't think he made his arrangements known to anyone. Great Uncle Gerhard was naturally the centre of attention at this time. Grigori from other far-flung throngs came long miles simply to attend social gatherings, and listen to Gerhard's lengthy and rambling tales of seductions and adventures in far lands. True to his word, he had brought many fabulous gifts; jewels and exotic fabrics and strange books and artefacts. To me he gave an elaborately worked golden head ornament, which I would not have been surprised to discover had been snatched from the brow of some entombed princess, long dead in the sands of Sumer. It was exquisite, but I could not imagine when I might ever wear it. Perhaps in the future I would be invited to some masquerade ball, when it could come in handy.

In the privacy of my chamber, I sat before my mirror and arranged the ornament on my head. I struck a dramatic pose and flared my nostrils at the glass. I was still quite a novice at summoning the intense concentration required for adjusting my physical appearance. Some Grigori don't even grasp the ability until they are nearly a hundred years old - well past puberty. Still, I fixed my attention upon my reflection and slowly willed the colour of my eyes to flow into a yellowy-orange hue and slitted the pupils, like a cat's. It was while I was indulging in this private display that I heard furtive movements in the hallway outside. Of course, I am used to the brisk steps of our servants as they go about their daily business in the upper storeys, but these steps were not at all brisk, and the very creak of the boards spoke of some sly commerce being enacted. Swiftly, I rose to my feet and, still wearing the golden ornament, opened my door and looked out. It was thus I surprised Peverel Othman in the act of creeping down the right side of the corridor, his head pressed to the door next to my own.

'Excuse me?' I said in a loud voice.

He did not start in surprise, but stood up and turned to face me in an insultingly languid manner, making me feel as if I was the one who'd been caught unawares.

'Are you lost?' I asked. Peverel Othman was staring at my head, so I snatched the ornament from my brow, tearing a few strands of hair from my scalp in the process. This was enough to bring tears to my eyes, and it was then I remembered they were orange and catty.

Peverel Othman folded his arms. 'Fortunate for you I was not some wandering human, who'd found their way into this house by mistake,' he said in an infuriatingly despotic manner. 'You should take care, Miss Gravewell, as to your appearance when you burst unannounced from your room.'

I decided to ignore his remark. 'What are you doing?'

He put the fingers of one hand against the door beside him. 'Whose room is this?'

'Why?'

'Just answer me,' he said.

'Indeed I will not!' I said, aghast he dared to use such a harsh tone with me in my own home, and he a guest of my family too. I went back into my room, slamming the door most emphatically. My heart was pounding. I felt furious. The room he had referred to was that occupied by Lathorne. Perhaps he had heard the hissing of the snake. Still, how dare he creep around our house, listening at doors. It was clear there was more to Peverel Othman than met the eye. Were my suspicions the product of his insulting demeanour towards me, or did my instinct speak truly that there was something sinister about him? My first reaction was to speak to Bayard about it, but, because of his partiality for the stranger, I felt disinclined to seek him out, sure that his infatuation would prevent him being a reliable ally.

I returned to my mirror and made sure my eyes were adjusted to their usual shape and hue. Then, after dragging a brush over the top of my head to quiet the frantic strands uplifted by the removal of the ornament, I left the room once more. There was no sign of Peverel Othman in the corridor outside. I walked purposefully towards the west wing to check he hadn't turned a corner, found nothing, then repeated the process to the east. Othman must have either gone downstairs or entered one of the rooms. Perhaps he had ventured up to the third floor, although this was unlikely as the doors to the stairs in this area were kept locked. Throng members in retreat slumber were secreted there, and we took all precautions to safeguard their rest.

I decided I must report our guest's eccentric behaviour to Letitia at once; at this hour, she would be found in her sitting room.

Unfortunately, almost as if he'd anticipated my move, Peverel Othman was also present when I entered the room. He was taking tea with Letitia, who seemed quite at ease in his company. Othman afforded me a curt glance as I crossed the carpet, and despite my pique at his rude treatment of me, I could not help but appreciate those finer points, of which Bayard seemed so enamoured. Othman was undeniably a fine-looking creature; aristocratic and finely-cast, his skin was white as bone. How well he sculpted himself, how beautifully. Humans must have died for his touch, I was sure.

'Celestine, I was not expecting you,' Letitia said, raking me with a cold eye. Clearly, she had plans of her own concerning the beautiful Peverel Othman.

'I was concerned about our guest here,' I said bluntly. He did not look at me, but smiled in a secretive fashion at the carpet.

'Oh?' Letitia oozed disinterest.

'Yes. He was quite lost upstairs just now. Did you find the room you were looking for, Mr Othman?'

He looked up at Letitia and laughed a little. It was a lovely sound, quite boyish. 'Yes... Miss Gravewell is angry with me, because I corrected her. Perhaps it was not my place to do so. Perhaps I should simply have reported to matter to you.'

'What matter?' enquired Letitia.

I could have turned to ice with fury, for my anger was not hot but achingly cold. How dare he!

Othman raised his hand. 'A trifling thing, of no consequence. I'm sure Miss Gravewell will not neglect her appearance in such a way again.'

'Celestine! What did you do?' Letitia demanded.

Cornered, I related the incident in detail, expecting Letitia to reprimand me further, thus increasing my mortified embarrassment. However, she merely turned away when I had finished speaking and said, 'Which room *were* you looking for, Mr Othman?'

Her response obviously surprised him, although he swiftly smothered his expression. He glanced at me. 'It hardly seems mannerly to explain,' he said.

Letitia laughed sweetly. 'Indulge me! I am not easily offended.'

'One of your youngsters,' he said. 'The boy. Bayard. We

had an assignation.'

I made an explosive sound of disgust and, pausing only to excuse myself to Letitia, left the room immediately, intending to seek my wayward nephew out and pull his hair. When had he had the opportunity to arrange such a liaison? I had been with him nearly all the time since Othman's arrival.

Bayard himself denied all knowledge of the arrangement when I found him in the music room. At first, I accused him of deceit, but his obvious excitement that our guest had at least used him as an excuse caused me to change my mind.

'Was he really looking for me do you think?' Bayard asked, eyes alight.

I shrugged moodily. 'Who knows! His antics were most suspicious. Why should he want to see you anyway?'

I was convinced Peverel Othman had lied. He had noticed Bayard's interest in him, so had used it as a convenient cover for his activities. And what exactly *were* his activities? I smelled malfeasance; I intended to root it out.

While changing my apparel for dinner that evening, I began to make plans. They necessitated involving Bayard, a course which initially I had shrunk from, because I did not consider him particularly intelligent. However, it seemed to me that Peverel Othman had created the very avenue for my intentions to traverse; therefore I must use it.

Having readied myself hastily for the meal, in order to have time to consult with Bayard, I went directly to my nephew's room. Usually, he spent more than an hour deciding which garments to wear, so I anticipated finding him there. Giving our coded knock - three-two-one - I entered the room without pause. Again, Peverel Othman had pre-empted me. To my astonishment, no less than my embarrassment, he had my nephew Bayard beneath him in the bed. Such was their engrossment in their activities, which indeed appeared ecstatic, neither of them seemed inclined to stop what they were doing. Othman turned his head to me and said, 'Get out!'

Which I did.

I was disappointed. It seemed Othman must have been telling Letitia the truth in some respects. Of course he would not admit to prowling round the house in order to sniff Bayard's chamber out, but in the light of what I'd seen, it certainly seemed that must have been his intention.

Lathorne had been having a bad day of it again, which meant she was not present at dinner. Peverel Othman came into the dining room, accompanied by Bayard and, after scanning the table, asked where Lathorne was. I could not bear to look at him, although it did strike me as unusual he should enquire after my aunt so soon after having lurked outside her room. *Did* his interest lie with her after all? If so, why? Did he suspect her defects? My mind was full of such thoughts as I tried to consume my dinner, although I was somewhat distracted by the clowning of Great Uncle Gerhard, who was on form as usual, telling jokes and playing tricks with the spoons. In truth, I was beginning to find his jocularity rather wearisome, and several of his stories had been repeated at least twice, without the slightest alteration of detail. Soon, I feared, we would all be able to recite them along with him. Why had our relative turned out to be so tedious? I wished he could be more like Peverel Othman, with his air of mystery and handsome shape, though perhaps without his malignance. Bayard, throughout the meal, was a nauseating picture of infatuation; I despised him deeply.

After dinner, I went to Lathorne's room, where Abisarah was feeding her a bowl of soup. Abisarah at least was interested in what I had to say concerning Othman's behaviour that afternoon. As a precaution, she decided that Lathorne should be confined to her room for the duration of Othman's visit.

'Do you think he suspects all is not well with her?' I asked. 'But if so, why? She has been a perfect lady in his company, as I recall.'

Abisarah pursed her mouth and shook her head. 'Celestine, there are Grigori among us who have taken it upon themselves... well, their sole function is to weed out those of us who are perhaps rather *non-conformist*, who might, to the over-cautious, be seen as a threat to our racial security.'

'Lathorne? A threat?' I had to laugh.

'It is not a subject for merriment,' Abisarah said. 'Perhaps I am being too cautious, but for all we know, Othman's purpose might well be the elimination of miscreants. I know these hidden invigilators regularly inspect all cases of suspicion. And, despite poor Lathorne's weak mind, her utter docility, she could be termed a threat in the manner I described. It is best to be circumspect.'

'Are you suggesting Othman might be here for the express purpose of examining Lathorne?'

Abisarah shrugged. 'As I said, I could be being too cautious, but the possibility should not be dismissed out of hand.'

'But how could he have found out about her?' I argued. 'It is impossible. Lathorne never leaves the grounds. Not even the males of this household are aware of her shortcomings.'

'Of that you cannot be sure,' Abisarah said grimly.

'But would one of our own betray her?' I found it hard to believe.

Abisarah nodded. 'It is possible. In truth, it is *we* who are at fault in concealing the problem. We are guided by our affection for Lathorne, I know, and sometimes I worry about it. However, I could never hand her to the Kerubim's arm.'

'Kerubim!' I had not imagined it could be that serious.

'But of course. What did you think? That miscreants are incarcerated somewhere - or simply told to behave? Celestine, have sense in your head, what else could happen to them? You know as well as I do it is imperative we conceal ourselves from the burgeoning humans in this world. And if you do not know that, it is time you reapplied yourself with zeal to the study of our history!'

I was stung by her sharpness, although I recognised the wisdom of her words. Was it possible Peverel Othman was here for the purpose of culling poor Lathorne from the throng? I shuddered to think there might be an informant within the family breast; a serpent who had nestled there, with fang concealed, until it dealt the fatal bite. Who could it be? Also, would I and my female relatives be seen equally culpable as Lathorne, because we had shielded her? Would we also be regarded as risks?

'Should we speak with Letitia?' I asked. 'Surely, we should do that!'

Abisarah frowned. 'Not yet. Letitia's first concern is the family unit. If she feels it is threatened, she might well take unprecedented action.'

'What do you mean?'

Abisarah turned her head to regard Lathorne preening

happily in her mirror, totally oblivious to our exchange. 'Sometimes, sacrifices have to be made, and as the Kerubim are creatures of the Parzupheim, their will cannot be contested.'

'Are you suggesting Letitia might let Othman kill Lathorne?' I hissed out the words, not daring to utter them too loudly, because they would surely penetrate the murk in Lathorne's mind.

Abisarah shrugged. 'I am not saying that. We must be vigilant, that's all. We have no proof Othman is what I fear he might be. I may well be over-dramatising the situation. It is just that I have dreaded something like this happening for a long time. I sincerely hope my fears are unfounded.'

As I left Lathorne's room with its sad perfume of reptile musk, I felt utterly depressed. I realised how little I knew of what went on in the world beyond our estate walls. Perhaps it was time I turned to the study of it.

Great Uncle Gerhard was in the library, smoking a pipe and enjoying a globe of brandy before the fire. Most of the family had gone to bed; it was a time of day I loved. I adored the quiet of it, when all the bustle had gone away. Nodding politely to Great Uncle Gerhard, I crossed to the lofty glass-fronted bookcase that Letitia kept locked. Fortunately, because on occasion I had been called upon to help with the accounts - having a mathematical mind - I knew where the key was kept. The accounts book resided in this cabinet, along with volumes of a more esoteric nature, ones which normally I would have to seek permission from Letitia to peruse. Assuring myself that Great Uncle Gerhard had his back to me, I pressed a certain section of panelling in the wall, revealing the shadowed slot where the small key lay. However, when he heard me opening the lock, Gerhard looked round his chair at me. I expected a facetious remark, but he said nothing. For a moment or two I felt strangely guilty, and reluctant to examine the spines of the books within the case. I felt a sense of disapproval emanating from my Great Uncle.

He took his pipe from his mouth. 'Hardly light reading to take to your bed, young lady.'

Nervously, I brushed my fingers over the books on the second shelf. 'No... But there was something I wished to look up.'

'And what is that, my dear?'

I saw little point in lying; it might open an unwelcome dialogue. 'A sensitive subject,' I said bluntly. 'Kerubim, and their office.'

Great Uncle Gerhard laughed in a manner I could only find offensive. 'And what possible interest could you have, my dear, in such a grim topic?'

'Soon, I shall begin my own travels,' I replied. 'I feel I know so little about the world, or even about my own people.'

'But this is such an odd time to begin your research; it's the middle of the night!'

I shrugged. 'The whim struck me.' Becoming annoyed with his patronising attitude, I took one of the books from the shelves. For the sake of security, all books concerning my people were carefully encoded, so that they appeared only to be fictitious travelogues, or fantasy histories. Many humans must have these books upon their library shelves, and had read them as novels. The book I had chosen was a double fiction; it was a novel that was supposedly written by a Kerub, yet the author was, by his own admission in the Preface, a teacher.

'*The Reaping*. Hmm,' said Uncle Gerhard. 'Most of that is conjecture.'

'How do you know?' I asked.

'I met the person who wrote it. It is dry reading too'

'But will this book tell me how to recognise the Keruim?'

Great Uncle Gerhard regarded me thoughtfully. 'Are you really afraid one of them might come after you, out there in the world? What transgression could you possibly commit, dear girl?'

'I find the idea of Grigori preying on Grigori repugnant, whatever the reason. Neither am I convinced that innocents might not, on occasion, be erroneously culled. I wish to protect myself.'

Gerhard nodded. 'That is sensible, I suppose. But come, put your book away. I can tell you all you need to know.'

I complied with his wishes and went to sit before his chair, next to the fire. He puffed for a few moments on his pipe and then sighed. 'Celestine - it *is* Celestine, isn't it? - you cannot recognise the Kerubim when they wear a human-like form. How could they possibly carry out their work if they were recognisable? And you are correct in assuming that some of them are somewhat overzealous in their vocation. Yes, the idea is repugnant, but these creatures are necessary, my dear. We cannot risk exposure - ever. If you follow the requirements of our laws, you will be safe from Kerubim. That is all you need to know. And if, in the future, you do feel the need to transgress - well, you will simply have to be extremely careful, won't you.'

I was shocked that my Great Uncle could even imagine I would ever transgress. 'I would never consider such a thing!' I said.

He gave me an astute glance. 'Of course not... pre-supposing you could help yourself, should the time ever come.'

I thought immediately of Lathorne. Was Gerhard implying he knew something about her? I shuddered inwardly and cast down my eyes, afraid my acquaintance with these unhappy facts would shine from my countenance.

'We embark upon our travels to learn,' Gerhard said, 'to experience life. It is not wrong that you know so little now. Your education awaits you and there will be many to be your teachers along the way; human and Grigori alike.'

'Human?' I did not understand him.

'But of course. Don't you know that we learn from everyone we meet in life? They themselves might not realise they are teachers, but they are. Every one of them. Books can teach you very little, Celestine. Lock that cupboard you were delving into with such secret intent. There is nothing for you there. Cherish your innocence while you have it. Later, you will remember this time with affection and, yes, even a little sadness.'

I wondered, at that moment, whether I should tell him what was on my mind. I felt he would be sympathetic and trustworthy, and yet, my tongue would not form the words.

'You look pensive,' he said. 'It is late. Empty your head of heavy thoughts and go to your bed. And kiss me goodnight before you leave. You are a bright little thing, Celestine. I feel confident your path will not crumble before you.'

I felt strangely buoyant as I went upstairs to my bed. However, this mood evaporated abruptly once I entered the corridor that led to my room. Peverel Othman was once again lurking outside Lathorne's door.

'If you are looking for Bayard, you are sadly off course,' I said. 'What do you *really* want, Peverel Othman? What interests you so much beyond that door?'

He said nothing, his expression unreadable.

'There is a snake in there,' I said. 'Have you smelled it? Can you hear it slither? Is that what fascinates you so?'

'And who is the snake?' he asked. 'A member of your family perhaps?'

'Nobody. Just a snake. It belongs to my aunt. She is very fond of it.'

He nodded, as if I had answered some question of import.

'You trust my answer?' I said.

He smiled. 'I can tell you are not lying.'

'How tedious of me to be so transparent,' I said. 'Well, I am glad to have been of service to you. Goodnight, Mr Othman.'

I began to walk past him, but he reached out and stayed my arm. 'I thought that was your Great Uncle's room,' he said. 'You have just been in the library with your Great Uncle, haven't you?'

'Your interest in my family seems unduly macabre and intense,' I said, in an amazingly calm tone, considering how unnerved I felt. 'You put such sinister inflection upon your words, Mr Othman.'

'Well, that might be because the Gravewell throng has a reputation,' he said.

'Really? For what? Tedium?'

He shook his head. 'No. I can see at one glance that you are ignorant of the situation, despite the fact you were in residence here some seven years ago.'

'I expect you are referring to the accident,' I said. 'Yes, I was here, but the tragedy did not occur in the house. Certain of the menfolk were preparing a bonfire for the celebration of Letitia's birthday. A barrel of fire-crackers ignited. It caused many deaths. Is that sorry episode the cause of our reputation? If so, our distinction cannot be for tedium as I imagined, but carelessness.'

Peverel Othman shook his head again. 'Poor child,' he said. 'I said this to your lovely nephew, and I will say it to you. If you would keep your innocence, get out of this house and seek sanctuary with another throng as soon as you can.'

I laughed. 'Whatever for? Are you planning something?'

He smiled. 'The majority of your people are ignorant, and act as an effective screen for the activities of those who are more worldly. You are part of the screen, and I suspect, as such, rather dispensable.'

'I'm afraid I have no idea what you are talking about,' I said coldly, although inside my curiosity was pricked into life.

'I have been monitoring the movements of Gerhard Gravewell for some months,' he said. 'And those of his immediate kin, who are widespread. Obviously, there are family secrets in this house, but I suspect that Gerhard's return heralds a more candid era. He will desire the recruitment of other throng members to his creed.'

'What creed?'

Othman narrowed his eyes at me. When he spoke, his words held disapproval, yet strangely, his mouth grinned widely around the words. 'The creed of the Anakim who disinter the past and what are seen as the least savoury aspects of our race.'

I was shocked by Othman's words. Anakim went beyond mere progressiveness. They were rebels of the first order, who worshipped the Hanged One, and whose views were regarded with the greatest disapproval by conservative Grigori. It was said they called upon the power of the Ahriman, the Great Lie, and made human sacrifice to attain power. Humans were an irritant to them, something to be used without compassion. Most Grigori saw Anakim as a great threat to our security. Great Uncle Gerhard's amiable visage sprang to mind. That he could conceal these sinister traits was a ridiculous notion. 'You are insane!' I said. 'By what authority do you speak this lunacy?'

'Celestine, your male relatives did not carelessly ignite themselves with fire-crackers seven years ago. If you were not so naive and shielded from the world, you would know that certain disappearances took place in the nearby human community at that time. A ritual was to be enacted, which went awry. Need I say more?'

'Frankly, I'd rather you didn't! There are no mavericks in my family.'

Othman uttered a caustic laugh. 'Oh, fold your wings about your face, my dear. Believe the feathers are not tinged with red! But if you are sensible, you will heed my warning.' He paused. 'Or, you could face the reality of the situation and become something greater than you are.'

I struggled to fix a scornful smile on my lips. 'I cannot tolerate such nonsense! Believe me, I yearn for excitement, and if there was any whiff of it within the house, I would sense it. But no, life is and always has been a staid, ordinary business at Gravewell Park.'

He studied me carefully for a few moments, almost as if he was considering my words seriously.

'You're no ordinary traveller,' I said. 'Tell me why are you here.'

He did not answer, saying only, 'Go to your bed now. I have further business to conduct.'

It was the second time some male in this household had ordered me to my room that night, and I was mightily sick of it. 'I think you are of the Kerubim,' I said. 'Or at least you *think* you are. Well, I'm afraid you're wasting your time here. Gerhard is a docile old gentleman. Anakim indeed! Hah! There's no-one here for you to slay, Peverel Othman, unless you're not particular about whom you kill or why!'

Othman looked thoughtful. 'Clearly, I have been too open with you,' he said. 'And perhaps overestimated your intelligence. But it does not matter.' With that, he turned on his heel and marched off towards the stairs.

For a few moments I stood without moving, totally aghast at this recent conversation. There was no doubt in my mind whatsoever now that Othman was all Abisarah feared he might be. Not only that: he was mad! Totally deranged and intent on victimising my relatives! Clearly, Letitia would have to be informed at once. I could not sleep with this unspeakable terror and outrage thrashing through my brain.

I went straight to Letitia's bed chamber, knocked once and entered directly. To my disappointment, the room was empty, lit only by a pleasant fire flickering in the grate. Now what should I do? Letitia could be with any of her husbands or wives, and I had little desire to invade every room to find out. Perhaps Great Uncle Gerhard was still in the library. He was the oldest and wisest of us all. I would go to him, unburden myself, pass on this dreadful fear. He, after all, was the one being slandered by Othman. I was convinced he would know how to deal with the situation.

Gerhard was not in the library. Surely he would not have retired to his chamber so early? Rather aimlessly, I went back out into the hall. The house was so quiet, as if everyone was hiding somewhere, holding their breath. My spine flexed and a wave of heat passed through me. Somewhere, something unusual was happening.

I was breathing quickly as I ventured down the long, dim-lit corridors of the house, searching for a sound or a feeling hanging in the air. I did not know exactly what it was I hunted, but I knew I would recognise it when I found it.

Instinctively, my feet led me to the cellar stairs. Below, beyond the labyrinthine, vaulted chambers where the wines and meats were stored - and perhaps one or two immobile relatives - lay the great doors to the family temple, the black room, the room of perpetual flame. Here, upon the eves of the great festivals, we would gather to commune with the memory of the Source, long lost to our race through the follies of the Fallen Ones.

Something moved in the air above the throat of steps that swallowed me down. I could feel it. Power and intention had passed this way. My heart was beating frantically now. I had yearned for adventure. Now I feared I'd found it. I replayed in my mind the conversation I'd had earlier with Peverel Othman. I realised now he had offered me an invitation.

The carved doors to the temple were closed, but orange light leaked from around their heavy frames onto the stone floor ahead of me. I went forward and pressed my face against the wood, listening for sounds. The cedar panels were warm beneath my cheek. Beyond, faintly, were the sounds of murmured chanting; a rite was taking place. To my knowledge, no private ceremonies were ever enacted in the temple, but then perhaps I knew less about my own family than I thought.

Would I be punished for intruding?

My curiosity was overwhelming. I knew I could not leave this place without seeing for myself what was happening beyond the closed doors.

They yielded to a gentle pressure from my hands, making no sound. I looked within.

Bowls of flame on stone plinths provided an eerie, flickering illumination. The air was thick with the pink-grey smoke of incense, more pungent than any I had smelled before. There were only four people in the temple. I had expected more.

Letitia was there, standing before the altar, her arms raised high, her fingers curled. She faced me, but did not seem to notice the doors had opened. She was naked to the hips, wearing a skirt of pleated, turquoise silk, her waist hung with metal girdles. Above them glared the crude painting of a great eye, which covered her belly. Her throat and chest were adorned with ropes of coloured beads and upon her hair, she wore a head-dress of peacock feathers and gold wires tipped with jewels, which towered above her.

Behind the altar stood Great Uncle Gerhard, dressed in a long cloak made entirely of peacock feathers. He looked suspiciously younger than when I'd last seen him, his long white hair flowing down over his shoulders, his face like that of a hawk. It must have been him whom I had heard chanting, for even now, his voice sang in a soft murmur the words of a rite unknown to me.

Upon the altar lay Bayard, quite naked. He appeared to be unconscious, one knee slightly raised, his head lolling to the side, long dark hair spilling down over the stone. One of his white arms hung down limply, as if he'd been reaching for the floor before losing awareness.

Before this tableau, in the centre of the circle which was inlaid into the floor before the altar knelt the figure of a man. I recognised him as Peverel Othman only by his glorious hair, which hung loose down his back, over a garment of black feathers. His head was bowed forward as if in prayer.

What were they doing? I had never seen such antics, and such was their preoccupation that my intrusion did not seem to register.

Uncle Gerhard yelled out unexpectedly, causing me to jump and gasp in alarm. I dashed into the temple and fled towards the thick columns stationed down its side. Here, I hid among the shadows, creeping nearer to the altar; every sense, every nerve of me, stunningly alive and alert.

'Peverel Othman, rise!' commanded Great Uncle Gerhard.

Slowly, as if drugged, Othman raised his head, his hair shifting over the feathers of his robe like the heavy gold fringes that adorned the hangings on the wall behind the altar. Awkwardly, he got to his feet, holding the garment of feathers around him. I was nearly opposite to where they stood now, a small, insignificant mote of watchfulness that they could not perceive.

Gerhard was now leaning on the altar, ignoring what lay on it. 'You have sought me out,' he said to Othman, 'and, through sinister means and threats, have exhorted me to grant you favours. Am I to take kindly to this?'

'There was no other way,' Othman replied, and his voice did not sound drugged at all, but musical and low, like a bell. I could not decide whether they were speaking from the script of a ceremony or merely exchanging remarks. Letitia remained silent, a motionless statue of flesh, her arms raised, her eyes staring.

'You desire power,' said Gerhard.

'I shall take it with me into the future,' Othman responded. 'And I shall use it in accord with the desires and directives of your own spirit.'

Gerhard drew himself erect, and stroked Bayard's white chest. 'Such jewels you will take from our treasure-house.' He shook his head and then, after only a moment's hesitation, turned round and flung wide his arms. A gout of flame roared upwards, revealing the wall behind the altar. I saw that the hangings with which I was familiar were drawn back and secured by golden cords, revealing a great stone face carved into the wall that I had never seen before. It was a face of unbearable beauty and sadness, nearly thirty feet high, framed by coils of hair interwoven with peacock feathers and sheaves of corn.

'My Lord Shemyaza, I call upon you to witness this rite, from your eternal prison in the stars. One of your children cries out for the light of your kingdom which was taken from you. Grant him your blessing.'

Upon these words, Peverel Othman threw out his arms, and I saw that his garment was a cloak, which when held out resembled a spreading pair of black wings. Beneath them, he was naked, his body glowing like marble, hairless and perfect. I sank to my knees beside one of the concealing columns. Never had I seen such beauty.

Behind them all, the great stone face seemed to become illumined from within. If that was the face of Shemyaza, most feared and revered of the Fallen Ones, it appeared he was signalling approval. I put my fingers over my lips to prevent any sounds coming out unexpectedly.

Great Uncle Gerhard had begun to chant in the ancient tongue, of which I knew very few words. But what I did pick up discomforted me sorely. It seemed he was speaking the words of a marriage ceremony, significantly changed from the usual form. Was he marrying Othman to Bayard? It was bizarre. Should Othman have desired such a match, it could have been conducted at a family gathering, indeed *should* have done. Also, I had never witnessed a marriage where one of the partners was lying comatose on the altar. How could Bayard possibly speak his responses?

It may seem strange that I did not realise at once that something sinister was afoot. I suppose I was influenced by the fact that Letitia was present, for I could not believe that she would be part of anything illicit or underhand. But ignorant as I was, I knew that what took place next could only be termed outside a traditional marriage rite.

Gerhard sprinkled Bayard's prone body with heavy white powder, which I took to be salt. Then, after uttering a few more incomprehensible words, he summoned Othman with one hand.

'He is ready.'

Othman walked up to the altar, while behind him, Letitia uttered a terrifying shriek. The sound of it sent me reeling back into the shadows with shock, my hands over my ears. How she could have created such a racket from her elegant throat I could not imagine. When I dared to peer around the column once more, I was greeted with a less than pleasant sight. Othman was standing against the altar, quite brutally sodomising my nephew, while Gerhard and Letitia shouted out strange, guttural words. They beat at the air with their clenched fists. I could feel a hideous presence forming within the temple, like a great, but invisible, black shadow. I could smell it; the stench of carrion. Yet at the same time, the sight of Othman's pale pumping buttocks was quite arousing. I was disgusted with myself. I knew I should leave the place. Whatever was occurring was horrible and corrupt. They were using the energy of Othman's act to conjure something. I didn't know what, but I did know I didn't want to be there to see it manifest.

I would have left the temple there and then, but a small, pathetic sound arrested my flight. Bayard moaned. It was a sound of such despair and pain, I knew I could not abandon him. I saw his head turn slowly from side to side, then his eyes opened. He seemed to look directly at me, and his expression was that of utter terror. Above them all, a swirling mass of dark matter slowly pulsed into being. It extended shadowy tendrils down towards the pale body of my nephew. He began to shriek in small, pitiful gasps. Othman was howling now and Letitia spun around on the spot, tearing at her hair. She uttered guttural obscenities. Uncle Gerhard's eyes were glazed. He was still, but for his right hand with which he was masturbating furiously.

Unconsciously, I had emerged from my position of concealment, so that I stood a few steps out of the shadows. Bayard saw me and screamed my name. The entity above him bunched and condensed, as if in preparation to lunge down upon him. It was too much. I emitted a howl of rage and ran across the temple. I leapt up the steps to the altar and beat at Othman with my fists. I clawed at his hair and pulled at his arms. He turned on me with a hiss and his blue eyes seemed to be on fire. I fell backwards, but in the act of defending himself, he left Bayard free to throw himself from the altar.

To this day, I cannot clearly recall what happened next. There was a sound of thunder, as of the earth splitting in two. A great crack of white light struck down and then all was in darkness. I came to my senses, huddled upon the floor. When I looked up, I could see Letitia dimly. She was hunched over, sobbing in a low, desperate manner. Bayard was crouched some feet away from me. He looked at me in complete bewilderment. Othman was like a marble statue, still upright, but with his head bowed towards his chest. 'The gate is closed,' he said. 'Still closed to me.'

All that remained of Uncle Gerhard was a dark, sooty stain on the floor.

There are two factions to my family. I'm not sure which one I'd rather belong to, but because of my curiosity, I've found myself in the position where I've been adopted by more *exotic* branch.

The rest of the family accepted without question Letitia's explanation of how Great Uncle Gerhard was called away unexpectedly. Othman left our premises by daybreak, and the implication was that he'd accompanied Gerhard on his business.

Bayard, though unharmed in body, seems like a stranger to me. He hardly speaks to anyone now.

I am surprised how ignorant I was in the past, how I never suspected that Gerhard's spouses and absent children were anything other than faithful adherents of conservative Grigori tradition. How blind I was. Kerubim came and killed my Great Uncle's husbands. Killed them in our own garden, under the noses of all my innocent relatives within the house. I still don't know exactly what the husbands were doing out there with the bonfire, and in all honestly I have little desire to know. I shall live my life, venture abroad on my travels, in possession of Gerhard and Letitia's secret. I might never act upon it, but then again, in the future, who can tell how circumstances might change, and whether I might desire to utilise some of this knowledge I have inherited. The tendency is in my blood; I am heir to it.

Spinning for Gold

In the land of Cos, many years ago, an important master miller lived beside a deep-flowing river. Widowed when his two children were very young, he had acquired along with his wealth a tendency to drink and gamble rather more than was advisable. So much so that quite often, his son, Jadrin and his daughter, Amberina, would lie trembling in their beds at night, waiting for the drunken homecoming of their father, for it was not unknown for him to behave irrationally under the influence of liquor. Sometimes, frenzied at not being able to find the whereabouts of his pipe or tobacco pouch, he would attack the furniture and even any household pets or servants who were too slow to move from his path. Having said that, however, he was not on the whole a cruel father. To be fair, his faults were merely the children of his grief, which had never healed completely, and in the faces of his son and daughter, he could often see the eyes of his dead, beautiful wife looking back at him; he loved the children passionately. Because of this, Amberina and Jadrin led a sheltered, luxurious life, which in creatures of weaker character would have led to them being altogether spoiled and petulant. Amberina and Jadrin, however, were gentle, kindly souls, without jealousy or any other evil temperament. Quite content in each other's company, the siblings spent most of their time in the great forest on the east side of the River Fleercut, or else scampering over the rolling, bosomy hills to the west, beyond which lay Ashbrilim, the city of the king; a place where they had never ventured.

Alike as twins, even though two years separated their births, they had both inherited their mother's dark, midnight hair and lustrous eyes. Visitors to the mill-house commented on their beauty to their father, although those of more sensitive nature could sometimes not easily repress an eerie shudder whilst looking into those fathomless eyes and forest-wise faces. Friends of the miller might comment to each other, over mugs of ale, in taverns far from the mill-house, that all was not right with the miller's children.

'They spend too much time out in the moonlight,' one might say, as if to explain their white, white skin.

'And too much time in the forest.' another might add, as if to explain their mossy hair and shadowed smiles.

Sometimes, in an attempt to bring Amberina and Jadrin out into the real world, some well-intentioned neighbour might send their own children to encourage the miller's progeny to enjoy more natural childish pastimes, but the other children always went home fearful and anxious. If their parents should question them, wondering if the miller's children had deliberately frightened them, they would always answer no. Amberina and Jadrin, though strangely distant, were always polite and friendly to visitors, leading them into the forest glades and weaving their hair with flowers. No, it was not fear exactly. The children could never explain exactly what it was that made sleep come with difficulty for several nights after a visit to the mill.

It was early Summer and Jadrin had just celebrated his sixteenth birthday. Soon Amberina would be fourteen years old. Their birthdays were very close together, both born under the sign of the moon and the water. After a large and cheerful tea-time, enjoyed only with the servants (as the miller had been gone to the city for some days,) the two youngsters went hand in hand down to the reedy edge of the river, some yards south of the tall, lichened mill-house, where the stream widened into a deep, dark pool overhung with waving willows. They knelt down in the soft, damp earth and gazed into the water, not yet brilliant with the reflection of stars, but lazily roiling, dark as if with unspoken secrets. Jadrin sighed and leaned out over the pool. Amberina moved quickly to untie his hair from the black ribbon at the back of his neck, so that the raven waves, like water itself, fell to kiss the surface of the pool, floating out like weed into the dusk.

'I feel a strange heaviness about me,' Jadrin murmured in a soft, sad voice.

'It is only your own hair floating in the stream,' Amberina answered, mischievously.

'No,' her brother replied, looking up and turning to face the hills behind which the sun was still sinking in a blaze of rich colours. 'It comes from that way, I think.' He pointed.

'Then it is probably just our father coming home from Ashbrilim,' Amberina said. 'Perhaps he will be drunk again and have lost all the money he earned in the city.'

They both looked at the huge, solid walls of the mill-house rising from the river up-stream, as if fearful it might crumble to dust in an instant. Jadrin sighed again.

'No, I don't think it is that either.'

'You are growing old, my brother!' Amberina sang and jumped up to dance in the pale owl-light, looking almost like the ghost of her mother; all floating white linen and midnight hair.

Jadrin smiled at her wistfully, but he could not share her joy. He gazed deep into the trees across the river, but could find no comfort in them either. After a moment, he stood up. 'I think I shall go back to the house,' he said.

His sister looked surprised. She held out her hand. 'Won't you come to the deepest, darkest glade with me?' she asked. 'The white deer gather there tonight. Perhaps they shall speak our fortunes.'

Jadrin could not tell his sister that he was no longer sure he wanted to hear his fortune, although it had been their custom to go to this place every year on his birthday. Once the deer had intimated where to find an egg-shaped quartz of power under the bank of the river. Sometimes, when the children gazed into it, they could see the lights of the city glowing within, the tall towers of Ashbrilim and the white road that led to it.

Now Jadrin shook his head and put up his hand in negation. 'I have to think,' he said and walked away from Amberina, soon lost in the half-light.

As Jadrin was climbing the bank up to the house, it happened that his father's valet, Tufkin, came down the path towards him. 'Be quick, master Jadrin,' he said, 'your father has sent me to find you.'

'Is all well at the house?' Jadrin enquired, noting the servant's worried mien. Perhaps Amberina hadn't been far from the truth in her conjecture about their father's financial affairs.

'The house still stands, aye!' Tufkin replied drily, jerking his head at the thick, grey walls. 'Come along.' Jadrin followed him.

If Jadrin supposed to find his father still reeling, red-eyed from the effects of last night's drinking, he was wrong. Skimblaze the miller stood sober and erect, leaning against the stout wooden table in the kitchen of the mill-house. Jadrin noticed immediately the suppression of a cunning glance steal across his father's face. All was not well. He waited for Skimblaze to speak.

The miller made several anguished noises, before turning his back on his son and saying, 'The time has come, Jadrin, for you to go to the city!'

Cool as mint, the boy replied, 'The time has come? I had no idea it would ever be due!'

'Come, come, you are nearly a man, Jadrin. What kind of education is it for you paddling about in the river and having only a little girl for a companion?'

'But why haven't you told me of this before?' Jadrin sat down. In his heart, he could feel a shred of guilt, a shred of deception winging its way about the room like a baleful spirit. He had no desire at all to leave the riverside, the forest, or his sister, his only friend.

Skimblaze cleared his throat. 'You need to learn more about life, my lad. One day all this will be passed onto you and I want to give it to a whole person, not some half-fairy changeling! You need your feet bringing down to earth!'

'You can't make me go!' Jadrin cried. He had never spoken out against his father before. 'I will hate it!'

'You're going, my boy! You're going! Tomorrow, and that's an end to it!'

'Tomorrow?' Jadrin murmured in bewilderment. 'Is Amberina to accompany me?' He asked this without much hope.

Skimblaze cast a quick, furtive glance over his shoulder. 'No. Amberina is too young. Come now, don't give me that face. You will learn to enjoy it. All travel is good for the soul. Run along now, you'd better start packing your things.' Skimblaze faced the window once more, looking out at the gently sloping bank. Perhaps he could see a faint suggestion of his lovely daughter down there, dancing lightly through the dusk, her mind far from cities and partings. Still Skimblaze could not fully face his son.

'Where am I to go?' the boy asked, in a small, husky voice.

'To the court. I've secured a place for you there. You're from a good family. Do you think I'd let you go if it was to anywhere else?'

'Have you been arranging this these last few days?'

There was a moment's silence. 'Yes,' Skimblaze said.

Jadrin climbed the curling, creaking stairs to the room he called his own. At the summit of the house, it had the smallest windows, all of ruby glass. It also felt near to the heart of the mill. Lying in bed at night, Jadrin could sense the great wooden machinery, turning, turning. The wall nearest to it, where he kept his bed, was always warm. Jadrin opened the window and gazed mournfully out over his beloved countryside. Half-heartedly, he threw a few belongings into a bag and then sat down on his bed, head in hands. He had no idea why his father should suddenly force such a thing on him, but he couldn't help suspecting the reason behind it might be connected with his father's weaknesses for good liquor and gambling for high stakes. He felt uncharitable thinking that, but the idea would not leave him. Jadrin shuddered. Inexperienced he was, and young, but as he watched the rising moon appear in the velvet sky beyond his window, as the wood cooled and creaked in the late evening, you could see, by looking at his eyes, that Jadrin would not be totally helpless out there in the unknown world.

In the morning, accompanied by Tufkin, Jadrin bid a mournful farewell to Amberina. As he leaned down from his horse, she placed a garland of woodland flowers about his neck, and offered him a velvet bag. 'Here is half of the quartz we found,' said she. 'I have the other. Guard it well, my brother, for it may help you in the world.'

Jadrin smiled and kissed the top of her dark head, already feeling a hundred years older than she. Then he lifted his horse's head with a swift command and glanced coldly at the mill-house door before cantering quickly off towards the west, Tufkin behind him.

In the doorway, Skimblaze drained the glass he held, grimaced, went back into the house and slammed the door behind him.

Amberina looked in at the kitchen window 'Why are you doing this father?' she asked.

Skimblaze sat upright in his chair, reached across the table for another mug of wine. 'You have magic, both of you,' he said, as if in explanation. 'Skills beyond the mortal man. I'm right. I know I'm right...'

Amberina shut the window without another word and went down to the river-pool. In the still, morning water, she could see an image of Jadrin riding towards Ashbrilim, his head held high like a prince.

The palace of the king stood upon a high hill at the heart of Ashbrilim. Jadrin and Tufkin rode right up to the palace gate, which were six times the height of a man, where Tufkin presented the letter he carried from Skimblaze. Eyeing Jadrin stonily, the guards let them pass through.

Rarely having left his country home, Jadrin was amazed by the sights he beheld. Such opulence! The noise overwhelmed him, the bustle, the smells. He caught sight of willowy figures in splendid clothes leaning over balconies above the yard they crossed. One or two fingers pointed; he heard a stifled laugh. It was late afternoon and the walls of all the courtyards were afire with blooming vines beginning to release their heady, evening scent into the air.

Tufkin paused to ask directions and dogs ran between the horses' legs as they found their way into the stable yard. Jadrin looked around, wide-eyed, studying all the day's-end tasks being completed in noisy joviality by the well-fed servants of the king.

A tall, gaunt man in dark, voluminous clothes ducked away from a forkful of yellow hay carelessly held aloft by a passing stable-boy, waving away the almost disrespectfully cheerful apology. Jadrin realised the gaunt man was heading in their direction.

'You are the miller's people?' the man asked and with a nod, Tufkin handed him Skimblaze's letter. The man smiled. 'Ah yes,' he said, looking up at Jadrin. 'Allow me to introduce myself. I am Galbion Floom, King Ashalan's secretary.'

Jadrin responded politely. He and Tufkin dismounted and their horses were led away to the stables.

'Now, boy, if you would follow me please,' Floom instructed, indicating the way with his hand.

Jadrin looked around. Tufkin was hanging back. 'Am I to go alone?' Jadrin asked.

'It is not my place to follow,' Tufkin replied edgily, stepping backwards. 'I'll just take a tankard of ale in the servants' quarters.'

Shrugging, Jadrin curled his hand more tightly around the velvet bag that hung from his neck on a cord, and followed the gaunt man through a dark doorway.

In silence they began to climb a winding staircase. They climbed and climbed. Soon, it seemed, the bustle of the courtyard was left far behind and they had entered a sleeping, ensorcelled place, deep in the core of the palace. Jadrin's guide did not speak. They walked down long, dusty corridors, silent, but lit by bars of golden evening sunlight, fighting its way through dusty glass. More stairs.

'Is it much farther sir?' Jadrin asked, wondering what desolate spot a miller's son (no matter how affluent) would be given in the palace of a king.

'No, my boy. We are here.'

Before them was an ancient, iron-studded door. Galbion Floom struggled with the heavy metal latch. No-one has come here for a while, Jadrin thought with a not altogether unpleasant thrill of dread.

Floom had managed to open the door and was now fastidiously wiping his hands on a large handkerchief. Without a word, Jadrin walked past him and into the room beyond. He dropped his bag onto the floor and dust lazily raised itself and eddied round his feet. He was in a high-ceilinged chamber, a gloomy place. What windows existed were narrow and far above Jadrin's head. Only a little of the evening sunlight came down onto the wooden floor, having to fight through shrouds of cobwebs and dust. 'Well!' Jadrin said, half amused, half aghast. In the shadows, he could see only a mean, narrow bed, a washstand and, of all things, a spinning-wheel. Whatever else the room might contain was hidden in the darkest corners, except for several neatly twined bales of straw, which had been placed just inside the door. Jadrin looked at these askance and said, 'Well!' again. Was this some kind of joke? Was he expected to bed down in straw like an animal?

'Am I to live here?' Jadrin asked, unable to hide the dismay from his voice.

'For the time being.'

Jadrin shook his head. Dismay gave way to anger. Surely he could not be treated like this. His father's animals lived in stables more comfortable and cleaner than this!

'And are all your guests accommodated in rooms of this type?' he couldn't help asking.

There was a moment's pause before Floom said, 'You do know why you are here, of course?'

Jadrin looked at him blankly. 'I don't believe I do!'

'You are Jadrin, the miller Skimblaze's son?'

'Yes.'

Floom stroked his chin. 'And you are, as he claimed, something of a... wonder worker?'

'What do you mean?'

'A magician,' the man said irritably. 'That was the term, I think.'

'Term? Magician? I think you'd better explain!' Jadrin, on the whole, was a stranger to anger. Now his indignation was tinged with fear. The gaunt man bowed, stiffly, smiling widely.

'Oh, forgive me!' he exclaimed. 'It was understood your father would have explained all this to you; the... er... circumstances of your being here.'

Jadrin remained silent, numb with the horror of betrayal.

'Obviously not,' Floom continued, with a sigh. He stepped over the threshold and pushed the door to a little. 'Several nights ago your father was involved in a... little wager. He played the King in a game of dice, making outrageous claims concerning his luck, which sadly for him, proved to be unfounded. The stakes were high, boy. King Ashalan does not play for trinkets. Debts were incurred and subsequently, agreements reached. Your father had lost everything, even the mill itself. But Ashalan is not a harsh man. They came to an arrangement between them. The agreement was that you should come to Ashbrilim to meet your father's debts.'

'He was drunk,' Jadrin said bitterly.

Floom shrugged. 'Wine had flowed, I believe. Don't look so forlorn, boy. I must say, the first thing your father said about you is true; you are one of the loveliest creatures on God's earth. The other, well, that remains to be seen doesn't it!'

'What do you mean?' Jadrin cried. 'What else did he say?'

'No idea at all, my lad?'

Jadrin shook his head fiercely, sick with fear at what his drunken father might have come out with.

'He thinks you can clear his debt for him. He says you have magical powers, so great, so potent, that you can even spin straw into gold!'

Jadrin could not stifle a surprised bark of laughter. 'What!'

'Use your magic, boy! Spin your father's way out of debt, as he claims you can. Spin this, all this, to gold!'

With a barely caustic grin, Galbion Floom gestured eloquently at the straw by their feet.

To spin straw into gold? Jadrin was left alone, the door firmly locked behind him. How could his father do this to him? he wondered with helpless dismay. Was this the education he had been promised? Did Skimblaze really think his son was the possessor of supernatural powers? No, Jadrin decided. He suspected that Skimblaze had merely sent him to the king, hoping (perhaps sure?) that Ashalan would be content with his beauty alone. Amberina had been spared, perhaps, because of the fact she was younger than her brother. Surely, all this business with the straw and the spinning-wheel was some dark joke on Ashalan's part, so that when Jadrin could not complete the task some other, more tangible, form of payment would be demanded? This much was obvious to Jadrin, who had little knowledge of the ways of men and their desires. The spinning-wheel stood in a diminishing pool of sunlight, its wheel gently rocking as if moved by an unseen hand. Jadrin put out his hand and touched it. He shook his head and sat down on the bed to wait.

Night fell. Nobody came to his door and silver fronds of moonlight came to replace those of the sinking sun, falling over the floor, over the skeletal form of the spinning-wheel, onto Jadrin's bed. The boy sighed, stood up and walked around the room. In a corner, he found bread and cheese laid upon a low table, next to a jug of red wine. He found a lamp and a tinderbox. Lighting the lamp, he took some wine and began to eat the bread and cheese. For comfort, he removed the quartz Amberina had given him from its bag and stared at the sharp lilac points of it, the hollow in its centre that shivered with the brightest threads. *Straw into gold indeed!* he thought. *No-one, nothing, can do that! Oh Amberina, if only you were here now!*

Dismally, he breathed on the stone, thinking of Amberina prancing, colt-like, beside the Fleercut; free as freedom itself. He felt so alone. Straw into gold...

A shadow fell over him. Something obscured the moonlight from the window, something that also caused the lamplight to flicker and dim. Jadrin looked up.

'Faithless boy! I can do that!' said a voice.

Jadrin squinted at the cobwebby ledge. A spirit was crouching there, almost featureless within a smoky veil. It hopped from the window ledge to the floor, leaving a trail of sparkling dust in the air behind it. Jadrin had seen spirits before. He was not afraid.

'You can spin straw into gold?' He indicated the forlorn-looking spinning wheel across the room.

'But of course... For a price.'

Jadrin inspected the quartz warily. Had his contemplation of it summoned the spirit? He knew the potential power of crystals. Obviously, this particular one possessed powers he and his sister had been unaware of. 'A price. Such as?'

The spirit cavorted around in front of him for a moment, emitting blushes of colour that made Jadrin's eyes ache. 'Something precious,' it said.

Jadrin held out the quartz. 'This is all I have.'

The spirit glowed pink. 'No! Something more precious that that!'

'Name it!'

'I want a kiss. A kiss from your warm, warm lips. A taste of life!' The spirit chittered and glowed and spun until the whole room was lit up like a firework display.

'Oh, is that all?' Jadrin replied guardedly. He was well aware of how the very life could be sucked from a person under the guise of a kiss.

'Just that. Nothing more. Oh, you think badly of me! You fear I will harm you! I won't! I won't!' The spirit's voice took on a sly tone. 'The king will ask for more, believe me!'

Jadrin considered for a moment, looking from the quartz to the wavering form of the spirit. He felt he had little to lose. 'Very well,' he said. 'Maybe, if you can do this thing, the king will be content with gold alone, and I can go home again. It will be a fine joke, in fact! Go ahead.'

'After you sleep,' the spirit said.

'As you wish.' Still suspicious, Jadrin went over to the narrow bed and lay down upon it. After a few moments, his eyes became heavy and sleep crept upon him, but not before it seemed, behind his closed lids, the whole room became radiant as if with the lustre of gold.

In the grey before the dawn, the spirit woke him up. Beyond its pale, gauzy body, Jadrin could see a glittering, unbelievable heap of coins piled upon the floor around the spinning-wheel. 'Now for my price,' said the spirit, in a low, chilling voice.

Jadrin offered up his mouth for the cold, cold touch of bodiless lips, dry as paper yet wet as grave-slime. He gasped, fighting for breath. In a moment, the spirit leapt, triumphant, into the air, whirled around a few times and vanished with a pop. Jadrin lay dazed upon the bed until the morning truly came.

First, it was Galbion Floom who looked in at the peephole of the door. Jadrin heard a gasp, then running footsteps. Soon, there was a babble beyond the door and it was thrown wide. Many brightly dressed people burst into the room, all talking at once. Jadrin sat up on the bed yawning. A tall young man with golden hair shouldered his way through the chattering crowd and stared, wide-eyed, at the heaps of gold. 'What is this?' he demanded.

'Look sire!' Floom spluttered. 'The scoundrel Skimblaze spoke the truth for once. The boy can spin straw into gold!'

Ashalan, king of Ashbrilim, reluctantly tore his gaze away from the shining heaps of coins and saw, for the first time, the shining thing upon the narrow bed, whose beauty of flesh easily eclipsed that of the treasure.

'Indeed he did!' the king agreed, but in a strange and guarded tone. He strode forward. 'Miller's son, I am most impressed by what I have seen. Surprised too, for I thought it was you yourself that Skimblaze had in mind to pay the debt he owed me. I did not, for one moment, really believe you could accomplish this magic.'

Jadrin thought, *And neither did I!* but considered it wiser to remain silent.

Ashalan eyed the gold once more. 'However,' he said. 'Beauty does not deceive me. Neither do I always trust the evidence of my own eyes. This may well be a fairy gold that turns to leaves within hours, or perhaps a single spell that you and your father have worked out between you. No, I must have more proof.' He strode to the door.

His cronies shrank back, allowing him to speak with his secretary.

'Bring more straw!' Ashalan ordered and left the room without a backward glance.

Jadrin was in despair. Now the lonely chamber was piled high with bursting bales of straw, the spinning-wheel nearly lost amongst it. All day, he sat on the bed with his chin in his hands, staring miserably at the straw. At nightfall, he took out the quartz from its bag, but without hope that he could be so fortunate twice. However, within an instant of his forming the thought, the spirit returned, once more nonchalant about the task in hand. 'And what price this time?' Jadrin enquired wearily.

'Well, that is simple. Merely this: to sleep in your arms,' it replied.

'Just that?' Jadrin asked.

'Just that,' the spirit answered.

By morning, the room was full of gold once more and Jadrin awoke feeling as drugged and chilled as if he'd spent the night under several feet of snow. He had not sensed the spirit beside him; neither did he see it leave.

To Jadrin, it seemed that Ashalan's greed was only whipped into further frenzy when he caught sight of the supposed fruits of the boy's night's work.

'Once more,' the king decided (without much consideration) 'One more night of this and, I promise you, you shall never see this room again. No more spinning! It is too incredible, this talent of yours. Tomorrow, I shall make you a gentleman of the court. You shall have apartments of your own within the palace, whatever you require...'

Jadrin thought he must already have produced ten times as much gold as Skimblaze could have owed the king. *No doubt he wants to keep me around to make further use of my magical abilities later on,* he thought cynically, for not once while he was speaking did Ashalan's eyes stray from the gold to Jadrin himself.

By dusk, hardly even able to find a space within the room in which to sit, Jadrin was desperate to call up the spirit again. Punctual, it materialised upon the window-sill as usual, preening its slim, glowing features with languid paws. 'Well, as you see,' Jadrin began, gesturing round the room, 'I begin to doubt whether you could ever spin enough gold to satisfy him!'

The spirit made a nonchalant gesture. 'Hmm. It would seem that way... Do you want to remain here at court, Jadrin?'

Jadrin shook his head. 'No, not really, but I can hardly go against the wishes of the king, can I?'

'Even after he has used you in this way?'

Jadrin paused for a moment to think. 'I have no choice. I doubt if my father would welcome me back if I ran away and where else could I go?'

'Oh, you are a foolish boy!' the spirit cried gaily, as if glad of the fact, hopping to the floor, dancing in the pale rays of the moon. 'And do you wish for me to spin?'

'If you will first tell me the price this time.'

For a moment, the shivery being glided from bale to bale, appearing to be seriously contemplating the matter. 'Mmm,' it murmured at length. 'I predict that, should I complete this task for you, the king will make you a celebrity of the court...'

'This much has been promised me, yes,' Jadrin interrupted, somewhat impatiently.

'After a while,' the spirit continued, unperturbed, 'Ashalan shall actually let himself see you. He is not a great lover of women. Perhaps this was why your father sent you here instead of your sister.'

'She is too young,' Jadrin said, wondering at the same time how the spirit knew so much of his circumstances.

The spirit shook its head. 'You are wrong. Where the lusts of the powerful are concerned, no creature is too young!'

Jadrin could sense in the spirit's words its great scorn of humankind, Ashalankind in particular.

'What is your price then ?' he asked irritably.

'The king will come to desire you,' it answered. 'I expect he will fight it for he is afraid of love and mistrusts beautiful things, but my price is that should do your best to encourage him and, when the time comes, submit to his desires. On the night that you go to his bed, you will allow me to enter your soul...'

'For what purpose?' Jadrin cried, aghast at all he had heard.

'That is not your concern.'

'But what will happen to me?'

'You will not be harmed. You will remember nothing. Agree now: yes or no? I can hear my brethren calling me from the starshine. I have little time to linger here!'

'One thing you must tell me,' Jadrin said quickly, half standing up. 'Do you intend to do the king harm?'

The spirit glowed a bright, aching white, intense as the heart of a star. 'And what do you care of that?' it asked.

Jadrin shrugged. 'I don't feel I can be part of a plot to harm anyone. It is wrong.'

The spirit spat out a stream of green sparks that made the air smell of sulphur. 'Jadrin, he will have you and use you, as he does with all whom he desires. You are nothing to him. He would kill you as soon as look at you if you displease him. My purpose is not your concern and you must put it from your mind. I dare say, when the time comes, you'll welcome what will happen. If you are afraid that I will kill him, then fear no more. I will not, but there are things that must be done and you will help me do them.'

Then the spinning-wheel began to turn, throwing off sparks of a hundred colours, like fireworks, and thundering like a galloping horse.

'Yes or no, miller's son?' asked the spirit. 'In the morning, if there is no more gold, you risk Ashalan taking your life to sate his monstrous greed. His moods change like clouds. He is mad and you are at risk.' The wheel spun and sang. 'Yes or no?'

Jadrin hung his head. His eyes felt hot with shame. 'Yes,' he said, and, looking up, added, 'Do it! Make the gold. I will do as you ask.'

In the morning, the great heavy door to the room was flung wide and golden coins spilled out around Ashalan's feet as he stood at the threshold. Golden light suffused his face, his long, braided hair and Jadrin, sitting on his bed, considered that there was a certain innocence playing around the king's features. *He is like a child presented with a new toy,* Jadrin thought.

'Boy, you are a true magician!' Ashalan exclaimed. He ordered that all the gold should be taken to his treasury, which lay deep beneath the palace. As for Jadrin, he was led bewildered into the sunlit courtyard where all the colourful ladies and gentlemen of the court cheered him and threw down petals to land on his hair and clothes. Jadrin held the piece of quartz tightly in its velvet bag and could not speak. He could only think of the bargain he had made and when it must come to fruition.

Jadrin was given rooms with marble floors where curtains of heavy silk fell to the floor before the windows, and beyond them, terraces of patterned tiles overlooked the gardens and lake. He was given servants of his own to tend him, who quietly awoke him in the morning and led him to a cool bathroom to douse his skin with fragrant water, spiced with cleansing herbs. A large bird with feathers the colour of green metal lived in a cage hanging from the ceiling of his living-room and sang to him in a lilting, almost human voice.

For the first week, Jadrin was utterly dazed by all this. The food his servants brought him was richer than anything he'd ever tasted but he could not eat. One mouthful of wine sent his senses reeling, so he lived for that time on iced mineral water flavoured with fruit juice, taking a small glass of warmed ewe's milk at bedtime. He did not leave his suite of rooms at all. However, this only served to aggravate the curiosity of the court so that Jadrin was visited daily by the arrogant and elegant, the softly-spoken and seductive, all seeking to court his favour, to add him to their list of satellites. Shining people with shining names who brought him presents, who squeezed his limbs with sharp fingers and calculating eyes, praising his talent and beauty. Of Ashalan and his immediate staff, Jadrin saw nothing. People spoke of the king, dropping his name to impress, speaking of the soirees and musical evenings in Ashalan's apartments to which only the most fashionable could hope for an invitation. Silent and in awe, Jadrin could only watch these tall, affected beings strut or lounge around his rooms, feeling that he could never hope to emulate their sophistication. It seemed to him that the spirit's price would never have to be paid. He would never be drawn into the elite, exclusive circle of King Ashalan's intimate companions.

Eventually, thinking Jadrin a true adept, several ladies of the court came to ask him whether he would weave spells for them. They spoke behind concealing hands of ineffable slimness and languor, complaining of lovesickness or being the victims of envy. Some gentlemen came also, begging Jadrin to scry their futures, worried about their incomes, their wives, lovers and rivals. But, if Jadrin knew magic at all, he knew only the magic of the earth, the water, the forest. The kinds of troubles his visitors spoke of meant little to him and he knew no spells to deal with them. However, willing to help in whatever way he could, Jadrin sat and listened, making soothing noises, and at the end of it, offered the only advice he knew. It was something that had always worked for him and which he considered ample medicine for any injured soul. He spoke of the quietness of the forest, where all mundane problems lose their sting, even their form.

'Go into the trees,' he said, 'And take off your finery. Crawl down amongst the great roots and smell the earth there. Lie down beside the forest pools. Forget the city, forget who you are and breathe in the freshness. In the peace that follows, the solution to your problems may come to you.'

The palace folk were usually somewhat taken aback by this advice, but those of them who were not too lazy to take heed of it, did as he told them. Unfortunately, the forest is a dangerous place for pampered souls who are not used to it; dangerous to the body and the mind. Of the ten people who sought Jadrin's advice, three came back to talk to him again, eager to share their enlightenment, five came back to the city angry and bedraggled, having experienced nothing except discomfort, and in one case a severe chill, whilst two, a particularly dizzy pair of ladies, never came back at all. It all caused rather a controversy.

Inevitably, because of this, Jadrin acquired a staunch following of supporters on the one hand and a bitterly venomous gang of opposers on the other. Rumours sprang up like fire. Jadrin was a necromancer. Jadrin was a devil. Jadrin was a saint. It could all have got ridiculously out of hand. Jadrin himself knew nothing of these rumours, locked as he was without friend or confidante in his rooms. Eventually, Ashalan himself was forced to investigate the matter.

Jadrin was summoned to the king's apartments. He went there dressed in black and bound up his hair so as to appear courtly and civilised. There was a painful, fearful beat in his chest as he followed Ashalan's servant into a small salon, where the king received visitors every morning. He sat down as he was bidden at the king's feet and Ashalan said to him, 'You must not do these things, boy.'

'Do what, sire?' Jadrin asked, in total innocence, confused as to how he'd misbehaved.

The king sighed thoughtfully. 'The people here are not like you, Jadrin. What is right for you can actually harm them because they do not have your strength. I know that some have sought your advice, and from what I have heard, the advice you gave them was straightforward enough, and little to do with magic, but they cannot understand it, you see. And what they cannot understand will never help them. What they desire is for you to speak a few words of mumbo-jumbo over a burning censer that will make everything right for them.'

'I cannot do that, sire,' Jadrin said, with lowered eyes and lowered voice.

The king leaned forward and lifted the boy's chin with his hands. 'I can see that,' he said gently.

Jadrin thought, *He is wiser than I imagined.* He smiled gratefully and, from that moment, victim of one of the most intense magicks known on Earth, Ashalan the king lost his heart to him.

'Let us speak together,' Ashalan said. 'I have troubles of my own. Is your advice to me to lie down naked in the wild forest? Shall I find myself there, perhaps?'

Jadrin detected a note of good-humoured mockery. 'I would have thought, my lord, that you would find yourself best in the presence of all your gold,' he said boldly.

The king laughed. 'Maybe!' he said. 'After all, gold can be trusted. Its beauty never fades, neither can it become fickle...'

'But it is cold,' Jadrin said.

'True,' Ashalan agreed, 'but at least it is an obvious cold and far less chilling than the coldness that may be hidden within a human frame.'

'Then go to the forest. Take your gold with you. All of it. Lie down there with all the shining cold treasures. Eventually, you shall die, but if gold is all that you desire from life, then at least you shall die happy.'

Ashalan still found this boldness amusing. 'I have heard that true magic is nothing but pure and naked truth,' he said. 'Your words convince me further. You are an artless child and yet a creature versed in wisdom. I think I shall seek your advice more often, boy!' Laughing, he called in his secretary and ordered that refreshment be brought to them, wine and sherbets. 'Tell me of the forest,' he said and Jadrin sat at his feet and told him.

'Your words must be saved for me alone,' Ashalan instructed, 'You do not have to advise any of the pampered hens around here anymore. That is my word and you must obey it.'

Wary in the soft but strengthening grip of a new feeling, Jadrin gave his word that he would.

Perhaps more subtle in the ways of love than those of accruing treasures, Ashalan courted Jadrin discretely. So discretely that the boy hardly even noticed it was happening. The occasional brush of fingers, the glances that lingered just a second too long; all of this the gentle but compelling language of desire.

Most days, Ashalan would summon Jadrin to his apartments in the late afternoon when they would sip cordials and speak together of many different things. Perhaps the king was surprised by Jadrin's lack of knowledge in so many subjects, perhaps delighted by his innocence.

Jadrin would listen, spellbound, as Ashalan spoke of far-flung corners of his kingdom. He learned about the Hell Mountains of Gash, those heartless crags inimical to humanity that smoked incessantly and vomited caustic showers of black ash. Reptiles with poisonous skin dwelt among the rocks, and basked in the steaming waters of the Lake of Insidious Sleep, whose toxic shores were forever wreathed in yellow fog. Jadrin, familiar only with the benign forests and hills of his childhood was thrilled to learn of these dangerous and exotic places. And there was more. Ashalan told him about the white waters of the Fleercut further north, a treacherous torrent far removed from the lazy, feminine flow that divided the fields of Cos. In the wilder places, naked barbarians lurked beneath the spray, leaping out onto unwary travellers along the banks. Then there were the secretive desert people of Mewt, who moved their black tents with the winds. They might sell a horse to you if the offer was right; fiery, temperamental beasts who were cousins of the winds themselves. But there was always the whisper of deviltry around those people, so only the foolhardy and reckless ever approached them.

Four evenings a week, Jadrin was dismissed at sundown, whilst on the other three Ashalan would bid Jadrin accompany him down to the Great Hall, where he would sit on a great, black marble throne. Dancers and musicians would come to entertain, sometimes gypsy fortune-tellers and most nights, gentlefolk would bow to seek an audience with the king himself.

Haughtily, Jadrin would sit at the king's feet, his dark hair curled and perfumed, his ears, his throat, hung with black jewels, his body adorned with splendid clothes of dark, rich colours, and he would think himself content. He was not exactly sure what his role was, for he did not like to ask, but it was easy to forget about the three days he had spent in the dismal, turret room and the deal he had made with a certain spiteful spirit. Ashalan was very kind to him, and gradually the boy came to realise that the king was not the greedy, lustful fool he had once thought him to be. He was a lonely, frightened man, surrounded by sycophantic idiots, half of whom probably conspired against him.

Slowly Ashalan began to trust the boy. 'You have brought a little peace to my life,' he said.

One evening, when the warmth of the day was being gently nudged east by a frivolous breeze, Jadrin and Ashalan walked together along the high tiled terrace that overlooked the gardens. Urns against the wall sprouted riotous haloes of yellow flowers, ivy swung in the breeze. It was an idyllic time marred only by the sound of revelry coming from the Main Hall below them, the high spiteful laughter of women, the responding drunken, male guffaws. Jadrin sensed Ashalan wince and he thought, *In some ways you are a very weak man,* and felt sorry for him.

'I do not think I was meant to be a king,' Ashalan said.

'Mmm,' Jadrin replied, non-committally.

They had come to the wide bowl of a fountain; the water was turned off. Ashalan sat down on the brim of the pool, shredding an ivy leaf he had picked along the way. 'I will tell you,' he said. 'My father died when I was too young to understand what power meant. He thought I would be fit to follow him. I was his only son after all. There was no-one else. For years he had been trying to groom me for the role. He had me instructed in hunting and fighting and reasoning. My brain was filled with the words of kings from great times; their heroic lifetimes filled me with dread. "You must have a wife," my father said. I did not want to marry. My father ignored my protests. He procured a young wife and a set of noble, upright young men as friends. It was not enough.'

Jadrin had never heard of the young wife before, neither was she in evidence about the court. He made a carefully worded enquiry. Ashalan sighed.

'Poor girl,' he said. 'It was no secret that she had harboured a kind of obsession for me for some time. We had virtually grown up together, for she was my second cousin. It was a liaison doomed to tragedy, I'm afraid.' He shook his head. 'I'm sorry Jadrin, but I have no wish to speak of it further.'

The king looked so forlorn that Jadrin went and put his arms around him, not caring whether it was a disrespectful thing to do or not. At that moment, he would have dearly loved to have taken Ashalan far from the palace, far from the city, back to the quiet mill-pool and the high, stone house; a place of dark and healing. It was the first time they had embraced.

'Jadrin, I love you,' Ashalan said, a whispered confession. Even as he savoured these words and wondered, in fact, what they meant to him, Jadrin felt the piece of quartz, still carried about his neck in its little bag, jump and grow quickly hot. The king bent to kiss him and he backed away, eyes wide.

Ashalan looked mortified. 'I have offended you. Forgive me,' he said.

Jadrin shook his head. 'No, no you haven't. It wasn't that.' His hand strayed to the pouch at his throat and he found that it was no longer warmer than usual; there was no hint of movement. Perhaps he had imagined it. Could the spirit have forgotten about their agreement? It seemed so long ago that it was made. He sat down beside the king, confused and perhaps a little afraid. He reached up with shy fingers to trace the smile on Ashalan's mouth, and then he kissed it, absorbed it, examining the rush of pleasure this new contact initiated. In its bag around his neck, the quartz remained still and cool. Jadrin sighed and smiled.

'What is it?' Ashalan asked him and the boy shook his head. 'Nothing. It is nothing.'

They continued their walk in silence, going down the sweeping, white steps at the end of the terrace and into the shadowed, rustling gardens. 'I am twenty-six years old,' Ashalan said, 'I am ten years older than you, Jadrin. Perhaps I am wrong to want to love you.'

'Go down to the forest,' Jadrin said lightly. 'Lie down naked in the damp leaves and perhaps the answer to your troubles shall come to you.'

Ashalan laughed sadly. 'You are oblique and rude. Only your loveliness allows you to get away with the things you say to people.'

'I am sixteen years old,' Jadrin replied. 'I am ten years younger than you, and perhaps it is wrong for me to want to love you, Ashalan, but in all frankness I do not care about what other people think is right. Most of them are fools whose behaviour would make a demon blush. Why should we consider their opinions?'

Ashalan smiled. He shrugged. Together, they returned to the palace.

Jadrin sat on a stool in the ante-chamber to the king's bedroom and combed out his hair. He could see himself shining like pearl and jet in the mirror before him. His flesh tingled with the presentiment of a delicious fear. His nervousness tasted like wine. Then, interrupting his private reverie, something cold touched his shoulder. It cast no reflection in the mirror before him. He gasped and turned round quickly on the stool. There, behind him, hovered the spirit from the turret room, malicious glee scrawled across its indistinct features. 'Now!' it hissed. 'Now! Let me in! Let me into your soul!'

Jadrin stood up. 'No!' he said, flinging out his arm. 'I will not! You must ask something else of me!'

'You gave your word!' shrieked the spirit angrily. Jadrin denied this vigorously.

'I was in no position to make such a bargain. Ashalan is not an evil man. I will not let you harm him. Tell me, what else do you want in payment?'

'Nothing!' the spirit spat petulantly. 'I will taunt you and haunt you until you do as I ask!'

'Then you will have to taunt me forever, for I never shall!'

269

'Hah!' the spirit snarled. 'That is where you are wrong, little boy, little, foolish boy. You have three days; that is all. At the end of that time, I am quite within my rights to force myself into your helpless, mortal brain and destroy you and the king together! We made an agreement, Jadrin, there is no going back now. You are bound by cosmic law!'

'And surely cosmic law is no friend of evil!'

The spirit pulsed with angry light. 'You are a child. You know nothing of evil.'

'Perhaps not much, but enough to know it when I see it. I am young, creature, I know that, but don't underestimate me. I know for a fact that it is always possible to wriggle out of situations like this, and I shall find the way, you can be sure of that.'

The spirit laughed. 'Brave words for a catamite, Jadrin! But I concede that you are right. You cast aspersions upon my character, but I shall prove my honesty and integrity by saving you the trouble. As you have guessed, there is a way to release yourself from our bargain and it is this. If, within three days, you can learn who and what I was on this earth, you can consider yourself free of our agreement. However, I think it extremely unlikely that you'll be able to do so. In my opinion, you are far too stupid!' It laughed again, a cruel and spiteful sound. 'See you in three days, my little friend!'

In a whirl of light, it disappeared, leaving only a trace of lingering laughter, an unpleasant smell and a cold spot in the room.

Jadrin sat down again, his heart thumping madly. He stared at himself in the mirror intently for some moments before coming to a decision. With tremorless hand, he picked up the brush once more and ran its bristles through his hair. By the time he rose and passed softly into the next room, the cold spot had gone completely.

In the morning, Jadrin awoke in Ashalan's arms, his body trembling to the echo of a hundred delightful pangs. The caress of mouth, the nip of teeth, the probings of tongue and fingers, and, above all, the invasion of spirit and body that is the most magical of all human activities if they could but know it. Jadrin knew. He said, 'Ashalan, I would like to visit my family,' and the king replied,

'Whatever you wish. I shall give you a white stallion to ride home upon, a retinue of six liveried guards, gifts for your kinfolk. Promise only that you will return to me.'

'Within three days, I promise.' Jadrin answered.

Once Jadrin could see the sparkle of the river in the distance, which signalled the proximity of his old home, he experienced a small, sad thrill. If only he could live here forever beside the tumbling water with the man he loved. That would be a life, showing Ashalan the mysteries of this beautiful land, benevolent mysteries that he felt the king had never experienced. However, Jadrin knew, that in becoming Ashalan's lover he had certainly bid farewell to his old life forever. Ashalan would probably never see the mill-house.

Amberina was waiting for her brother upon the road, half a mile from the house. 'I knew you were coming,' she said.

Jadrin dismounted and walked beside her, leading his horse.

'You have such fine clothes now,' Amberina said.

'Yes. I have brought you a gown of crimson linen sashed with gold rope.'

'Thank you, Jadrin! Are these men your servants?' Amberina gestured towards the six liveried riders following behind them at a respectful distance.

'Indeed they are. And do you see the girl riding behind them on the grey pony? She is Psydre, the daughter of a witch from a far land. She was bored of life at court, so I have brought her to be your companion.'

'Thank you, my brother.'

'She carries a small chest of jewels to adorn your throat and wrists.'

'You are too generous Jadrin.'

Amberina narrowed her eyes and looked at him slyly. 'If only you had not had to leave such a large part of yourself in the city!'

Jadrin glanced at her sharply, but her eyes were twinkling with merriment. 'I am glad to see you so happy,' she said.

'My happiness is not yet complete,' Jadrin replied. 'I think I may need your help, Amberina.'

'Ah,' said she.

Jadrin had brought gifts for all the household. Excitedly, they gathered around him in the large, warm kitchen of the mill, crying out in pleasure as the rich colours of silks and jewels spilled out over the table. Psydre, a gregarious creature, danced around the room, flinging the shining bolts of cloth around the servants' shoulders. Within minutes, they had taken her to their hearts.

Jadrin beckoned his father aside. 'This is for you,' he said, and took from his jacket a jewelled, white-gold pin, which had been found deep beneath the ground and was far more valuable than all the rest put together.

Skimblaze looked at it thoughtfully as it lay in his son's outstretched palm. 'No,' he said. 'I cannot take it, Jadrin. I virtually sold you, my only son and the first-born of she whom I loved above all things, to pay off the miserable debts of my weakness! You owe me nothing but scorn.'

'On the contrary,' Jadrin replied smoothly. 'I owe you everything, father.'

Skimblaze smiled ruefully, but let Jadrin pin the jewel onto his jacket. 'And did you spin the gold?' he asked.

'In a fashion.'

'Oh, my son!' Skimblaze, unaware of all that had happened to Jadrin in Ashbrilim, drew him close, but one thing he was sure of, in his heart; the boy he held belonged now, wholly, to another man.

In the evening, Jadrin and Amberina stole away from the impromptu party that was raging in the house in celebration of Jadrin's visit. Neighbours had materialised from miles away to congratulate Jadrin on his good fortune. Now, brother and sister walked hand in hand down to the riverside, where the long shadows fished the water's surface and balls of flimsy flies hung, dancing, in the dusk. 'You seem taller,' Amberina mused aloud.

Jadrin did not answer. He lifted the velvet bag from around his neck and tipped out the quartz onto his palm.

'Ah yes,' Amberina said, 'I still have mine. Was it useful?'

Jadrin told her just how useful it had been, and also the situation he had got himself into because of it. 'Perhaps,' he said, 'if I'd refused the spirit's offer, Ashalan would have come to love me even though I couldn't spin straw into gold.'

'Do you really think so?' Amberina asked drily, in a voice far wiser than her years. Jadrin shrugged. He did not really know.

'Now, I have to learn the spirit's name, its identity, but how?'

'Perhaps in the forest...' Amberina gestured across the lazy water. Jadrin wrinkled his nose.

'That is why I have come home, I suppose.'

'There is a place in the forest,' Amberina said, 'where the spirits gather, they who will not leave this earth or who are held here by the cruelty of their souls and their love of carnal things. You must go to this place, all pathways lead there, to see what you can learn, but it will not be easy. They can smell a living heart from miles away and will scatter if they sense you or, worse, attempt to possess you.' She sighed. 'It's not much, but I don't know how to advise you other than that. Naturally, I will come with you if you want me to.'

Jadrin took one of her white hands and pressed it against his face. 'You are more help to me than you know but how we'll be able to conceal ourselves I just don't know. It seems hopeless.'

Amberina was just about to answer when they were disturbed by the unmistakeable sound of low chuckling coming from the bushes beside them. The branches shook and separated to reveal the slim form of Psydre, the witch's daughter. She stood up, still laughing and pulling twigs from her hair. Amberina and Jadrin drew closer together in surprise. 'There are ways and means to everything!' Psydre announced.

Jadrin bristled. 'Spying being one of them, I suppose?'

Psydre shook her dark, wild hair and smiled with her red, red mouth. 'I wasn't spying. I just overheard. Couldn't help it, although I must confess, I am surprised to learn that it wasn't you who spun the straw into gold. Does Ashalan know of this?'

Jadrin growled and Amberina laid her hand fearfully on his arm.

'Hush now,' Psydre said sweetly. 'I can help you.'

'You?' Amberina sounded sceptical. 'Why should you want to?'

'What a suspicious little thing you are!' Psydre exclaimed. 'I don't mean you harm. You can trust me.'

'As I did the spirit in the turret?' Jadrin reminded her.

273

Psydre waved his comment away with a careless hand. 'Poosht!' she said. 'Come on now, listen to what I say. I can help you and I do not lie. Your sister is right, Jadrin. You must find the desecrated shrine where the spirits congregate to emulate the ways of men. If you walk there in your flesh, you have no chance at all. No, you must leave it behind you.'

Jadrin laughed. 'Fine. I'll kill myself then to be able to spy on the spirits! Such action seems a little extreme.'

'Do you know nothing?' Psydre asked. 'I can help your soul leave your flesh and be able to come back to it as many times as you like. It's a simple art and one that is taught to all where I come from.'

Jadrin was still a little sceptical but Amberina confirmed Psydre's words by saying that she too had heard of such abilities. 'We have nothing to lose,' she said.

'You don't,' Jadrin replied, rather frostily, but he agreed to let Psydre help him.

Well-guarded are the arts of the witch-women of the east. Jadrin hardly knew what was happening to him other than Psydre's soft, compelling voice seemed to lure him into infinity. She made him lie down on the damp grass and stroked his limbs, murmuring in a sing-song voice until he was nearly asleep. Then the pull. For a second he seemed to hover between sleep and waking, before leaping up with a yelp as if tugged sharply to his feet. Psydre was smiling up at him.

'You see?' she said.

'Perfectly!' Jadrin replied. 'So what?'

'So look down at your feet, young magician.'

There on the grass lay the body of a pale young man, eyes closed, perfectly motionless. Jadrin recognised it as himself. He was free! His soul was really out of his body! Amberina was on hands and knees, stunned, squinting at the spectral form of her brother's soul whom only Psydre could see with any clarity. 'Go now, Jadrin, quickly, before the moon rises,' Psydre said. 'When you want to return, merely think it so and you will be back within your flesh.' She patted the ground beside her. 'Come, Amberina, and sit with me. Your brother must go alone. We shall have to keep each other company while I weave a protection around his body. After that, perhaps we can gaze into the pool together for some moments...'

Jadrin moved away from them, downstream, where he crossed the water and so ventured into the trees.

It was nearly morning by the time he came once more to the widest path that led out of the forest. Although he did not truly need to follow it, he was enjoying the freedom this astral movement afforded him. When the trees opened out upon the banks of the river, he thought himself back to flesh, and sat up as if waking from a dream, with stiff limbs and an aching back. Amberina and Psydre had returned to the house hours before, confident that Psydre's power was strong enough to protect the corporeal bits of Jadrin left beside the river. Above the trees, behind him, the sky was flushed with pale dawn. Jadrin walked to the mill-house and let himself inside. On the kitchen table, he found a bottle of wine which he took with him to the best parlour. Sprawled out in his father's favourite chair, he drained the bottle. By the time the servants were stirring, he was dozing, half drunk.

By mid-day, Amberina could contain her curiosity no more. She went to shake him awake. 'What happened in the forest?' she asked.

'I know the answer,' Jadrin said wearily, but it looked as if knowing it hadn't lightened his burden at all.

On the morning of the third day, Jadrin and the six liveried guards took their leave of the mill-house to return to the city. Jadrin said to his sister. 'Give me the other half of the quartz' and she did so. He kissed her goodbye, inclined his head to the silent Psydre and embraced his father fondly. They spoke vaguely of reciprocal visits in the near future.

In the afternoon, some miles from Ashbrilim, Jadrin bid his companions wait for him whilst he visited a cottage set some yards back from the road amongst a snuggle of gnarled trees. The guards raised eyebrows at each other and sniffed, although none of them spoke. It was well-known that the cottage was the home of a witch of less than savoury reputation. Jadrin stayed within for maybe ten minutes. When he emerged, he offered no explanation to the others, but urged that they should hurry towards the city.

On reaching the palace, without even pausing to refresh himself or brush the dust of travel from his clothes, Jadrin went straight to the king's apartments. He threw open the doors and five of the king's servants looked up in alarm. Ashalan was playing a game with counters and a chequered board with one of his courtiers. Jadrin said, 'Send them all away!' and from the darkness in the boy's face and voice, Ashalan did so.

'What has happened?' he asked, once they were alone.

'You must tell me the truth,' Jadrin said, quietly.

'What truth? What are you speaking of?'

'Of Angeline...'

At the mention of that name, Ashalan's face fell dramatically. He was silent. He turned away.

'I shall be truthful with you,' Jadrin said, 'and my truth is that I cannot spin straw into gold. Now I shall tell you who can...'

Calmly, omitting no detail, Jadrin told the king how he had gone into the forest on the previous evening. He had followed the winding, hidden paths until he had come to the white, stone shrine, all covered in creepers and moss. There, he had lurked among the ruins, waiting for the spirits to gather. Eventually, two wavery forms had come to sit upon the tumbled stones at the front of the shrine. They were wearing forms that approximated human appearances, though their faces were terrible and their hands merely sticks of bone. Presently, others drifted through the misty ferns, coming to pluck at their companions and chitter together as children do. Jadrin had moved from cover a little. He noticed some of the shades were inclined to hover apart from the rest. He wasn't that conspicuous. Eventually one of them had said, 'One of our company is seeking justice this moon!' and another had replied,

'Seek it? She shall have it dearest, have it, have it!'

Then another had murmured, 'Hush now, she is here.'

Jadrin could barely differentiate between one spirit and another, but there was something balefully familiar about the blade of light that had come dancing into the centre of the glade. It danced and sang and preened, cavorting with smug merriment.

'Are you happy, dear one?' cried the spirits.

'Indeed I am!'

'And why is that, beloved?'

'Because Ashalan is to die in the arms of his whore!'

'But why, lovely sister?'

'He has my blood on his hands, my sisters, my brothers, and I desire to live once more with his on mine!'

The spirits swayed towards her like a fog. 'And how shall you do that?' they asked together.

Here the spirit grew into a great and pulsing flame.

'Quite simply,' it replied. 'Tomorrow night, I shall possess the boy Jadrin. I shall possess his body and, through that, experience all that was denied me; the passion of the man I once loved. After that, my dears, Ashalan will experience the true, keen blade of my revenge. As he still penetrates the body that I possess, I shall take a knife and kill him! It will be very easy. Naturally, after such a terrible crime, Jadrin will have to flee the city, but then Jadrin, as he lives and breathes on this earth, shall be no more. He is too weak and no match for me! In Mewt, I think, I will discover a new and rewarding life...'

'But are you quite sure, my dear, that the boy Jadrin shall have no defence?' one of the other spirits asked.

The spirit glowed red. 'Quite sure!' it said. 'There is only one way he can defeat me but, as he will never know by whose shade he is to be possessed, there is no chance of his victory. Tomorrow night, Ashalan shall die and I shall live again! I who was once Angeline Hope De Vanceron! I who am the murdered, slaughtered, butchered, dead queen of Ashbrilim!'

Ashalan's expression of disbelief as he listened to this tale gradually changed to one of pale horror. At the end, he said, 'I did not kill her,' which Jadrin had expected and also dearly wanted to believe.

'Then tell me the truth,' he said. 'Who was this woman and why is she so bitterly seeking revenge from beyond the grave?'

Ashalan looked at the floor. It was clear he was considering memories best left forgotten. 'She was my wife,' he said.

Jadrin sat down beside him. 'Then how...?'

'I did try to dissuade her,' Ashalan butted in, slamming a clenched fist into his cupped palm. 'I told her marriage to me would be a barren, joyless venture, but she would not listen! She was obsessed! What could I do? She was a strong-willed creature and clearly intended to try and change my nature, even make me love her. A fruitless task!'

Ashalan told of how he and Angeline were married, to the delight of Ashalan's father and those who had previously considered Ashalan to be a weak and sickly creature. Surely the strong and tempestuous Angeline with her fiery beauty would fill him with life and strength?

Unfortunately, their relationship, which had started off badly, never came to anything. Ashalan found Angeline terrifying: a succubus of a creature, hungry and grasping. He knew his nature and refused to go anywhere near her bedchamber at night, never mind share it. This behaviour only served to stoke Angeline's pain and grief into a vicious rage. She tried to win Ashalan over, but eventually, exhausted by her efforts, resorted to extreme and desperate measures. A boy of whom Ashalan was particularly fond was found poisoned, his flesh black and burned. Ashalan knew who was responsible, but had no way of proving it.

Angeline stalked the battlements crying out her marriage vows, shrieking of fidelity and the painful fate awaiting those who discredited those vows. In numerous ways, Angeline sought to cause trouble for Ashalan, especially with his father, the king. She knew Ashalan had no desire to rule, so in some undiscovered way, persuaded the old king to abdicate in favour of his son. Then she was queen and for a while the power of that position put a binding over her wounds, but it did not last. Ashalan's original indifference towards Angeline developed over the years into an abiding aversion. He wished her dead a thousand times a day, longing only to be free of her obsessive vigilance, her troublemaking, her carping demands. What she saw in him, he could not fathom. He was powerless to end her pain. She would not listen to reasoned argument. She would tolerate no compromise.

One night, as she had done many times before, the queen followed Ashalan to the high tower on the north wall of Ashbrilim. She knew that Ashalan was friendly with a captain of the guard there, and through her spy network had discovered the two men had arranged to meet that night. Ironically, it was not a lovers' meeting. Ashalan and the captain were good friends, yes, and with similar tastes but had never been physically close. In fact, since the episode of the poisoning, Ashalan had not been close to anyone. Angeline did not believe this for an instant. She followed Ashalan up the winding, yellowstone steps to the battlements and concealed herself among the shadows of the buttressed wall. She must have watched them for a long time, perhaps becoming disappointed, for all they did was share a bottle of wine and talk together. However, as Ashalan got up to leave, he bent and kissed his friend on the cheek. That was enough evidence for Angeline. She waited until Ashalan had gone back to the palace before leaping out of hiding. All that the captain saw was a frenzied, shrieking shape, hidden by robes, rushing towards him, brandishing a long, curved knife. He rightly presumed it meant to murder him.

Angeline did not have much time to regret her reckless behaviour. She did not think about how the captain was one of Ashbrilim's best warriors, well trained in self-defence. She had no chance. He did not know who she was. Perhaps he thought she was a mad woman from the town. After a brief scuffle, he disarmed her, but still she would not give in, frenziedly tearing at his face with clawed hands, her face unrecognisable with the insanity of her rage. Afterwards, the captain said he could not recall exactly what happened, but during the struggle, Angeline fell or was pushed over the city wall.

She did not die at once. The captain, remorseful for using violence against a woman, no matter how crazed, ordered his men to look for her body. They found her still alive, crawling brokenly among the filth and offal of the city that was thrown regularly over the walls at that point. It was the rubbish that had arrested her fall somewhat, although both her legs were ruined. Because her face had been cut, they found her with rats clinging to her head, devouring even as she crawled along, head wagging to dislodge them. She was clearly a mad woman, some poor wild soul, tormented by demons. It was also clear that she was dying, beyond the help of any physician. The soldiers carried her back within the walls. They never expected anyone to claim her, but made her as comfortable as they could and sat with her, waiting for her to die. No one recognised the ruined figure as Angeline Hope De Vanceron. No one, until a priest passed the lodge and the soldiers called him in to bless the dying woman. The priest lifted her hand and there, on a ring, he recognised the symbol of the house of her parents, which the soldiers had not known. A frantic search was organised and it was discovered that the queen was missing from her rooms.

She died before they could carry her home, in discomfort and filth, halfway down the main road to the palace.

'The whole business was tragic and sordid,' Ashalan said, which Jadrin thought was rather an understatement. 'None of us had realised the depths of her feelings, nor how they had dragged her into insanity.'

Jadrin thought this was rather stupid. Angeline must have had these tendencies from the beginning and in Ashalan's position, he was sure he would have identified them.

Ashalan rubbed his face. 'My father tried to persuade me to have the captain executed, because, no matter what the reason, he had killed the Queen of Ashbrilim. Perhaps I should have ordered this execution. Perhaps it was my duty, but I couldn't. You see, in the depths of my heart, no matter how hard I tried, I couldn't feel grief for her death. Secretly, I felt I owed that captain a favour, not the death sentence. Do you see, Jadrin? Do you see how terrible a creature I am?'

'You were caught in a difficult situation,' Jadrin said carefully. He was unsure how he felt about these disclosures.

'Ultimately,' Ashalan said, 'I had the captain posted to the border of Cos, where he was out of harm's way. My father never understood me, or sympathised with me at all. He made sure I was punished for what had happened in small, subtle ways until the day he died.'

'Angeline's spirit must have been waiting for the chance to wreak its revenge,' Jadrin said, unwilling to comment on Ashalan's story. 'Unwittingly, I gave it that chance. I gave it power: my breath and my warmth. Oh, to live those few days again!'

'You sound bitter,' Ashalan said. 'I have disappointed you and it has killed our love. She has won.' He put his head in his hands.

Jadrin stared upon the king, caught in a maelstrom of conflicting feelings. In his view, the main tragedy of the story was that Angeline had obviously been very ill: no sane woman would have behaved and felt as she had done. No one had helped her. She had suffered alone, and for that Jadrin felt very sad. Still, despite the wretchedness of the story, he thought there was no excuse for the queen's spirit to continue her obsessive vendetta beyond the grave. He knew now at least that he was dealing with a mad ghost, and in some way, that gave him courage. 'Do not crumble, my lord,' he said in a cold voice. 'Angeline has not won yet. Perhaps you are to blame to some degree, but who among us acts always in complete wisdom? The fault is not entirely yours.'

Ashalan made an anguished sound. 'It is certainly my fault that she has this advantage over you. If I had been content after the first night of your spinning, this would never have happened. All she wanted of you then was a kiss. Oh, I was blind to the true gold that was in you all the time!' He put his head in his hands once more.

'Do not punish yourself with guilt any further,' Jadrin said. 'What is done, is done. Now leave me to resolve this matter, once and for all. I shall go to the bedroom. Wait here for an hour and then come after me, but no sooner, mind.'

Jadrin went alone to the king's bed chamber and drew all the drapes against the balmy evening. He lit pungent incense on a brass saucer and robed himself in white and let down his hair. From the velvet bag, he withdrew the two halves of the lilac quartz and laid them on a table next to the smoking incense. It lay like two halves of a broken egg, glowing inside, reflecting the light of the smouldering charcoal upon which burned the perfume. Jadrin sat down on the bed, calmed his mind and made a call. Within minutes, the spirit appeared at the window. It looked a little confused. 'Let me in Jadrin,' it said. After a pause, the boy arose and opened the window.

'It is time, Jadrin.'

'Indeed it is!'

'If only you'd had true magic eh?' it giggled.

'If only !' Jadrin agreed.

'Well, I must give you the chance, I suppose. Have you thought of my name?'

'I have pondered it deeply,' Jadrin said. 'Would it be... Grizelda?'

'No.'

'Nanune, Riboflax, Tanteberry, Archimund?'

'No, no, no!' The spirit flickered with delight. Jadrin patiently recited every name, both male and female, that he could think of. All the while, the spirit glittered and spat light and laughed.

'No,' it said, 'none of those. You have just one more try. Your time has run out.'

'Ah,' said Jadrin, 'in that case, would you, by any chance, be the shade of Angeline Hope De Vanceron, dead queen of Ashbrilim?'

At these words, the spirit shrieked wordlessly in horror, manifesting itself more definitely into the form of a gaunt, bedraggled woman, clothed in the rags of a shroud, with terrible, staring eyes. 'Sorcerer!' she shrieked.

'I am learning,' Jadrin said mildly. 'Be at peace, Angeline. You are free of flesh, so be free of pain. Why carry it with you? Fly!'

'Never! I must have my revenge, for my broken body, my broken spirit!'

'Broken long before you became queen,' Jadrin said. 'Be healed, Angeline. Fly!'

The spirit uttered a horrifying squawk and flew at Jadrin, spectral claws reaching for his face.

Jadrin stepped back swiftly and picked up the broken halves of the quartz. 'If the earth cannot contain you maybe stone can!' he said and, reciting a spell that the witch at the roadside had sold him, he issued an Irrefutable Order that the spirit of the dead queen could not ignore or fight. She was sucked like smoke into the quartz, whereupon Jadrin snapped the two halves together. They sealed in an instant as if they had never been apart. For a few moments, the quartz glowed as if it contained a small flame within its heart, but by the time Ashalan came through the door curtains, it lay innocent and cool upon the table.

The next morning, Jadrin took the quartz and buried it deep beneath the garden of the palace. Over its grave, he planted three creepers of ivy to bind it into the ground. He surrounded it with scented flowers, and called upon the spirits of the earth to heal the essence of Angeline. In time, he hoped, when all that was dark had left her tortured soul, she would seep through the stone as a radiant light and soar to the celestial realm. He could do no more. But whether his actions in this regard were successful or not, the spirit of Angeline never bothered him, or

Ashalan, again. But there is no doubt that what Jadrin did upon that night changed him forever. He took a little of Angeline's darkness into his being.

The Nothing Child

Jadrin, consort of the King of Cos, desired a son. He pondered long hours upon this vain hope, sitting among the dappled shadows on the palace terrace, pacing the marble stairs, watching the stars from pointed windows. Between them, it was impossible for two beings of masculine physical aspect to conceive life, but neither was Jadrin composed to commit some sordid infidelity with a woman. As for encouraging Ashalan to do so, this was beyond him, beyond the hot, possessive passion of his love. There seemed no solution to his problem, yet the yearning would not leave him. He watched the palace women with their children. Perhaps he could sate this uncontrollable and inexplicable longing by adopting somebody else's offspring? He considered this idea and then put it aside. No, it was a child of the flesh that he wanted. Nothing else would do. So obssessed was Jadrin with this desire that others came to notice a dark and poisonous aura about him, violet with the intensity of his feelings. It was mentioned to the king in careful terms. Was Jadrin perhaps not quite in the full flower of health?

Ashalan questioned him, at first tenderly, then sharply, fearing some other reason for the change in behaviour.

Jadrin was reluctant to speak his thoughts aloud; surely the king would think him mad. His excuses only fuelled Ashalan's suspicions. An argument ensued. Fleeing from hostile words, Jadrin ran blindly from the more inhabited areas of the palace. When his anger had left him and his breath, clutching furiously in his chest, forced him to pause and rest, he found himself amongst a clutter of abandoned buildings, far from the rich apartments he was used to. Curiosity at his surroundings chased the bitter words with Ashalan from his mind. Entranced, Jadrin began to explore. Some of the doorways had been boarded up, others left open to the elements, so that the winds had scoured the buildings barren. Naturally, it was the boarded entrances that interested him most. Especially that of a structure embellished with weathered, stone fetishes. Tearing the boards from their rusty nails, Jadrin forced an entrance into the building. All was dark inside, dark and silent. Jadrin's flesh prickled with excitement.

This, he thought, *this is a place trod by other than mortal feet.*

He was right. And, as in the tradition of magical tales, it was within that place he found a great, old book...

That evening, the court noticed a change in Jadrin. He seemed more like his old self. Not everyone present at dinner was gratified to see he and Ashalan seemed to have settled their differences, but on the whole, the atmosphere was one of relief. Jadrin smiled secretively into his purple wine.

Ashalan watched him carefully, mollified by Jadrin's apologies, but still wary. He had seen this strange and guarded smile on Jadrin's face before. It spoke of power, the kind of which Ashalan had only a cursory grasp. It made him feel as if he was sitting next to a total stranger, and someone not entirely human. It made him afraid.

Unbeknown to the king, on the night of the next full moon, Jadrin robed himself in black cloth and flowed like a vapour through the midnight gardens of the palace. He sought out a sylvan grotto, decorated with tumbled stones that had been designed to resemble an ancient temple, artfully strung with trailing arms of ivy and convolvulus. Pale, glowing blooms exuded a secret, aching perfume into the moist darkness and above the cracked and mossy stones of the garden, the moon swam, pregnant with light, in a smooth, velvet sky, sequinned with stars. Jadrin felt energy course through the fibres of his flesh. He stood upon the stones and raised his arms to the moon. The cloth fell from his back and he was an aloof and dignified courtier no longer, but a witch-boy, the creature of his childhood, he who had sung the water spirits from their gnat-gauzed homes: Jadrin, as white and deadly as the hottest of consuming flames.

He conjured forth a rare and capricious angel, whose hair burned the moss at his feet, whose eyes were pale as milk, as if blind. Jadrin had memorised an ancient invocation from the old book he had found. Some of the words made his teeth ache, some made his tongue stumble and become thick in his mouth, but he persisted. The angel swayed, sometimes fading a little as if to reprimand the boy when his words slipped.

'Lailahel, angel of the night, prince of conception, I implore you...'

'Implore me, nothing,' the spirit interrupted. 'You desire a child, yet you know this cannot be under the sway of the laws of the earth mother. You are male, Jadrin; your lover is male. There can be no issue from your union. This you know.'

'This I know!' Jadrin answered defiantly. 'Yet I have summoned you, Lailahel; your power can facilitate my need. You would not have come otherwise.'

The angel shimmered - a vagueness that could have signified amusement or displeasure. 'I have been called on pale, cold moon-nights by the fairest and most ill-favoured, youngest and oldest of women, yet never, in my experience, have I been summoned by a boy! Maybe I can ease your difficulties, but the Goddess will not be pleased. You risk needling her wrath.'

'My Prince, I work magic, thus do I understand I must take responsibility for my actions. Make it happen. The child will be consecrated to the Goddess as soon as it is named.'

'It will not be a normal child, Lord Jadrin.'

'What is? I ask only for its body to be fair, its face to be the mirror of the moon, its mind to be swift and canny as the hounds of the Maiden.'

'So few specifications?' The angel laughed; a sound both musical and sepulchral. 'Very well. I shall instruct you in what to do.'

Jadrin bowed deeply. 'I thank you, Lailahel.' He raised his head. 'So what is your price?'

The angel smiled. 'My price? By the Heavenly Spheres and all their Motes, dare I ask a price for such a boon? My price is this: nothing. I want nothing from you, Lord Jadrin.'

Jadrin frowned. 'Forgive me, but this is not the usual way.'

'Nevertheless, it is what I ask.'

'At least permit me to light a temple candle in your name and blend a sacred incense to be burned for the next three nights.'

The angel shrugged. 'If such fripperies appease you, then by no means let me prevent you from realising them. If I should ask for anything, I should ask for your silence, but, as I said, I ask for nothing.'

'You have my silence anyway. You may also have my blood, if you wish.'

The angel shook its radiant head, causing the cascade of hair to wave like weed under water. 'No need. I want nothing from you.'

Jadrin could not help but feel uneasy. He understood that there is always a price for everything and he had been fooled by sly spirits before. However, the intensity of his desire forced him to ignore any misgivings in his heart.

He knelt upon the stones and Lailahel, prince of conception, whispered instructions as to what he must do.

The moon fell to her rest and Jadrin hurried back, like a shadow, insubstantial and furtive, to the palace and his king.

On the night of the first crescent of the waxing moon, the Maiden's time, Jadrin bathed himself in salt water. Emerging, dripping and stinging, from the pool, he stood in the unlit bathroom of hollow echoes and slick water sounds, gazing towards the skylight, where hasty clouds muffled the stars. He closed his eyes and quickly, with a knife as sharp as a blade can be, cut the pale skin of his breast above the heart. Blood rilled eagerly over his fingers as he pressed the wound. Shaking, he knelt and lifted a silver chalice, catching a measure of the dark, warm liquid in the bowl. Inky, diluted streams ran down his body into his wet footprints. Perhaps he had cut too deep. He had not expected so much blood from a wound in that place. The air was still, watching. Magic, then. Magic. He hurried from the room, not even bothering to cover himself with a robe or towel. By the time he reached his dressing room, the wound had dried.

Ashalan slept on his back in the huge, canopied bed. Jadrin paused to regard him, filled as he always was with gratitude that such a magnificent creature could belong to him.

'Ashalan,' Jadrin called softly, a voice of the new, horned crown itself, 'look, my love, to the window, the moon.'

Ashalan stirred, woken more by the invisible reverberations of the unseen blood-harp than Jadrin's words. What he saw was the willow pale, willow slim form of the witch-boy, robed now in black, whose hair was an indigo smoke, whose eyes were black as the shadows of his hair.

'It is late, where have you been?' asked the King, who could not see the dark smear upon Jadrin's breast.

'Bathing,' Jadrin replied in a strange, distant voice. He stared for a moment at the sky beyond the window. When he turned his gaze once more upon Ashalan, the king was almost afraid. Almost. His heart beat faster and Jadrin slipped between the sheets, cold and salty, feverish and hungry.

If Ashalan thought it odd that his lover should whisper strange words throughout their pleasure, the heat of the moment put it from his mind. Not even when Jadrin speared himself on Ashalan's lap and screamed and screamed a hundred arcane words, his body arched and tense, his hands clawing air, did Ashalan suspect that anything was different from usual. He knew Jadrin to be a bizarre and magical creature and after three years of his acquaintance knew better than to anticipate his moods and caprices. Spent and exhausted, he fell quickly into a contented sleep, where his dreams were innocent.

Jadrin did not sleep. He waited, lying motionless on his back, until Ashalan's breathing proclaimed him unconscious. It took only a moment then to reach down for the knife that was concealed in his discarded robe. Ashalan murmured as Jadrin drew out his arm and winced as the sliver of steel licked into the soft flesh above the wrist, but he did not wake. Into the cup, to mingle with the caking ichor already within it, Ashalan's blood dripped down. One spot fell upon the sheet. Jadrin stilled his shaking hands. No mistakes in this - no. He carefully placed the chalice on the floor, away from the heavy, swaying curtains that moved in the early morning breeze. Morning was coming through the window; there was little time. Jadrin sealed the wound on Ashalan's arm with his own saliva. Into the dressing-room then, where a small, silver dish waited beside the mirror. Jadrin smeared the surface of the dish with Ashalan's seed that he held in his body, blended it with a powder of his own essence. Blood and seed, dried over a flame, laced with wine, thickened and perfumed by the gums of karaya, tragacanth and myrrh, blended with a little warm milk; this was the basis of Jadrin's elixir. Whatever else he cast into it, has not been recorded, but, by the time the sky outside was shedding its night robe for the pearl of dawning, Jadrin was slipping and darting down into the gardens once again, past the drowsing peacocks, the hanging terraces, the silent statues, to the rose garden. Here, in the yellow-rose light of dawn, he scrabbled with his bare fingers in the earth and buried the thing he had made, the blood-seed icon of desire, the egg of the dream-child. If anyone should have seen him working there, his hair and eyes all wild, they would have hidden themselves from his sight, for Jadrin in a frenzy of need was a fearsome and dangerous object to behold.

In the morning, Ashalan's servants were intrigued by the stripes of blood upon the bathroom floor, the bloody handprint upon the doorframe. Ashalan himself was somewhat disturbed to find he had cut himself in the night and that he had bled upon the sheets. Jadrin walked through the day in a daze, but there was evidence of a smile upon his face.

Months passed, the Wheel of Life turned, seasons changed. Every day, Jadrin strolled in the rose garden, trying not to peer at the rich soil in an obvious manner. He never quite stopped believing in the spell, but as time went on and the soil remained undisturbed, the daily visits became more of a habit than an eagerness. Other matters took precedence in his life.

In the east of the country, near the border of Candeleen, there lived a warrior king. His tribe was small, admittedly, but he had grand designs on the territory of Cos, and his swift, cunning warriors had become adept at worrying the skirts of the eastern duchies. Flustered and irritated, the dukes had approached Ashalan together, demanding that he employ Ashbrilim's forces to quell the nuisance. Therefore, in the late Summer, Ashalan led his army away from the city to do battle.

Jadrin stood with the court on the battlements of the highest tower and watched the shining, prancing steeds kick dust from the highway, carrying the jewels of Ashbrilim's manhood towards the east. Jadrin was not overly concerned about Ashalan's safety, having worked a number of protective spells to ensure it, but he had no way of knowing how long the king would be absent, and that caused him grief.

One crisp morning when the smell of Autumn surged across the palace gardens for the first time that year, the head gardener came hurrying to Jadrin's quarters himself, begging the servants for an interview.

'Go away,' Jadrin's valet said, haughtily, 'Lord Jadrin may not be disturbed by trifles. Take your business to the Chamberlain.'

'The Chamberlain be damned!' the gardener insisted. 'I wait here until Lord Jadrin comes himself; this matter is too grave for the ears of anyone else.'

Sniffing derisively, the valet retreated and was consequently surprised by Jadrin's animated reaction to the gardener's request.

Maybe it was the turning of the season, the crescent of the new moon, but Jadrin knew that, at last, his spell had borne fruit. The gardener told, with wonder and amazement, how one of his underlings had been passing through the rose garden that very morning. A strange, mewing sound had attracted the boy's attention and there, beneath the trained branches of the grandest bush, he had seen a pale-skinned baby writhing in the dirt.

'Bring the child to me,' Jadrin commanded and the gardener hurried away, to pluck the babe from the arms of the maids in the kitchen, where they were trying to tempt it with warmed milk.

Many grisly suppositions were whispered around the palace of how some cruel wench must have buried the child, perhaps because it was illegitimate. Perhaps she'd thought it dead. Wiser women pronounced the child a changeling, too pale, its eyes too knowing to be wholly human. Jadrin, keeping secret the occult origin of the baby, made it known that he intended to adopt it. 'The king and I shall never have an heir,' he said. 'Perhaps it is this babe's good fortune to be found upon our land.'

Some secretly questioned Jadrin's judgement in this respect while others praised his charity.

The priests said, 'Dedicate the child to the Goddess quickly. If it is evil perhaps the consecration will dispel all negative aspects. The boy must have a name.'

Jadrin merely shook his head. 'The ritual must not be performed until Ashalan returns,' he said. 'It would not be right to do otherwise, however pressing it might seem. Let the king himself choose a name for his adopted son.'

The most cynical members of the court wondered how Ashalan would greet the news that Jadrin had adopted a child found buried in the rose garden as the heir to the kingdom, but they complied with his wishes and kept their suppositions amongst themselves.

A year passed and still Ashalan had not returned from the east. The boy who had no name blossomed and filled out in the arms of his wet-nurse and beneath the dark, smoky gaze of his adopted parent. True, he did not seem an ordinary child. Occasionally, the women were frightened by the intensity, the ironic humour, of his gaze and yet, physically, he appeared normal if perhaps a little slight in build.

'Whose soul are you?' Jadrin asked the child and in response the tiny fingers would grip air, the petal mouth smile and sigh. He had no name, and the servants, his only company, jokingly referred to him as Nothing, because it was impossible for them not to address him in some way. 'Where is Nothing?'

'Asleep on the terrace.'

'Nothing never cries.'

'Nothing has the bright eyes of a bird - a very old bird!'

Jadrin watched his magical son grow and in his heart warmed the secret of his birth, forever silent.

Ashalan and his army had a hard time of it in the east. They had ridden out to battle light-hearted and confident, unprepared for the astute organisation of the warrior king and his tribe. It was like trying to dispel a mist; swords and lances were of very little use. Here and there the ragged warriors ran, under cover of cloud and branch; shadows themselves in the night, pricking Ashalan's soldiers as they slept, loosing their horses, spoiling their water, stealing their food. Morale slumped; it was a slow business driving the enemy back, though by sheer weight of numbers it was considered inevitable by all that, eventually, Cos would have to succeed and carry the banner of victory back to Ashbrilim.

One evening, as Ashalan and his elite guard returned to their camp through a thick forest, a storm came up from the south, suddenly and fiercely. Trees above them shook leaves and sharp twigs onto the heads and shoulders of the men, rain sluiced them cruelly, wind tore their sight from them. Ashalan's stallion took a fright, being more spirited than the rest, and plunged recklessly off the path, tearing madly through dense undergrowth. All

Ashalan could do was lean forward and close his eyes, trusting that the animal would quickly spend his strength and not fall. The frantic calls of his men faded behind him and he gave himself up to a nightmare of lashing branches and furious galloping. Eventually the horse burst from the trees on the banks of a raging torrent. The storm had passed but the river was swollen. On the other side, unbelievably, Ashalan could see the lamps of his camp twinkling through the dark. How could he reach it? His body ached, his clothes were torn, he was drenched and tired. As for the stallion, it was unlikely he retained enough strength to brave the fast-moving water. The camp glowed, welcoming and secure. Savoury smells of cooking meat and fresh bread drifted across to him. Ashalan tried to urge his horse forward, but he dug in his heels and wheeled about, making noises of distress.

'Either you cross the river, or we perish from cold and fatigue!' Ashalan said wearily.

The stallion would have none of it, which was more good sense than stubbornness.

Ashalan dismounted and stared miserably at the water, at the trunks of trees mashed carelessly in its foaming ribbons, the rocks that moved sluggishly downstream that had not moved for a hundred years. Human flesh would be shredded like old lace in that torrent. He sighed, hugging himself, preparing to spend the rest of the night out in the open. In the morning, he might be able to find his way back through the forest. Wistfully, Ashalan let his thoughts linger on Ashbrilim and the warm mystery of his beloved consort. Would he ever see them again.

'Why so glum, my lord?'

Ashalan turned quickly at the sound. Behind him stood a figure concealed in a hooded robe. He could not quite see the face.

'As you see, I am stranded. This damned beast took a flight through the forest. I lost my company and can't see how I can cross the river. There's no sign of a bridge.' It did occur to him that the stranger might be some creature of the warrior king, his enemy, and his hand strayed nervously to the pommel of his sword.

'No need for alarm,' the figure said, noticing his move. 'Allow me to assist you. I am a builder of bridges.'

Ashalan laughed. 'And can you build me a bridge before my fingers freeze off?'

The stranger did not laugh. 'My lord king, I can build you a bridge before you blink your eyes.'

'How did you know who I...' But Ashalan never finished the question. Even as he blinked, he beheld a shadowy shape spanning the foam, high and arched, that had not been there before. 'You are a magician, then,' he said.

The stranger shrugged. 'Of sorts. The bridge is yours, King of Ashbrilim. Why not cross it?'

Ashalan fixed the black, lustreless bridge with a narrow stare. Perhaps this man was an enemy and the bridge would dissolve to nothing when he was halfway across it, leaving him and his horse to drop helplessly into the furious swell beneath.

'Oh, do not doubt me,' said the stranger in a low, cajoling voice. 'I am no foeman of yours.'

'You are generous, my friend, but tell me the extent of your generosity. What payment do you require for this service?'

'Why nothing, king Ashalan,' the stranger replied. 'I want nothing from you. Let us just say that I have your interests at heart. What do you say to that?'

'If you want nothing then take nothing and I shall cross the bridge. I thank you sir.' Ashalan remounted his horse and with a further grateful wave to the stranger urged the animal into a canter across the sombre planks. Around them the pitchy wood groaned and creaked, below them the river tossed and snarled. Behind them, the river bank was empty and it was without incident that they crossed to the other side.

On a day of great celebration, Ashalan led his men home once more, along the wide, yellow highway from the east, to the great, gilded gates of Ashbrilim. The air was full of petals as the maidens of the city thronged the balconies, tossing handfuls of bright blooms into the air to be crushed beneath the feet of the snorting horses. Two long years had passed since the army had left the city. In the end, it had happened that the warrior king had been bought off rather than routed. Now everybody in the east seemed satisfied - at least on the surface. Ashbrilim gave the returning soldiers its best, shining with the last of the summer sun, giving off a heady aroma of shaded flowers and rubbed ferns.

Jadrin, with the elite of the court around him, waited on the steps of the palace, dressed in deepest blue that was the blue of midnight, with heavy, waxy blooms fixed in his hair. Behind him stood a woman holding the changeling child. Ashalan could have wept when he beheld his household. There was Jadrin, more lovely than he had remembered in his loneliest hour. There was Jadrin who came running down the steps, courtly aloofness forgotten, to reach up for his hands and say, 'My lord, you are home.' Ah, the homecoming was sweet.

Long and riotous was the feasting in the palace that day. Ashalan felt as if he was being swept along on an intoxicating wave of exotic perfume. His body was tired but it was carried high on the euphoria of his return. The fact that Jadrin carefully placed a young boy-child in his arms and, equally carefully, informed him that he now had an heir, seemed only another heady facet of the glorious day. He raised the child on high and laughed, and the court laughed with him, spilling wine onto the marble floor, singing his praises. 'You are home, my lord.' Yes.

In the evening Jadrin led Ashalan into the gardens, saying, 'The boy was found here, among the roses...'

'How cruel! He seems wise for his years, such knowing eyes...'

'Yes. We thought that too.' A silence fell. They sat upon the grass, beneath the boughs of a drooping salix tree.

Ashalan began to speak of some of his experiences in the east. When he came to the tale of the strange bridge-builder, Jadrin's gaze became more intense, his expression fixed and wondering. Ashalan laughed at the end of the telling but Jadrin was silent. He stood up, his back to the king, and stared hard into the trees behind them.

'What is it?' Ashalan asked.

Jadrin raised an impatient hand. 'I... don't know. Only this. I should have thought. I should have realised. It may not be important, I don't know.'

'What? What?'

'The child. I refused to have him named until you returned.'

'So? I don't understand what you're trying to say.'

'Don't you see... the servants, they call him "Nothing"! You promised nothing. Your son is nothing. Don't you see?'

Ashalan was quite stupefied by Jadrin's outburst. He uttered a small but nervous laugh. 'Jadrin, what you're saying is ridiculous! How could that stranger have known about your... adoption... when not even I knew myself!'

'There is more to it than you know, or could even guess.' Jadrin punched the air in frustration. 'Goddess, I should have realised!'

'This means nothing to me!' Ashalan said coldly. 'Perhaps you'd better explain.'

Jadrin opened his mouth to say, 'I can't' but a sudden and bitter wind swept the words from his lips. His hair blew across his eyes and he heard Ashalan swear in surprise. All the trees rustled furiously around them. The air smelt of acrid smoke and stale flowers. 'No,' Jadrin said.

'Such a welcome!' said a ringing hollow voice.

Ashalan turned to follow the direction of Jadrin's gaze and beheld the same cloaked figure who he had encountered on the banks of the river back east.

'Lord Jadrin,' the figure said in a silky voice, 'would you give me any less welcome than you gave the king when he returned? After all, I granted you your heart's desire.'

'Who is this?' Ashalan demanded, cold on the inside with a sick dread.

'Tell him, Jadrin,' said the angel.

'It is Lailahel, prince of conception,' Jadrin replied.

'I have come for my payment,' said the angel.

'You asked for none.'

'I asked for nothing.'

Jadrin sighed deeply. 'It is plain to me what you really want. You tricked me.'

Lailahel laughed. 'Nothing is a magical child, Jadrin. More my son than yours. Both of you promised him to me; you can't deny that. He does not belong with you and your kind.'

'Very well.' Jadrin took a deep breath. 'Tomorrow. Give us until tomorrow.'

'As the cock crows. No more.' And without further manifestation of any kind, the angel vanished.

Ashalan had no more than looked on in horrified disbelief; now he demanded an explanation. Feeling he no longer owed the angel anything, including silence, Jadrin told him the whole story.

At the end of it, he stood back, expecting Ashalan's rage, but the king merely shook his head and held out his arms. 'Beloved,' he said, 'you are a dreaming romantic boy.'

Jadrin's body stiffened in affront. 'I am no longer a boy and there was nothing romantic about what I did. When Lailahel returns tomorrow another child shall be in Nothing's place. Nothing shall be in the temple being consecrated to the Goddess!'

And so, long before dawn, Jadrin carried Nothing to the creamy-stoned temple. He roused the priests, who sleepily shuffled into the Hall of Naming and lit the candles and incense.

'Hurry,' Jadrin said, glancing through the windows. Only grey light showed outside.

They named the child Jadalan, for his parents, and crowned him with myrtle leaves. Surely no malefic entity could touch him now. Jadrin knelt before the altar and entreated the Goddess to protect the child. Perhaps he had done wrong in invoking the angel, but it had been done for love and without evil intent. Feeling reassured, Jadrin went back to the palace, leaving Jadalan in the care of the priests.

At dawn, the angel came to him in his sitting-room. Jadrin was holding a child on his knee, a happy, bonny creature. 'Then take him,' Jadrin said and held the child out, turning away as the angel's glowing fingers closed around the plump, pink body.

'You had your wish, Lord Jadrin,' Lailahel said, 'and several years' enjoyment of it too. Think yourself blessed that I concurred with your desires at all!'

'Forgive my ingratitude,' Jadrin replied curtly, 'but I can find no comfort in your words. Just take the child and go.'

Lailahel put the child onto his back and flew up through the ceiling, manifesting himself on another plane of existence. There was quite a journey ahead to the angel's palace of light, but travelling through the aether is an intense pleasure in itself and time means nothing there. Pausing to rest, Lailahel put the child down upon a glittering crystal rock.

'Well,' it said, 'Soon you will be a long, long way from the place you know as home. Do you wonder what your parents are doing now, little nothing child?'

'I know what,' the child said frankly. 'My mother will be feeding the hens behind the kitchens and my father will be putting new loaves into the oven.'

With a horrified howl, the angel realised that he had been tricked. Furiously, he cast the child back into the world of men, some yards from the city gates. 'Find your own way home!' it boomed. 'And tell Lord Jadrin I will be back at sunset!'

'It was a mistake,' Jadrin said mildly when Lailahel returned.

'Mistake? Don't try my patience. Don't try to tell me you don't know your own child, Lord Jadrin!' The angel glowered, emitting a poisonous aura of brown and livid red.

Jadrin shrugged. 'Nothing is very similar indeed to the baker's son. I was distraught at losing him, blind with grief. The child you want is playing with the dogs on the terrace. Take him, take him.'

'You should apologise for the inconvenience you have caused me,' said the angel in a peevish voice. 'Otherwise, I could cause all of your hair to fall dead upon the floor and really blind you, forever, grief or no grief.'

'I am mortified!' Jadrin clutched his throat, a picture of wounded innocence.

Lailahel experienced a pang of satisfaction that such a beautiful creature had formed the magical child he intended to abduct. 'Very well. Have no fears for the boy, Jadrin. He shall grow in power and magnificence far more than he could have done under your care.' And in a whirl of light, Lailahel, formless and spiralling, swept out of the window and across the terrace.

A black haired boy sat upon the chequered, marble tiles whispering to a pair of panting, grinning hounds. Light enfolded him, warm and strong as hands. Still giggling, the child was borne aloft, tossed onto the angel's back and away.

This time, they travelled overland; fields and forests passed beneath them as they rushed towards the sinking sun. Lailahel listened with pleasure to the delighted cries of the child as the world flashed by beneath them. However, a faint but persistent niggle of doubt caused him to sigh, 'You will soon be far from the world you know, little nothing child. Do you wonder what your parents are doing now?'

'That's easy!' responded the child, precociously, 'My father will be waiting on table in the king's apartments while my mother mends lace in the butler's parlour.'

Only the fact that he was prince of conception and thus, in some ways, a patron of children, prevented Lailahel from hurling the unfortunate boy to the ground and hurtling straight to Ashbrilim to raze the palace to the ground. He swallowed his fury and with a graceful curl, skimmed around and flew back the way he had come.

Jadrin and Ashalan, as the child had predicted, were indeed sitting down to enjoy their evening meal. The light had not yet vanished from the sky when all the long, arched windows of the dining-room burst asunder and the angel Lailahel gusted into the room. With frightening calm, he strode over to the table and placed the butler's child among the tureens of vegetables. 'Your servant may be missing this,' the angel said dryly.

Jadrin attempted to bluster some reply but the angel raised his hand and shook his head.

'I don't want to hear your excuses, Lord Jadrin. There is only one thing to be said and it is this. Unless the real child of your blood is brought to me immediately, I shall be forced to shake this magnificent and historic building to rubble and then curse you and your beloved king with a dreadful plague, which you shall unwittingly spread to all your subjects before dying a particularly painful and undignified death. I hope I've made my intentions clear.'

'I don't think there can be any doubt as to your determination,' Jadrin said in a choked voice. He turned to Ashalan. 'We have no choice. We will have to give up our son.'

'You should never have done this, Jadrin,' Ashalan said. He called for the butler. 'Your son is returned to you,' he said. 'Have no fear, we appreciate the service you did for us and you and your wife may keep the gold we gave you. Be thankful that events have turned out this way. Now, be so kind as to have your good woman bring out Prince Jadalan.'

With great sorrow, Jadrin handed his son to the angel, who smiled and said, 'In future, have the good sense to adopt some earthly child, Lord Jadrin. I believe there are plenty of them about. Good evening to you!' And with a spiral of blinding effulgence, he whisked the child onto his back and flew away, towards the red sky of the west.

As they streaked between the rosy clouds Lailahel felt to compelled to ask, 'What do you suppose your parents are doing now, little nothing child?'

Prince Jadalan curled his perfect little white fists in the angel's streaming hair and said, 'You know very well, Lord Lailahel. They will be grieving my loss and perhaps ordering somebody to sweep up the glass in their dining-room.'

Thus, with a deeply satisfied laugh, the angel looped and wheeled and disappeared from the world of men taking Jadalan the changeling child with him.

Living With the Angel

Lailahel, prince of conception, lived in a far and mystical realm, high above the souls and aspirations of mankind. His home was a wondrous palace, wrought of light and sound, where every room had a mysterious tale to tell and strange aethers roamed the tall, echoing corridors.

Jadalan, the abducted son of the King of Ashbrilim, was very impressed with this new home. Because he was only a child, because he was only half-human and because of the angel's potent power, the memory of his old life soon began to fade. Away went the vision of green fields stretching beyond the city walls. Away, the sight of rolling forests to the north, skirting the great purple mountains where the night eagles lived. Forgotten too, were the faces of Jadalan's parents; the witch-boy Jadrin and the king himself. Estranged from the lands of men, Jadalan became more angel than human.

Now, sometimes angels stretch and stretch so far that they release a portion of themselves into new reality. Lailahel had done this once and had formed for himself a son of his own - though son is not really the word for an angel child. As all angelic creatures, they are neither one gender nor the other, but something of both and sometimes nothing of either. Lailahel's child was named Variel. He was pleased to have a companion, especially one as strange and unethereal as Jadalan. Wherever Jadalan walked in the palace, things came into being as if he called them from the air. Variel could not do that and was delighted when Jadalan made him dogs and jewels and bizarre furniture. 'It was there all the time,' Jadalan would say.

'But no-one can make them real like you can,' Variel would reply.

They played together in the crystal fields beyond the palace, where ferns the size of houses swayed and sang to them. Jadalan learned all about the spirits that live beyond the senses of a human and how to call them up and speak with them. The air always smelled of jasmine in that place and at night the sky became a deep, rich purple, but there were no stars. Jadalan slept in a bed of sighing mist and ate from bowls of honeyed ambrosia whenever he was hungry. Lailahel, obviously genuinely fond of the boy, taught him many arcane things and would brush out his hair with the sparks that flowed from his fingers. Jadrin's childhood, therefore, was nothing other than idyllic, but Lailahel was careful to teach the boy about the dark side of existence; misery, loss, privation and pain. The angel knew that if the boy remained ignorant of these things he could only ever exist as a powerless half-creature. However, Jadalan's journeys through such experiences were always necessarily those of the mind and he would always wake up to the soothing light of his wondrous home and the cries of his nightmares would fade away to mere lessons in his head.

Nonetheless, he learned and grew to be a wise yet joyful sixteen year old, with more angel in him than he'd ever have had growing up in the gardens of Ashbrilim. As he grew in wisdom, so he grew in beauty and eventually because of the close proximity in which they existed, Jadalan and Variel fell in love. Neither of them particularly understood what they were feeling because they were very innocent and neither of them had any idea what the strange sensations in their bodies could mean or how they could be satisfied. Lailahel noticed their growing closeness with unease. He knew that if they discovered the pleasures of the flesh, they might want to leave and form their own astral palace. Lailahel would no longer have control of either of them. Caught up in a maelstrom of jealousy, that had more than one cause, Lailahel decided that Jadalan would have to leave the palace of light. Variel was of his essence; the angel could not bear to lose him.

One morning soon after this revelation, Lailahel said to Jadalan, 'You are nearly a man, or as close to a man as you can get, therefore the time of testing has come. You must undertake a series of tasks, which, if you fail them, will mean you'll have to return to the world of men.'

Jadalan looked horrified. In many ways, he had lived an idle life.

'It may sound hard,' Lailahel said, 'But believe me, it's for the best. Beyond the blue fields of the north, you will find a single stone sticking from the ground at the boundary of my lands. It is the last stone of the spire of a buried temple. By sundown tonight, you must have excavated that temple or else be cast out into the world of men, where you will be cold and the light may burn you.'

Miserably, Jadalan trudged down the blue fields until he saw the stone that Lailahel had spoken of. Using a spade which he'd manifested into being on the way, he tore at the crumbling, fragrant, crystalline soil, but as fast as he dug a hole the crystals fell back into it. The land was too dry, the spade too small. By the time Variel came down the field to bring him a lunch of ambrosia, Jadalan was in despair, clawing at the ground with his bare hands. 'Oh Variel, tonight I must leave here,' he cried. 'As fast as I try to dig up the temple, it is covered again. There's no hope.'

'Don't fret,' said Variel. 'Go over to that hill and lie down and rest. You'll get nowhere if you're tired. Perhaps I can think of a way to help you.'

Jadalan and Variel went to the hill and sat down together. Jadalan ate his dinner and then collapsed on the short, alien turf, exhausted by his work. As soon as he saw this, Variel got to his feet and went back to stand by the temple stone. He held out his arms and cried out to the sky,

'All ye beasts of field and stone,
All ye beasts of woodland throne,
Attend me now and dig this earth,
Bring the temple to rebirth.'

And in a great flash of blue light, strange creatures hastened out from the trees of glass and metal, burrowed up through the crystal soil and flowed round Variel's ankles like a sea of fur and spines and fluff. He directed them to their work and, by the time Jadalan stretched and yawned and sat up on the hill, in the valley there stood a magnificent, gleaming temple. Jadalan knew that Variel had done this for him and ran down the hill to take the angel's child in his arms. 'You have saved me,' he said and kissed Variel on the mouth. It was an impulsive gesture and one they had not thought to try before.

However, Variel was afraid of experimentation. 'We must return to the palace,' he said. 'Lailahel will be pleased that you have passed the first test.'

This, of course, was not altogether true. Lailahel suspected that Jadalan must have had some kind of outside help but it never crossed his mind that Variel might have had anything to do with it. 'You will find tomorrow's task just as simple, I'm sure,' he said silkily. 'To the west of the palace is a lake that is seven miles long and seven miles wide. Your next task is to drain it so that I may walk in the ruins of an ancient angelic city that used to stand there.'

Jadalan was again filled with alarm. At daybreak, after a mostly sleepless night, he set out for the great, still lake to the west of the palace. In the weird, morning light, it appeared as a polished, silver tray. Surely, some liquid other than water lay there. Jadalan went to the shore of the lake. White sand of fragrant resin crunched beneath his feet to release a pungent perfume that made his head ache. The lake was absolutely motionless - and vast. He sat down in the sand and rested his chin on his fists to stare helplessly out over the object of his task. He had no magic strong enough to deal with it. By tonight, he was sure, he would once again be treading the rough earth of the world of men, homeless and unwanted.

After a while, Variel came down to the lake, bearing a pitcher of milk for Jadalan's refreshment. 'As you can see, I've made very little progress in draining the lake,' Jadalan said scornfully and with a dismal, humourless laugh.

'Don't worry,' Variel replied. 'Drink this milk and lie down to rest on that bank of wild myrhh-moss over there. Perhaps I can think of some way to help you.'

Gratefully, Jadalan did as he was told. The milk made him sleepy and presently he fell asleep.

Then, Variel went to stand at the edge of the lake and raised his arms to the sky, calling out over the shining surface,

'Silver beasts of foam and wave,
Attend to me, my friend we'll save,
Drain the lake and drink it dry,
Reveal the city to the sky.'

Immediately, the calm, mirror surface of the lake began to stir. Fish of every shape and size swam up through fizzures in the lake-bed from other water-ways, underground rivers, and hidden oceans. Being angelic by nature they swallowed the liquid of the lake and took it with them back to their shadowy aquatic realms, far beneath the ground. And in its place, the ancient city stood revealed, purple weed clinging to its ragged spires, its proud avenues choked with silt and stones. Jadrin awoke and ran to the edge of what was now an enormous crater. 'Variel, how did you do it?' he exclaimed.

'It was done because it had to be done,' Variel replied. 'Let us return to the palace, so we may tell Lailahel.'

'If first I may kiss you again,' Jadalan said.

Variel looked surprised. 'Well, if you want to, then you may.'

Jadalan put his arms around the angel child, and thought about how slim he was, how fragile. He took a handful of Variel's silver hair and thought about how fine it was, how pure and fragrant. 'Variel, you are beautiful,' he said. 'I could never tire of looking at you.'

'Tire, maybe not. But Lailahel will lock me away if we don't return home. It is late.'

'Are you afraid of me in some way, Variel?'

'Perhaps I am. After all, you are an earthly creature.'

'Then maybe I should return to the place where I came from!' Jadalan cried, surprised at the pain those words inspired.

He ran away from Variel, up the swaying fields towards the palace. *I belong nowhere*, he thought. *I am neither man* nor angel. What am I? Is there anywhere I can truly belong?

Lailahel could not disguise his agitation when Jadalan summoned him to a western window of the palace and showed him the drained lake and the city that lay there instead.

'I would advise you to wait until the mud has dried before you attempt to walk the streets of that place,' Jadalan said, trying to be helpful. 'It looked very deep and smelled most unpleasant.'

'Don't presume to lecture me, boy!' Lailahel snapped. 'So you completed the task?'

Jadalan looked away. He found it very difficult to lie. 'The task is completed, yes,' he said.

At this, Lailahel gripped his arm with talonned fingers. 'You don't fool me! By the elements, you surely have the blood of Jadrin in your veins. A minx, a trickster, like him! Who helped you, boy? Who drained the lake for you?'

'I did it myself!' Jadalan cried, feeling his face grow hot.

Lailahel appeared to withdraw into an icy tranquillity. His temper sloughed away. 'Very well. Tomorrow, complete the last task or it's back to the earth for you! In the centre of my neighbour's garden is an image of the Tree of Life. I want you to climb it and bring me back a pearl from the crown you will find in a nest at the top of the tree.'

'Your neighbour's garden?' Jadalan repeated in a small voice.

'Just so,' replied the angel.

Jadalan went directly to his room, threw himself on the bed and wept. He knew that Lailahel's neighbour was a crusty demon of truculent and unreasonable nature, who guarded his land with basilisks and cockatrices, who devoured first and asked questions later. Even before he reached the Tree of Life, Jadalan knew his task was doomed. He realised that Lailahel really meant to kill him, and in a flash of insight saw the tasks for what they were. Lailahel had no intention of testing him, he could see that now. *He only wants to be rid of me,* Jadalan thought miserably. *It is because I am half human.*

There was no alternative but to leave the land of angels immediately and find his way to the world of men himself. Perhaps there, he could find a secluded corner in which to meditate on his woes until death took the hand of age and left him lifeless. The thought of solitude gave him some comfort. Lailahel had spoken of earth as a crude and uncomfortable place, but Jadalan now remembered the dreams he had once had of green fields and shady glades in creeping forests filled with the bright eyes of woodland beasts. Let the angels keep their stark, beautiful purity; he would go to the land of his fathers. Only the thought of leaving Variel caused any real pang in his breast.

As he packed his most treasured belongings, he kept seeing the huge violet eyes of the angel he loved. He saw the smile, the hair, the quickly moving hands. No matter! Hardening his heart, Jadalan crept from his bedroom and tiptoed down the misty corridors of the palace, out into the purple night, where moths the size of dinner plates flickered and glowed among the curling branches of a grove of maiden trees and the road shone white and hard towards the north.

Jadalan walked through the night, past the temple he'd been ordered to excavate, past the boundary of Lailahel's lands. As he walked, he found he was weeping and that his body was aching for a final embrace. But he was alone under a moonless sky and no-one heard him.

In the lilac morning, Variel awoke and hurried down to the gleaming terrace where he, Jadalan and Lailahel were accustomed to break their fast. Only Lailahel was seated at the table sipping a distillation of amber crystals and staring with unreadable expression out towards the mud-limned city where the silver lake had once stood.

'So where is Jadalan?' Variel asked. 'Have you set him another task?'

Lailahel turned a speculative eye towards his son. Maybe there was a note of sarcasm in Variel's voice that morning that was not usually present. 'As you ask - yes,' the angel replied stiffly.

'What is it this time?'

'What business is it of yours?'

Variel shrugged. 'Curiosity only.'

'Someone has been helping the boy, I'm sure of it. Therefore, I consider it more prudent to keep to myself what I've asked him to do this time.'

'Forgive me,' Variel said smoothly, 'but I fail to see why these tests are necessary. Hasn't Jadalan been as much of a son to you as I am?'

'A son to me, but what to you?' the angel raged suddenly.

Variel was taken aback. 'A brother,' he replied, 'what else. I'm very fond of Jadalan and it upsets him that you should test his loyalty or his suitability to remain here like you're doing.'

'Variel, you are blind! I should send you too to the world of men to learn a little common sense. Jadalan desires you. He will violate your mind and body if he remains here. Don't speak! Just think about my words. He will bring the crudity of humankind to our dreaming land. I won't have it.'

'What if he completes the tasks?' Variel said quickly before Lailahel could silence him.

The Angel of Conception stared long and narrowly at his son who, though small beneath his father's gaze, stared back bravely. 'If he completes the tasks?' Lailahel laughed. 'If he does that, he can have you. He can have you across my own dinner table if he likes! If he completes the task! Hah!'

And with that, Lailahel drained the rest of his amber liquor and swept back into the palace of light.

Variel sat trembling for a further pleat of light and shadow. Lailahel had left a lot of his rage behind, which lingered over the table like a pungent smoke. Variel was concerned for Jadalan, suspecting that this final task would be the hardest of all. He realised that Jadalan would have no hope of completing it without his help. Sighing, he rose and glided into the palace, gazing at the marvellous things that Jadalan had wrought for them. Climbing the white crystal stairs, he went to Jadalan's room, hardly daring to hope that he would be there, but perhaps to gain some clue as to where Lailahel might have sent him. The room felt very different to how it usually did. This was because Jadalan had left a fume of grief and despair in the air - alien aromas to the palace of light. It also felt very empty. Variel sat on the bed and absorbed the atmosphere. After a few minutes, he gave a short gasp and shot to his feet. A cursory search confirmed his fears; Jadalan had gone. He had not gone to complete the task either, but just to wander away and find some corner in which to grieve. All this, Variel gleaned from the air of the room, but one thing he could not grasp - what the task had been. He must know! If he could complete it himself then he could find Jadalan and bring him back. Hadn't Lailahel himself said that Jadalan could stay if the task were completed? Hadn't he? Almost in a panic, Variel ran from room to room, trying to glean some clue, some pervading atmosphere, some phantom word or sigh that could tell him what he needed to know. There was nothing. Eventually, he paused in the salon where Jadalan had told Lailahel the lake had been drained. Naturally, the angel had been prudent enough to clean the atmosphere in the place; he wanted to be sure there was no way anyone could discover Jadalan's final task, but he had forgotten one thing. On the far wall, almost obscured by a heavy curtain, hung a large, oval mirror. This was one of Jadalan's creations and Lailahel had admired it, which was why it now hung on the wall. Variel passed through the room like a ghost himself and he heard the mirror whispering as it revolved the images it had absorbed over the past few days in its cold, glass soul. Variel paused and stared at the bright surface. Only his own reflection stared back. 'Tell me,' he said. 'Is Jadalan in there? Is he?'

'Demon tree,' the mirror whispered. 'Crown of the tree. A pearl. A pearl...'

'Demon tree?'

'The tree of life. Its image.'

'A pearl from the crown? Is that what he asked for?' Variel could not believe his ears. Sabbalom, their neighbour, was notoriously solitary. It required aeons of negotiation even to secure a social visit, never mind permission to climb the image of the Tree that hung over his lawns. Variel was not sure whether even he could complete such a task. He sighed. Sure or not, it would have to be done. Why? He kept on staring into the mirror. He had lived for an age in this place before Jadalan came. Why risk danger just to keep him here? Couldn't life resume its old pattern now? Variel considered. He thought about the barren days that would ensue without Jadalan's bright company; the absence of his humour, the absence of his beauty. *I would rather travel the world of men myself to find him,* Variel thought. *My father's house is a wasteland without him.*

Thus a decision was made and without further hesitation, Variel transformed himself into a spiralling column of light-shot mist and whirled up and away towards the demon's garden.

Jadalan had come close to the edge of the angel's kingdom. Ahead of him, a golden gate hung in the sky, flanked by winged sentinels holding drawn swords. The gate was so vast that he felt he could touch it, but it was some leagues off yet. Jadalan put down his bag of meagre belongings and stared back up the road for a moment. He could no longer see any of the shining dwellings of the angels, only a strange, flat plain of sparkling stones. Here the dominion of Earth crept over the threshold and the magical stuff of angelic creation drew back its toes in distaste. Jadalan allowed himself to shed a few last tears of farewell. His vision was blurred by them, to the extent that it seemed a shimmering vortex spun along the road towards him. Jadalan blinked and the rushing spiral was still there. He made a sound of distress and picked up his bag to run and run. He was sure it was Lailahel coming after him and he feared for his life. All misery was forgotten in that moment of stark desire for survival. He began to run, but the sparkling stones of the road had become slippery beneath his feet so it seemed that, as if in a dream, he could not go forward at all. The rushing wind was nearly upon him and, uttering one last despairing, defiant wail, Jadalan fell to his knees, covering his face, letting the vortex engulf him. But then there was no cold, furious embrace but only a sudden stillness and a voice he knew saying, 'Jadalan, Jadalan, get up. Get up quickly.' The voice was almost unrecognisable because of its hollow ring of fear but he could tell it was Variel.

The instant relief and joy that recognition gave him soon subsided to a more bitter, spiteful human reaction. 'You should not follow me, Variel,' Jadalan said. 'I am returning to the land of my fathers, as Lailahel wants, and, if you were truly honest with me, you'd say you wanted too.'

'Don't be a fool, Jadalan!' Variel said, surprised.

'I won't return! I can't!'

'I know that. Neither can I. Look.' Variel held out his hand and uncurled the long, pale fingers. In his palm rested a single, enormous, perfect pearl in which the colours of the universe shifted and writhed. Variel looked at the light of it reflected in Jadalan's face.

'The pearl. You took it.' He looked at Variel. 'Why?'

'I'm not sure. It seems senseless, I know. When Sabbalom comes cursing over the wall, Lailahel will know that it was me who took it. I've exiled myself. For you. It's senseless. I don't know why. I thought I could sneak in and steal it and bring you back. We could have said you'd taken it yourself and everything would have been alright. I must have been out of my mind. The place was crawling with sentinels who kicked up such a cacophony when they saw me that Sabbalom himself came out onto the lawn. He saw me and was furious. He will know who I was. I can't go back. You must take me with you.'

Jadalan looked wretched. 'No, Variel, I can't do that,' he said. 'You'd hate it and then you would hate me. Say, I bewitched you, anything, only go back to your father's palace. I beg you.' He had clenched his fists helplessly in front of him.

'How strange you are Jadalan. You don't want me to go back at all,' Variel said. 'Neither am I going to.'

'I'm human, you're an angel. You'd pine for your home. Please. Go back. Let me go.'

'No. I don't want to live here without you. I can change. I can live in the world of men. Others have done it. I want to be with you, Jadalan.' He held out his arms and wrapped Jadalan in them.

Then Jadalan was lost and could not have sent Variel back for all the freedom in the world. They clung to each other, tiny as pins on the wide, glittering road, with the great gate of creation hanging over them.

'Come,' Variel said. 'Lailahel will follow, I'm sure of it. We must go.'

Jadalan kissed Variel one last time and picked up his bag. Together they walked towards the gate, swiftly, not looking back. After a few steps Jadalan said, 'What is that odd noise, Variel?' He made to turn and look behind them, but Variel hissed.

'No, don't look, don't look! It is just a breeze passing over the stones, nothing more.' They increased their pace.

'Variel,' Jadalan said in a low, tense voice. 'I am filled with fear - filled with it! What is that noise?'

Variel clutched his arm, bringing pain. His face was almost translucent, his eyes wide and completely black. 'Don't look back, don't say what you think it is. There are just soul birds flying above us, that's all. Quick! Quick!'

They were almost running. Hot air blew the hair up on their heads and a whistling scream penetrated through the wind; a scream of fury and potency.

'Variel, it's him! It's Lailahel!' Jadalan screamed, unable to keep the name inside him any longer.

'Then run! Then run! Then run!' Variel replied, and half swooping, half running, he dragged Jadalan along the road, which roiled like smoke beneath them, a writhing black shadow between them and the gate.

Jadalan felt tears of sheer terror sting his face. He could hardly see the Gate now and swore he could feel the hot breath of the avenging angel on the back of his neck.

Suddenly, Variel pulled him to a halt. 'Keep going, Jadalan,' he said, 'I shall distract Lailahel in some way. I will come to you. Keep going.'

'No,' Jadalan craoked. 'You won't. Lailahel will kill you. Let's keep going - together...'

'Hush, no time for that, no time at all. Run. I love you. Run.' And Variel let out one shuddering gasp of breath and blew Jadalan up the road.

Jadalan wailed and waved his arms, calling out, until Variel disappeared into the black smoke. His voice came faintly to Jadalan's ears or maybe into his mind. 'I'll come to you, I promise. But you'll only know me if nobody else touches you in love before I come. Otherwise your memory of me will fade completely. Take care, Jadalan, and wait for me!'

Then the black mist enclosed Variel completely. The Gates of Creation creaked open and Jadalan was sucked, head over heels into the world of men.

Variel stood small and straight upon the road, facing the approach of Lailahel, with Jadalan's wails fading behind him. All he had as protection was the pearl from the Tree, and his knowledge of such things was far from all-encompassing. Lailahel appeared as a black storm, eyed with golden orbs of anger. The raging column paused in front of Variel, its spin decreasing until the tall, slim form of the angel could be seen hovering within it. 'What are you doing?' he asked in a reasonable voice.

'I am following Jadalan to the world of men,' Variel replied. 'You cannot stop me Lailahel. I have made up my mind.'

Lailahel uttered an indulgent laugh. 'A pretty show of loyalty, dear child, but woefully misplaced! Do you realise what will happen to you in that place?'

'Nothing worse than the emptiness I'll feel should Jadalan go from my life.'

'Such loneliness would be a boon in comparison! Foolish child! If you turn from our world and live upon the Earth, you will become mortal as they are, doomed to age and die. But neither will you become one of them. You can't. Neither man nor woman can you be, and they will fear you because of that. They will cast you out and pelt your body with stones, a body that will be an abomination to them, because they will not understand it. They will desire you and loathe you. And as for your beloved Jadalan, well, under the light of his own sun you will appear as a demon to him, a creature of darkness. What is translucent and holy here in our lands will become freakish clay beneath the sun. Follow him, Variel, and you condemn yourself to a misery as eternal as mortal life can be.'

Variel hesitated. Then he said, 'You lie,' in a small, uncertain voice.

Lailahel laughed. 'Lie, do I? In your heart you know that I do not. Come home with me. If you desire closeness then I can give it to you, but do not turn to mortal beings for that - ever. They will destroy you, as they destroy all things they do not understand. And, it must be said, he could never give you pleasure, Variel. It is beyond his capabilities. Stay with your own kind. Come home.'

Variel still hesitated. He stared hard at Lailahel, whose golden eyes were impenetrable as the metal itself. 'I shall have to see this for myself,' he said at last.

'You won't be able to return if everything goes black. You do know that, don't you?'

'I gave him my word I'd follow.'

'They expect us to break promises. We are angels, unpredictable and contrary. Forget him, Variel. Come home.'

'In my mind, I see the sense in your words, Lailahel, but my heart is telling my mind to be silent. I love Jadalan. I must follow him, for good or bad. I have no choice.'

Then Lailahel grew in stature until the image of him filled the whole, glowing sky. He turned the sky livid violet with his fury. 'I will not let you go, Variel. You are my son.' And poisonous tendrils of semi-solid fume snaked towards him.

Variel screamed, unsure of what to do. He found that he had tossed the pearl from the crown of the Tree of Life high into the air, where it spun and spun; a single bright mote against the shadows of the angel's rage. The pearl contained the sum of all knowledge, a blinding ache that burst into the air of the land of angels, a thousand thousand sharp thrusts of light and meaning. In an instant, Lailahel was given the vision of Variel, bound and helpless, chained in the palace of light and the light was gone from him. He was given the vision of himself suffering the pain of love unrequited as Variel watched the windows for a Jadalan who could never return. All life would be sterile should Lailahel force Variel to return home. With a wail that equalled Jadalan's in despair and wretchedness, Lailahel was sucked inside the vortex of his own ire and disappeared with an eerie hiss in the direction of the palace of light.

Variel was left upon the road, alone. He turned around. Above him the giant sentinels spread their wings and drew back the Gates that he should pass. He flew towards them. They did not look at him directly. Variel followed Jadalan into the world of men.

Jadalan meanwhile had emerged from the realm of angels in the land of Cos and, as fortune was with him, very close to the city of Ashbrilim, the home of his parents. It was early morning there and Jadalan found himself walking along a wide, dusty road with fields on either side. He stared at the marvels of the mortal world; the jewel colours of the trees and grasses and flowers, the impossible hue of the morning sky as the sun rose in the east. Horses galloped through the dew, mad with the joy of simply being alive. He walked and walked, and, as the hour drew on, came across other people setting out for their day's work in the fields, the markets, the villages. At noon, he paused by a well to drink and a pretty girl with green eyes and a brown dress offered him a cup of milk instead. She took him to her cottage and fed him and then offered him more than food or drink. 'Kiss me,' she said, pouting prettily. 'I've never seen a lad more handsome than you.'

'I can't,' he replied, smiling.

'And why's that? Spoken for, are you?'

'In a way. I'm waiting for an angel.'

The girl laughed good-humouredly and pestered him no more. Jadalan could tell she thought him strange, perhaps mad. He left the village, still heading west. By late afternoon, the spires and turrets of Ashbrilim could be seen like a mirage in the sky. Jadalan asked an old man scything grass by the road, 'Is that the city of King Ashalan?'

'It is,' the old man replied.

'My parents live there. I'm going home,' Jadalan said and the man nodded and smiled; perhaps he too saw a madness there.

Jadalan wandered the streets of Ashbrilim, eyes wide, steps dragging with fatigue brought on by the assault of stimuli to mind and senses. A thousand brutish odours filled his nose, far removed from the vague perfumes of the land of angels. Everywhere colour and noise whirled around him, indecipherable to his alienated condition. He was almost blind, shaking and nauseous by the time he reached the gates of the palace. The reason for his being there was fading fast in his memory; his body was unable to cope with the drastic differences. Out in the country, those differences had been pleasant, challenging, new. Here in the city, they were cruel and overwhelming. The close proximity of thousands of human souls and human bodies oppressed him; he could sense all their petty cruelties and jealousies, all their dark secrets. Jadalan sank wearily to the ground, leaning upon the closed gates. Never had he felt so ill.

Then, with a shattering burst of noise, the gates were thrown wide open, causing the wilting Jadalan to cringe further towards the dirt, hands to ears, his stomach churning. Loud shouting and laughter, and the sound of horses' hooves sounded from within the courtyard. Jadalan crawled to the side, just in time to avoid being trampled by a group of riders trotting smartly out into the city. Jadalan squinted. Shapes blurred before his eyes. He did not know it was Ashalan himself, setting off for an evening's hunting in the forests and fields beyond Ashbrilim's walls. Dogs swarmed around the horse's feet and it happened that one of them was the puppy with which Jadalan used to play, in those days before the angel came. Time moves in a strange way between the worlds. Though Jadalan had been away for many years in angelic terms, only eight seasons had passed in the land of Cos. If Jadalan had returned a different way, or on a different day, it might have been that he'd come back to a place where his family had been dead for years. It might have been that the city itself had fallen to dust. There was no way of knowing. He'd been lucky and the dog that he had petted as a baby recognised his scent, broke away from the pack and bounded up to him, tail wagging wildly. Before Jadalan could move, the animal had covered his mouth with affectionate licks, the touch of love that Variel had warned against, thus effectively destroying any vestiges of memory that Jadalan had retained of the recent past. He lay back in the dust with the dog nuzzling his face, eyes staring vacantly at the sky.

Ashalan noticed the commotion and sent one of his aides to see what the dog was doing.

'Why sire, it is a lad,' the man said.

Ashalan dismounted and went to see for himself. It was as if Jadrin himself lay there, stupidly gazing, but a Jadrin of even finer aspect and ambience.

'The boy is ill,' someone said. 'Perhaps diseased.'

'Have someone take him into the palace,' Ashalan said.

'Is that wise, sire?'

'Have someone take him into the palace.' The king's tone was not to be argued with.

In this way, Jadalan returned home, but without the capacity to say who he was or what had happened to him.

Because of his beauty, he was taken to the royal apartments, bathed and laid in a soft bed. Ashalan had even considered that this was some relative of Jadrin's come to seek him out, but Jadrin claimed no recollection of such kin. He watched the boy coolly as the servants tended to his body. He felt he ought to be angry at the way Ashalan had brought him in; it was obvious why, and yet, some part of him, deep within, was drawn to the pale stranger.

Perhaps I find him attractive myself, Jadrin thought and yet, it did not feel that way.

When the servants had finished, Jadrin sent them away. He stood and stared at the boy lying there. *Yes, he looks like me,* he thought. *How odd.* A vague memory stirred, of a moonlit bathroom and blood, black in the moonlight, pooling on the floor. Jadrin shuddered and the boy opened his eyes. They were the colour of violets.

'Who are you?' Jadrin asked and the boy struggled to speak. 'Who are you? Who are you?' Jadrin had leaned right over him, his voice filled with a tremor that could have been fear. Then a whisper: 'Who are you?'

The boy sighed. 'I don't know,' he said. 'I am no-one. I am nothing.'

Jadrin found himself pressed against the far wall, one hand to his mouth. He dared not think. He dared not hope. Nothing.

Jadalan recovered slowly, but his mind seemed almost empty. He wandered, pale and lovely, through the corridors of his parent's palace, sat with them to eat, smiled and nodded at their friends, walked in the gardens with his arm through Jadrin's, became beloved to them. Jadrin suspected who he might be, but never voiced his thoughts. Perhaps Ashalan too had some intimation of the boy's identity, but a weird kind of fear kept the king and his consort from discussing the matter. Jadalan simply was. He was with them and they were fond of him. People seemed afraid of the boy so Jadrin named him Ailacumar, which was a deity name, seldom used by the populace, but which represented the god in his aspect of wandering youth. Ailacumar hardly ever answered to his name. There seemed within him a deep and secret sadness. He slept for most of every day and though he smiled, would never laugh.

Variel came to earth in the middle of a forest. He crouched shuddering, beneath the branches of a giant oak, his gossamer angelic robes torn to shreds, his amber skin bruised and scratched. For a while, he could not remember who or what he was, why he was there or where he had come from. The earth claimed him. Stupid with terror, senseless to a degree even more than Jadalan had been, he was unaware of urine pooling beneath him, melting the last of his clothing. He had come to earth and its coarseness claimed him instantly, as if resentful of his aetheric origins. *Learn reality,* She said. *Feel pain and fear; piss yourself.*

By nightfall, under the softer caress of the moon, Variel stumbled painfully along a forest track. The ground beneath his feet tore his flesh, even the light of the moon burned him. He was unprepared for a visit to Earth. Lailahel was experienced and knew what precautions to take, how to modify his form. Variel was virgin and ingenuous and the Earth mocked him.

Eventually, he found shelter in a byre at the edge of the forest. Lights burned in a farmer's cottage nearby, but he was too terror-stricken to seek aid there. Animals moved patiently in the musty darkness and he lay down in the hay, shivering himself to sleep. There were no thoughts of Jadalan, not even any thoughts of home, just a bewildered and helpless vacuum in his mind. All he desired was rest and warmth.

In the morning, the farmer's daughter came to milk the cows in there and found him. She ran shrieking to the cottage. 'There's a dead person in the byre, Papa!'

The farmer, his sons and his wife hurried out to see. They thought Variel was a girl at first, until they carried him back to the cottage and saw the finely formed organ between his legs. The farmer's wife made a sign to protect herself from spirits. 'It's a man-woman,' she said. 'A faery messenger.'

'We must put it back where we found it,' one of the sons said to his father. 'Its people will come for it.'

'It's near dead,' said the daughter. 'I'll fetch a blanket.'

As the family debated what to do with their unearthly visitor, Variel groaned and writhed and opened his golden eyes. The family gasped as one, which under other circumstances would have been comical. Variel put his hands over his face and made a terrible sound of despair. Bravely, the daughter went and wrapped the blanket round his shoulders.

'Who are you?' asked the mother.

Variel stared up at them helplessly. Their odour, their physical strength, their animal forms virtually made him feel sick. He shook his head and closed his eyes, hot tears squeezing between his lids.

'Are you of the faery?' asked the farmer, gruffly.

Variel shook his head. He could not speak.

'Obvious what this creature is,' said one of the sons proudly. 'A freak. Probably from one of the travelling fairs. Probably got lost, and separated from its people. Is that right, stranger?'

Variel could sense these people desperately wanted answers about him. He was weary, sick and afraid. He nodded his head. It seemed the best thing to do. And they accepted that.

The farmer's daughter's name was Phoebe. A kind-hearted soul, she took Variel into her care, nursing his constantly solidifying physical form back into health. Variel simply lay on a low cot in Phoebe's room, staring at the far wall for three days, watching the sunlight and the moonlight cycle and slide and feeling himself change, become clay. He lay there thinking about what his angelic father had told him and how all those words were becoming truth. He was conscious of the heaviness of his body, the unweildy solidity of his flesh. He could smell himself beginning to emanate the animal odours of humankind. He could feel all that was magical about himself draining away.

On the morning of the fourth day, Phoebe woke before dawn as usual to attend to her chores and then, as sunlight burned away the grey, came to bring Variel a bowl of cereal foamy with warmed milk. Previously, Variel had been unable to stomach more than a mouthful, so Phoebe was rightfully surprised as she watched her unearthly charge heartily consume half of the bowl before clutching his stomach with a groan. 'You

feel better today then,' she said, eyes round as coins. Variel had
not spoken to her yet. She had to sit down when he said,

'Yes. In a way, I think so.'

What a strange voice this person had. 'What are you?'
Phoebe asked. 'What is your name? Where do you come from?'

Variel remembered what Lailahel had told him about
humans pelting him with stones and thinking him a freak. He was
unsure of what to say and merely opened and closed his mouth a
few times.

'You are afraid,' Phoebe said. 'Don't be. You are among
friends here. We will not harm you or send you back, if that's
what you're afraid of.'

'No-one can send me back,' Variel said, and told her his
name.

Phoebe seemed content with that for the time being and
offered him some of her youngest brother's clothes to wear.

The family gathered for breakfast and, for the first time,
Variel joined them. The kitchen was dark and pungent. Dogs and
cats continuously put their paws onto Variel's lap where he sat,
begging food. Variel was afraid of them. He was less than an
animal in this world, for even animals knew the way of things
here and how to behave. He was also uncomfortably aware of the
curious glances cast his way, disgusted by the brutish table
manners of Phoebe's male relatives. Even though Phoebe tried to
encourage him to drink a glass of apple juice, he dared put
nothing in his mouth, for fear of bringing it right back onto the
table.

At length, Phoebe's father pushed his plate away, uttering a
resounding belch of satisfaction and announced, 'Mother, it is not
right that wench, strange as she is, should be dressed up as a
boy. See to her togs and have Phoebe show her the chicken
runs.'

Thus Variel learned that in this world at least he was
destined to be a she, however odd, and from that moment it was
true things became easier for him.

So Variel learned the lore and customs of working the land.
She found that, after a while, it came as a natural and enjoyable
thing to do. She did not mind the long hours or the hard toil and
found her new human body became less of a burden as time went
on. With Phoebe's encouragement, she began to take care of her

appearance, and took joy in the lissom athleticism of her form. Slim as a whip she was, sinewy as a boy and fast as a hare. She could wrestle with Phoebe's brothers and not be bested, she could fell a tree with the heaviest axe and still be a fey, languid beauty in the lamplight at dinner. The family came to adore her and could not remember what the days had been like before the flame of Variel's presence had come to warm their home.

Variel could not believe that the world of men could offer such pleasures as she now beheld. The miracle of life, the changing banner of the seasons, delighted her and filled her with awe. As an angelic being, isolated in the realms of light, she'd had no thought for the Great Goddess of the Earth. Now, Variel embraced her as did all the farming families in the community.

One night she and Phoebe went down to the pool hidden in a sunken spinney in the farthest paddock. It was the night of the full moon and Phoebe wanted to bathe naked in the waters to entreat the Goddess for the powers of attraction. There was a young lad working for a neighbouring farmer for whom she'd developed a craving. Variel was happy to comply with her friend's wishes. Indeed, she looked upon Phoebe as a sister now. As she sat on the bank of the pool, watching the farmer's daughter raise her wet, pale arms to the sky, Variel reflected on how long she had been in this place and for the first time was visited by a pang that reminded her of Jadalan. He seemed a creature of her dreams nowadays, an insubstantial idea that bore no relation to her life as she now lived it. Her past life had become similarly unreal. Now she was a young woman, with a young woman's needs and feelings, if not possessed utterly of a young woman's physical form. This was what the Goddess had decreed and Variel considered that the Goddess was indeed a benevolent Being to have so tolerated her on the Earth. It was almost as if she'd been rewarded. How wrong Lailahel had been and yet, how right too.

Phoebe came swimming to the water's edge. 'You look thoughtful, Variel. Are you alright?' she asked.

Variel smiled. 'I was thinking of my father,' she replied.

'Do you miss him?' Through veiled remarks made by Variel, Phoebe had gleaned Variel had been found in such a distraught condition because of being exiled from home by her angry parent. It was a subject they rarely discussed, for Phoebe sensed it gave Variel pain to think about it.

Variel wrinkled her brow. 'Miss him? How odd. I never thought of it that way. I suppose I do, but there's no point grieving. I'll never see him again.'

'What was he like?' Phoebe asked carefully. From Variel's dreamy expression she was thinking the father must have been a wild and handsome creature.

'He was an angel,' Variel replied, laughing. 'I was an angel too and he kicked me into the world of men.'

Phoebe laughed too. 'You are a strange one, Variel. Your sense of humour is peculiar at times.'

Variel frowned. 'No, I lied. I was not kicked into the world of men. It was my choice. I loved a man. I followed him. But now it's like a dream.' She turned and stumbled away from the water, one hand to her eyes, the other blindly reaching forward.

Perplexed and concerned Phoebe scrambled from the water, her wet skin gleaming like silver, and hurried after her, not even pausing to dress herself. 'Variel, stop! Come back!' She ran after the swiftly marching Variel and laid a restraining hand on her arm.

Variel spun around, shaking her arm from Phoebe's hold. 'Am I human, am I?' she demanded angrily.

Phoebe was frightened and confused. Had Variel gone mad? 'Of course you are,' she soothed, and then remembered the weird, shimmering body she had found in the byre, the odd sexuality of it, the alien feel of it. 'You are *now*,' she amended.

Variel snarled. 'Don't be so sure!' she snapped and then with another lightning change of expression began to cry and raised her face to the moon. 'Goddess, what am I? Can I truly live here in contentment? Am I worthy of such a thing? Or will I one day petrify and shatter and break like a crystal shard? Oh, help me! Help me!'

Phoebe was concerned that one of her brothers on his evening chores might hear the commotion and come to investigate. She dragged the protesting, wailing Variel back into the hollow, where the surface of the pool was ruffled by the night breeze. The water grasses rattled as if the Goddess herself was concerned at what was happening. 'Get into the water!' Phoebe ordered, tearing Variel's clothes from her back. 'Come on, hurry!

321

Get into the water!' Above them, a vast, pale moon sank towards the trees at the edge of the meadow.

Shivering and weeping, Variel removed the petticoats and undergarments that were gifts from Phoebe's mother. 'Do not look at me,' she said.

Phoebe turned away her face. She did not look back until she could hear Variel splashing into the pool. Crouched down below the surface, only Variel's face showed above the water, her eyes wide and black, her white-gold hair floating around her head like wet silk.

Phoebe stepped into the pool and held out her hands. 'Pray,' she entreated. 'Pray, Variel, pray! Don't lose it all. Gain more! Pray!'

Phoebe's hands ached from the iron grip of Variel's weirdly strong limbs. Tears squeezed from between her own eyelids with the pain. The water felt like ice around her legs and stomach. Everything hurt and Variel's face was pinched into an ugly expression of helpless pleading, of determination, of angry strength. Suddenly, with a final agonising squeeze of her hands and a shuddering gasp, Variel threw back her head, and releasing Phoebe from her grip raised her arms to the sky. With a fluting peal of triumph, Variel rose up from the water, her wet hair clinging to her body, and Phoebe backed, splashing, towards the bank, wiping her face. It was as if she beheld an embodiment of the Goddess herself. From between the strands of Variel's encompassing hair, proud, blooming breasts jutted like perfect fruit; an area that had been rather devoid of swelling before. The waist curved in as if carved from perfect wood and, as Variel strode through the water to the bank, Phoebe could clearly see that was no longer the slightest evidence of masculinity between her legs.

Wild-eyed, Variel stood upon the bank. 'I have been answered!' she cried, fists clenched and raised above her head.

Phoebe scrambled up the bank. She could not speak. She knew she had witnessed some kind of miracle but it had been so awesome, so strange, she was unsure whether gods or demons had been responsible for it.

The next morning, Phoebe was awoken by a chilling cry from Variel's bed. In an instant she hurried to her friend's side, throwing back the blankets, fearing some reversal of last night's event. There was no need to worry. Clutching her stomach, Variel struggled from the bed, where the bottom sheet was stained with red. There could be no mistake. Variel was truly a woman. The Goddess had visited her with the indelible mark of femininity. As the earth, as the beasts, as the birds themselves, Variel was one of the Goddess's creatures now. A fertile female. It was then that she knew it was time for her to seek the city of Ashbrilim.

The family were hardly pleased that Variel wanted to leave them. At breakfast, she told them she must seek the city of the king. She was grateful for all the help they had given her, and one day hoped to reward them for their troubles, but she knew she had a destiny and had to fulfil it.

'What business do you have in Ashbrilim?' asked Phoebe's father.

'I must find the man I love,' Variel said. 'I made a promise.'

Reluctantly, the family gave her provisions and fondly wished her farewell. Phoebe wept openly and begged Variel to return to her one day. This Variel promised to do, if she was able. She too was sad to leave her friends, who had given her so much, but she had a purpose and could not deny it.

For many days and nights, Variel travelled to Ashbrilim. Along the way, she questioned people about Jadalan. 'Does the king have a son?' she asked.

'Of sorts,' she was told. 'Though some say he is not of this world.'

Variel was then sure that Jadalan had found his way home. She had only to present herself at the palace for them to be reunited.

However, once in the city, Variel quickly discovered that a common person simply could not walk in through the gates of the palace. She spoke to the guards on duty at the main entrance and said she had come to see Jadalan, the son of the king.

'There is no such person,' said one of the guards. 'The king's son is Ailacumar.'

Another guard laughed. 'Perhaps she has come to offer herself as a bride to the prince!'

'Then she should get his name right!' said the first. 'Jadalan died as a babe. Be off with you, wench!' They clearly thought Variel was mad.

Variel pondered the situation until nightfall. Then, because she was more agile than a human could be, she climbed an ancient oak next to the high wall that surrounded the palace gardens. She crawled along a wide limb that hung over the garden and dropped down onto the wide lawn beneath. The palace gleamed before her in the moonlight. She could see guards stationed around it. For while longer, she must think and plan.

At the back of the palace was an orchard and a kitchen garden. Variel made her way to this place and climbed into an old apple tree, next to a clear pool of water. Here, she went to sleep and trusted that her dreams would advise her.

In the early morning, the head gardener's daughter passed by the pool and looked into it. She saw the reflection of Variel's face in the water and mistaking it for her own, said, 'Why, how beautiful I am! I should not be working in the garden. I shall ask my father to go to the king at once and tell him that I am the true bride he seeks for the handsome boy he calls a son, who sighs and sleeps so much.'

A short while later, the gardener's wife happened to be passing and she too paused to look into the water, and as her daughter had done before her, mistook Variel's radiant reflection for her own. 'Well, look at me!' she declared. 'I am beauty itself! Why should I be married to a mere gardener? I will go to the king at once and tell him I am the true bride he seeks for that boy he calls a son, who sleeps so much and speaks so little.'

The gardener was faced with his womenfolk, who he could only presume to be demented. There they were in the kitchen of their house, putting on finery and talking about being so beautiful they must wed a prince. To him, they looked the same as they always had. In between arguments with each other about who was the most beautiful and fit to become a princess, they told the gardener about how they'd seen their reflections in the pool that morning. Suspecting capricious magic at work, the gardener went himself to investigate the matter. He saw the beautiful face in the pool and looked up, spying at once the young woman hiding among the green leaves.

'Are you a witch?' he asked her.

'No,' Variel answered. 'I am a lady from a far land, and I have come to see the prince.'

'Get down,' said the gardener. 'You are charming my womenfolk in strange ways, and it must not be.'

Variel climbed down out of the tree, and the gardener told her that because Prince Ailacumar was so listless, his parents had decided to find a bride for him, in the hope that vivacious female company might coax him from his lethargy. 'Girls and women from all quarters of the world have come to the palace,' said the gardener. 'And now, I have heard, King Ashalan and Lord Jadrin have chosen a suitable bride. The wedding takes place very shortly.'

'Will you help me?' Variel said. 'I am the prince's one true love.'

The gardener stared at her, 'I should think you mad,' he said, 'but I have never seen a girl like you.'

'If you'll take me to the prince, you'll not regret it,' Variel said.

Sighing, the gardener nodded and took her into the palace. They went to the room where the royal family took their breakfast, and here Jadrin and Ashalan sat with their adopted son, whose head was sunk on his breast in slumber. Variel recognised him at once as the one she loved. Also seated at the table was an exotic princess from a far land, who was indeed very beautiful, but she might as well have been a horse for all the notice Jadalan took of her.

'What is this?' King Ashalan demanded as the gardener ushered Variel towards the table.

'This young woman claims to know the prince,' he explained.

'Indeed!' said Jadrin. 'You must tell us all you know of him, girl.'

But Variel barely heard Jadrin's words. She rushed to Jadalan's side and knelt beside his chair. 'Hear me,' she said, 'I have come to you as I promised I would. Awake and look upon me.'

Jadalan did not stir, but uttered a soft sound as if his dreams were pleasant.

Variel knew then that some creature must have touched Jadalan in love before she'd come to him, and that all memory of her had faded from his mind. Part of him was lost, perhaps, in the land of angels.

Variel took hold of his hands and no one stopped her. Jadalan's parents and his prospective bride looked on in curiosity and perhaps some hope that this stranger could awaken the prince. Variel began to sing, 'For you I raised the city dead, for you I drained the lake, for you I took the pearl of life with both our lives at stake. For love of thee, beloved one, I fell for love of thee. And to this world I came a girl, your one true love to be.'

When Jadrin heard this song, he asked Variel what she meant, for their son had not spoken of any of these things to his parents.

Variel looked at him and said, 'Three times I completed the tasks that Jadalan had been given by my father, Lailahel. He is my one true love, but now he will not awaken or speak to me. I have travelled here in vain.'

'Jadalan!' Ashalan exclaimed. 'How is this possible? Our son was hardly more than a baby when he was taken from us. We dared not hope this person might be him.'

'This is your son, Jadalan, have no doubt,' Variel said. 'Time passes differently in the land of angels. And I was an angel's son, banished from my father's realm for daring to love a human.'

At once, Jadrin jumped out of his chair and went to his son's side. He put his arms around Jadalan and kissed his face and told him to awaken.

The sound of his name drifted through the fog in Jadalan's mind and he opened his eyes. The first thing he saw was Variel's face and she leaned forward quickly and kissed him upon the mouth. Jadalan's memory returned, and it quickly became clear that the exotic foreign princess would not become his bride.

Jadalan and Variel were married very soon after, and lived long and interesting lives. Of the angel Lailahel, nothing was heard again.

The Oracle Lips

Sheila met the woman she should have been in the ladies wash-room at Euston station. It was very early in the morning, two o'clock; a time of day when memories of Old London seem very near to this reality, perhaps seeping up from the drains. People like Sheila were like bright flames to these fleeting ghosts. She didn't want to be there; the empty, echoing chamber, with its weirdly dull strip lights, felt like an abattoir or an operating theatre. Sheila saw blood on the tiles in some places. Ghost blood.

She had seen ghosts all her life; one of her many unusual talents. She read cards for her mother's friends; that sort of thing. Sheila felt it was only her abilities that made her interesting to other people. Nobody would want to know her otherwise. She was like a ghost herself.

She wasn't used to being out so late; the night often unnerved her. It was when the whispers were loudest and it was hard to shut them out. She had washed her hands and gone to the mirror to comb her hair, which was so wispy, it needed to be brushed every half hour; an inconvenient task that Sheila rarely had time to attend to.

Shadows wanted to manifest, but she fought them. She was exhausted, having been awake for nearly twenty hours. Perhaps she should have stayed overnight in London with her sister. Her mother would have approved. But Tess gave Sheila a head-ache - too energetic, too noisy. The trip had been meant to be a treat - Mother had paid - but to Sheila, outwardly grateful, it had been nothing but a trial. Her craving for the solace of her bed-room, which had begun virtually the moment she'd stepped off the train that morning, had become more painful as the day progressed. In the end, she had fled, mumbling about an appointment she had in the morning. Dentist. A good excuse. Tess would not have believed anything more exciting.

Hard to retain control now. Too weary. At the corner of her vision, a tired shadow woman mopped the floor in endless silence. What kind of life had she led only to end up haunting this joyless place? But the shadows weren't only of the dead. Flickering images of other, busy lives hovered round, buzzing from cubicles to hand basins to mirror. Their energy made Sheila dizzy.

Then, behind her, she heard a lavatory flush and, in the mirror, saw a tall figure march out of one of the cubicles. A real woman, not a shadow or a memory of a thought. Flesh and blood. At once, the shadows disappeared and Sheila felt a weight lift from her body. She and this singular other were alone.

The woman wore a beautiful long dress of soft moss-coloured fabric, quite severe in cut, which described eloquently the perfect lines of her body. Over her arm, a mass of black velvet coat hung. Ignoring Sheila, this vision stalked up to the mirror and placed a large shoulder bag on the shelf before her. For a moment, her hands lay long upon the leather, and she flared her nostrils at her reflection. Then, with business-like economy of movement, she opened the bag and withdrew a lipstick. Thoughtfully, almost reverently, she removed its cap.

Sheila's comb was stilled in her hair. Her heart, unaccountably, ached. If only her hands understood the tools of beauty magic. If only her hair hung lush and dark and foaming around straight shoulders. Such eyebrows - a statement of command and control. No fear. None. This woman was not plagued by shadows, for her life was full and absorbing. She was more than whole, at home in her skin, pausing here to preen, before whirling back into adventure and experience. Her movements were concise yet graceful. She was not pretty, but had strong, striking features and the proud stance of a woman who was comfortable with her body.

Sheila was not disposed to envying other women. She liked to look neat, but otherwise never fussed over her appearance. There seemed no point. Where nature had given some women poise and arresting faces and bodies, it had spent little time crafting Sheila's mortal form. Plain but homely: her mother's description; meant to be a palliative, she supposed. She was not fat, but not shapely either. Straight up. Straight down. A sort of solid chunk.

The woman caught Sheila's eye in the mirror. Her hand froze half-way to her face, her fingers curled around the bullet of brilliant red lip-stick. Tightly, she smiled. Pity. A moment of it.

Sheila withered in its beam. Then, the woman focused in upon herself and pressed the waxy colour against her mouth. The movement was sensual, almost choreographed. Sheila's lips were thin, but this woman's were autumn ripe, the lower lip fuller than the upper. Their cushiony flesh sank beneath the invading stick of pigment. Round and round. Twice. Colour so thick it must surely dry to a hard, gloss finish.

Sheila became aware of staring, and coloured up. She stuffed her comb back into her own small purse and leaned forward to rub at her nose. It was shiny.

Beside her, the woman took a tissue from her bag and pressed it to her mouth. She dropped the kissed paper onto the floor, didn't even look at it. For a moment, she pouted at herself, then frowned and applied another layer of colour.

It seemed purposeful.

The woman gazed haughtily at her reflection, smiled to herself, and leaned forward to press her mouth against the mirror. A guileless act of self-love. It seemed as if another woman behind the glass leaned forward to accept the kiss. Then, she dropped her lipstick carelessly back into her bag, slung it over her shoulder, patted her luxuriant hair and walked regally out.

Sheila stared at the ghost of the lips on the mirror. Shockingly red. The woman was still here. She had left a part of herself behind.

Outside, the public address system announced the imminent departure of a train, Sheila's train. Hurriedly, she zipped up her purse and scraped her hair behind her ears. But she could not walk past the lips on the mirror. They glared out at her, summoning.

Almost without thinking, Sheila found herself standing on tip-toe to place her own mouth against the print. The glass was cold and unyielding. She could not feel the thick colour.

Suddenly self-conscious, she jumped backwards. Her reflection showed a startled pale face, its mouth daubed with a gash of raw red that engulfed her own narrow lips. She rubbed anxiously at this invasion and bent down to pick up the tissue the woman had discarded. This, she shoved into her rain-coat pocket, then scurried out to the concourse. Her face was flaming, she could feel the heat. Platform 15. Hurry. Hurry.

Defences down, shadows assailed her from all sides. She felt as if she was pressing through a throng, although the station was unusually empty, just a few clots of people staring up at the board announcing arrivals and departures. All the shops were shut, fenced off by metal grilles. Sheila ran down the ramp to the platform, where the train panted softly. There was hardly anyone on it. She leapt awkwardly through the nearest door and found a seat quickly. Her face was still burning. She could see herself reflected in the window. A wounded mouth. Remembering, and wanting to scrub her lips, she took the tissue from her pocket. It was white as a towel, the blot like a flower of blood upon it. Sheila stared at it in her hand. The ghost mouth was an oracle, it might speak. She laid the tissue out on the table in front of her, smoothing carefully around the print. Someone sat down opposite her, but they were not really there, so she ignored them. The lipstick had sunk into the fibres of the tissue, revealing every line of the lips they had touched. It was perfect, like a painting. Red on white. The lines, Sheila thought, are so personal, like those on a palm. A woman's life might be encrypted in the print of her lips, or her future.

The train shuddered, creaked. A guard stamped past the window, blowing a whistle. Doors slammed. And they were moving, away from London, out into the darkness of the sleeping land.

Sheila could not sleep. She stared at the red lips on the table, and when she closed her eyes, the pouting shape burned behind her lids, neon green. She wanted to know the woman who belonged to their shape.

Sheila's mother let her sleep without interruption until one o'clock the following afternoon. Sheila had arrived home at four thirty in the morning, creeping into the house as quietly as possible, although her mother, whose hearing seemed as acute as a bat's, called her name as she tip-toed up the creaking stairs.

'Sheila!'

'Yes, Mum.'

Silence.

In her bedroom, Sheila had laid out the tissue carefully on the dressing table where her tortoiseshell brush and comb set lay on a lace mat. The lines in the lip print were more defined now, as if the colour between them was bleeding away. Hyper-sensitive with exhaustion, Sheila's eyes had blurred as she stared at the shape. The lines were widely spaced, most of them without fork, which to her spoke of an open personality, but at the corners of the mouth, a series of links hinted at secrecy and deceit.

Sheila's mother breezed into her room without knocking, bearing a large mug of weak tea. Sheila loathed weak tea.

'Morning, love,' said Sheila's mother, whipping open the curtains.

Sheila blinked in the light and accepted the warm mug. It had clearly been standing on the kitchen table for some time. Full-cream milk fat made oily puddles on the surface of the liquid. Sheila looked up at her mother's face. She wore thick lip-stick too - some of it had smeared onto her front teeth - but the effect was not the same.

'Good trip? Why did you come back at that godawful hour? Why didn't you stay with Tess?'

Sheila began to reply, formulating excuses, but her mother breezed on,

'Oh, Sheila love, Marj is round, with her sister. I told her you'd do the cards for them in a bit. You won't be long, will you?'

Sheila sighed. 'No.'

Sheila's mother paused, frowned at her daughter. 'What's that on your face? Lipstick?' She laughed. 'Don't tell me Tess gave you a make-over!'

Sheila felt her face grow hot. She mumbled incoherently.

'Right,' said her mother. 'I'll pop down and put some toast on for you.'

Left alone, Sheila stared glumly into her tea. Why must her mother make her feel like a freak show? Her gift was special; it was wasted on divining the narrow lives of her mother's friends. This was not the first time Sheila had thought it, but now there was anger behind the thought rather than simply numb acceptance.

Sheila dressed herself and went to her mirror to brush her hair. She was taken aback by the red stain, which still covered her lips. Rubbing it, she found it would not come off. Soap and water, then. She glanced down at the lip-stick print on the tissue, which seemed to smile up at her provocatively. Those lips had not felt soap and water for years, not since their owner had been a child. Only the best, silky cleansers and toners had stroked them clean, only the richest of moisturisers had nourished their soft folds. Sheila lifted the tissue and sniffed at the print. A faint aroma of fading perfume, cinnamon or ginger. And something else. Tobacco smoke, wine, the bloody smell of rare meat; the tinkle of silver against china; the glint of candlelight reflected from diamonds and eyes. Sheila closed her eyes and inhaled. A glimpse of that life, the sureness of it.

Among Sheila's many prognosticative talents, psychometry and palmistry ranked high. She knew that the lipstick print was a gift. It would give her a story, a life to invade and explore. What was she doing now, that woman who had kissed herself in the mirror?

I need a name, Sheila thought, and willed it to come to her, but then her mother was calling, 'Are you coming down, Shee? Marj has only got an hour.'

The impressions fled; back into the print, back into the past. Sheila sighed again, more heavily, and carefully placed the tissue in the top drawer of her dressing-table, so that her mother wouldn't inadvertently throw it away.

Downstairs, Sheila came across Marj and her sister, Joyce, who were sitting with her mother at the kitchen table. On the stove, greens boiled for later consumption by her timid father when he returned home from work.

'Oooh, Sheila!' Marj exclaimed. 'Bit of a cold sore there, is it?'

Sheila rubbed her lips, went red. She had washed her face thoroughly, but the scarlet stain still haunted the corners of her mouth. Her mother swept over to investigate, and gripped Sheila's jaw in a fierce squeeze. 'Dearie me,' she said, squinting. 'Does seem inflamed, you know.'

'It's nothing,' Sheila snapped, pulling away. 'Lip-stick.'

Sheila's mother nodded to her friends. 'Tess has really fancy make-up. Expensive, you know.' She shook her head. 'Not really your thing, is it, Shee!'

'Oh, I don't know,' Marj rejoined. 'She is looking a bit perky. Must've done you good, girl, a nice day out.'

Sheila had to admit she did feel more energetic than usual. She associated it with the anger she'd experienced after her mother had left her bed-room. She felt more alive than she had done for months.

Breakfast eaten, she spread her old tarot cards on the kitchen table. What could she tell Marj and Joyce? Nothing. Because nothing much happened in their lives, other than petty squabbles with friends and families, along with the occasional unexpected pregnancy from younger and wilder relatives. 'You will be feeling reckless,' Sheila said, 'but there could be disappointment.' An extra round on the lottery perhaps - to no avail.

As the women stared down at the cards, Sheila couldn't help but examine their lips. Could they possibly reflect what lay in the readings? Joyce, silent and with a perpetual worry line between her eyes, had flaking lips; dry and bitten. They didn't seem to have lines, as if she'd nibbled away all her personality. Marj's upper lip was virtually non-existent, while her lower lip stuck out petulantly and always appeared slightly wet. Marj was hungry - for gossip and control. Sheila smiled to herself. Over the years, she had trained herself in many disciplines of divination. Now, she had something new to work on.

The lipstick woman's name was Francesca. It came to Sheila as she went back upstairs after giving Marj and Joyce their reading. She wasn't entirely sure whether she'd simply dreamed up the name because it seemed so appropriate, or whether it really belonged to the woman whose mouth print lay hidden in the dressing table drawer. Francesca. She could not be called anything else.

Looking at the print once more, Sheila strained her psychic sight to acquire more details of Francesca's life. She was a woman who lived on the edge, who was often disliked, especially by other women. Sheila saw an indolent selfishness in the lines of Francesca's mouth, perhaps even a streak of cruelty. But she also had humour and hedonistic desires. Sheila glanced at herself in the mirror and was surprised by the expression she saw on her face; a watchful sneer. *Do I want to be like her?* Sheila wondered. Francesca was glamorous and beautiful, but had few female friends. Sometimes she felt lonely although she never admitted it. Sheila realised that she herself never felt lonely, despite her own lack of close friends and the gulf between her and her family. She liked her own company and was not totally dissatisfied with herself. Her part-time job at the local news-agent fulfilled her modest financial needs and gave her more than enough contact with the world. Why then this growing obsession with an alien creature, this woman of secrets and dangerous passions?

Sheila put the tissue back into her drawer. She shivered involuntarily, suddenly craving a walk in fresh air.

Sheila strolled across the common, where people walked their dogs and children played in the cold, winter sunlight. The trees were stark against the sky and crows rasped from the naked branches. The town beyond the expanse of grass looked squat and grey. There was so little colour in the hibernating world. Sheila thought of red lips and heard a peal of free laughter in her head. A ghost of giant lips kissed the grainy sky and Sheila knew that somewhere Francesca was sitting in a wine bar with a group of men, her eyes restlessly scanning the room, searching for someone. She despised her lecherous, overweight companions, but she had information now; information to sell. Sheila could feel Francesca's impatience and also a shred of uncertainty. It was a seed of fear, hidden in darkness. Perhaps Francesca could not sense it herself.

Sheila closed her eyes to blink away a band of pain that gripped her temples, her eyes. Her glimpse into Francesca's life scared her, but she was still curious, still wanted to know more.

On the High Street, Sheila ambled along gazing in shop windows. It was one of her favourite pastimes. She passed an array of satiny continental chocolates, then the winter coats of the ladies' dress shop, on to the garish jumble of children's toys and the sleek, sinister pyramids of electrical goods. The shoe shop, Sole Partners, lay at the end of the street, where what had once been a market square had been turfed over, flower-bedded and stuck with benches, bearing the names of dead town councillors on small, metal plaques. Sheila decided to go and sit there for a few minutes, watch the clouds of scavenging pigeons lift and fall, before making her way home via the coffee shop in Church Street. She looked into the shoe shop window as she passed, and her attention was caught by a pair of shoes in the display before her. Shiny black patent leather with high, high heels. A strong impression assailed her: they were power shoes, designed for treading on human flesh; figuratively if not literally.

Sheila wanted the shoes immediately and with a hunger she had never experienced before. The lust to acquire flooded her system. Her heart beat fast.

The shop assistant looked at her strangely when she stammered her request and pointed at the window. Sheila knew she did not look like the kind of woman who would buy shiny, spiky shoes. As the assistant flounced out from behind her counter, she glanced down, taking in the worn-down, flat-heeled pumps that currently encased Sheila's feet in scuffed, tan leather. The black shoes were removed from the window display and presented with reverence for the customer to inspect. Sheila looked at them nervously and the assistant suggested she try them on. For a moment, Sheila considered saying that they were for someone else - a gift - but then she was told the size of the shoes, which was hers, and it seemed too much of a coincidence. 'All right,' she said, and sat down on a plush-covered seat and bared her stockinged feet.

The stiff patent leather slid over her right foot, crushing her toes. 'They're too small,' she said, with some relief, but the assistant frowned and lifted Sheila's foot, declaring that no, they were a good fit.

'You're just not used to wearing shoes like this,' the assistant said. 'Slip the other one on. Stand up, walk around.'

Of course, Sheila could not walk in them and suffered the humiliation of staggering up and down in front of the mirror, while the assistant chewed the inside of her mouth in a clear attempt to stem her laughter.

'Yes, I'll take them,' Sheila said.

What am I doing? she thought as she numbly made out a cheque for what was to her an extortionate amount. The assistant packed the shoes into a box amid a froth of black tissue paper.

Out in the street, the maroon and gold carrier bag weighed heavily in Sheila's hand. She could no longer face sitting among the empty flower beds of the square and made her way directly home. She would never wear these shoes. Why had she bought them?

The answer was obvious. These were Francesca shoes, worn with sheer black stockings, the toenails hidden within lacquered to a red gloss.

Back home, Sheila scuttled into her bedroom and sat

panting on the bed, the carrier bag lolling between her feet on the floor. After some minutes, while her ears strained to detect the approach of her mother, she took the shoe box from the bag. She could hear her mother's voice downstairs; a monologue to her father, who was silent. Sheila lifted the shoes from the box, held them in one hand. She felt guilty, ashamed, as if she was about to examine a pornographic magazine.

Her feet seemed to slip into the shoes more easily now. She looked down at her feet, the toes pointing inwards. Her ankles looked slimmer, although her beige tights spoiled the effect somewhat. Sheila stood up in front of the mirror and was surprised at how tall she appeared. She took a few tentative steps. Away from the deriding eyes of the shop assistant, she could take her time, and realised she could learn to walk in these torturous contraptions, if she wanted to. But still, the feeling of shame persisted. Sheila knew that in some way she was stealing something, from a woman who was unaware of the theft. Like a magpie, she had snatched up the glittering fragment of Francesca's life and taken it back to her nest to gloat over. She could never truly appreciate the glittering thing, because she was not a creature who could make use of it properly. She could only admire its lustre.

Sheila paused before her mirror and straightened her spine. She lifted her hair in both hands and held it on top of her head. With the extra height of the shoes, she did not appear so chunky, and her face, free of its customary veil of drab hair, looked stronger somehow. Sheila was suddenly filled with fear. She sat on the bed and kicked off the shoes. *Do I want this?* She asked herself. *Do I really?* The shoes lay on their sides before her, provocative and gleaming. Waiting.

Sheila took to walking in the shoes at night. She would leave the house at seven o'clock, her clandestine purchase hidden in a large shoulder-bag that Tess had left in the cupboard under the stairs. Once she had sauntered a couple of blocks away from home, she would change her shoes. They hurt her at first. She would walk with her hands deep in her pockets, the collar up around her ears. She liked the sharp tap of her heels against the damp sidewalks, although the new leather, stiff with cold, ate into the soft flesh of her feet. She carried the lip-stick print in her coat pocket, her fingers barely touching it. As she walked, impressions of Francesca's life would flood her mind: impromptu parties, city lights, music, laughter. And Francesca's shadowed profession; the secrets of the enchantress had been revealed.

Sheila was now sure that Francesca was involved in dangerous business. She had visualised Francesca seducing men of power, stealing information from them with soft words and deft hands, then selling what she had learned to other men, who paid her highly: politicians, industrialists, high priests from the inner cabals of mega-corporations. Francesca was cold and greedy, wrapped in a veil of ice, yet she slunk with movie star gloss through the adventures that Sheila applied to her. The evening walks were spiced with endless day-dreams of Francesca's exploits, yet even as she fleshed this fantasy out, Sheila couldn't help feeling impatient about Francesca's failings. The woman had so much, yet abused her privileges. She was the kind of person Sheila normally despised - spoiled, selfish and avaricious - yet their lives had inexplicably become entwined. It could be no coincidence. They were linked by more than a chance meeting at Euston.

About a week after buying the shoes, Sheila went into a cosmetic store on the way to work and bought the brightest red lipstick on sale. She did not attempt to use it, but removed it from its paper bag several times during the afternoon and twisted the colour up out of its casing. Later that evening, during her walk, Sheila went to rest her aching feet in a cheap café. A couple of down and outs mumbled at one another in the dim light, and the only other occupants were a group of teenagers who were clearly on their way to somewhere more interesting. Sheila ordered coffee and spread out the tissue on the Formica table top. The fibres were fragmenting badly now and would soon would be nothing more than wisps of fluff in the bottom of her pocket. The lipstick print had faded to a mere filigree of lines and looked aged. When the tissue had fallen apart completely, would she lose this strange half-life she had begun to enjoy? *No,* Sheila thought, determined. *I took some of her into me. I kissed the mirror. The print has sunk into me.* These thoughts made her heart beat faster, shortened her breath.

She stared at the lip print without blinking, until her eyes watered. *Tell me, tell me...* She had exciting images of

Francesca's life, but she wanted more: the future. Some of the lines were broken, perhaps because of natural decay. Perhaps they had always been broken, but the details were only now becoming clear. The print itself, while fading, had spread outwards, almost as if the lips were bloated.

Strangled lips. Breath squeezed out. The heat. The darkness. Gasping, struggling.

Sheila shuddered, and nausea churned through her body. She almost cried out, but managed to control herself and stuff the tissue back into her pocket. Her heart was pounding now and specks of light boiled before her eyes. She mustn't faint - not here.

She lurched from her seat and felt her way between the tables to the rest room at the back of the café. Here, she pushed open a door and virtually fell into the cramped cell beyond. She leaned over the stained sink, taking deep breaths. A bare electric light-bulb hummed over her head, echoing the buzzing in her mind. She splashed some cold water on her face. *Mustn't think about what happened. It's fantasy. I dreamed it up.* Her hand dipped into her coat pocket, seeking the tissue in reassurance. She found instead the smooth plastic case of the lipstick she had bought. Sheila couldn't remember having put it into her pocket. Her fingers were steady as she took it out. She removed its case and with one twist exposed the rod of colour. Almost involuntarily, she applied a layer of it to her lips. The colour glowed like neon in the dim electric light. It made her look startled. Shoes and lips. Top and bottom. But what about the expanse in between? Was it still hers? She shuddered and remembered she'd left her bag outside at the table. She must go back: someone might steal it.

By the time she returned to her seat, Sheila had managed to compose herself, and was relieved to find her bag where she'd left it under the table. She forced herself to examine the lipstick print again. Red waves of danger and darkness seethed up to her, yet she could fix on no definite image. The fading image of Francesca's mouth looked misshapen, bloated. Sheila took a sip of coffee to calm herself and an unusual craving crashed through her. She wanted a cigarette, badly, but she had never smoked.

Numbly, she found herself outside, tapping down the sidewalk to a convenience store, where she knew exactly which brand to ask for. The implications of what was happening disorientated her, yet at the same time she felt calm and focused.

Back on the street, Sheila lit a cigarette, took the smoke into her lungs. Her body coughed and spluttered, yet her inner self revelled in satisfaction. Leaning against the shop wall, Sheila closed her eyes to the night and forced herself to examine what had happened in the café. *She can't be dead, can't be...* Yet how could she doubt her talent? It had never failed her before. What she'd experienced in the cafe must have been an intimation of the future. Sheila opened her eyes. She had no choice now but to find Francesca, seek out her home, make sure the dreadful prophecy never came true. Although she did not wholly like the woman, Sheila realised she looked upon her as a wayward sister. She could not judge Francesca for her actions; she could only love her - unconditionally. Sheila glanced at her watch. Was it too late to start looking now? There was a train to London in fifteen minutes. She could make it; if she hurried, if she ran.

On the train, breathless and hot in her raincoat, Sheila removed the tissue from her pocket once more. She needed to direct all her energy and intention into the print now. She needed hard information. Her vision blurred as she stared unblinking at the red stain, and an image of a cat filled her mind; an animal wholly suggestive of Francesca's nature. *No, no, concentrate!* Sheila saw a hill, a spire and superimposed over it, a cat's face. Cat, church, hill. Perhaps the cat was relevant then; part of a road name. She would have to buy a street guide as soon as she got into town.

Sheila sat in the smoking carriage, lighting cigarette after cigarette. Her body protested, but her mind ignored the physical pleas, some distant part of her mind.

The station shops were just closing as she charged up the ramp from the platform into the concourse at Euston. She marched into a Menzies shop and snatched an A-Z street guide off a shelf, setting her face in a determined expression. The bored assistant behind the till clearly wasn't going to argue the shop was closed.

Sheila made her way down to the tube station. It was only ten o'clock; there was plenty of time to search. She could look all night if necessary. Her body bubbled with energy. If by any chance tiredness overcame her, she could go to Tess' place.

Some explanation would be needed, but it just didn't seem important now.

As she glided down an escalator, Sheila scanned the index of the book. It was almost too easy. There it was. Catchurch Hill. Virtually tearing the pages, Sheila found it in the map section: a tiny curl of a road on the fringe of the West End.

The last time she had been in London, the tubes had terrified her, with their crowds and labyrinthine lines. Now, she marched directly to the escalator for the Northern Line, ignoring the people who pushed past her in needless hurry. Some part of her seemed to know already exactly where she was heading.

The streets were empty around Catchurch Hill. No raucous crowds, no brightly lit bars. It was a quiet little corner of London, a place where it was easy to forget you were in the heart of a sleepless city. It was a cul-de-sac, used mainly by vehicles belonging to the residents. At the end of the street, beyond some black and gold painted iron bollards, the bulk of a gas-works rose ghost-like in the non-dark of the city night. Naked lime trees reared before it, promising that in warmer seasons, the power plant would not seem so imposing. The street did have a slight rise to it, but could hardly be termed a hill. Its lights were ornamental, and the four storey houses, which ran down the right side of the road, had an almost continental appearance: wrought iron balconies girdled it on every floor and it was plastered a pale pink. Ivy seethed up the walls, gripping the curlicues of the balconies, where lanterns burned softly. On the other side of the street, bare magnolia trees in bud murmured of spring. Sheila thought of summer evenings, and what it would be like to own one of these apartments, to sit outside in the warm air among sighing trees, sipping icy wine, with music drifting out into the perfumed dusk. She could almost see herself in that situation, as if she'd already experienced it, or would.

All of the residences were apartments, but which one was Francesca's? Sheila became aware of her throbbing feet, and also the fact that she hadn't felt or seen any spirit presences since she'd boarded the train back home. Her vision had been wholly focused on the search, eclipsing all other thoughts and impressions. She stared up at the curtained windows. Too close now. Hard to tell. She dug into her coat pocket and took out the tissue and with one hand, flung it up into the air. It seemed the scrap of crumpled paper would fall immediately back to earth, but then a breeze took hold of it, and it was swinging up and up, spread out like a white leaf, until it came to rest among the dead twigs of an ornamental shrub that stood in a pot, decorated with dragons, on a balcony of the third floor.

There must be security locks, Sheila thought, and sure enough a dimly-lit intercom system was placed next to each front door. She went to examine the list of residents of the building she was interested in. Most were listed only by their surnames, without even an initial to give a clue. Green, Chevalier, Elstone, Buckingham. None of them seemed to fit Francesca. But she could be wrong? A disorientating moment of panic spun through her. What if she was in the wrong place entirely? The list of names blurred before her, and then she saw it. Flat 7. On the third floor. Sancha. That was it. She just knew it.

Sheila reached out and touched the plastic covering the name, then pressed her finger against the buzzer button. When Francesca answered, what would she say? Now, her adventure was real. She would have to explain herself.

There was no response at first. Perhaps Francesca wasn't at home. She pressed the button again. After a few seconds, she heard the intercom click into life, but there was no voice at the other end, just the rushing of empty wires. 'Hello,' Sheila said. 'Ms Sancha?'

There was still no response. Sheila leaned forward and pressed her cheek against the intercom, willing her intention into the mechanism. *Answer me, answer me...* There was nothing but the hiss, and a sense of waiting, of observation. Then, the front door clicked too, and Sheila realised its lock was open.

Quickly, she went through it, afraid she was being offered only a fragment of time during which to enter the building. She found herself in a plain hallway of dark grey stone. Two black doors clearly led to ground floor flats. Against one of the walls, a large dead yucca plant listed in an earthenware pot, but otherwise the hall-way was unadorned, disappointing. The steps leading up to the next floors were concrete with a functional metal hand-rail. Sheila began her climb. Her heels clicked dryly against the stone.

On the third floor landing, the ceiling lights were set into the plaster and covered with metal grilles. A corridor yawned before her, disappearing into darkness, because a couple of the bulbs had blown. Sheila did not like the atmosphere. It seemed polluted somehow, or perhaps essentially unclean. There was an emptiness to it; loneliness too. She couldn't hear a single sound of human habitation. Shivering, she made her way to the door of flat 7. The tap of her heels seemed dull against the bare floor. The building seemed like a representation of Francesca herself: decorative on the outside but bare and cold within.

There was a small spy-hole in the centre of the door. Sheila approached it cautiously. Was Francesca looking out at her now? She placed her hand against the door, then knocked. She could hear nothing, aware only of an air of desolation. She knocked again, and again, then tried the handle. It was unlocked. Sheila froze, afraid of opening the door. What might she find beyond? Someone was in there, because someone had activated the intercom and the door mechanism downstairs. That someone might not be Francesca. Francesca might be…

Sheila opened the door and flung it wide. It took a moment for her senses to register what she saw. The door opened directly onto a large living room. The windows must be open, for it seemed to be full of a whirling wind that had sucked up tatters of paper and scraps of cloth, creating a tornado of debris. But the room was derelict. Sheila could see that through the maelstrom. The plaster had fallen from the walls in places, revealing a skeleton of wooden slats. There was no furniture, just bare brown drabness. No-one lived here. No-one had lived here for a long time.

She felt compelled to step over the threshold. What did this mean? Was she seeing reality now, or something else? She had lived with strange phenomena all her life. This was no different. She just had to interpret it. The wind snatched at her hair and flapped the skirt of her coat. The air smelled acrid, and it was very cold.

How dark the room was. Shadows swirled and spun amid the litter circling in the wind. As Sheila observed, the shadows coagulated to form a figure in the centre of the room. At once the scene before her became flooded with brightness, bleaching out like an over-exposed photograph. The figure was its dark core. Francesca. Her body was erect and rigid; the eye of the storm. Her hair was a writhing halo around her head and she was wrapped in a black cloak or sheet. One white hand was visible where she clutched the cloth at her throat and her face was startlingly pale. The red gash of her mouth seemed painted onto the black and white image. Her eyes were black holes, open wide.

Sheila stared at this vision, involuntarily holding her breath. Francesca's full lips opened up. It looked as if she was screaming, but there was no sound. There could be no doubt now. This was not the image of a living woman. As the red mouth worked noiselessly, the lips became engorged, their colour bleeding from red to blue. A series of bright flares dazzled Sheila's eyes, like the acidic splash of a camera flash. She glimpsed broken images, in black and white, what she assumed were freeze frames of the past. A hotel room. A man. Francesca's wide eyes. Furniture falling. A struggle. But when? In the past? Recently? Soon?

Sheila felt as if the images were crowding in upon her, until she would be crushed beneath their weight. She had to take a step backwards into the hallway, and the door slammed shut immediately in her face. She was held in a caul of silence; there was no hint of the chaos beyond the door. For a few moments, she stood motionless in shock, then began to back slowly away down the corridor. She heard a sound of a woman's voice, speaking low and quickly. It came through the walls of the flat opposite Francesca's. A domestic dispute or a heated debate. She passed the door to flat 8, which hung open. It too was derelict. There was no-one there.

Sheila fled the building, out into the night. The stars wheeled crazily over-head and the gas-works pumped like a bellows. Spirits fled in scraps of mist through the branches of the trees, wailing in torment. Litter pursued her out of Catchurch Hill into the main street beyond. Traffic flashed past too fast; she could see only the coloured blurs of their tail and head lights. She knew where she had to go, what she must do.

As she marched back to the nearest tube station, her feet were bleeding in their high, spiky heels. Her mouth was bleeding red lipstick. All she could see in her mind was the wide expanse of mirror in the ladies' rest room of Euston Station. She was compelled to return there, hoping that by going back to the beginning, she would somehow acquire more information, answers.

By the time she reached Euston, Sheila was surprised at how late it was. Perhaps she had stood, transfixed, in the strange apartment for longer than she'd thought. Had that really been Francesca's home? The experience was blurred in her mind now. It didn't seem real.

Two women came out of the rest room as she pushed her way through the turn-stile. Inside, she was relieved to find it empty. This time, there were no shadows to distract her.

Before she turned to face the mirror, Sheila experienced a moment of pure fear. She could turn back now, abandon this ridiculous obsession. Her life waited for her - grey, temperate and safe - at the end of a line. If she followed this through, there would be no going back.

Sheila turned round. The room in the mirror looked larger than reality, an endless tiled corridor, a clinical representation of Hell. The first thing she saw in her reflection was the red of her lips, then she realised the face was not hers, and that it was Francesca looking back at her. Her eyes were steady, full of knowledge, yet hooded. The mirror was a veil between the worlds of the dead and the living, and the realm of the dead lay beyond the glass.

With business-like economy of movement, Sheila delved into her pocket and removed the lipstick. Thoughtfully, almost reverently, she removed its cap.

It was then she became aware that someone else had come out of a cubicle behind her. Another woman stood next to her, dragging a brush through her drab hair. The woman caught Sheila's eye in the mirror. Sheila's hand froze half-way to her face, her fingers curled around the bullet of brilliant red lip-stick. Tightly, she smiled. Pity. A moment of it. The other woman withered in its beam. Then, Sheila focused in upon herself and pressed the waxy colour against her mouth. When she had finished, she took the old tissue from her pocket, and pressed it to her mouth, then she dropped the kissed paper onto the floor, didn't even look at it. For a moment, she pouted at herself, then frowned and applied another layer of colour.

Francesca smiled back at her from the mirror. Sheila leaned forward to press her mouth against the glass and it seemed as if Francesca dipped towards her to accept the kiss. When Sheila drew away, she saw only her own reflection looking back at her, the mark of her lips and also the surprised expression of the woman beside her. *I was her, once*, Sheila thought.

Perhaps the other woman might have lingered, waited to pick up the tissue, kiss the glass, but she hurriedly stuffed her hair-brush into a shoulder bag and almost ran from the room. Sheila smiled to herself. She saw, in the mirror, a woman of medium height, with soft, fair hair, whose square face was not pretty, but strong and striking. She looked as if she'd escaped from a 'Thirties film with her raincoat collar up around her ears.

Sheila now had all of Francesca's knowledge. It no longer mattered whether she had lived in the past or very recently, or whether she had lived at all.

The woman in the mirror. She is a ghost of life, like clothes hanging in a wardrobe, devoid of feeling or essence. The body, the feelings, the depth, stand before her in the world of the living. Now they are one. She is on her way somewhere, urgently. She might not come back.

Sheila had business to finish. She put her lipstick back into her pocket and walked out of the station to an assignation. Her feet would lead her there, in their high, spiky shoes. The future in the lip-stick print had been hers, but now she had kissed another future over it, and the outcome would be different. Her hands were strong and steady, deep in her raincoat pockets.

Afterlude: Story History

The stories in this collection have a very loose angelic theme. Some are set in the worlds of my novels – Wraeththu, Magravandias, and the Grigori. Most were inspired by the legends of angels and fallen angels and associated mythology.

Paragenesis

I was asked to contribute a story to James O'Barr's anthology, 'The Crow: Shattered Lives and Broken Dreams', published by Del Ray in 1998. The main theme had to be based around vengeance. The story didn't have to be set in the Crow universe, so I decided to write the Creation Myth of Wraeththu. This is the story of how Thiede was created and his unwitting inception of the new androgynous race. The Wraeththu themselves were originally inspired by angelic legends, specifically the idea that angels could be either or both genders. This was mixed with alchemical ideas and eventually, brewed in the alembic of my imagination, gave rise to the world of Wraeththu.

The Law of Being

This piece originally appeared in the 'Euro Temps' collection (Roc 1992), edited by Neil Gaiman and Alex Stewart. This anthology was a follow up to 'Temps' for which I wrote 'The College Spirit'. 'The Law of Being', however, is far darker in mood than the previous story.

There are certain motifs and archetypes that appear regularly in my writing, and the doomed prophet is one of them. Emory Patrick is also Resenence Jeopardy (from Sign for the Sacred). The story explores the concept of celebrity, in this case both a religious and a musical one. I've noticed that people often elevate musicians to a kind of quasi-spiritual status, when their words are treated like the outpourings of a guru-sage. But what of the person behind the words and the flamboyant act? Are they real or not? Or can we somehow make them real? Is Emory Patrick a paranorm, a charismatic charlatan or a messiah? These were the concepts behind this story, and as usual the characters took over and had their own tale to tell.

The Green Calling

I seem to run into trouble with my gender politics, because 'The Green Calling' was another example of a fairly feminist editor being offended by the content. This story, in one way, examines the concept of ageing and what people feel about it, women in particular. The editor who read this story didn't like it at all and said that no women would ever think or talk that way. This amused me immensely because a lot of the lines in this story had been taken from real life conversations with friends, when we'd been discussing the subject. So I know for a fact that women do think and talk this way! The discussions had actually inspired me to write the story. As in another similar case, with the story 'Priest of Hands' (that eventually developed into the novel Sign for the Sacred), 'Interzone' magazine came to the rescue and accepted it for publication.

Reading this piece again now, when I am more sanguine about the ravages of time, I do think the piece is quite savage and brutal. It's like a rant against the temporary nature of the human vehicle. It was written when I – and my friends - first began the notice the changes that had begun to take place in our bodies as the years advanced. As women, we're supposed to accept this situation gracefully and quietly, but none of us felt like that. We were, to put it mildly, resentful. 'The Green Calling' is a female snarl against the tyranny of time.

Angel of the Hate Wind

This story first appeared in 'Destination Unknown', edited by Pete Crowther, published by White Wolf, in 1997. Sometimes, when I begin to write a story the narrator will just spring to life with a strong voice of their own, speaking authoritatively about their world, as if it has existed for eternity. Such was the case with this piece – similar in fact to 'The Time She Became', which will appear in another collection. As with many of my stories, I felt that here was a world ready and waiting to be visited time and again, and which I could go back to in the future when further stories would await me. As yet, I haven't had the time or the specific inspiration to return to this particular world, but the story does remain one of my favourite pieces and I think one of my strongest.

The Feet, They Dance

Again written in 1997, this was a story that was originally written for a gay themed fantasy anthology, but didn't make the final selection. Eventually it appeared in my story collection, 'The Oracle Lips', published by Stark House in 1999. The piece was inspired by all the research I'd been doing for the Grigori trilogy. The story involves a rogue Nephilim deity called Sin-na'el – wholly fictional. I came across so much intriguing material during my research, and a lot of it didn't make it into the Grigori novels, so several of my stories written during this period include the unused ideas.

One thing about this story, which I acknowledge is rather unlikely, is that a physical anthropologist attached to a museum might have mystical leanings, or be affected by an exhibit in the way I describe. In my experience, those who study ancient cultures academically have the least romantic notions about them. I discovered this quite painfully when approaching Egyptologists for information while researching a book on Egyptian magic. So perhaps Grigor in this story is wishful thinking on my part.

A Change of Season

This story was written for the Midnight Rose anthology 'The Weerde' (1992). The Weerde were a race of shape-shifters, hidden among humanity. Later, in a much reworked form, this piece became the opening chapters of the first Grigori novel, 'Stalking Tender Prey'. As I was writing the story, I knew there was more to it than the constraints of the short form allowed. I can see novels in many of the short pieces I write, but in this case, the ideas became reality and I was able to expand upon the original version. I'd always wanted to write a novel about the fallen angels in a modern setting, and 'A Change of Season' was perfect for the beginning of the book. Again, this was published in 'The Oracle Lips' collection.

How Enlightenment Came to the Tower

This story was originally written with a male protagonist, but one of my writing advisors at the time suggested I should change it to female in order to try and sell it. This was the mid 80s when publications were less open to the idea of shifting or ambiguous sexuality. It did eventually appear in print in 'Scheherazade' magazine, quite a few years after it had been written, and later appeared in Meisha Merlin's 'Three Heralds of the Storm'. I've since re-edited the story, restoring the protagonist to his original gender. This piece was written during the time I was writing the first Wraeththu trilogy.

Return to Gehenna

This story first appeared in 'Dante's Disciples', edited by Pete Crowther, (White Wolf, 1996). The contributors were asked to write about gateways to hell. My idea of hell is the mundane reality the protagonist, Lucy, lives in before all the weird stuff starts happening to her! I've had day jobs very similar to Lucy's, and they were often a torment to me. I'd sit there watching the clock, desperate to go home, wishing my life away. There must be more to life than this, I'd think, and thankfully there was, because through sheer tenacity, if not a hideous fear of having to return to that existence, I've made a career out of doing something I really love. Another thing touched upon briefly in this piece is the sadness of seeing people you love being sucked away from you into a life of mediocrity and mundaneity. So many times in my life I've had to watch the birds of bright plumage shed their gorgeous feathers to become drab and grey. Why does that happen? Why do people feel obliged to conform and shed all the vivacity, sparkle, sense of wonder and exuberance they enjoyed in youth? I didn't believe that this was the way things had to be when I wrote this story and I don't believe it now. But still it happens, and I still have a lot more to say on the subject at some point! In 'Return to Gehenna', the protagonist's gateway to hell is actually her doorway to sanctuary.

By the River of If Only, in the Land of Might Have Been

Another story of the Wraeththu, this piece was written way back in 1988 and appeared in a fanzine I published with friends called

'Paragenesis'. We had formed a creative collective called 'Thirteenth Key', which sadly had only a short life. It was a wild, exciting time, when anything seemed possible and the first Wraeththu novels had only just been launched. At the time, I'd planned to write many more Wraeththu novels, but my hopes were crushed by the publishing industry, so that I wasn't able to return to that world until 15 years later. However, 'By the River of If Only...' captures the spirit of that optimistic time. The piece also appeared in 'Fear' magazine in 1991.

Fire Born

This story was published in the magazine 'Science Fiction Age' in 1996. It is again one of my Grigori spin-offs, and was created while I was writing 'Scenting Hallowed Blood'. 'Fire Born' derives from a vision experienced by a psychic I knew who helped me with the research for the Grigori novels. There wasn't really a place for this material in the trilogy, but it was too good to waste.

To me, this story has a mood and flavour all of its own. To write it, I interviewed the psychic about their experience and recorded our conversation. They had visualised meeting a strange community of fairy chimneys, which are towering rock formations like those found in Cappadocia. It was almost as if they had visited this place in waking life, because their recall of the scene was incredibly detailed. In the visualisation, the psychic met a peculiar old woman who showed them the secrets of a potent elixir that could bestow either immortality or death. With base material this strong and vivid, it was fairly easy to come up with a plot.

Re-reading this story, I do find it rather harsh and bitter – perhaps a reflection of how I was feeling at the time. It was republished in 'The Oracle Lips' collection.

Heir to a Tendency

This story was written for the second volume in Roz Kaveney's shared world anthologies, 'The Weerde'. Unfortunately, my contribution, 'Heir to a Tendency', wasn't taken up. However, I never like to waste stories, and as my first Weerde piece had transformed neatly into a Grigori story, I decided to do the same for the second. 'Heir to a Tendency' became a prequel to the

Grigori trilogy. Peverel Othman appears in it, and the time frame is round about a hundred years before 'Stalking Tender Prey'. I have never bothered to send this piece off anywhere and for quite some time the transformation process wasn't quite finished. There were still a few Weerde serial numbers that needed filing off. Then I needed unpublished stories to be included in 'The Oracle Lips' collection, so got round to finishing it.

Spinning for Gold

Back in the 80s, I wrote a series of stories that were retellings of fairy tales. 'Spinning for Gold' was based upon 'Rumpelstiltskin'. These pieces languished unused for decades until Stark House republished my novella 'The Thorn Boy' in 2002. The editor wanted me to include several short stories in the book. As 'The Thorn Boy' was set in the world of the Magravandias Chronicles, I decided that I'd revamp my fairy tales to be in the same universe.

In folklore, you acquire power over supernatural creatures, in particular goblins and fairies, when you can learn their true names. Another version of this story can be found in the Scottish folk tale 'Whoopity Stoorie'.

'Spinning for Gold' is set in the land of Cos, and its king is called Ashalan, as he is in the Magravandias trilogy, but this is a distant ancestor of that character. If the Magravandias stories are set in an alternate Victorian Age, then these fairy tales are in the Medieval Age of that world. This story, and its two sequels, 'The Nothing Child' and 'Living with the Angel' can be seen as different chapters of the same tale.

The Nothing Child

This piece retells a lesser-known Scottish fairy tale, 'Nicht Nacht Nothing'. It illustrates how magic takes the path of least resistance and you should be very careful indeed when making deals with supernatural beings, especially in the choice of words used to make the deal.

As he grows older, Jadrin, the protagonist of 'Spinning for Gold', becomes a distinctly darker character, which to me made him more interesting. When I wrote this piece, my fascination with capricious angels was already in full flight, and Lailahel, the angel of conception, is a precursor to the fallen angels of the Grigori trilogy. This story also appeared in Stark House's production of 'The Thorn Boy and Other Dreams of Dark Desire' in 2002.

Living With the Angel

Part three of the short series of stories begun with 'Spinning for Gold'. There are echoes of the androgynous Wraeththu in this piece, probably because it was written while I was working on 'The Enchantments of Flesh and Spirit' in 1985. At the time, I a pondering deeply the concept of gender and identification, although probably wouldn't have thought of it in those terms. I must have been playing with these ideas when I devised Variel's fate in this piece, because if I had followed the premise and theme of the previous two stories in the sequence, it wouldn't have happened.

The Oracle Lips

Ideas for short stories strike me at odd times. The seed of 'The Oracle Lips' occurred in the back of a friend's car, in an underground car park in Wolverhampton, a town in the Midlands. A group of us were there for a day's shopping, and before we left the car, I touched up my lipstick. I blotted my lips on a tissue and then the idea came. I said to my friend, 'Lip prints are as personal as marks on a palm. I wonder if you could tell someone's fortune from them.' I thought about this again throughout the day, and by the end of it, I had the beginning of a story. It was fortuitous, because I'd recently been contacted by Laurence Schimel to submit a piece for his 'Fortune Tellers' anthology, which was published in 1998. Clearly, the subject of prognostication was burning away at the back of my mind. I wanted to do something different with the theme, rather than resort to a tale about crystal balls or tarot cards.

The setting for the character Francesca's flat in London is a real place near King's Cross. In the middle of the city, there's a quiet alley, with these amazing Italianate buildings. I just had to put them in a story some time.

Did You Like What You Read?